Sheila O'Flanagan is the author of many No. 1 best-selling novels, including *How Will I Know?*, *Anyone But Him* and *Too Good To Be True*, as well as the short story collections *Destinations* and *Connections*.

Sheila pursued a very successful career in banking, becoming Ireland's first woman Chief Dealer, before she decided to become a full-time writer. She has a weekly column in the *Irish Times*, and she also plays badminton at competition level.

My Favourite Goodbye

Sheila O'Flanagan

headline
review

First published in Great Britain in 2001
by HEADLINE BOOK PUBLISHING

First published in paperback in 2001
by HEADLINE BOOK PUBLISHING

This edition published in paperback in 2006
by HEADLINE REVIEW
An imprint of HEADLINE BOOK PUBLISHING

3

ISBN 978-0-7553-2997-7

Typeset in Galliard by Palimpsest Book Production Limited,
Polmont, Stirlingshire
Printed and bound in Great Britain by
Clays Ltd, St Ives plc

Headline's policy is to use papers that are natural, renewable and
recyclable products and made from wood grown in
sustainable forests. The logging and manufacturing processes
are expected to conform to the environmental
regulations of the country of origin.

HEADLINE BOOK PUBLISHING
A division of Hodder Headline
338 Euston Road
London NW1 3BH

www.reviewbooks.co.uk
www.hodderheadline.com

Author Note

In December 1999 I attended a long and liquid lunch organised by a charity called To Russia With Love (website www.torussiawithlove.ie) which does tremendous work for orphaned Russian children. At that lunch various items were auctioned including the right to the inclusion of a name of the bidder's choice in my next book. This is that next book – and the successful bidder was Mr Paul Howett, whose choice of Kate Coleman appears in these pages. I hope Paul thinks it was worth the top-of-the-range sum he donated which has been of great benefit to the charity and that when Kate is old enough to read she won't be too embarrassed at having her name hijacked.

Acknowledgements

Once again to all those who have worked so hard to keep me working hard . . .

My wonderful agent and friend, Carole Blake.
My editor Anne Williams who had to haul me back on to the rails a few times but who did it so nicely and with such skill.
Every single person at Headline, all of whom are so brilliant to work with and so passionate about books.
Patricia and the girls for allowing me to have regular breakdowns in a calm and collected way.
My family for being such a great support group.
Everyone who offered their recipes and who can actually cook.
Colm for putting up with me even though sometimes it was a lot of putting up with.
And, once more and above all, to those of you who buy my books – thank you very, very much!

Chapter 1

Vegetable Stir Fry
Peppers, mushrooms, green beans, carrots, baby corn
Fry briefly in oil over hot flame

Ash was packing five dozen mini-pizzas into foil containers when the buzzer sounded. She swore softly and glanced at her watch. Molly was early. Ash hadn't bargained on her aunt being early when lateness was a family trait, although not one she possessed herself. She covered the remaining pizzas with paper towels and stacked the full boxes on the counter. She'd have to finish packing them when Molly was gone even though she'd planned to sort them out before her aunt arrived. Now she had no time to tidy herself up. Ash could hardly believe that Molly had picked today to be early for the first time in her life.

She glanced in the mirror as she walked into the living room. Her pale pink lipstick had faded, there was a smudge of flour across her cheek and a lock of hair was trying to escape from the ribbon that had held it back

1

while she was working. She didn't bother to retouch her lipstick but she rubbed at the smudge of flour and pulled the thin black ribbon from her hair, allowing it to flow loosely around her shoulders in a sheen of white-gold. She looked OK, she thought. Not hassled, which was the main thing. She always felt it was important not to look hassled in front of Molly.

She pressed the intercom.

'It's me,' said Molly. 'Let me in, Ash. It's starting to rain.'

'Not again.' Ash had been too busy to notice the change in the weather. 'This is turning into the wettest autumn in living memory.'

She held the door open and waited while her aunt walked up the stairs to the fourth floor of the apartment building. A silver and grey cat streaked past her. He sat by the window, licking his front paw and rubbing it behind his ear accusingly.

'Sorry, Bagel.' Ash looked at him apologetically. 'I would've let you in earlier if I'd realised it was raining again.'

'Hi, Ash,' Molly gasped as she stopped outside the door. 'Those stairs get steeper every time!'

'Give me your bags.' Ash held out her hand and took some of the carrier bags from the older woman. Molly had hit almost every shop in the Jervis Shopping Centre. Ash couldn't bear the thought of trudging around so many crowded shops in one day, but Molly enjoyed it. Nevertheless, her aunt sighed in relief as she handed over the bags and walked into the apartment.

2

'You'll have to get over this phobia about lifts, Molly,' said Ash sternly. 'One day you'll have a heart attack walking up the stairs. Especially when you go on shopping sprees like this.'

'It's a keep fit thing,' said Molly. 'Although I think I may have overdone it this time. My feet are killing me, even in my flat shoes.'

'Never mind,' said Ash as she placed the bags in a neat row along the wall, making sure that they were grouped according to the store. 'Why don't you give me your jacket, sit down and I'll get you a drink.'

Molly took off her jacket and handed it to Ash who hung it on the brushed steel coat rack beside the door. Molly stretched her legs out in front of her and wriggled her toes. 'You know, I don't usually feel any older,' she told Ash, 'but a day tramping around the shops takes it out of me.'

'Buying up half of Dublin would take it out of anybody. And you don't look a day over fifty,' said Ash loyally.

Molly, who was fifty-nine, made a face. 'Thanks.'

'I like your hair,' added Ash. 'Shorter suits you.'

'It's easier to manage,' said Molly. 'And grey hair looks better short.'

'It's not grey, it's white,' objected Ash.

'I suppose so,' Molly said. 'At least it makes me look so pathetic it sometimes gets me a seat in the bus!'

Ash laughed. 'You could never look pathetic. You're far too strong a woman to look pathetic.' She stepped over to the maple sideboard and opened one of the opaque glass doors. 'What would you like to drink?'

'What have you got?' asked Molly.

'I've got everything,' Ash told her. 'Gin, vodka, Bailey's, Jemmy . . .' She looked round at Molly and shrugged.

'Jameson would be nice,' said Molly.

'On the rocks?' asked Ash.

'And ruin a good whiskey?' Molly grinned. 'Neat is just fine.'

Ash poured the amber liquid into a crystal glass and handed it to Molly. 'It's nice to see you again,' she said.

'And you,' Molly replied. She looked around at the cornflake-yellow walls of the apartment. 'You've had this done up since last time I was here.'

The last time Molly had visited, a few months earlier, the walls had been maroon and covered with charcoal drawings of old Dublin.

'It was too dark before,' explained Ash as she sat down beside Molly, a glass of white wine in her hand.

'What about the drawings?' asked Molly. 'They were nice.'

'Oh, I gave them back to Kieran,' Ash told her. 'I didn't want to keep them and I really only bought them as support.'

'And how is Kieran?' Molly sipped her whiskey and looked curiously at Ash.

She shrugged. 'Fine, I guess. I haven't seen him. Well, I wouldn't, really, Molly. We don't tend to go to the same kind of places these days.'

4

'You did for nearly six months,' said Molly tartly.

Ash sipped her wine. 'Too long,' she said lightly, after a pause.

They sat in silence for a moment. Ash glanced at Molly who was surveying the apartment. Ash preferred the new décor, she hadn't really liked it in maroon. It was too old-fashioned for a riverside place that was only a couple of years old but it had suited her mood while she'd been going out with Kieran. He was a dark, brooding kind of man and he'd made her feel dark and brooding too. When they'd split up she immediately redecorated.

'Why did you break up with Kieran?' asked Molly.

Ash sighed. 'Oh, Molly, he just wasn't for me. I liked him but not enough for it to go anywhere.'

'Maybe you didn't give it a chance,' suggested Molly.

'I gave it plenty of chance.' Ash shook her head. 'Can you imagine me living with a man like Kieran for the rest of my life? It'd be so depressing.'

'There are worse men out there, Ash.'

'That's not saying much.' Ash stood up. 'Food in ten minutes,' she told Molly. 'Salmon cutlets. Stir-fried vegetables and a light sauce. It was my summer special this year. Salmon was such a good price and nobody likes eating heavy food when it's hot.'

Molly glanced at the window where the rain was running down the floor-to-ceiling glass in torrents. Ash laughed. 'Well, it was hot last month.'

She went into the galley kitchen, followed by Bagel, while Molly sat on the sofa and sipped her whiskey. The cat jumped lightly onto the deep windowsill and watched Ash as she slid the cutlets under the grill.

'How's Michelle?' Ash called out to Molly. 'I keep meaning to ring her but I've been so busy lately . . .'

'She's fine.' Molly pushed herself out of the sofa and padded to the kitchen door. 'She was complaining that she hasn't seen much of you since the christening.'

'It's my fault,' admitted Ash. 'I keep saying that I'll ring or call out there and I just don't.'

'You should.' Molly watched while Ash tipped green beans, slivers of carrots and peppers into a wok. 'It's not as though she can drop everything and visit you, Ash.'

'I know.' Ash bent down to take plates out of the warm part of the oven. She stood up, pushed her hair out of her eyes and smiled apologetically at Molly. The older woman bit her lip. The gesture was pure Julia, she thought, as she looked at her niece. Even if Ash's unusual combination of fair hair and brown eyes suggested somebody else completely.

'Sit down and I'll bring the food out,' said Ash. 'What train are you getting home, Molly?'

'The later one,' Molly told her. 'We've plenty of time.'

'Particularly since you were early.'

Molly smiled. 'I knew you'd notice. I slowed down specially when I got to the quays but I wasn't slow enough.'

'I didn't mind you being early,' Ash lied. 'Although you have to admit it was a bit out of character.'

'I ran out of energy,' said Molly. 'I was standing in

Debenhams and there were hordes of people round me and I just thought that I'd had enough. But I bet I threw your timetable into total disarray.'

'That's how I feel in shops all the time. And I didn't have a timetable.' Ash handed her a pepper mill. 'Here, eat your food.'

'This looks delicious,' said Molly. 'You really didn't have to go to all this trouble, Ash.'

'It's no trouble.' Ash looked surprised. 'I could do this in my sleep, Molly.'

'I'm more interested in your waking life,' Molly said. 'Is there anyone in it now? Post-Kieran.'

Ash shrugged. 'Brendan.'

'Tell me about him,' said Molly enthusiastically.

'There's nothing to tell,' Ash said. 'I like him but . . .'

'But what?' asked Molly.

'But – oh, you know how it is. You meet someone at a party, you have a few drinks, they seem perfect . . .' Ash sighed. 'Then you go out with them a few times and you realise that they're not.'

'Oh, Aisling.' Molly looked disappointed. 'How long have you known him?'

'A few weeks,' Ash was noncommittal.

'Is he good-looking?'

'Molly, how he looks makes no difference,' said Ash. 'Maybe I just meet the wrong sort of man.'

'Maybe you're looking for the kind of man who doesn't exist, Ash. You want somebody who'll fit your life perfectly and that'll never happen. There has to be a bit of give and take, you know.'

'I know,' Ash said sharply. 'But I don't want to do all of the giving and none of the taking.'

Molly's expression was worried. 'It would be nice, though, if you did find someone special soon,' she said hopefully.

'Oh, Molly!' Ash laughed. 'Just because Michelle is married with a squadron of kids! I'm happy, really I am.'

'I don't doubt you think you're happy,' said Molly. 'But you don't want to be on your own for ever. You can't keep going through men like a box of tissues.'

'Don't be so old-fashioned.' Ash dropped a flake of salmon onto the maple floor and Bagel, who'd been sitting under the table expectantly, ate it in one gulp.

'It's not old-fashioned,' protested Molly.

'I'm twenty-nine,' said Ash. 'I've loads of time to find Mr Perfect.'

'I was married with three children at twenty-nine,' said Molly acidly.

'That was then,' said Ash. She dropped another flake of salmon onto the floor.

'What about Michelle?' added Molly. 'She has three of her own and she's only a few months older than you.'

Ash shrugged. 'She's different to me. She's your daughter, Molly. That's why she's into the whole family thing.'

'I worry about you,' Molly told her. 'And don't laugh at me for worrying about you, Ash.'

'I wouldn't dream of laughing at you,' said Ash seriously. 'But you've got to understand, Molly, that

8

I'm perfectly happy the way I am. I enjoy my work, I know loads of people and I can go out anytime I like—'

'Then you come home to a solitary bed and your cat,' finished Molly.

'Not always.' Ash's eyes twinkled at her.

Molly flushed. 'I don't really want to know about your sex life,' she said.

'I've no intention of telling you about it either.' Ash grinned at her. 'I know we've always got on, Molly, but I draw the line at that. You don't have to worry, I don't sleep with all of the men in my life. And I quite enjoy spending evenings alone with my cat too.'

'What worries me is that you seem utterly incapable of staying with anyone for any length of time,' said Molly tartly. 'I'm all for playing the field, Ash, and I agree that women now don't have to settle down and start having kids at twenty. But you need someone.'

'I haven't met one special person,' said Ash reasonably. 'And I don't *need* anyone. If I find a bloke, fine. If I don't – so what?'

She stood up and took the plates into the kitchen. Bagel padded after her and mewed as she scraped her leftover salmon into his bowl. She rubbed his head and he purred furiously.

'I don't mean to nag you,' said Molly as Ash came back into the living room.

'I know.' Ash looked at her appraisingly. 'You're just afraid I'll end up like Julia, aren't you?'

Molly flushed.

'Oh, Molly, I can read you like a book!' Ash laughed. 'You know perfectly well that I'm nothing like Julia.'

'In lots of ways you're very like Julia,' objected Molly.

'Don't be ridiculous,' said Ash hotly. 'Much as I loved her, Molly, she was the most disorganised, flightiest, silliest woman I've ever known. I am certainly not like Julia.'

'You're not disorganised or silly, I'll admit,' said Molly.

'I'm not flighty either,' cried Ash.

'Not in the sense that Julia was flighty,' admitted Molly. 'But she couldn't settle with one man, Ash, and neither can you.'

'For completely different reasons,' Ash pointed out. 'She started out on this free love thing. And then she did a one hundred and eighty degree turn and thought all men were prospective husbands! I'm not like that at all.'

'Ash, you do the same thing as Julia only in a completely different way,' said Molly.

'That is so untrue,' said Ash furiously. 'I don't sleep with hordes of men and I haven't yet got pregnant by someone who I can't even remember!'

There was an awkward silence.

'Look, Molly,' said Ash eventually. 'I loved my mother to bits. She did her best for me no matter how daft she was. But she never settled in one place and she fell in love at the drop of a hat. Do you know how many blokes were in her life after I was born? I've lost count! And she really thought that each one of them was the right man for her.

When actually none of them were. It was insane, Molly. Absolutely insane.'

'I know.' Molly looked at her niece sympathetically.

'And then she goes and does something incredibly stupid like—' Ash broke off. 'Well, it doesn't matter now. Water under the bridge and all that sort of thing. But I'm telling you now and telling you for the last time, I will settle down with someone when I know for sure, when I'm absolutely certain that he's the right one and the only one.'

Molly sighed. 'I understand that, Ash. I really do.'

'So we don't need to talk about this any more, do we?'

'I guess not.' Molly shook her head.

'Great.' Ash stood up. 'I'll get the desserts. After such a healthy main course I thought you might like some pure indulgence.' She went into the kitchen again. Bagel was sitting beside his empty bowl and he looked anxiously at her. 'Still hungry?' she asked. 'Even after the salmon?' She took a foil packet out of a cupboard and tore it across the top, making a face as the smell of cat food escaped. 'This is so disgusting you're bound to love it,' she told the cat. 'Liver and kidney with a touch of mouse.' She emptied it into his bowl and he pushed her hand out of the way. She took two plain white plates from the dresser and eased her speciality, sticky toffee pudding, onto them.

'You wretch!' Molly smiled at her as she carried the plates to the table. 'You know that's not on my list of allowable items.'

'Special treat,' said Ash.

Molly dug her spoon into the pudding. It came apart in a waft of sweet sauce and golden sponge. 'A minute on the lips,' said Molly resignedly.

'Oh, you probably walked it all off earlier,' said Ash. 'What did you buy today? Were there sales on?'

'In some of the shops. I got some really pretty beach wraps, a gorgeous cashmere cardigan and a really lovely pair of trousers. Nice swimsuits too – I picked up a few in M and S.'

'Molly, there are about a hundred bags in the corner. I wish I could stand being in shops, then I'd have more than just white T-shirts and black jeans in my wardrobe. What else did you buy?'

'Oh, things for the children, you know. Tops. Sweatshirts. Jumpers. Lovely dresses. I love buying things for the kids, everything is so cute!'

'I'm sure the boys won't thank you for calling them cute,' said Ash.

'But Shay junior is only nine months old.' Molly beamed. 'You can buy some awfully cute things for babies. And I like to get things for the others too. Michelle hardly has the time and the other two are so fussy.'

Ash shrugged. Having lived with Michelle since she was eleven years old, Ash still found it hard to believe that her cousin had three children. She frowned as she tried to remember the ages of the other two.

'Lucy is six and Brian is three,' said Molly helpfully.

'I knew that.' Ash was annoyed that Molly knew what she was thinking. 'Would you like some coffee?'

Molly nodded. Ash brought the cafetière in from the kitchen. When she'd poured the coffee, Bagel, who'd followed her, jumped onto her lap and started to knead her stomach furiously. Ash winced as his claws penetrated her cotton top.

Molly spooned some brown sugar into her coffee. 'How's business?' she asked.

'Booming.' Ash liked talking about her business as a freelance chef. She worked mainly for corporate customers who needed people to cater for business lunches and dinners, although she also did a lot of cooking for private dinner parties. In the five years since she'd left the small restaurant where she started out, her business success had exceeded her wildest expectations. 'I'm booked up every day. The summer was incredible. I thought things would drop off because they often do when it's warm, but any slack on the lunchtime work was taken up by doing garden parties and things like that. Today I was baking for a rugby club fundraising do tonight. Fortunately I don't have to be there. It's all nibbles and someone will be along later to pick them up.'

'What did you cook?' asked Molly.

'Party food,' Ash told her. 'Sausage rolls, vol-au-vents, pizza, that sort of thing.'

'Is it profitable?' asked Molly.

'Very.'

'And you're kept busy.'

'I'm so busy you just wouldn't believe, Molly,' said Ash. 'I'm thinking of getting someone else with me but I'm not sure. I don't want to lose the personal thing, you

13

know. And then you get someone working with you and next thing you know they're pinching your clients – so I haven't made up my mind yet.'

'It might take some pressure off you, though,' said Molly.

'Maybe,' Ash conceded. 'But it brings a whole new set of pressures and I don't know if I want them. The way things are now, I can be booked up every single day if I want. I try to keep a balance between regular bookings and special events.'

'I wish I knew where you got it from,' said Molly. 'I can cook, but not like you, Ash. And Julia—'

'Was good at takeaways,' Ash interrupted her. 'More coffee?'

Molly shook her head and changed the subject. 'Any plans for Christmas yet?'

'Give me a break, Molly, it's only the end of September.' Ash looked aghast.

'I know you,' said Molly. 'If I open your diary you've probably got every day planned until December the twenty-fifth.'

'I have my bookings filled in,' said Ash defensively. 'I have to do that, Molly. And they're not in a diary, they're on my computer. I'm a technology-minded chef, you know. I set up my own website last month.'

'Whatever.' Molly hated anything to do with computers. 'You'll still have it all planned. So what do you plan for Christmas?'

'I always come to you, don't I?' said Ash. 'The traditional O'Halloran–Rourke family gathering?'

Molly nodded.

'So why should this year be any different?'

'I don't know,' said Molly. 'Maybe I think that you're fed up with us.'

'Of course not!' Ash looked shocked. 'Of course not,' she repeated.

'It's just that you visit us less and less,' said Molly. 'Shay was only saying so the other day.'

'Yes, well, I don't often get the time to go to Drogheda,' Ash said. 'I'm too busy during the week and Saturdays – well, the last month I've had a function every single Saturday night. Which means that it's late when I get up on Sundays and the train service isn't all that wonderful . . .'

'You don't have to explain,' said Molly. 'I'm merely telling you that you don't see us very often. That's fine. You don't have to.'

'It's not because I don't want to,' Ash said. 'It's because I—'

'I know,' said Molly. 'I do, Ash. Honestly.'

'You don't know,' said Ash fiercely. 'You think you know everything, Molly, but you don't.' She bit her lip. Bagel looked up at her and leaped from her lap. He sat by the window again while Ash folded and refolded the linen napkin she'd left on the table.

'Michelle and her family are coming of course.' Molly returned calmly to the subject of Christmas dinner. 'And the boys and their wives.'

'That's a lot of people.' Ash looked up from the napkin. 'Are you sure you want that many people?'

'I've done it before,' said Molly. 'When everyone was at home.'

'I know,' said Ash. 'It was different then.'

'It's only a meal.' Molly grinned. 'You told me that, Ash, the first time you cooked for us.'

Ash's smile wobbled slightly. 'I remember.'

'It was fantastic,' said Molly.

'Turkey isn't difficult.' Ash shrugged. 'Let's face it, you just shove it in the oven and leave it there. Christmas dinner is all about timing, nothing else.'

'Who better than you, in that case?' said Molly wryly. 'But I promise you, Ash, you don't have to cook. You'll be sick of it by then anyway, I'm sure.'

'Probably,' admitted Ash. 'But I like doing it, Molly. I feel—'

'You don't have to do it because you want to be useful,' said Molly. 'Or out of some misguided sense of gratitude.'

Ash felt her cheeks redden.

'I love you,' said Molly. 'When you love someone you don't have to keep doing things to prove it.'

'You did rather a lot for me,' said Ash.

'You're Julia's daughter,' said Molly. 'What did you expect?'

Ash sighed. 'It's just that I sometimes wonder what it'd be like not to have been Julia's daughter.' She rubbed the back of her neck. 'When your mother was like Julia – well, you can see how people would look at you and expect you to do something odd sooner or later.'

'I suppose Michelle's said something,' surmised Molly.

'Michelle is always saying something,' said Ash ruefully.

'Don't let it bother you,' advised Molly.

'I don't,' said Ash. 'I know she's your daughter, Molly, but she gets under my skin sometimes.'

'I know,' said Molly.

'Is there anything you don't know?' asked Ash.

Molly laughed. 'I don't know how I'm going to get out of this chair and back to the train station. I haven't eaten as much in ages.'

Ash laughed too. 'I'm glad you enjoyed it,' she said.

'You'd want to be insane not to enjoy your food,' said Molly ruefully. She yawned then stood up from the table. 'Give Michelle a call, Ash. She'd love to hear from you.'

'Sure,' said Ash. 'I will.' She glanced at her watch. 'You've loads of time.'

'I'm trying to be more like you,' said Molly. 'Punctual to the second! Besides, with this rain . . .'

'You should get a taxi,' said Ash. 'I'll phone.'

'It's a ten-minute walk to Amiens Street at the most,' Molly told her. 'You're out of your mind if you think a taxi will call here just to cross the river.'

'Maybe,' said Ash. 'But let me come with you. I can carry some bags.'

'You don't have to.'

'No. I want to.' Ash took a long waxed jacket from the coat stand. 'I haven't been outside today, the walk will do me good.'

'What about the person collecting the party food?'

asked Molly. 'Won't you need to be in the apartment in case they call?'

Ash glanced at her watch. 'Not for another hour,' she told Molly. 'It's fine.'

Molly shrugged and then waited as Ash turned off all the electrical equipment in the apartment. 'You're only going to be out for a few minutes,' she told her niece. 'You don't need to unplug the TV.'

'I know. But I feel better if I do.' Ash took as many bags as she could and pressed the lift button. 'Come on,' she told Molly. 'It takes about five seconds. And I'll be with you, you don't need to worry.'

'I just don't like it,' said Molly. 'I'm not worried.'

She got into the lift with Ash and squeezed her eyes closed while the lift glided downwards.

'I like it that you're afraid,' Ash told her as they got out on the ground floor. 'It makes you seem human.'

'Me – human!' Molly laughed nervously. 'I'm super-human, girl, didn't you know? Raising all of you? What else would you call it?'

Ash smiled. 'Super-human. Naturally.' She pushed open the door to the apartment building and looked out. 'Not too bad,' she told Molly. 'Drizzling, but otherwise OK.'

Molly followed her outside. The lights along the quayside reflected onto the puddles of water on the street as well as onto the black water of the River Liffey. On the other side of the river the buildings of the financial services centre were bathed in the green and white lights that played on the façades. The wind was easterly, from the mouth of the river, and Ash shivered as she scurried across the road, Molly's bags bumping against her legs.

They walked quickly and in silence past the entrance to the gleaming office buildings and along Amiens Street to the mainline train station.

'Plenty of time,' said Ash as they entered the concourse.

'Told you.' Molly smiled at her. 'Thanks for dinner, Ash.'

'You're welcome.'

'You will phone Michelle?'

'I told you I would.'

'And you're OK for Christmas?'

'Molly, I'll definitely be talking to you before then.'

'You'll look after yourself, Ash, won't you?'

Ash nodded. 'Sure, I will.'

'And maybe you'll even give this Brendan guy a chance?'

'Oh, Molly!' Ash looked at her in exasperation.

Molly smiled. 'Sorry, sorry. It's your life. I know.'

'Yes,' said Ash firmly. 'Please don't worry about me, Molly. I'm fine. I always have been.'

'I know.'

'So, here, take your bags and get on your train. Tell Shay I was asking for him. And Rob, if you see him.'

'I see Rob every day, Ash.'

Ash shrugged. 'Well, you know, tell everyone I was asking for them.'

'It's not much of a journey,' said Molly. 'You know you can come anytime.'

'I'd probably come more if it was more of a journey,' said Ash wryly. 'When people aren't that far away you tend not to bother. I'm sorry, Molly. I will try and visit before Christmas. But you know you can come and stay with me anytime you like.'

Molly nodded. 'I know.'

'Great.' Ash kissed her on the cheek. 'It was really lovely to see you.'

'And you,' said Molly.

'Talk soon,' said Ash.

Molly nodded and walked towards the train.

Chapter 2

Pizza ai Funghi
Dough, mozzarella cheese, tomatoes, mixed herbs, mush-
rooms
Bake at 200°C for 20/30 minutes

The rain was coming down more heavily again and Ash pulled her jacket round her neck as she hurried back to the apartment. Traffic was heavy at the Matt Talbot Bridge and she grimaced as the rain was swept against her face by the wind. Her hair was getting wetter by the minute too.

The lights at the junction changed and she ran across the bridge, not looking at the churning river. A container lorry drove past her, spraying her with water.

'Oh, bloody hell!' she cried as a mini tidal wave engulfed her, soaking her from head to toe. 'Bloody, bloody hell!' She sprinted the rest of the way back to the apartment still cursing the rain and the lorry driver under her breath.

Viking Quay was one of the smaller blocks that had sprung up as private development of the waterside areas of the city had begun. Ash had bought her apartment on the top floor just before prices had spiralled beyond belief, though it had still been shockingly expensive. One of the reasons she worked as hard as she did was to meet the mortgage payments that took such a chunk out of her earnings every month. But she loved having her own place and Molly had encouraged her to buy although Ash knew that her aunt had hated the idea of her moving out of the house in Drogheda. But Ash had to move; she knew she couldn't stay with the Rourkes for ever.

She opened the door of the block and stepped into the lift, smiling as she thought of Molly's aversion to it. Strange that Molly should hate it so much, Ash mused, when she was such a practical sort of person.

Bagel was mewing behind the apartment door. He wove his slinky body around Ash's legs as she walked in and purred frantically when she leaned down and scratched him behind the ears. She looked round the apartment anxiously, then relaxed.

'A shower for me,' she told him as she took off her coat. 'I'm cold and I'm wet, Bagel, and I hate it when those bastards in lorries drive too fast in the rain and don't give a toss about pedestrians.'

The bedroom and bathroom in Ash's apartment were on a mezzanine level. She hurried up the wooden stairs, peeling off her top as she went. Bagel followed, almost tripping her up when she reached the top of the stairs. She threw her clothes onto the bed and walked, naked, into the white tiled bathroom. She turned the water to its hottest so that the mirrors and the glass shower door steamed up almost instantly. Then she stood under the jet of water and let it run through her hair.

Molly was right, she didn't visit Drogheda often enough. Worst of all, she'd been to Belfast the previous Friday and she could have stopped on the way back to Dublin and visited Molly, Shay and the rest of the Rourkes. She'd even thought about it very fleetingly. But she'd made excuses – that she had a job on Saturday, that it was late, that she hadn't called in advance to tell them she'd be there. She knew that these were only excuses because Molly and Shay would have loved her to simply drop in. I don't do that, she reminded herself as she added conditioner to her hair. I don't drop in unannounced.

Unlike Julia. Ash shivered as she thought about her mother. Julia, who'd gone through life dropping in unannounced. Julia, who couldn't bear organisation and planning and having things mapped out for her. Go with the flow had been Julia's motto. Ash shook her head. She hadn't thought about her mother in ages; it had been Molly's visit that had brought some of the memories back.

Well, she wasn't going to think about Julia now. She took her robe from the hook on the back of the bathroom door, rubbed her hair vigorously with the fluffy white and blue striped towel, then draped it neatly back on the towel rail so that the edges of each side were perfectly aligned. Very non-Julia. She smiled to herself as she checked it again.

Bagel was sitting on the bed, his head on her jumper. He looked up at her, his green eyes wondering if she'd be mad at him for getting silver cat hairs on her black cash-mere. He leaped from the bed and ran past her. Ash sighed and plucked the cat hairs from the jumper before folding it neatly and putting it away. Then she went downstairs.

She walked into the kitchen and shrieked. Bagel was sitting on the table, sniffing at the pizzas. She scooped him up and dropped him on the floor.

'You devil! Have you touched any of them?' She surveyed the food. The cat had taken a bite out of one pizza but the rest looked untouched. 'You little git!' she shouted at him. 'These weren't for you! And I gave you salmon earlier!'

She looked at them more closely. It looked like he'd only sampled one, but there were half a dozen others beside it and Ash knew that she couldn't take the chance. She visualised the headlines if she did. 'Chef kills party-goers with deadly pizzas. Blames cat.' Her business would go down the toilet. She scooped up the ones she thought he'd sniffed at and threw them away.

'Little bastard,' she muttered as he stalked into the living room, his tail high in the air. All the same, she said to herself as she packed the remaining pizzas into boxes, that'll teach me not to get so caught up in things that I forget that I've left unprotected food and a cat in the same apartment. She couldn't believe she'd actually done that. Usually she would have checked. But when Molly had started talking about Julia . . . Ash sighed deeply; she wished they hadn't talked about Julia. She didn't even want to think about Julia right now.

She'd just snapped the lid onto the last container when

the buzzer sounded. Laura Pearson, who was calling to pick up the food, was early too. What was it with people today!

Ash pressed the button to let her in. In the meantime she raced upstairs and pulled on a warm red jumper and pair of jeans.

'Hi.' She opened the door just as Laura arrived.

'Hi.' Laura shivered. 'Horrible, horrible weather.'

'I know,' said Ash. 'Is your car outside?'

Laura nodded.

'OK,' said Ash. 'I've done everything you ordered. Plus, I've thrown in a few extra samosas. They're light curry and I know that the blokes love them.'

'You pet,' said Laura. 'I just hope they all turn up.'

'I'm sure they will.' Ash packed the containers into a big box for Laura to carry to the car. 'What time are you starting?'

'Oh, some of them are in the bar already,' said Laura. 'It's casual.' She took her chequebook out of her bag. 'Will I make this payable to you?'

Ash shook her head. 'Celtic Dream Food,' she told Laura. 'That's the name of my company.'

'Oh, right.' Laura wrote the cheque. 'Don't lodge it too quickly,' she told Ash. 'Or else it'll bounce.'

'It better not.' Ash threw a baleful glance at Bagel who was curled up on the sofa, completely oblivious of her. 'I've a mortgage to pay and a cat to feed. Thanks for the order, Laura. Let me know how things go.'

'I'm sure the food will be fine.' Laura sighed. 'Let's face it, they'll eat anything really.'

Ash laughed. 'That's my ego shattered!'

'I didn't mean—' Laura broke off in confusion. 'I'm sure they'll love the food.'

'Have a good night,' said Ash. 'Drive carefully in this weather.'

'I will.' Laura lifted the box and grunted.

'Can you manage?' asked Ash. 'Do you want a hand to the car?'

'No, it's fine.' Laura made a face at her. 'I raised two bloody rugby players, didn't I? I have the strength.'

Ash called the lift for her and then looked out of the landing window to make sure that Laura managed to get the box into the car without difficulty. When Laura had driven away, she went back to the apartment.

'Peace at last,' she said to Bagel as she flopped onto the sofa. She flicked through the newspaper to look at the TV listings and the phone rang. She groaned.

'Hello.'

'Hi, Ash.'

'Jodie, how's it going?'

'Not bad. Well, OK.'

Jodie worked with Ash whenever Ash was catering for enough people to need a waitress. Most of the time she did, and Jodie had been working with her for the past two years. When Jodie wasn't being a waitress she sang the blues in one of the Temple Bar restaurants where she hoped that, one day, she'd be noticed by someone who'd offer her a huge contract leading to fame and, hopefully, fortune.

'Only OK?' Ash said. 'What's the problem?'

'It's not a big problem,' said Jodie. 'Not insurmountable, Ash, but . . .'

'But what?' asked Ash impatiently.

'I've sprained my wrist,' confessed Jodie. 'I'm sorry. I slipped, landed awkwardly and it's pretty sore.'

'Just a sprain?' asked Ash.

'Well, yes, but I'm struggling to use it,' Jodie said. 'It'll probably be OK by next week but I thought I'd better warn you. We're doing Chatham's on Monday, aren't we?'

'Yes,' said Ash. 'That's not so bad, Jodie, there's only eight of them.'

'I know. And I'll be able to manage, I know I will. I might just be a little slow, that's all.'

'Let me know tomorrow if it's a real problem,' Ash told her. 'I could always get Margaret or Seamus to do it.'

There was a pause. Jodie didn't want anyone else to do her job. Ash paid well and she made a lot more money working for her than she did singing in Temple Bar. 'I'll be fine,' she assured Ash.

'OK. Well, call me tomorrow anyway.'

'Sure,' said Jodie. Her voice brightened. 'Why don't you come to the restaurant tonight? I'm on in about twenty minutes.'

Ash glanced at the clock. It was after nine. She didn't feel like going out again and, besides, she wanted a night at home. 'I'm having a night in,' she told Jodie. 'Me and Bagel are curled up on the sofa watching the telly.'

'Oh, Aisling!' For a moment Ash could almost believe

she was talking to Molly again. 'I swear to God you prefer that cat to humans.'

'Don't be daft,' said Ash mildly.

'Why don't you give Brendan a call?' suggested Jodie. 'I can't believe you're not going out with him on a Saturday night.'

'I don't want to see him,' said Ash sharply. 'And I certainly don't want to give him a call.'

'Why not? He's your boyfriend, isn't he?'

'I don't want to go out with Brendan tonight,' said Ash firmly.

'Come to the restaurant then,' begged the younger girl. 'You shouldn't be at home on your own at the weekend.'

'I'm alone by choice,' Ash said. 'It's not something that's been forced on me. Besides,' her tone was warmer, 'my aunt was here earlier and I walked to the train with her. I got soaked, I've just had a shower and I honestly don't feel like getting dressed again.'

'Oh, all right.' Jodie conceded defeat. 'It's just that I don't like to think of you being lonely.'

'Jodie, being alone doesn't mean being lonely,' said Ash. 'I'm fine. I'll see you on Monday.'

'OK,' said Jodie. 'But I'm going to insist that you go out next weekend.'

Most nights Bagel went out, but the wind and the rain meant that when Ash opened the kitchen window to allow him outside the cat turned round and immediately ran upstairs. I should have just chucked you out of the window, she muttered to his retreating tail, for nibbling on that pizza. And cats aren't supposed to like olives or cheese!

The kettle, which she'd filled earlier, clicked itself off and she took down a jar of instant hot chocolate. She heaped three large spoonfuls into her mug and poured hot water over it. Then, to undo all of the good work that its being fat-free might have given her, she broke off a square of Cadbury's milk chocolate and dropped it into the drink. She wrapped her hands round the mug as she carried it back to the living room and sat down. She hoped nobody else would ring tonight. She really and truly did want to be on her own even though all of the magazines and books she read told her that she should be out there having a good time, swilling Chardonnay and meeting Mr Right. Or, at the very worst, sitting in with all her best friends to moan about the fact that she wasn't out there having a good time, swilling Chardonnay and meeting Mr Right. Oh well, she thought as she ate a piece of chocolate, at least I'm comfort eating.

Bagel woke her the following morning, kneading her stomach with his claws and mewing raucously to tell her that he wanted to go out. Ash blinked a couple of times and then realised that the rain and the clouds had cleared away – she could see clear blue through the skylight of her bedroom.

She pushed the duvet from the bed and pulled her dressing gown round her. Bagel raced down the stairs ahead of her and jumped onto the windowsill.

'Wait,' she said as he head-butted the glass. 'For good-ness' sake, give me a minute! And, by the way, don't think I've forgiven you for last night yet.'

The cat stepped outside, then leaped gracefully onto a nearby ledge and ran vertically up the wall to the roof. Sometimes he wandered across the roof and sat on the bedroom skylight, which both amused and terrified Ash.

She yawned and rubbed the sleep from her eyes. These last two weeks had been so busy she hadn't had time to relax. She'd had a lunch every day and a dinner almost every night and she knew that she was stretching herself too thin. But when you worked for yourself and you only got paid every time you cooked a meal the temptation was to accept every booking. Jodie encouraged her to take every booking too, on the basis that Ash would never know just when she might have a very important guest who could take her on as a private chef. Jodie thought that Ash agreed with her that working as a private chef would be great, but Ash didn't think so. She liked having the freedom to plan for herself, to be in control of her own work every day. If she worked for someone else then she'd have to listen to their ideas of what was a good menu, stick to their faddish eating habits, do things someone else's way. Ash didn't want that.

She went upstairs and stepped under the shower, this time protecting her blonde hair under a shower cap. She didn't feel fully awake until she'd stood under the jet of water but too much washing made her fine hair unmanageable. On Sundays she liked to have breakfast in Bewley's in Grafton Street. She would buy the papers on her way, sit at one of the dark wooden tables and read the supplements while drinking their frothy coffee and eating fresh croissants. Sometimes, in the depths of winter, she'd even have a mixed grill for breakfast and feel guilty about it for ages afterwards.

Since she'd met Brendan he'd often joined her for her Sunday breakfast. At first she'd enjoyed his company but now he seemed to take it for granted that they'd meet every Sunday and Ash didn't want to meet him every Sunday. She didn't quite know why because, despite the fact that they enjoyed different things, he was fun to be with and had a nice sense of humour. Everyone said that it was important to have a boyfriend with a good sense of humour. It was practically mandatory in the Lonely Hearts columns. And it was a refreshing change from Kieran who'd had no sense of humour whatsoever.

She opened the kitchen window and whistled for Bagel. There was no sign of him and she hadn't really expected that there would be. When he spent the night in he always liked to prowl around for a few hours the following day. Besides, he knew that she was still pissed off with him. She closed the window again and pulled on her fleece. Then she checked the apartment.

Ash knew that what she did was irrational. But she couldn't help it, she was afraid that if she forgot to check one item before she went out it would bring her bad luck. Last night, going to the train with Molly, she'd worried that she'd left the immersion heater switched on and she'd been afraid that the whole thing would explode from overheating before she got back. She'd worried about it all the way to the train station and back again even though she knew that she was being stupid.

She began her ritual by ensuring she'd switched off the central heating. She checked to see that the taps weren't dripping. She checked that all the right electrical sockets were switched off. And, finally, she checked to make sure that the kitchen worktop surfaces were clear of any mess and that the alarm was on. One day, she murmured, as she clicked off the socket to the kettle, I'll walk out and leave everything switched on. One day. But not today.

She loved the streets of the city on Sunday mornings. When she'd first bought the apartment there were very few people around before midday. But in the last couple of years the streets were busier and Ash loved the buzz that they created. She walked past Trinity College where a couple of American tourists were arguing about whether or not they'd have to queue to see the famous Book of Kells, past the bronze statue of Molly Malone – Ash's aunt emphatically denied being named after the city's most famous probable prostitute – and along the red-brick pavement of Grafton Street, with its cornucopia of shops where she bought her newspaper supply. Ash loved the Sunday papers. She bought the Irish ones and the English ones and sometimes, to keep up the Italian she'd learned in school, she bought the Italian ones too.

There was an autumn theme to the Grafton Street window displays, she noticed, and the clothes were now in muted shades of green and grey. She stopped in front of Brown Thomas and wished she could justify spending nearly a thousand pounds on a red wool coat with a black velvet collar which she knew would look well on her. She pulled the warm grey fleece round her. Better value at a tenth of the price, she told herself, and probably far more practical.

Bewley's Café was as noisy and clattery as always and enticed her with its aroma of freshly ground coffee. She looked around for Brendan and saw him checking out the coffee display.

'Hi, Ash!' He waved at her. 'You're late.'

She looked at her watch. She was exactly on time. She was always exactly on time. Why was it that people were suddenly turning up early?

'Hi,' she said, turning her head slightly as he kissed her so that his lips brushed her cheek and not her lips as he'd intended.

'I'm starving,' he told her. 'I'm having everything. How about you?'

She shook her head. 'Coffee and croissants.'

'Come on,' he said. 'Let's get a table.'

She chose a table in the corner while he ordered their food.

'Guess what?' He beamed at her.

'What?'

He reached into his jacket and pulled out an envelope. 'That's what.'

She looked at him in surprise and slid her finger under the flap of the envelope. A shiny blue ticket folder was inside.

'Go on.' Brendan grinned. 'Open it.'

The tickets were to the Canaries. They were made out in her name and in Brendan's.

'What on earth is this about?' Her brown eyes looked at him in puzzlement.

'What do you think?' He laughed. 'It's a holiday. I've booked it.'

'You've what!' She stared at him.

'You said last week that you hated the idea of autumn and the evenings closing in and the weather getting cooler. Not, mind you, that anyone expected it would get this cold this quickly! A friend of mind works in the travel agent's. He told me about this deal and I took it.'

'For us?'

'We're the named parties. It'll be great fun.'

'Brendan, I can't possibly go on holiday with you,' said Ash.

'Of course you can,' he said.

'I have a business to run,' she told him. 'When I take holidays I have to work it out very carefully.'

'Oh, live a little,' he said carelessly.

'I'm sorry?'

'Live a little, Ash. Sometimes you're so tensed up. I know you've got your own business. So have lots of people these days. But they find that it gives them more flexibility, not less.' Brendan worked in a credit union.

'Don't be so silly,' said Ash tartly. 'I can't believe you just went and did this, Brendan.'

'I did it because I want to be with you,' he said. He reached across the table and took her hand. 'I really care about you, Ash.'

She swallowed. She liked him even though they were so different. But she didn't like him enough to go on holiday with him. And she definitely didn't like the way he thought she would drop everything and do what he wanted. Who the hell did he think he was?

'I love you,' he said.

'You hardly know me.'

'I want to spend more time with you. Alone. That's why I booked it.'

'Look, Brendan, I'm really sorry.' Ash bit her lip. 'I – I'm flattered that you feel like this. I really am. But I'm not ready to do something like this with you.'

'What do you mean, something like this?' he demanded.

'Going on holiday.'

'But—'

'You should have asked me first.'

'And what would you have said?'

She bit her lip. 'I'd have said no.'

'Why?'

'Because I'm not ready.'

'It's only a bloody holiday! It's not a declaration of undying love,' he said.

'You said you loved me just now,' she pointed out.

'I know. And I do. But it's still only a holiday. Ash, you can't possibly ask me to cancel it.'

'Brendan, I didn't ask you to book it.'

He stared at her. 'Most girls would love to be taken on holiday.'

'I'm not most girls,' she said.

'I know.' He sighed. 'I'm sorry. That was patronising.

Look, Ash, think about it. Don't just say no without thinking about it.'

She pushed her blonde hair behind her ears. 'I have been thinking about it,' she told him. 'I'd been thinking about us, anyway. And I don't think it's working out, Brendan.'

'What?'

'I like you,' she said. 'You're fun to be with. But, well . . .' She shrugged.

'I don't believe you.' He looked at her in surprise. 'You're breaking up with me? Because I booked a holiday?'

'Not really. But—'

'I just wanted for us to have a good time together. I thought it would be fun.'

'It's not that it wouldn't be fun,' she told him. 'But I—'

'You just don't want to have fun!' He stared at her. 'You don't give a shit about me, do you? You never really did.'

She sighed. 'It's not like that.'

'I don't bloody well know what it's like then,' he said finally.

'I'm sorry,' she said.

He was silent. He picked up the navy blue wallet. 'Thanks for letting me make a complete arse of myself.'

'You didn't,' said Ash. 'I know you probably feel bad about it now, Brendan, but I swear to you I didn't want to hurt you. I'm not ready for the commitment thing.'

'It was only a damned holiday.'

'I know.'

'I thought you enjoyed being with me,' said Brendan. 'I thought we had fun.'

'We do. We did. It's just that I'm not ready to be with anyone long-term.'

'I'd hardly call us long-term,' he said.

'I'm sorry,' she said again.

'Right.' Brendan got up from the table just as the waitress arrived with his breakfast. He took twenty pounds from his wallet. 'This should cover it,' he said.

'I'll pay,' said Ash hastily.

'Don't bother,' he snapped.

'Goodbye, Brendan,' she said as he turned and walked away.

She sat for five minutes before leaving the café, skimming through the newspaper headlines and trying to ignore the rapid beating of her heart and the tingling sensation at the tip of her nose. But the words on the pages were just a jumble of letters and she knew that she couldn't sit still for very much longer.

She walked out of the café and hurried down Grafton Street. I'm OK, she told herself. I'm calm. I'm relaxed. I'm fine.

She stepped off the pavement at Suffolk Street and jumped back again as the driver of a Rover blasted her with the horn. She hadn't noticed him, hadn't realised that the lights were against her. He was gesticulating at her, angry that she'd stepped out in front of him, probably relieved that he hadn't run her over.

Stay calm, she told herself as she waited for the lights to change. Stay cool. There's no need to get hassled.

But she could feel the panic welling up inside her. She could hear her heart beating faster and feel her legs begin to tremble and then the sudden sensation of floating out of her body that always scared her. She clenched her fists until she could feel her nails digging into her palms.

You're OK, she said under her breath. You're fine, you're OK, you've nothing to worry about.

Her lips were starting to tingle now and her heart was skipping beats. She told herself that it wasn't really skipping beats, Dr Mullen had explained it all to her years ago. And she'd read a lot about it since then. She knew that it was the adrenaline rushing through her body that made her feel the way she felt. There was no other physical reason. She wasn't going to faint, she wasn't going to collapse and she wasn't having a heart attack. Dr Mullen had told her that a heart attack was like a golf bag thrown onto your chest. She didn't feel as though a golf bag had been thrown onto her chest.

She recited recipes as she walked alongside Trinity College, along Poolbeg Street, towards George's Quay. Reciting recipes helped her to focus on the fact that she wasn't about to die.

Chicken main courses. She was good at chicken main courses. Chicken breasts. With pasta. Chilli pepper. Cumin. Oregano. Red peppers. Garlic. Chopped tomatoes. Fromage frais. Fresh basil. Put the chicken in a food bag with oil, the spices, herbs and seasoning. Rub together. Leave for a while. Cook pasta. Stir peppers and garlic in heated oil. Mix tomatoes and peppers in some water. Cook for five minutes. Add basil and fromage frais. Add pasta. Sizzle chicken strips on pre-heated pan. Turn. Serve on top of pasta. That was a comfort recipe. An easy one. Looked good, didn't take long.

She crossed the road at City Quay and began to count her footsteps. Counting was her other way of dealing with the panic attack. She knew it was exactly six hundred and three paces to her apartment. Five hundred and ninety, she said under her breath as she passed the office building next door. Six hundred. And one. And two. Six hundred and three. Her hands were shaking as she put the key in the lock. She forced herself to breathe slowly, to calm herself down. Finally the door was open, she ran up the stairs, let herself into the apartment and grabbed the brown paper bag that was on the side unit.

She held the bag to her face and breathed in and out. She always felt stupid doing this, as though she was a fraud. There was nothing wrong with her. She didn't have a fatal disease. She didn't have asthma, emphysema or cardiac problems. She was simply hyperventilating. Dr Mullen said it was nothing to be ashamed of. Lots of people hyperventilated when they were worried or anxious or upset. When she'd been younger, when Molly had brought her back to Ireland, it had happened a lot. Now the attacks were much rarer but they still scared her all the same. Mostly they happened when she broke up with someone, or if she was very late for an event or, sometimes, after she'd met Michelle.

But breaking up with someone shouldn't upset her any

more. She'd broken up with so many people by now that it should be easy! What would Brendan think if he could see her now with her head stuck in a paper bag? He'd be glad he'd managed to make her feel this way, she supposed, and she couldn't really blame him. It was a nice gesture, booking the holiday. It really was. But he shouldn't have done it. He shouldn't have tried to pressurise her. She didn't like being pressurised. Anyway, she thought as she finally took the bag away from her face, they would have split up sooner or later. And better now, before she got to care for him too much. Before she got some mad idea like maybe he was The One. Before she made a complete fool of herself. Like Julia.

Besides, this feeling only lasted a few hours. It was horrible when it was happening but she could cope with it. And she knew she could cope because she'd learned to cope. She'd had to.

Chapter 3

Chicken with Tarragon
Chicken, lemon, tarragon, white wine, crème fraîche
Roast at 200°C until cooked through (a little over an hour)

Sometimes Ash got up very early and went to the fruit and vegetable market in Smithfield. She liked wandering around the stalls, looking at huge boxes of vegetables and breathing in the smell of bananas, oranges and ripening fruit. She liked the noise and the bustle and the fact that the market was so close to the Four Courts and the legal centre of Dublin. The contrast between the greengrocers appraising the merchandise and the legal eagles striding around the streets later on in the day always amused her. And she liked, too, the fact that it was an area of the city that had been regenerated over the last few years, with new apartment blocks and people living in renovated buildings that had once been derelict.

But Smithfield was usually for the high summer months,

when she used lots and lots of salads and enjoyed getting out of bed at dawn. Once September came, Ash reverted to buying her fruit and vegetables in Moore Street, which was where the people who'd gone to Smithfield earlier actually sold their goods. Fruit and vegetables were inexpensive in Moore Street and Ash wouldn't have dreamed of buying them anywhere else.

For the lunch she was doing at Chatham's stockbrokers on Monday morning, Ash had planned chicken with tarragon sauce, green peas and baby potatoes. Chatham's didn't want anything heavy for their once a month board meeting lunch, and Ash had a rota system of six different dishes which she cooked for them. As well as the regular lunch, though, she also cooked for them whenever they entertained clients, which was usually at least one other day during the month. But not everyone came to those lunches and she had a different set of menus for them.

She liked her bookings with Chatham's. The people were friendly and relaxed and they paid her well. Some of the partners had also asked her to do the catering for them when they had dinner parties at home, which was even more lucrative. And potentially the most lucrative of all, Ash thought, as she turned on her computer before going out to pick up her produce, was the fact that she had an account with Chatham's stockbrokers which allowed her to buy and sell shares for herself.

She'd asked Kate Coleman, the girl who had first booked her to do the lunches five years earlier, exactly what buying and selling shares was all about. And Kate had explained it to her and told her that, in the long term, shares were nearly always a good investment.

'I don't have any long-term money,' Ash had said gloomily. 'Right now I don't even have any short-term money.'

'When you have you should buy some,' Kate advised her.

By the end of that year, Ash had amassed more savings than she'd expected because her career as a self-employed chef had really taken off. It wasn't a huge sum but it could have paid for a very nice holiday. Instead, she'd kept Kate's words in her mind and she'd listened at the lunches when the partners were talking about different companies and how well they were doing and what that might mean for the share price. She started to read the financial pages of the newspaper and relate the stories she saw there to the discussions that she heard at lunchtime. She never tried to eavesdrop on the partners, but if she heard an interesting piece of information she stored it away in her head.

At Christmas, when Kate gave her an envelope which was an additional gift cheque for her work during the year, Ash asked her about opening an account. Kate told her it was a great idea and set it up for her with Steve Proctor, one of the junior dealers. Ash, having decided that interest rates were coming down and that that was good news for anyone in the financial sector, bought some shares in the major banks. By January, she was in profit. By February, she'd made enough to go on a much more expensive holiday than she could have done previously. By July, she'd made enough to go away again during the winter. Sometimes, though, she lost money and she'd feel panicky and scared. But she kept Kate's words in her head, that it was a long-term investment, and she never put more than a few hundred pounds into shares.

She clicked on the folder called 'my portfolio'. She always smiled to herself at the term portfolio, which sounded far too grand for what it really was, but all of the stockbrokers called their clients' holdings portfolios and so that was what she called it too. It was linked into prices that were fed from the stock exchange through to Chatham's which meant that, at a glance, she could see whether her shares had gone up or down in value. Ash got a kick out of watching her share prices move even though, in the whole scheme of things, it wasn't that much money.

There were no big moves so far today so she closed 'my portfolio' and opened the Chatham company folder instead. She'd known it was the chicken and tarragon month but she wanted to check all the same. Ash knew that she had a reputation for thoroughness. She liked to live up to it. She printed off the menu with the little boxes beside it where she filled in the price of everything she'd bought and folded the sheet of paper into her Filofax. Despite her love of technology, Ash hadn't quite got around to an electronic personal organiser yet. She put the Filofax beside her bag while she did her check of the apartment. Then she picked up her bag, checked to make sure that her purse was in it, and opened the door of the apartment.

Bagel came running up the stairs and she swore as she nearly tripped over him. 'Where did you come from?' she demanded. 'I opened the kitchen window for you earlier but you couldn't be bothered to show up! You'll make me late.' The cat wound himself round her legs. 'And who let you in the front door?' she asked. 'You know I hate you wandering outside the front of the apartment block and along the quays.' Bagel's green eyes regarded her thoughtfully. 'I suppose you want food,' Ash said as he bounded into the apartment and headed directly for his bowl. She opened a fresh tin of tuna and salmon and heaped some into it. 'There,' she said. 'Enjoy.'

Bagel stuck his face into the food and began eating. Ash sighed. 'You are a pig,' she told his round body. 'An absolute pig. I asked for a cat and I got a porker in disguise. An insane pizza-stealing porker!' And if anyone heard me talking out loud to you right now, she thought ruefully, they'd probably have me admitted to the funny farm. 'Goodbye,' she said as she let herself out again. 'Behave yourself until I get back. Fortunately you haven't yet learned to open the fridge.' Or they'd think of me as a poor, demented single girl living a sad and solitary life with her cat, she murmured aloud, and then wondered if they'd be right.

There was a new receptionist at the desk in Chatham's. Ash had to wait while the girl checked with Kate that Ash was who she said she was. I wonder if she thinks I'm going to hold the place to ransom with a bag of tomatoes and some overripe bananas, mused

Ash. It was an interesting image but, before she had time to plan her takeover, the receptionist handed her a swipe card that allowed her access to the fourth floor where the dining room and kitchen were located. The real work went on in Chatham's on the second floor where, Ash knew, they huddled in front of computer screens for ten or twelve hours a day.

Ash shuddered at the idea of sitting in front of a computer screen from eight in the morning until eight at night. She couldn't imagine anything more soul-destroying than working with numbers all day long. She could understand the buzz they got when the shares they bought went up – she got a buzz out of that herself – but all day, every day! That was surely more than most people could take.

She put down her bags at the security door on the fourth floor and swiped her card. The door clicked open and she carried the bags into the kitchen. Her job was much more satisfying than reading pages and pages of research before buying and selling, she thought. She could pick up her ingredients and look at them. Turn the peppers over in her hands and marvel at the fact that a couple of days earlier they'd been picked in Spain. Sniff her mushrooms and know that they were freshly out of the earth. Crack open her eggs and know that she'd actually been to the farm where they came from. Cooking was creating. What the people in Chatham's did was just bean-counting.

Although, she had to admit, the bean-counting certainly seemed profitable. Chatham's offices were luxurious and the kitchen was one of the best she'd ever used. The double oven was a top of the range Neff with a gas hob, there were two microwaves, an American-style fridge and freezer and her favourite cool granite worktop surfaces. Chatham's also had a wine cooler which kept up to 140 bottles stored at the perfect temperature.

She stood at the kitchen window and stared across the river. From here, she could see the corner of her apartment building, the rest of it hidden behind yet another office block. But she could also see the Dublin mountains and the spires of the churches as well as the cranes that still jutted up from the building sites around the city. Black clouds scudded across the sky. It looked horribly like it would rain again.

She turned away from the window and put on an apron. Then she poured herself a glass of Ballygowan, dropped a slice of lemon into it, and started to prepare her ingredients.

She was rubbing the chicken with lemon when Jodie arrived. Ash smiled as the dark, elfin girl pushed open the kitchen door, then winced as she saw the heavy strapping on her wrist.

'I thought it was a sprain,' she said accusingly.

'It looks worse than it is,' said Jodie. 'And I know I can manage.'

'You won't be able to serve vegetables,' Ash said. 'You'll never hold a serving dish and manage with the cutlery.'

'I thought you could put them on side plates instead of in serving bowls,' said Jodie.

'What about drinks?' asked Ash. 'How are you going to pour drinks?'

'I'll manage with their aperitifs,' said Jodie. 'But I thought, maybe, you could pour the wine.'

'Me!'

'Oh, come on, Ash. Just at the start. And I'll let you know when they need to be topped up.'

'I'll be doing dessert when they need to be topped up,' said Ash.

Jodie looked at her pleadingly. 'The strapping will be off soon. Please, Ash. I really need the work.'

Ash rubbed her forehead. She didn't want to get someone else – she couldn't today in any event, it was far too late – but it would be almost impossible for Jodie to wait on the table properly with her wrist in that condition. Ash could feel a sense of panic welling up inside her and she clamped down on it. Whatever she felt inside, it wouldn't do any good to panic in front of Jodie who hadn't ever seen her with her face in a paper bag! She counted to ten. Jodie was a good waitress, dependable, personable and efficient. She knew when to engage the diners in a little conversation and when to melt into the background so that they forgot she was there. And if Jodie thought she could manage then Ash felt as though she owed her the benefit of the doubt.

'We'll give it a go, I suppose,' she told her. 'Only please take care. Don't spill anything on them!'

'I won't,' Jodie assured her. 'I've been practising all weekend. I filled an empty vodka bottle with water and tried pouring it with my left hand. I'm quite good by now.'

Ash laughed nervously. 'In that case everything's fine.'

'Well, not quite,' Jodie conceded. 'I dropped the bottle a couple of times. But that was at the start.'

'How did you sprain it?' Ash pushed the remainder of the lemon and some tarragon into the chicken cavity.

Jodie blushed and didn't answer.

'Jodie?' Ash smeared butter over the chicken then seasoned it with sea salt and ground pepper.

'I was fooling around with Chris,' she admitted.

Ash looked at her. 'Fooling around with Chris?'

'You know.' Jodie looked embarrassed. 'We were playing games and I slipped. And I can tell you,' she added quickly, 'that it's not very easy to get dressed and go to hospital when you're covered in baby oil and your wrist hurts.'

Ash exploded with laughter. 'At least you were having fun!'

'I can't even remember the fun part,' said Jodie. 'And Chris was less than amused afterwards. We were waiting in casualty for four hours before anyone saw me.'

'I suppose the enjoyment had worn off by then.' Ash put the chicken into the oven.

'Somewhat.' Jodie sighed. 'Still, he was nice to me yesterday. Brought me breakfast in bed and everything.'

'Lucky you,' said Ash. She refilled her glass with Ballygowan.

'What about you?' asked Jodie.

'What do you mean, what about me?'

'Do anything nice yesterday? Go anywhere with Brendan?'

Ash grimaced. She hadn't even thought about Brendan since yesterday. She never did think about them once she'd got over her panic attack at breaking up with them. It was as though they'd never even existed as far as she was concerned. She never wished that she'd done it differently because she always knew that she'd done the right thing. Even though Molly would be mad at her, and her cousin Michelle would make some barbed comment about her rate of attrition with men the next time she saw her.

'We split up,' said Ash shortly.

'Oh, Ash!' Jodie looked at her. 'I liked him.'

'Well, I didn't,' said Ash.

'I thought you did! How did he take it?'

'He wasn't over the moon,' said Ash. 'He'd wanted us to go on holiday together.'

'And you split up because of that!' Jodie shook her head. 'Ash, you know that's weird, don't you?'

'He booked it and everything,' said Ash. 'I don't like being pushed around.'

'But – he was sweet, Ash.'

'You only met him once,' Ash told her. She looked at her watch. 'Get a move on, Jodie, it'll probably take you twice as long to set the table today. The starter is mixed salad and there'll be eight for lunch.'

Jodie knew when she was beaten. Ash wasn't going to talk any more about her relationship with Brendan, just as she never talked about her relationships with any of the others. Ash was the most private person that Jodie had ever met. Occasionally she would mention the name of someone she was going out with but invariably the relationship didn't last. She'd only been going out with Brendan for a few weeks. Jodie liked Ash but she thought that her boss was clueless about men. Except, Jodie mused as she walked into the dining room, Ash always seemed to be the one to end the relationship. Jodie had never seen her plunged into the depths of despair over a failed romance. Maybe there had been someone in the past but whoever it was had obviously scarred Ash for life because – and Jodie was sure of this – despite her offhand manner about boyfriends, Ash was certainly wary of them. One day, Jodie told herself as she set the Newbridge cutlery on the table, one day I'll find out everything there is to know about Ash O'Halloran. But not today by the look of things.

She cast an appraising eye over the table. It looked good. She liked the floral arrangement that had arrived earlier in the morning. Chatham's had a standing order with their florists for new arrangements every Monday, one for the reception area, one for the managing director's office and one for the dining room. Sometimes the florist went a little crazy and sent weird and ultra-modern designs that Jodie liked but she knew the partners didn't. This one, she knew, would suit them both.

She went back into the kitchen where Ash was washing fruit. The aroma of roasting chicken had begun to waft through the room.

'So, we've nothing tomorrow but we're doing Butler's

on Wednesday, Bank of Hamburg on Thursday and Houghton and Company on Friday,' she said.

Ash nodded. 'I'm cooking more party food tomorrow,' she told Jodie. 'A twenty-first. I'll be delivering it tomorrow evening but, thank God, don't have to stay.'

'Don't tell me you're feeling your age.' Jodie grinned.

'Sometimes,' admitted Ash. 'But twenty-firsts were never my thing.'

'I enjoyed mine,' said Jodie. 'It was the first time I ever got legless in front of my parents.'

Ash smiled but said nothing. Jodie grimaced. She hadn't meant to mention her parents; she hated talking about them in front of Ash who, when Jodie had first asked about them, had simply stated that her parents had died. She'd said it in such a way that Jodie knew there was no point in even trying to find out how long ago it had happened. Jodie couldn't imagine what it would be like to have lost your parents as a child and, because of that, she made allowances for Ash's too-serious way of looking at life sometimes. And her habit of breaking up with boyfriends far too regularly.

The partners arrived at a quarter to one for lunch. Jodie carefully poured their drinks – two mineral waters, two gins and tonics, two tomato juices with a dash of Worcester sauce, and two orange juices. Her left arm ached afterwards. She handed around dry roasted peanuts and wondered, as she always did, what it would be like to be the person being waited on instead of the person doing the waiting. She'd never been a diner at a lunch in a private dining room in a busy company where the conversation was all about business and all about making money. Jodie didn't care about money, not in the same way as the suits did. Jodie wanted enough to live on. Enough so that she could make some demo tapes that might, one day, lead to a recording contract. Which in itself might lead to untold riches and fame but, and this was the important point, she often said to herself, that would just be the very nice side effect of someone appreciating that she could sing.

'I think we'll sit down now.' Ross Fearon, the prematurely bald managing director, nodded towards the table and the other partners took their places. Jodie slipped back into the kitchen and told Ash that they were ready.

'If you come out and pour the wine now, I'll dish out the salads,' she said.

Ash nodded. Mixed salad was boring, she knew, but she'd intended to keep one of the quiches she'd made yesterday to go with the salad for today's lunch. Bagel had put paid to that because she'd had to include the quiche with Laura Pearson's order to make up for the loss of the mini-pizzas.

'Am I OK?' she asked Jodie. 'No stray bits of tarragon in my hair? No splodges of butter anywhere?'

Jodie grinned at her. 'You look great,' she said. 'As always. I wish I knew how you do it. If I ever cook I always end up red-faced and flustered. While you, you cow, you look as though you've just stepped out of *Vogue*.'

'That's a bit extreme.' Ash smoothed back her hair which was tied in a tight plait and secured by one of her many black ribbons. 'I'm wearing an M and S T-shirt and an ancient pair of trousers. And no make-up. So I really don't think that I'd get past the before and after pictures in any magazine!'

'It's just that you look so cool,' complained Jodie.

Ash laughed. 'I wish.'

She carried the bottle of wine into the dining room. It was a rectangular room with a long, narrow table which seated ten. Ross Fearon sat at the top, as always, with John Minihan, the financial controller, at the other end. Ash knew the others by sight but she couldn't remember all of their names. The only two she knew for certain were Adrian Leigh who specialised in Japanese shares and Dan Morland who spoke to her about her account when Steve Proctor wasn't around. Ash liked Dan who was usually easy to talk to and never minded the fact that she had only a few hundred pounds to invest at any one time. She knew that some brokers wouldn't be bothered to talk to anyone with less than a few thousand. She stood beside him and poured wine into his glass. As she finished, he turned abruptly in his seat and jolted her arm. Wine glugged onto the table before she could do anything about it, spreading across the polished walnut in a golden pool.

'Shit.' The word was out before she could stop it and she flushed. It didn't do to swear in front of the clients. It made them uneasy.

'Oh, sorry!' Dan looked at her. 'My fault, honestly.'

'It's OK.' She tried not to appear annoyed although she couldn't believe that Jodie was the one with the sprained wrist but she'd actually managed to spill wine. She was normally so careful, attuned to the movement of people around her, alert for something untoward to happen. But she hadn't been paying enough attention, she'd been watching Jodie struggling with the plates of salad. 'I'll get a cloth,' she said.

She could feel her cheeks burning as she went into the kitchen and returned with a white napkin. There was no way she was using some bedraggled dishcloth to mop up the spills in Chatham's dining room.

'It was my fault,' said Dan as she wiped the table. 'I was about to adjust the blinds on the window behind me. I didn't notice you there.'

That's me, she thought. Trying so hard to be unobtrusive that I'm bloody invisible. And how can you say that you didn't notice me when I even asked you whether or not you wanted wine.

'No problem,' she said calmly. 'And at least your glass is still full. I hope you enjoy lunch.'

'I'm sure I will.' He smiled at her and his face was suddenly softer. Less dynamic suit and more, well, she thought, still dynamic suit really. None of the guys around the table looked anything other than businessmen, dressed to impress.

She finished serving wine and went back into the kitchen. She'd taken the chicken out of the oven and carved it earlier, now she poured a small glass of wine into the juices and brought it to the boil.

Jodie walked in. 'Maybe I should have done the wine after all.'

'It wasn't my fault,' said Ash. 'He wasn't looking. Honest to God, Jodie, those blokes don't give a shit about ordinary people.'

'They're not ordinary people?' Jodie took a sliver of chicken and popped it into her mouth. 'Um, Ash, this is gorgeous.'

'Oh, good,' said Ash dryly. 'And no, none of these people are ordinary people. None of them have to worry about their mortgages or have to save up for their holidays or think about how they'll afford to trade in the car.'

'You don't have to worry about that either,' said Jodie.

'Only because I don't have a car! But I do have a mort-gage.' Ash stirred some crème fraîche into the juice.

'You have shares too, don't you?' Jodie watched as she added tarragon to the sauce.

Ash nodded. 'But not many. I'm not rich, Jodie. I don't have a secret stash of savings or anything like that. I wish I had!'

'It wouldn't make you happy,' said Jodie. 'I bet none of them are happy.'

'I bet they bloody are,' said Ash.

Jodie went back to the dining room to collect their plates. 'More wine,' she mouthed to Ash as she carried them into the kitchen. Ash rinsed her hands. The last thing she wanted was to let a bottle slip out of her grasp because her hands were greasy.

They were talking about the Japanese market. Adrian had been to Tokyo the week previously and he was letting them know what he thought. It'd be lovely to go to

Tokyo, she thought as she walked round the table. It'd be lovely to go somewhere abroad and get paid for it.

Back in the kitchen, she arranged the food on the plates and handed them to Jodie. Doubling as the chef and the wine waiter was hard work. The meal wasn't flowing as seamlessly as it should. She'd splashed oil on the kitchen floor too and had nearly gone on her ear twice already even though she'd mopped it up as best she could. Meanwhile, Jodie scurried in and out with the plates and side plates, managing to avoid the slippery part of the floor.

'It'd be just my luck to end up on my bum and sprain the other wrist,' she said.

'I hope your other wrist isn't in your bum,' said Ash and the two of them giggled.

'I'll pop out again in a little while,' said Jodie. 'Let you know how they're doing on the wine front.'

'I should have let you pour anyway,' said Ash. 'It wouldn't have made much difference, given that I nearly drowned Dan Morland in the stuff.'

'Which one of them would you fancy?' asked Jodie.

'Pardon?'

'The partners. Which one of them, given the chance?'

Ash wrinkled her nose. 'Jodie, they're my clients. I don't think of them as potential – potential . . .'

Jodie giggled. 'I rather like Ross myself. I know he's bald but it's a sexy kind of baldness, don't you think?'

'What about Chris?' asked Ash. 'How d'you think he'd feel if he knew you were lusting after the managing director of Chatham's?'

'It's only pretend,' said Jodie. 'Harmless fantasy.'

Ash said nothing.

'So, in a pretend situation,' continued Jodie, 'which of them, Ash?'

'None of them.' Ash shrugged. 'I told you, I don't even notice them.'

'Oh, come on, Ash!'

'Seriously. I don't.'

'What about Gordon O'Sullivan? Don't you think he's rather cute?'

'Which one is Gordon?' asked Ash.

'The blondie one,' said Jodie. 'He's sitting beside Daniel Morland. Daniel's the one you tried to spill wine all over.'

Ash flushed with annoyance again. 'I know who Dan is. I've spoken to him about my account once or twice.'

'He'll think you're pissed off with the return on it.' Jodie laughed. 'He'll think that you're sending him a message by drowning him in Meursault.'

'Some message,' said Ash. 'It should have been house plonk and then he'd know all about it.'

'He's sexy in a glowering kind of way.'

'Dan?' Ash took the bowls of prepared fruit out of the fridge so that they wouldn't be too cold when she served them.

'I think so,' said Jodie appraisingly. 'Nice face, good body, dresses well. And, unlike Ross, he has lots of hair!'

'Stop lusting after the clients and check that everything's OK in there.' Ash gave Jodie a shove in the small of her back and sent her into the dining room again.

'You could do a wine top-up,' suggested Jodie as she came back. 'And Adrian's looking for more potatoes. That bloke is a pig, he really is.'

Ash took a bowl of potatoes from the oven where she'd been keeping them warm. 'Will you be able to manage?' she asked. 'It's heavy.'

'I'll just put it in the centre of the table,' said Jodie. 'They'll all dig in, I bet.'

Ash nodded, although she didn't like the idea of simply leaving them to serve themselves. But she couldn't do everything and Jodie wouldn't have been able to hold the bowl and serve them as well. I should have told her not to bother, she thought, as she adjusted her T-shirt. I should have got Margaret instead. Even if she's not half as much fun to work with.

They'd moved on to the US economy by now. A small, thin, extremely unprepossessing man was talking about the prospect of a merger between two big automobile companies in the States.

Boring, she thought, as she refilled their glasses. She wondered whether they'd be more or less likely to take risks after lunch. That was what their business was, after all. Buying shares and hoping they'd go up in price. Selling shares and hoping they'd go down. Would a few glasses of white wine alter their perspective on things?

The rain began to fall just as they started dessert. Ash stood in the kitchen and watched it roll in from the river. The sound of laughter from the dining room made her smile. Obviously the risk-taking had taken a turn for the better.

She turned away from the window and sat down. Once the meal was over, she was finished. Jodie was the one who cleared everything away, polished the fine wood dining table and stacked the dishes in the dishwasher. One of the reasons that Ash liked working with Jodie was that she could trust her to wait until everyone had left the dining room and clean up properly. She'd had an unnerving experience once with a waiter called Odhran who had simply gone home after pouring the coffee so that she'd received a frantic phone call later that day to tell her that the dining room was a mess. That had been in Banco Brava and it had taken her months to build up her reputation with them again.

Jodie grimaced as she picked up the coffee pot. Ash watched her.

'Do you need any help?' she asked.

Jodie shook her head. 'I can manage.'

'Sure? I don't want you to drop it.'

'Certain,' said Jodie. 'I won't drop it. I have the knack.' Although, she thought to herself, she'd be lucky if she didn't end up with a second sprained wrist.

'All OK,' she said to Ash as she returned. 'I don't think they'll be much longer. Ross looked at his watch when I came out with the coffee. Do you want a cup yourself?'

Ash nodded. She was never hungry when she cooked but she loved to drink coffee afterwards. She liked strong Kenyan blends with a bitter aftertaste although the coffee she served at Chatham's was fairly mild. But she gratefully accepted a cup from Jodie.

'Thanks,' she said.

'No.' Jodie put the glass pot on the hotplate. 'Thank you, Ash. I know I wasn't really fit for this today but you put up with me anyway.'

'Oh, it's good for me to meet the clients from time to time.' Ash smiled at her.

'You would have been better with Margaret or Seamus.'

Ash nodded. 'Yes. But you've been with me a long time, Jodie, and I like working with you. If I get anything bigger to do than today, then I'll have to have someone else. But we're OK for the others this week. The bank is the biggest and that's only for six.'

'You're a gem,' said Jodie.

'I know.' Ash stood up and stretched her arms over her head. 'Everyone says so.'

A flurry of activity from the dining room made the two girls look at each other in satisfaction. The partners were going back to work. Ash picked up a cloth and began scrubbing at the oily patch on the floor again.

'I'll go in and tidy up,' said Jodie. 'Get everything over and done with. Oh, sorry!' she gasped as she opened the door at the same time as Dan Morland and almost collided with him.

'Sorry, Jodie,' said Dan. 'Hope I didn't damage the other wrist.'

'I'm fine.' Jodie wrinkled her nose. 'I didn't realise you were still here. I was going to clean up.'

'I just wanted a quick word with Ash,' said Dan. 'If you're not too busy doing a Mrs Mop impression, that is.'

Ash flushed as she stood up. She tugged at her T-shirt

and pulled her hair more tightly in its plait. She hated any of the partners coming into the kitchen after a meal. She liked her clients to think that the food had appeared on their plates as if by magic but Dan Morland would hardly think that after seeing her on her hands and knees.

'Hi, Dan,' she said as Jodie disappeared into the dining room. 'Is there a problem?'

'Not at all.' Dan smiled and Ash felt a sudden surge of relief. For a horrible moment she'd thought that maybe he was going to tell her that she'd ruined his obviously expensive designer suit by pouring wine over it earlier, which she knew she hadn't but all the same . . . Or – much worse – that something awful had happened in the stock market and that she'd lost all her money. The idea of losing her money gave her a spasm of pain in her stomach.

'Are you OK?' he asked. His dark blue eyes looked concerned.

Ash nodded. 'Fine,' she said. 'For a moment I thought you were going to say I'd poisoned you all.'

He laughed. 'I wouldn't be standing here if you had. And lunch was delicious, Ash, as always. That's what I wanted to talk to you about.'

She looked inquiringly at him.

'I wondered – I know you do private dinners some-times. I wondered if you'd be available to do one for me?'

'When did you have in mind?' Ash reached into her bag and took out her organiser.

'Either Friday or Saturday fortnight,' said Dan.

She looked at her engagements. 'I can't do Friday,' she told him. 'I have a big lunchtime presentation that day and I simply wouldn't be finished early enough. At least, I might be finished but, honestly, Dan, I'd be exhausted and that wouldn't be fair to you or me. I could do the Saturday, though.'

'Saturday would be fine,' he said.

'How many people?' she asked.

'Just two.'

She thought he was blushing. It was hard to tell because his face was tanned and healthy anyway, but she was almost certain that he was blushing.

'Where?' she asked.

'At my house.'

'Special occasion?'

'Sort of.' He was definitely blushing now. She smiled to herself. It was nice to think that a man could blush. She'd never met a blushing bloke before.

'Birthday? Anniversary?' She grinned at him. 'Engagement?'

'Well, I . . .' He stopped in confusion. 'I'm not sure yet.'

'Dan, there's a difference between the three! I know you might want to keep your options open but aren't you taking things a bit far?' Her tone was amused.

'Possibly.' He looked at her wryly.

'I don't mind what sort of occasion it is,' she told him. 'I don't need to know.'

'It's just that—'

'It really doesn't matter.' Ash closed her organiser.

'I'll do you something really great which will raise your stock no matter what. I'll give you a call next week and we can plan the menu. Different menu, different price per head.'

'That sounds fine,' said Dan. 'Thanks, Ash.'

'No problem,' she said. 'It's my job.'

Chapter 4

Sweet and Sour Kebabs
Assorted meat, pineapple, lemon juice, soy sauce, garlic,
olives
Marinate overnight. Cook over hot grill

Ash felt extremely guilty about not having met with Michelle since Shay junior's christening. Her cousin had called her once or twice but Ash had always been busy, either in the middle of cooking something or just about to go out to cater for an event. She'd been offhand with Michelle, told her she was rushed and that she'd call her back. But she hadn't.

Molly liked to think that Ash had been closer to Michelle than she actually was, simply because they were nearly the same age. And she'd hoped that the constant rows that they had were simply because they knew each other so well. But Ash had known, from the moment she arrived in the house in Drogheda, that she and Michelle would never be close. Michelle had resented her cousin's arrival into the family where she was the only daughter.

She'd never been able to accept her. Besides, Ash was small and fair, not dark and sturdy like her, so they could never have been mistaken for sisters. Michelle had hated all the attention Ash received from her parents even though Molly had always done her best to be even-handed. But it didn't matter. Ash had a glamour that Michelle would never have because Ash was Julia's daughter.

Julia had never been close to her family. She had been the wilful one, the rebellious one, the one who'd decided that Ireland, and certainly Drogheda, were places that she'd be better off leaving far behind. Julia had been a sixties girl, her curls held back from her face by a variety of multi-coloured bandannas, her arms and neck decorated with love beads and a wardrobe that consisted of denim jeans and calico skirts.

Julia was the one who'd practised what she preached and spent a couple of years living in a commune in San Francisco. She became pregnant with Ash while she was living there but by the time the baby was born, the commune had disbanded and Julia was a single mother who neither knew nor cared about the father of her daughter. Julia had been disappointed when the commune had broken up; she'd enjoyed being with lots of people and she'd enjoyed the sense of community. Afterwards, she'd drifted from town to town and from job to job. At first, having a baby along hadn't bothered her. But as Ash grew older, Julia decided that her previous belief, that a girl didn't need a father, was completely wrong and she'd set about finding a man who wanted a ready-made family. Julia was a woman who believed things fervently. Just as she'd been convinced that the commune was the only way to live, later she believed that only by finding a man and marrying him would she and her baby be secure.

Only nobody she met wanted a ready-made family. They wanted Julia, who was still attractive and fun and full of life, but they didn't want Julia and Ash. Ash had watched different men come and go – sometimes with relief and sometimes with disappointment – but Julia had never found Mr Right. And every time a man left, Ash watched Julia cry and worry and she swore that she'd never let anyone make her feel like that. Ever.

Ash got off the DART at Killester and walked along the narrow roadways of the Demesne and Middle Third until she came to Michelle's house. Ash had been surprised that Michelle and Emmet hadn't bought a house in Drogheda, closer to Molly and Shay, but she had to admit that the quirky bungalow where the Somers family now lived was a great family home. It was set back off the road on a big corner site and surrounded by high hedges which gave it added privacy. There was plenty of room for a family of five – or more, as Michelle often joked while Ash smiled blankly.

She walked up the short gravel path and rang the doorbell.

'Hi, Ash.' Emmet, Michelle's husband, opened the door. Emmet had been Michelle's boyfriend since she was fifteen. Ash remembered how he used to hang around the house when they were kids, waiting to see Michelle.

He hadn't actually spoken to her for ages, he'd just looked at her from afar, but eventually they'd gone to some party or other together (Sarah Murphy's birthday, Ash remembered suddenly; she'd gone too and hated it) and they'd been an item ever since.

She hadn't spoken to him since the christening. He was a handsome man, well-built and broad-shouldered with fair hair and bright blue eyes. He looked relaxed and at ease as he ushered her into the house, his jeans frayed at the ankles, his red and black cotton checked shirt hanging out over them.

'Have you been keeping well?' It was trite, she thought. Surely she could think of something brighter and more interesting to say. But Emmet wasn't the sort of person who brought out the brightness in her. Emmet was like a pet Labrador, warm, comfortable and dependable.

'Not so bad,' said Emmet easily. 'Business has been great, of course.'

'It's a good time to be a builder,' she agreed as she followed him into the living room.

Michelle was watching TV but hit the mute button when she saw Ash. 'Hello, stranger.'

'Oh, Michelle, I'm sorry I haven't been out before. Really I am.' She handed a bottle of wine to her cousin. 'How are things?'

'We're fine.' Michelle took the bottle. 'Not that you'd know much about it, of course.'

'I said I'm sorry I haven't been around,' said Ash. 'I know I should come more often.' I'm like a record, she thought. Every time I meet Molly, every time I meet

Michelle, I say the same thing over and over. And I'm not sorry really because every time I see them I feel . . . she wasn't sure how she felt. She knew that she should have felt grateful because they'd taken her into their home and into their family and they had, truly, made her feel welcome. But it wasn't what she'd wanted. And, ever since she'd got married herself, Michelle always made Ash feel totally inadequate for not having a husband by now too. Besides, Michelle and Molly and the rest of the Rourkes knew too much about her to make her feel relaxed. She preferred going out with people who didn't know her. That way she could be someone completely different, someone who was fun to be with. It was easy to be a fun person when you only saw somebody once.

'The kids like to see you,' said Michelle.

'Molly called last week.' Ash sat down beside her cousin.

'I know. She told me,' said Michelle. 'So I knew you'd be out soon. On a guilt trip.'

'Michelle.' Emmet's voice held a warning.

'It's just that we have to drag you over,' said Michelle. 'I'd have thought that living on your own like you do you'd welcome the company.'

'I do,' said Ash. 'But I work at home a lot and . . .' She shrugged helplessly. 'Time goes by. I don't mean it to but it does.'

'Mum tells me that you've broken it off with Kieran.'

'It's a non-event.'

'Oh, come on, Ash! She said you've even had another boyfriend since then. Getting round a bit, aren't you?'

She smiled to show she was joking but Ash didn't smile in return.

'I split up with Kieran because it wasn't right between us,' she told Michelle. 'And Brendan was just a bit of fun.' She closed her eyes for a moment as she remembered his face in Bewley's. It was meant to have been a bit of fun. It wasn't her fault that he'd got so bloody serious.

'So who's your current victim?' asked Michelle.

Ash sighed. 'Why do you and Molly always ask the same questions? And they're not victims. There's no one around at the moment. I don't need there to be. I'm fine. I'm busy.'

'Sure.' Michelle reached over the arm of the sofa and picked up a wallet of photographs. 'I thought you might like to see these,' she said. 'Lucy had some friends over for tea last week.'

Ash took the photos and flicked through them. Her niece was like Michelle, she thought. Black hair, sallow skin, a defiant look in her eyes. Her own father's genes must have been particularly strong, she mused, to have turned her into the blonde in the family.

'She looks great,' said Ash.

'She's pretending to be you,' said Michelle.

Ash looked at her cousin in surprise.

'She insisted on cutting the sandwiches into shapes, like you did for her birthday, remember? And she wanted me to make that chocolate Rice Krispie cake that you did for them – the one that you made in the sandwich tin and filled with ice cream and broken biscuits.'

Ash smiled. 'I rather liked that myself.'

'She loved it,' said Michelle. 'And she demanded it. The other kids loved it too and she told them exactly how you'd made it.'

'I'm surprised she remembered.'

'Kids don't forget,' said Michelle. 'They come out with the most amazing things months after an adult has long forgotten them.'

'How are the others?' Ash closed the wallet.

'Oh, fine. They're all in bed. Want to go inside and have a peep?'

Ash nodded. She got up from the sofa and went into the children's bedroom. For the time being, Lucy and Brian shared while Shay slept in Michelle and Emmet's room. The two children were both sleeping – Lucy cuddled up beneath her duvet, Brian with his pushed down around his knees. Ash pulled the cover gently to his shoulders and he heaved a sigh before turning over, still asleep.

For years after Julia died, Ash had been afraid to go to sleep. She'd lain in the bed and fought it, terrified that she'd drift off and never wake up again, not believing for one second that Julia was in heaven watching over her as Molly had insisted. That was when she'd panic, trembling under the sheets and wishing that it was the morning. When she knew that Michelle was asleep she'd switch on the bedside lamp and read books until she couldn't keep her eyes open any longer. Every morning Molly would come in to wake them, every morning she'd find Ash lying with her face on the open page of whatever she was reading and every morning she'd tell her that it wasn't good for her to read in the middle of the night and that she'd have to stop. She'd taken away the bedside lamp but Ash bought a torch with her pocket money and read by torchlight instead. It had cost her a fortune in batteries.

She left the children's room and tiptoed into the main bedroom. Shay was asleep on his back, looking utterly content. She hugged her arms across her body. She couldn't imagine herself with a child of her own even though sometimes she wanted to gather Michelle's kids to her and never let them go.

'They're asleep,' she told Michelle as she walked back into the living room.

'They're exhausted,' Michelle said. 'Thank God, because it's a nightmare when they're not tired and you can't get them to settle.'

'We used to be like that.'

Michelle made a face at her. 'But I was always the one who got into trouble. Molly never gave you a hard time, Ash.'

'No,' admitted Ash. 'And I suppose that wasn't fair.'

'Of course it wasn't fair,' said Michelle. 'But she was never fair when it came to us, was she?'

'She was trying to make it up to me.' Not this again, thought Ash. How come we always end up raking over the past?

'And because of you she changed towards me.' Michelle's tone held a touch of steel.

'Michelle, I don't want to have a row about it,' said Ash. 'It was years ago. It doesn't matter.'

'Not to you, of course,' said Michelle. 'Why should it matter to you – you were the favourite.'

'Oh, grow up!' Ash's tone was bored.

Emmet, who'd been reading the paper, glanced at the two women. Ash looked far too calm, while Michelle had two spots of red on her cheeks.

'I have grown up,' said Michelle spiritedly. 'It's you who hasn't.'

'And what exactly does that mean?'

'Michelle, Aisling, there's no need to argue,' said Emmet.

'I'm not arguing,' said Michelle. 'I'm just saying that Ash is a case of arrested development.'

'I beg your pardon!' Ash stood up. 'Just because I haven't surrounded myself with a husband and a brood of kids doesn't mean there's something wrong with me, you know.'

'It's nothing to do with a husband and kids, as well you know.'

Emmet looked at them helplessly. 'I don't think there's any point—'

'Oh, shut up, Emmet!' said Michelle tersely. 'This is between Ash and me.'

'What's between us?' asked Ash. 'What in God's name is your problem, Michelle? Why do you always criticise me? Why do you constantly harp on and on at me? I know you resented me, but you don't have to keep on resenting me.'

'I didn't resent you,' cried Michelle. 'How can you say that? I let you into my home and into my room and I let you hang around with me and I was bloody nice to you, Aisling O'Halloran, but you never gave anything back, did you? You were Miss Bloody Ice Cool the whole time, with your cute little blonde ponytail and your neat and tidy ways.'

'Michelle!' Ash stared at her.

'Tidying the bedroom. Stacking the books on the bookshelves. Spending hours in the bath. Helping around the house. Learning to cook!'

'I—'

'And so you wormed your way into our lives and you made us all feel so sorry for you because you don't know who your father is and your mother was so silly she got herself killed.'

Ash thought that she was going to be sick. She could feel her stomach turning over, feel the lump in her throat and the metallic taste in her mouth.

'Michelle, that's enough.' Emmet's voice was firm.

Michelle watched Ash, her teeth clamped together, her eyes bright.

'Why do you ask me here?' Ash swallowed. 'Why are you always inviting me to your house and when I come why do you always say something horrible?' It was true, she realised. Which was why she didn't visit Michelle very often. Every time she did, Michelle would say things – never as bad as this but, despite her smiles, she would say things to make Ash feel unwelcome.

'She needs to cop on to herself,' said Michelle. 'Everyone's always so bloody careful around her. Whenever I talk to Mam about her she always says things like "Poor Aisling, she's had a hard time of it." God knows, she was only eleven when Julia died. It's time she got over it.'

'I am over it,' said Ash tightly. 'I've lived with it for the past eighteen years and I am over it. And just because your mother was nice to me when I was a kid doesn't mean that I shoved you out of the way or that she loved me any more than she loved you. And if you think that she did then it's you who needs help, Michelle, because you're too damned insecure. Which is maybe why you rushed into marrying someone you'd known your whole life instead of looking around a bit and why you feel the need to populate the planet every three years.'

'You bloody cow!'

'Ash, I think you—'

'Oh, who cares what you think. Either of you.' Ash grabbed her bag and her jacket. 'I'm fed up with the pair of you. I'm fed up with the way everyone gets at me all the time. I'm fed up with trying to be nice!'

She strode out of the living room, down the hall and opened the front door. Part of her expected either Emmet or Michelle to come after her but they didn't. For a moment she thought about slamming the front door closed, but she remembered the sleeping children and she closed it gently instead. Although I should have, she thought as she walked back towards the train station. I should have slammed the fucking door and woken the kids and let her deal with three of them screaming and roaring at her and it would have been her own damned fault!

She stood on the platform and shivered in the wind which whistled down the tracks. She'd always known that Michelle had resented her, seen her as an interloper.

Sometimes she imagined the conversation that Molly must have had with her before she came to live with them. 'You've got to be nice to Aisling,' she'd have told Michelle. 'She's had a terrible time. She doesn't have a daddy. And now she doesn't have a mammy either. So Aisling has no one to love her and we have to love her instead.'

And she imagined Michelle nodding and thinking to herself that there was no way on earth that she was going to love the cousin she'd never met before and that there was no way on earth that she was going to let her share her toys and that Molly could say all she liked but she would do exactly as she pleased.

The green commuter train slid into the station and Ash pushed the button on the doors. She sat down and leaned her head against the window. She'd thought that all this stuff was over, forgotten about. She closed her eyes and remembered Michelle telling her that she couldn't have her Barbie doll or her in-line skates. But she also remembered Michelle asking her what it had been like living in America and living in England, and Michelle had asked her as though she actually cared.

She felt her heart begin to race. Not now, she thought. Not now. I don't want to feel like this, I really don't. But the familiar tingle was spreading through her body and she knew that she was breathing far too quickly. She stared out of the window and tried to remember the train stations between Howth and Bray. It was like counting, like recipes, it took her mind off the fact that she was afraid that she was going to die.

Howth Junction, she thought. Bayside. Kilbarrack. Harmonstown. Raheny. Killester. Clontarf.

She swallowed as the train slid into Clontarf and a woman sat in the seat opposite her. If I faint now, thought Ash, at least the woman would notice. They'd look in my wallet and find my ID and they'd know who I was. So everything would be OK. She felt her breathing beginning to slow down and the feeling of panic subside.

And she began to feel angry with Michelle again. Really and truly, her cousin was a pain in the neck. If Michelle still had a problem about events that had happened eighteen years ago then it was Michelle who needed help, not her.

She'd dealt with her own demons herself. She had it all sorted out by now.

Chapter 5

Seared Tuna and Salsa
Tuna steaks, lemon juice, olive oil, garlic, chopped tomatoes,
salt and pepper, fresh basil
Marinate tuna in lemon juice, olive oil, salt and pepper.
Cook over high heat. Brown garlic in more olive oil, add
tomato and basil, spoon over tuna

As she'd promised, Ash rang Dan Morland the following week to discuss his dinner for two. She was put on hold while he finished another call. While she waited for him, she scrolled through her portfolio and thought, for the thousandth time, that it was assets that mattered in the end. Julia had been right to look for security but she'd looked for the wrong sort. People could hurt you, Ash decided, but money in the bank never did.

'Hi, Ash, sorry to keep you.' Dan sounded cheerful.

'Is this a convenient time?' she asked. 'I can always call you again, it doesn't matter.'

'No, this is fine. Just hold on another second, will you?'

Ash wondered how he could live with the pressure of watching those prices going up and down every day. But of course it didn't matter to him. Dan made money by buying and selling shares for his customers, not for himself. Although he must have a portfolio of his own. It wouldn't make sense if he worked in a stockbroking company and didn't have a portfolio of his own.

'Me again.' His voice was still cheerful. 'I just had to pass on a message to someone. I'm all yours now.'

'Well, actually, I'm all yours,' said Ash. 'Whatever you want, Dan, I'm your woman.'

'Good God, that sounds like an offer I can't refuse.'

'Not that sort of woman,' said Ash.

'Oh well, can't have everything, I suppose.' Dan chuckled. 'You haven't bought anything from me lately, have you?'

'Nope. I had my apartment redecorated and I needed the money for that,' Ash told him. 'I can't afford to splash money around on stocks and shares when I'm paying off my loan for paint and wallpaper.'

'Probably much better value,' said Dan.

'I should buy shares in a paint company, the cost of it!'

'Never mind,' said Dan. 'You can pay it all back when you cater for me.'

'Dinner for two?' Ash laughed. 'I'll have to charge you a fortune.'

'You won't say it to anyone, will you?' he asked anxiously. 'Only I don't—'

'Of course I won't say anything. This is a private

arrangement between you and me.' Ash sounded shocked that he'd asked.

'I know. I know.' Sitting at his desk, looking at the bank of screens in front of him, Dan Morland thought that dealing with numbers was a lot more straightforward than dealing with women. Dan liked women, he'd gone out with plenty of them, but he'd never met anyone he wanted to live with. In fact the idea of living with any of his previous girlfriends made him shudder. But Cordelia Carroll was different.

Cordelia was an analyst at one of the big American investment houses which had recently opened a division in Dublin. She was tall, olive-skinned, with red-brown hair, bewitching green eyes and a brain that was razor sharp. He'd met her at an investment seminar in the exclusive St Helen's Hotel where she'd been giving a lecture on technology stocks. She was a natural speaker, she'd kept the audience interested, imparting information in a friendly, down-to-earth way, in complete contrast to the previous talker. Dan had been impressed by her knowledge and captivated by her smile. Afterwards, he'd spoken to her and, surprising himself, he'd asked her to dinner. Cordelia had accepted and it was at dinner that Dan discovered that, despite the slight twang in her accent, she was actually from Wexford.

'But I've been in the States since I graduated,' she told him. 'I pick up accents far too easily – you should hear me when I visit my pals in Kerry.'

'Are you thinking of relocating to Kerry?' he asked lightly.

She shook her head. 'Nope. But I'm back in Dublin now so you'll soon think I was born and reared in the Liberties.'

'Since you're back, any chance you'd like to meet for dinner again?'

Cordelia smiled her wide, beguiling smile. 'You bet.'

And that had been the start of a relationship that Dan considered to be almost perfect.

It would be perfect, he decided, when she agreed to marry him. And he was determined to ask her. He'd wanted to ask her before now but it had never seemed the right time or the right place.

'Dan?' Ash's voice brought him back to the present.

'Sorry,' he said for the third time. 'I'm a bit distracted.'

'Look, I called you at work because it was the only number I had,' said Ash. 'If you want me to call you at home, I will. I'll need that number anyway.'

'No, Ash. Let's get this whole thing sorted out now,' said Dan decisively. 'What have you got in mind?'

'It depends on you,' she told him. 'Is there anything special you'd like? You can have your dream menu, you know!'

He laughed. 'I don't have a dream menu. Well, if I did it'd probably be fish and chips, which isn't exactly the world's most – most . . .' He broke off, aware that his colleagues could overhear his conversation.

'How about your girlfriend?' asked Ash as though he'd finished the sentence. 'Anything she likes?'

'I don't know.' Dan furrowed his brow. 'I think she

likes ethnic food – we've eaten Chinese and Thai and Indian quite a bit. She mentioned liking fish too . . .' his voice trailed off. 'This is bad, isn't it? I should know.'

'Not necessarily,' said Ash. 'Don't worry about it. I'll do something suitable.'

'Great, thanks.' Dan sounded relieved.

'OK,' said Ash. 'I promise you'll like it. What's her name?'

'Her name?'

'Yes,' said Ash patiently. 'It would be nice for me to be able to use her name when I'm flinging the plates around.'

'Cordelia,' said Dan and he loved saying it. 'Her name is Cordelia.'

'Great,' said Ash. 'What time do you want to eat?'

'Oh, around eight?' suggested Dan.

'Fine,' said Ash. 'I'll be there by six. Do you want to organise the wine or do you want me to do it?'

'You should do it,' said Dan. 'Since you're deciding on the menu.'

'And you don't have any red or white hang-ups?' asked Ash.

'No.' Dan sighed. 'It's much more complicated than going to a restaurant, isn't it?'

'Only because I have to cater for every eventuality,' said Ash. 'If you were in a restaurant, everything would be to hand.'

'I suppose so,' said Dan. 'OK, then.'

'Have you an upper limit on the cost?' asked Ash. 'Per head. So that I know.'

'No.' Dan was decisive about that. 'However much it takes, she's worth it.'

It was amazing, he thought on the Saturday morning, just how caught up in the whole thing he was. He hadn't thought he'd be so nervous about it, hadn't imagined that it would all matter so much to him. The thing was, he wanted to get it exactly right. He knew that Cordelia was the perfect match for him. Sometimes, at thirty-three, he'd wondered if he'd ever find the right girl. But Cordelia was, he knew she was. She was good for him, made him take himself less seriously, made him take her more seriously – he'd been somewhat chauvinistic about women's careers until now – and he knew that Cordelia would be the kind of woman he'd be happy to settle down with. After making mistakes in the past, he wanted to cement this relationship. And he knew that she was good for him. Whether he was good for her, he was less certain, but she'd told him she loved him, she'd whispered it to him over and over again when they made love together on the king-sized bed in his house and she wrapped her long, long legs round him and made him feel so bloody wonderful. Women didn't say 'I love you' lightly. He'd been told that before and he believed it. Women meant what they said, they were more into the whole relationship thing than men. Cordelia loved him as much as he loved her and tonight he was going to ask her to marry him.

He'd toyed with the idea of doing something heart-meltingly romantic like putting an engagement ring on the side of her plate, or (as he'd once seen in a movie) freezing it in an ice cube and dropping it into her drink, but that would mean choosing a ring without her and he didn't want to do that. He didn't think that she'd actually like him to choose the ring without her because she was the kind of person who knew exactly what she wanted and he could understand that. There'd be nothing worse than making the wrong choice, picking something that he liked but that she didn't. So he held back from the great romantic gesture and hoped that dinner would be good enough instead.

Actually, he admitted to himself, the one thing he was confident about was dinner. Ash O'Halloran was a good cook – no, chef, he knew that she called herself a chef – and Ross had sung her praises when she'd catered for an anniversary dinner for himself and Sarah a couple of months ago. She'd also done the Chatham's summer barbecue, held in the grounds of Landsdowne Rugby Club, and that had been fantastic. The one thing he didn't have to worry about tonight was the food.

Ash's taxi was twenty minutes late. She stood at the doorway to the apartment block and fumed that it was utterly impossible to get anyone in this city to do anything on time. But she'd taken the altogether necessary precaution of booking the taxi for half an hour earlier than she needed. In all the years that Ash had used Dublin's taxi service, a cab had only once arrived early.

She watched as the driver pulled up outside the building and checked to see if he was at the right place. The other irritating thing, thought Ash as she opened the door and waved at him, was that she used this company regularly. But they never seemed to know her, or her building.

She loaded her bags into the car and gave Dan's Rathgar address as she got in beside them.

'On a date, are you?' The driver pulled away from the apartment.

'No,' said Ash shortly although there was a part of her that felt as though she should be out there again, looking for someone.

'Saturday night and a young one like you should be out and about.'

Ash sighed. 'I'm working,' she said.

'Times have changed, haven't they?' The driver cut in front of another car and Ash grimaced and grabbed the door handle. 'There was a time when nobody except taxi drivers worked on a Saturday night.'

'Taxi drivers and waiters and waitresses and bar staff and doctors and nurses—'

'I get the drift,' said the driver. 'And which of those are you?'

'I'm a chef.'

'Cooking, that's great. I'm a great fan of Indian myself. Know any good recipes?'

'I do a nice chicken Korma,' said Ash.

'I liked Vindaloo myself. Puts a bit of fire in the belly,' said the driver. 'So where do you work? That address you gave me isn't a restaurant, is it?'

'No,' said Ash. 'It's a private function.'

'Wouldn't it be great to have the money?' asked the

driver. 'To be able to afford to hire chefs for private functions.'

'Yes.' Ash leaned back in the seat. 'It sure would.'

Although traffic was heavy they arrived at Dan's house on time. Ash paid the driver and hauled her bags out of the car.

'Nice place,' he said as she tipped him.

'Not bad at all,' said Ash.

Dan Morland's house was in the centre of a terrace of red-brick Victorian houses on a narrow side street. Ash had been in this type of house before – they looked deceptively small from the outside but many of them had annexes and returns at the back, which made them much larger than they first appeared. She pushed open the iron gate, walked up the stone pathway and pressed the bell.

Dan opened the door and smiled in welcome. His hair was still damp from a recent shower and he was wearing black jeans and a black T-shirt. Ash had never seen him in casual clothes before and was surprised at how much younger and how much more relaxed he looked. The staff had worn jeans to the barbecue during the summer but Ash couldn't remember seeing Dan at it. She remembered remarking to herself how different the bean-counters had looked in their casual clothes. Everyone, even the receptionists, in Chatham's wore suits. Kate had told her that they all received a clothes allowance.

'Come in,' said Dan. 'You're on time.'

'I do my best.' Ash carried her bags into the hall and looked around. 'This is a lovely house.'

'Only some of it,' said Dan. 'I bought it a couple of years ago and it was a complete mess. It had been divided into flats. I'm doing it room by room but it's a slow process.'

'You're doing well,' she said.

'But it takes for ever,' said Dan. 'And it's cost me every spare penny I have. Plus some.' He grinned at her. 'Everyone thinks brokers are loaded but I don't earn enough to do more than a room a year. Come on, I'll show you the kitchen.'

She followed him along the hallway which was decorated in warm shades of terracotta, down a short flight of stairs and to the kitchen. She gasped when she saw it. The kitchen was obviously one of the rooms he'd got around to renovating. And, looking at it, she wasn't surprised he could only do a room a year.

'This is unbelievable!'

He grinned. 'Which part?'

'The whole thing. It's like – it's a professional kitchen!'

Long stainless steel Gaggenau units, set with a very discreet double oven, lined one wall. Two free-standing units took up the centre of the floor – one was a double sink with exceptional workspace, the other a series of gas, electric and ceramic hobs. A stark stainless steel extractor fan hung from the ceiling over the cooking unit which had no pots or pans on it at all. The severity of the room was tempered, though, by the beech flooring and by the fact that, between two full-length units on adjoining walls, the walls themselves had been replaced by glass so that it was possible to look out into the garden beyond. And even though it was dark outside Ash could see that the garden was big because it was lit by soft outdoor lights which followed a meandering path through the evergreen shrubs.

'Is it OK?' asked Dan.

'It's utterly fantastic.' She turned to smile at him. 'But you've terrorised me – do you cook much yourself?'

'Actually,' he looked shamefaced, 'my major area of expertise is that piece of equipment there.' He pointed to the stainless steel microwave. 'I'm a dreadful cook – but great at heating up frozen lasagne.'

'You're joking,' said Ash. 'Why on earth would you do up such a fantastic kitchen and not bother cooking in it?'

'For one?' He shrugged. 'It's hardly worth the effort. And I eat out a lot. But the kitchen was so bad that I had to do something. So I ended up with this.'

'It seems such a shame.' Ash sighed. 'I'd love to have this kind of space in my kitchen at home.'

'Where do you live?' asked Dan.

'On the quays. Almost opposite the Chatham building in fact.'

'The apartments?' Dan nodded. 'Nice building. Especially if you're on the top floor.'

Ash smiled. 'I am. And you're right, they're lovely apartments. But, as the estate agent said at the time, compact.'

He grinned. 'Surely not that small! Not compact!'

'Slightly bigger than compact,' she conceded. 'But

nothing like this.' She slipped out of her jacket. 'Anyway, I'd better get to work. Where will you be eating?'

'The dining room is upstairs,' said Dan. 'There's a kind of breakfast area off the kitchen but obviously I don't want to eat there. Don't worry, though, it's not a big walk with plates or anything to the dining room.'

'Best show it to me,' suggested Ash. 'Let me get the feel of it.'

She followed him out of the kitchen and into his dining room. It was another renovated room, coolly elegant, with what were obviously the original floor-boards sanded and varnished, barley-white walls hung with occasional prints and swathes of gauze draped over the windows. The dining table was made of heavy smoked glass supported by wrought iron and surrounded by eight cream-coloured chairs, also of wrought iron. Ash bit her bottom lip. Stylish, yes. In fact some of the colours weren't a million miles away from her own apartment décor, but she couldn't see an intimate dinner for two in a room like this. It was too cool. Too classy. Too damned designer!

'What do you think?' Dan looked at her hopefully. 'Dinner won't get cold en route from the kitchen, will it?'

'No-o,' said Ash doubtfully.

'Is there something the matter?' he asked.

She shrugged. 'I think I need to work on the table a bit, Dan. There's only going to be two of you and it's so – so big!'

He looked at it consideringly. 'But according to my interior designer this room needed a big table.'

89

'It does,' said Ash. 'But you and Cordelia need a more intimate table, don't you think?'

Dan scratched his head and looked worried. 'I suppose you're right.'

'It won't take much,' she assured him. 'I've brought a few bits and pieces with me anyway.' She smiled. 'You go ahead and do whatever you have to do, leave me to worry about everything here.'

'You sure?' he asked.

'Positive.' Ash nodded. 'And I work better when someone isn't hanging over my shoulder.'

Dan laughed. 'Point taken. Don't worry, I've things to do. When Cordelia arrives I'll bring her into the living room for a drink anyway. The living room is across the hall. I'll show you.'

I feel like a pet dog or something, thought Ash, as once again she followed Dan.

If the kitchen in his house was utilitarian to the point of starkness and the dining room was icily elegant, his living room was warm and relaxed. The sofa was midnight-blue and well-worn, the walls were painted burnt sienna and the floors were covered in an assortment of rugs with Aztec designs that were both warm and colourful.

'OK,' she said. 'I'll aim to have dinner ready for you by eight o'clock. You can either come into the dining room or I'll come and get you. Whatever you like.'

'There's an intercom.' He looked almost apologetic.

'Pardon?'

'Between the different rooms in the house.' He shrugged. 'There's a lot of technology floating around here, one way or another. A friend did it. He works for an electronics firm and he's a whizz with anything that operates with either a button or a mouse. He thought that the intercoms would be a good idea.'

'So you'll buzz me when you're ready to eat?'

'Is that awfully pretentious?' asked Dan.

'Fairly,' she said. Then she grinned. 'But whatever you want. You're paying the bill, Dan.'

She giggled to herself as she went back to the kitchen. Men and gadgets! They were all the same about anything that you could press or click or turn. The Rourke family was no different; all of Michelle's brothers had been into things you could tinker with. At least it had meant that there was always someone ready to try to fix something for you. She sighed as she began unpacking her bags and thought of her cousins. She wished she hadn't argued with Michelle. But really and truly the girl sometimes drove her mad. Could she blame her? Ash asked herself wryly. I'd probably have thrown a wobbler if someone had foisted an unwanted cousin on me too.

Dan stood in front of the mirror and looked at his reflection. Pretty good, he thought, courtesy of his soft biscuit-coloured Calvin Klein jumper and his Levi's, although I should really work out a bit more. He turned sideways and looked at himself critically. All those business lunches piled on the pounds and although he certainly wasn't overweight he knew that his body wasn't as good as it had been when he was twenty. But then, whose is? he asked himself. He ran his fingers through his hair and dabbed

Polo on his cheeks, flinching as it stung. Girls were lucky, he thought as the pain subsided. No shaving.

He looked out of the bedroom window just as the taxi pulled up outside the house. He stepped back straight-away, hoping that Cordelia hadn't seen him looking out. It would be so utterly naff, he thought, to be caught peeking from behind the blinds.

He waited until she'd rung the bell before he went downstairs and opened the door.

She smiled at him and he felt the now familiar tingle of desire run through his body. She was gorgeous, really gorgeous.

'Hi.' She offered the side of her cheek for a kiss and he leaned towards her. At just over six feet tall he was used to bending down to women. But he hardly needed to with Cordelia who almost matched him in height when she was wearing high heels.

'Come in.' He ushered her through the hall and into the living room. She sat in one of the armchairs and stretched her long legs out in front of her. She was wearing a green dress and long green jacket, both of which matched the colour of her eyes. Her earrings were emeralds and so was the stone in the necklace she wore.

'You look stunning tonight,' said Dan.

'So do you,' she told him. 'Hardly as though you've spent the day slaving in the kitchen.'

He laughed and handed her a gin and tonic. 'I don't slave,' he told her. 'I never slave.'

'So what's on the menu?' she asked. 'Takeaway?'

He shook his head. 'The girl that does the cooking for us in Chatham's. She's pretty good.'

'Excellent.' Cordelia smiled at him. 'Presumably we have some time before dinner is served?'

'Presumably we have.' Dan sat on the arm of the chair. This time he had to bend down to kiss her. And this time she pulled him closer and wrapped her arms round him.

Ash had prepared everything for the Thai prawn soup but since it only took a few minutes to make she didn't want to start until Dan buzzed her. The worst thing that she could do to the soup would be to overcook it. She looked at her watch. A quarter past eight. Soon, she thought.

'Hungry?' Dan kissed Cordelia behind her ear.

'Not any more,' she replied lazily.

He laughed. 'All the same, there's a girl cooking like a mad thing in the kitchen just for you.'

'Not on my account.' Cordelia sat up and rearranged her dress. She pushed her fingers through her hair.

'I'm starving,' admitted Dan. 'Making love always makes me hungry.'

'How romantic,' said Cordelia dryly. She stood up and looked at herself in the mirror over the mantelpiece.

'You look gorgeous,' said Dan.

'Good enough to eat?' She turned round to him and smiled.

'God, Cordelia, you do things to me . . .' He held out his arms to her and she fell into them again.

*   *   *

93

Ash wondered if the intercom was actually working. She remembered the Meccano crane that Rob Rourke had once made. It looked absolutely fantastic, was authentic down to the last detail, even to a row of tiny bulbs along the gantry which, he told her, could be lit up for Christmas. But it hadn't worked. He'd tested everything over and over again but never managed to get it working properly. He'd thrown it out the window eventually.

'Hungry now?' asked Dan.

'I think so.' Cordelia yawned. 'Though maybe more sleepy than hungry.'

'Should have organised to have dinner in bed,' said Dan.

'What a good idea.' Cordelia kissed him on the forehead. 'But since you've gone to so much trouble . . .'

'Come on.' Dan crossed the room and hit the intercom button. 'Hi, Ash, we're ready now.'

About bloody time, thought Ash as she turned on the heat under the chicken stock. Honestly, if he'd said that it would be nine before they were actually going to eat then I wouldn't have been ready to go at eight. Why aren't people punctual? I am, why can't they be? Because he's paying the bill, she told herself as she added lemon grass to the stock. When I'm rolling in it I can be as late as I like.

'Goodness, this looks fantastic!' Cordelia looked around the dining room while Dan stood beside her equally impressed. Somehow Ash O'Halloran had transformed the room which he privately thought was rather too glacial into a softer, more relaxing area. She'd spread a white tablecloth over the centre part of the table, effectively making it seem much smaller than it actually was. She'd moved some of the chairs away from it too and had dotted small candles in glass holders around the room. White wine was chilling in a bucket on the sideboard while a bottle of uncorked red stood beside it.

'Sit down,' said Dan.

'Your little waitress knows her stuff,' Cordelia told him.

'She's a chef,' corrected Dan.

'Waitress, chef, whatever.' Cordelia unfolded one of the neatly pleated napkins and placed it on her lap just as Ash arrived carrying a serving dish of soup. She placed the dish on the sideboard and brought the bottle of wine to Dan.

'It's a Sancerre,' she told him. 'Would you like to try it?'

He shook his head. 'Just pour.'

She glanced at him. He looked more self-satisfied than she'd ever seen him before. Not, she told herself, that she'd seen him that often but tonight he looked like a man who had got exactly what he wanted. Which, she supposed, looking at Cordelia who was also bathed in a contented glow, he obviously had.

She served the soup and left them.

'That was really good.' Cordelia put down her spoon and looked at Dan. 'She can cook, can't she!'

'Told you.' Dan looked pleased with himself.

'Wish I could cook like that.'

'Cooking isn't everything,' said Dan loyally.

Cordelia grinned. 'But it would be nice to be able to do it all the same.'

'Leave it to the experts,' Dan advised.

'I suppose if you can afford to have someone cater for you every day . . .'

'I couldn't eat this sort of thing every day,' Dan said. 'My waistline is bad enough already.'

'So there's something to be said for being useless in the kitchen!' Cordelia was laughing when Ash arrived to clear away the soup bowls and serve the main course.

Dan watched Cordelia silently as they ate the seared tuna with tomato salsa. She was so self-assured, he thought, you'd never believe that she was twenty-four. He loved that self-assurance, that belief that she was invincible. He wondered when he should ask her. 'Will you marry me?' wasn't a question you could just blurt out while someone was eating! But he didn't quite know how to bring up the subject now that she was here in the setting he'd so carefully arranged. Somehow he'd imagined that she'd guess when she'd seen how much trouble he'd gone to and that the whole question of marriage would just bubble into the air between them without having to bring it up at all. Which, he had to admit, was a pretty silly thought on his part.

The best thing would be to ask her straight out. The worst that could happen would be that she'd say no. He shuddered at the thought of the fool he'd be making of himself if she said no.

'I just wanted to—'

'I have to tell you—'

They both spoke at the same time and stopped, laughing.

'You first,' said Cordelia.

He shook his head. 'No. You.'

'What I was going to tell you is . . .' she popped the last piece of tuna into her mouth and swallowed it, 'that the bank is sending me to New York for a while.'

Dan stared at her, aghast. 'New York!'

'Yes.' She nodded. 'Isn't it great? I loved it when I was there before but of course I was only a junior then. This time I get to work with some of the senior analysts and it's a much better position for me.'

Dan didn't know what to say. He could hardly believe what she'd just told him. 'How long will you be away? What about your job here?' he asked finally.

'I work for the company, not for the Dublin office specifically,' she explained. 'And this assignment is both promotion and training. Six months or so in New York and then I can get sent anywhere. They still need people for Ireland so I can choose to come home.'

'But what about us?' asked Dan.

'It's not like we don't have phones and e-mails so that we can keep in touch. And I can fly home as much as I like if work commitments allow.'

'Well, yes, sure, but I thought – I wanted to—'

'And it's such a brilliant opportunity! I can't pass it up, Dan, I really can't.'

'I wanted to marry you.' The words came out before he could stop them.

Cordelia stared at him. 'Marry me?'

'Yes,' said Dan.

Cordelia fiddled with her emerald earrings. 'Dan, I—'

'It's OK,' he said fiercely. 'If you don't want to, if I've stepped out of line—'

'It's not that.' She slid the earring out of her ear. 'It's just that I didn't expect you to ask me.'

'Why?'

'You never said anything before.'

'I'm saying it now,' said Dan.

'I thought that . . .'

'That what?'

'That you had problems with the idea of settling down.'

'Not with you, I don't,' said Dan.

'Do you love me?' she asked.

Dan looked at her in surprise. 'Why the hell do you think I'm asking you to marry me? Of course I love you. Who wouldn't?'

'You don't say it very often,' she told him.

'I love you,' he said passionately. 'I really do.'

'And I love you,' said Cordelia. 'But I love my job too. And I want to go to the States.'

They looked at each other in silence, then Ash came in to clear away the plates.

Chapter 6

Crème Brûlée
Single cream, double cream, vanilla pod, caster sugar,
egg yolks
Make custard and refrigerate overnight. Sprinkle caster
sugar over top. Pop under hot grill until sugar caramelises.
Chill before serving

S he could feel the tension as soon as she walked into
the room. She glanced from Dan to Cordelia and back
again. It was clear that the atmosphere between them was
electric. But not with the electricity of people who had just
decided to get married. Surely to goodness, she thought,
the beautiful Cordelia hasn't refused the eligible Dan.
Once she'd seen Cordelia she'd immediately thought
that she and Dan looked perfect together, both tall and
attractive and obviously well off. But not perfect for each
other after all?

Ash cleared the plates. 'Would you like dessert now?'
she asked, feeling her words dropping like bricks into
the room.

'Not yet,' said Dan tightly.

'I'm not sure I should have a dessert,' said Cordelia. 'I lost a stone last year through a terrorising regime at the gym. I try to steer clear of sweet things.'

'That's OK,' said Ash. She glanced at Dan. 'Buzz me when you want something.' She left the room as quickly as she could for the sanctuary of the kitchen. It didn't look as though she'd need to caramelise the top of the crème brûlées after all. Somehow she got the feeling that whatever was going on in the dining room, dessert was never going to be part of it.

Dan and Cordelia looked at each other.

'Dan, I won't be in New York for ever. I'll be coming back.'

'But you'll meet someone else in New York, won't you? Or you'll decide that business is more important than anything else. I've been to Wall Street, Cordelia. I've felt the buzz.'

'I worked there before and I came back,' said Cordelia reasonably. 'I'm not taken over by it. But I have to go, you understand that, don't you?'

'Marry me before you go,' he said impulsively.

She turned her earring between her fingers. 'That'd be crazy.'

'Why? Why would it be crazy?'

'Because – oh, Dan, I do love you. I really do. But I just need a bit of space for me, that's all. Anyway,' she smiled at him, 'I don't think we've time to get married! I'm going in a few weeks.'

'Yeah, right,' said Dan sulkily.

Cordelia looked at him. 'You've got to understand how important this is to me, Dan. It's only six months, give or take a little. I'll be back then.'

'Six months is a long time.'

'Oh, come on.' She slid the earring back into her ear and fastened it. 'Six months is nothing. You know it's nothing. And if you really loved me—'

'I do really love you,' said Dan.

'Then you'll understand why I have to go.'

He sighed. He did understand, of course he did. If the opportunity had been his, he wouldn't have let anything stop him. But he wished she'd told him this last week so that he hadn't made such a complete and utter fool of himself tonight. She must have known about it then but she hadn't said anything. Wanting to make sure, he supposed, that everything was in place for her big job back in the States. He'd thought that she was happy to be in Ireland, happy to be with him, happy with how things were.

'Dan, I'd like us to stay together,' said Cordelia urgently. 'We work well. We like the same things, we want the same things – I see a future for us. I do. Honestly.'

'A future with me in Dublin and you in New York?'

'Some time for my career,' she said. 'That's all I'm asking for.'

He looked at her. 'We could get engaged before you go. It wasn't quite how I planned it but if you love me and you're coming back – why not?'

'Of course I'm coming back! And I *do* love you, Dan.'

'Well then,' said Dan.

'You really want to get engaged now? Even with me going away?'

'I wanted to get married!' he cried. 'I was going to buy you a ring straightaway. There wasn't exactly any need for us to hang around.'

Cordelia laughed. 'You sound so determined.'

'I am determined,' said Dan. 'You're the only girl for me, Cordelia. You're the only one I've ever even considered marrying.'

'I'm supposed to be flattered by that.'

'I'm sorry.' He looked abashed. 'That sounded—'

'It's OK,' she interrupted him. 'It's not that I don't want to get married or don't even want to get engaged but I want to be practical. How will you feel when I'm away and you're here? Happy about it still?'

'Not happy,' said Dan. 'How can I be happy when you're not with me? But if we're engaged I'll feel as though everything will turn out all right.'

'It'll turn out all right,' said Cordelia. 'Of course it will.'

'So, we'll do it then,' said Dan. 'Get engaged.'

Cordelia twirled a lock of her curly auburn hair between her fingers. 'Why not?' She smiled at him suddenly. 'Yes, Dan, why not? It's not like I don't want to marry you. It's just – you know – I need to do this.'

'I understand,' said Dan. 'I really do.'

She reached across the table and took his hand. 'It's the right thing for us.'

'OK.' Dan twined his fingers round hers. 'OK. So we'll go and get you a ring and then we'll be engaged and you'll come back in the spring and we'll do the whole marriage thing.'

'Right,' said Cordelia. 'Sounds good to me.'

'OK,' said Dan again. 'Sounds good. OK.'

Ash sat in the kitchen and waited for the intercom to sound. She hadn't heard raised voices or angry shouts, which was something. But she still doubted that dinner was going exactly as Dan had planned it.

Dan watched Cordelia who was sipping her wine. It didn't feel like they'd just got engaged. He didn't feel like someone who was going to marry the girl sitting opposite him. He felt as though it could all be torn away from him before he knew it.

Cordelia drained her glass and looked at her watch. 'I know you'll think this is really unfair of me,' she said, 'but I have to go.'

'What!'

'I'm meeting with our European president before he goes back to the States tomorrow,' she said. 'And the only time he can meet me is six o'clock in the morning. So I need to go home and get some sleep.'

'You can stay here,' said Dan.

'Normally I would.' She smiled at him. 'You know I would, Dan, but that'd mean getting up before the crack of dawn to go home and change. I can't meet Mr Kelley in this particular outfit.'

Dan looked at her seductive green dress. 'Maybe not.'

'Definitely not,' said Cordelia.

'So why don't you come back after you meet him?' said Dan. 'We can go out for breakfast or something.'

Cordelia nodded. 'That sounds good.' She stood up.

'You're going now?' asked Dan.

'I'm knackered,' she told him. 'Making love twice . . . and the food . . . and getting engaged.' She grinned. 'I need my sleep.'

Dan sighed. 'This isn't exactly what I'd planned, Cordelia.'

'Hey!' She grinned again. 'What is it they say about the best laid plans?'

'It's just that on the night we got engaged I kind of thought – well, you know.'

'This isn't the night we got engaged,' she told him. 'We'll get a ring next week and that'll be our official engagement night. This is just a – a preliminary engagement discussion.'

Dan laughed. 'You sound like you're talking to those Wall Street honchos now.'

'I know.' Cordelia hung her head but peeped at him from under her black lashes. 'I'm sorry.'

'It's OK.' He got up and walked over to her. She allowed herself to be held by him. 'I love you,' he said.

'I love you too,' said Cordelia and kissed him, slowly, on the lips.

Ash heard the door closing. She couldn't see the front of the house from the kitchen so she wasn't certain that

Cordelia had left but she found it hard to imagine any other outcome to the tension she'd felt in the dining room. She felt sorry for Dan. He'd gone to so much trouble for Cordelia; he'd wanted everything to be so right and it clearly hadn't been. She wondered where it had all gone wrong, what had happened to make Cordelia walk out on him like this.

She glanced at the intercom on the wall, waiting for Dan to call her and tell her not to bother about dessert and coffee. But it remained silent. She bit her lip. Maybe he was getting blitzed in the living room and he'd forgotten all about her. In which case she'd have to go up there and . . . She rubbed the side of her nose. It hardly seemed sensitive to walk in on a distraught man and ask for her cheque! Of course he might not be distraught. He might suddenly be relieved that Cordelia had turned him down, realising that he'd had a lucky escape. Somehow Ash didn't think so.

She poured herself a cup of coffee. She'd give him some time to get his act together and remember that she was waiting for him. But if he hadn't buzzed her within twenty minutes then she would have to go up to him. She had better things to do than wait here all night. And then she wondered, exactly, what better things she had to do? Go to bed on her own, maybe Bagel lying at the foot of the bed? She should get out and find someone new again. Someone she could have fun with for a while. But, she thought agonisingly, someone new was such hard work. She hadn't always thought of it as hard work. She used to like the fact that every man she went out with was different. But now . . . She sighed. Perhaps most of them weren't so different after all.

She drained the cup and put it into the dishwasher. Time to go upstairs, she decided. Whatever had happened was well and truly over by now and she had no desire to sit in Daniel Morland's kitchen for the rest of the night.

He wasn't in the dining room. She cleared away the remains of the meal and retrieved her white linen table-cloth which she folded neatly despite the fact that she would put it in the wash that night. She brought every-thing back to the kitchen, stacked the dishes in the dishwasher and put her own equipment into one of the cardboard boxes she'd brought with her. She put the two crème brûlées back into Dan's fridge on the off chance that he might like to eat them later. Then she folded her invoice and went upstairs again.

He was in the living room, gazing out of the window into the darkness of the garden. Ash cleared her throat and he turned round.

'Ash!' He looked surprised to see her.

She smiled awkwardly at him. 'I cleared everything away. I left the desserts in the fridge. Just in case you might want one.'

'Thanks,' he said. 'I'm sorry. I forgot about you.'

'So I gathered,' she said. She looked around. 'I heard the front door closing . . .'

'Yes.' Dan nodded. 'Cordelia had to go early. She has a meeting tomorrow morning.'

'Oh.' Ash nodded. 'And did everything – was every-thing OK?'

'Absolutely fine,' said Dan. 'Great meal, Ash. Absolutely great. Wonderful.'

'And you and Cordelia?'

'Engaged,' said Dan.

'Great!' Ash's smile hid her surprise. 'Great.'

'Yes.'

'So – you're sure everything went OK?'

'Couldn't have been better,' he said brightly.

'In that case, I suppose I'd better give you this.' She handed the invoice to him.

He glanced at it. 'Excellent value.' He took a chequebook from a drawer in the bureau. 'You're a great cook.'

'Thank you.'

'And you did a fantastic job on the dining room.'

'Thank you,' she repeated.

'She's going to the States.' Dan signed the cheque and handed it to Ash.

'Oh?'

'She was promoted,' he said. 'She thinks it's a great opportunity and she won't marry me because she'd prefer to be in the US slugging it out with the big boys.'

'But I thought you said—'

'We're engaged.' Dan couldn't stop himself from telling Ash what had happened. 'Oh yes, I popped the question! More or less. And tonight we had the preliminary engagement discussions. We'll actually be engaged next week when we get the ring.'

'That's what you wanted, isn't it?' Ash was intrigued by the idea of preliminary engagement discussions. Sounded like a reasonable idea, she thought, although probably not many people would agree. She wasn't sure that preliminary engagement discussions were what Dan had in mind when he'd asked her to cater for dinner tonight.

'I thought it would be different,' admitted Dan. 'I thought it would be – romantic.'

'It looked romantic,' said Ash.

'But it felt more like business,' said Dan. 'She says she loves me but it felt like a business arrangement.'

'How long will she be spending in the States?' asked Ash.

'Six months. Well, she says six months but I have the horrible feeling it might be a bit longer.'

'I bet she'll be dying to get back!' Ash looked at him sympathetically. 'She'll probably be really busy while she's there. And you *are* engaged to her. Why are you so worried?'

'I'm worried that she'll get there and think that she'd like to stay there,' said Dan. 'Or that she'll meet some Wall Street bultibillionaire and decide he's a much better proposition than a humble Irish stockbroker.'

'Not so humble.' Ash glanced around the room. 'You have a lovely home.'

He smiled at her. 'Thanks. But I couldn't compete with someone who has a private jet and a house in Malibu.'

'And is there someone with a private jet and a house in Malibu?'

'Not yet,' said Dan darkly.

'I don't know what you're getting into such a state over,' said Ash although she knew perfectly well. But he was her client and she had to make it sound good. 'She said she'll marry you but she's going to America for six months first. No big deal.'

'That's what she said. But how would you feel,' he asked her, 'if you got engaged and the guy disappeared for six months?'

She shrugged. 'Not likely to happen,' she said.

'Are you engaged?' asked Dan. 'Are you married? I'm sorry, I don't know.'

'Neither,' she said.

'And would you like to be?'

She laughed. 'Not right now. Is that an offer? Do you usually propose to two women in one night?'

Dan laughed too, a little shakily. 'Not this time.'

'She'll be back.' Ash kept her tone confident. 'Maybe she just needs to get the States out of her system.'

He was silent then he poured himself a brandy from the decanter on the sideboard. 'Want one?'

Ash shook her head. 'I don't think—'

'Have a drink with me,' said Dan. 'You deserve one. You did a great job and – and . . .' He swallowed the brandy in one gulp. 'I'd like you to have a drink with me.'

'Dan, I'd love to have a drink with you. But not now.'

'Why not?'

'Because I'm not sure that it's a good idea.'

'It's a celebration drink,' Dan told her. 'To celebrate my engagement to Cordelia.'

Ash looked at him uncomfortably. 'A celebration?' she said doubtfully.

'Even though she's deserting me straightaway.' Dan smiled crookedly. 'But she has to because she's going to be a very successful lady. Which is why I love her. And I need to celebrate.'

'You do?'

'Absolutely.' Dan waved the decanter at her. 'Join me.'

'I'll have a Baileys if you have it.' Ash didn't drink brandy.

'One Baileys coming up.'

'Great,' said Ash carefully.

She watched while Dan poured the creamy fudge-coloured drink into a cut glass tumbler. 'That's enough!' she cried as it reached the brim. 'There's about six measures in there.'

'A quiet drink,' said Dan. 'A celebration.'

'Congratulations,' said Ash. She raised her glass and tipped it gently against his. Brandy sloshed over the side of Dan's glass and landed on the floor.

'Oops,' he said. He grinned at her. 'Just as well it's not carpet! Cordelia would hate to think of me messing up the carpets.'

Ash wondered how much Dan had drunk since Cordelia's departure. She'd been sitting in the kitchen for at least half an hour while she waited for him. She suddenly realised that Dan might be a good deal more drunk than she'd thought.

'Do you mind if I call a cab from here?' she asked. 'I'm sure it'll be a little while before it arrives.'

'No problem,' said Dan. 'I'll call one for you.'

She warmed her hands in front of the fire while she heard him ask the cab company if it wasn't possible to get a taxi to the house in under half an hour.

'Busy night,' he told her as he hung up. 'Thirty minutes is the soonest one will arrive.'

'That's fine,' Ash assured him. 'I can do a few things in the kitchen.'

'No,' said Dan. 'Sit down. Finish your drink.'

Ash had barely sipped the Baileys. She looked at Dan and then sat down in one of the loosely covered armchairs. He sat down opposite her and closed his eyes. Ash looked at him anxiously. She didn't really want him to fall asleep before she left. It wouldn't be any great deal, she supposed, she could just get up and walk out when the taxi arrived. But it seemed inappropriate somehow. She'd catered for evenings when the hosts had got very drunk before but usually that meant they gave her an extra tip, or squeezed her arm or pinched her bum as she was leaving. She'd never quite been in the situation where one of her clients had fallen asleep.

He opened his eyes again. 'What do you think?' he asked.

'Pardon?'

'Have you ever had preliminary engagement discussions?' asked Dan.

Ash shook her head.

'Have you ever been in love with someone?'

Ash shook her head again.

'My parents had a shit marriage,' said Dan. 'It's what made me realise that the most important thing in your life is your relationships.' He drank some brandy. 'Oh, sure, the work is important. Obviously. But the relationships are the most. I usen't to think so. But I do now.'

He's pissed out of his brains, thought Ash as she watched him.

'What about your parents?' he asked vaguely. 'What sort of marriage did they have?'

'My parents weren't married,' she told him.

'What?' He sat up in his chair and focused on her.

She shrugged. 'Nothing special. They weren't married.'

'Why didn't they get married?' asked Dan. 'Was one of them married already?'

'It's none of your business.' She hadn't meant to sound so abrupt.

Dan looked abashed. 'I'm sorry,' he said and for the first time in a while his words were distinct. 'I've been really, really rude. I didn't mean it. I'm sorry.'

'It doesn't matter.' Ash pulled at her plait. 'They didn't get married because she wasn't sure who my father was.'

'What?' He stared at her and she sank back into the chair, pulling at her plait again. What had possessed her to blurt out information to Dan that she normally kept to herself? And now he was trying not to look surprised but failing miserably.

'My mother lived in a commune,' she said dismissively. 'It was the late sixties, early seventies. You know. Free love, all that sort of thing.'

'You're joking.'

'Why should I be joking?'

'You don't look like the product of a free love home.'

Ash couldn't help laughing. 'What would you expect me to look like? Flowers in my hair or something? Hand-me-down bell-bottomed jeans?'

'I don't know.' Dan reached for the decanter again. 'I never thought that – I suppose you don't think about the children, do you, when you're doing the free love thing?'

'No,' said Ash. 'Children were the last things on their minds.'

'So tell me about it.' Although he was clearly drunk, Dan was alert now. 'What was it like?'

'I don't remember,' said Ash. 'I didn't actually live in the commune. It broke up before I was born. My mother travelled around.'

'Wow.' There was admiration in Dan's eyes. 'So you've lived a really different life to most people.'

'No,' said Ash. 'I haven't.'

'Look, most people don't live in a commune and not know who their father is – did she sleep with loads of blokes, was that it?'

'Lots of people don't know who their father is these days,' said Ash. 'And sleep with loads of people too, I guess. But it was different then. The commune was supposed to be egalitarian and all that sort of thing. You weren't supposed to have relationships with one person. So they didn't. And all the kids were brought up as though anyone was their father.'

'I don't believe you.'

'It's true,' said Ash. 'There was a documentary about

it on TV a while back. Well, about communes generally, not Julia's, though it did feature.' They'd interviewed a woman in her fifties who'd talked about having sex with four men in one night as though she was describing a dinner party. Ash found it impossible to believe that the very ordinary grey-haired woman was the naked Afro-permed girl in the photos that she'd displayed.

'Julia is your mother.' Dan broke into her memory.

'Was,' corrected Ash.

'What happened?' asked Dan.

She'd never told anyone about Julia before. None of her friends in Dublin knew anything about her mother or her childhood. And she really didn't think that telling someone who was a client, and of whose company she herself was a client, about her personal life was really a good idea. But he was drunk and she was comfortable and it seemed right to tell him. For the first time ever she really wanted to tell someone about Julia.

'Julia was a nutcase,' said Ash baldly. 'After the commune broke up she travelled around and then she thought that she should find a father for me so she went out with loads of blokes. But of course it was crazy. They weren't interested even though she used to think that they were. Eventually she moved to England. I've no idea why, unless she thought she might get a better class of man in England.'

'And what happened then?' Dan was intrigued.

'She was the most disorganised person in the history of the universe,' said Ash. 'I used to get myself to school because she'd forget about it. It was like living with an older sister rather than a mother. A completely scatty older sister.'

'But you loved her,' said Dan.

'She was my mother.' Ash sipped the Baileys. 'She was my mother and of course I loved her.'

'So what happened?' asked Dan again.

'She was always doing things off the top of her head,' said Ash. 'She would never, ever do anything to a routine because she thought that it was bad for the soul. We used to go shopping on different days of the week so that she wouldn't get into a rut.'

'Actually she sounds quite fun,' said Dan.

'Maybe.' Ash shrugged. 'But it killed her in the end.'

'Killed her?'

'A friend called for her.' Ash tried but failed to keep the bitterness out of her voice. 'Another one of the men that she thought would take us on. God, she was stupid. I was eleven then. Would you have proposed to Cordelia if she had an eleven-year-old daughter?'

'I see your point.' Dan drained his glass again.

'Anyway, Tyke was into motorbikes. He called around, asked Julia if she'd like to go for a spin and she said yes. I told her that she was supposed to be taking me to my ballet class – all eleven-year-olds were into ballet then – and she said that I shouldn't be so hidebound by timetables. And that I had to learn to do things whenever I felt like it. And that she'd be back soon.'

'And?' Dan looked inquiringly at her.

'They ran into the back of a lorry at the bottom

of the road,' Ash said baldly. 'Killed outright. Both of them.'

'I'm sorry,' he said. 'Really sorry. I shouldn't have asked you about it.'

'It doesn't matter.' Ash shrugged. 'It was a long time ago and I'm over it now. Obviously.'

'But it was such an awful thing to happen.'

'It was her own fault,' said Ash. 'Silly lifestyle, silly woman.'

'She was your mother.'

'Just because she was my mother doesn't make her any less silly,' said Ash.

'So what did you do next?' asked Dan.

'Oh, I came back to Ireland to live with my aunt and uncle and their kids,' said Ash. 'I was fine.'

'All the same—'

'It's not the kind of upbringing I'd recommend,' said Ash. 'But I hardly remember my life in the States at all. And, in the end, it was kind of a relief when Julia died. I used to have to look after her, you know?'

'You don't really mean it was a relief, do you?'

Ash sighed. 'When I was with Julia I had to be grown up all the time. When I lived with Molly I was encouraged to be a child.'

'And now you live on your own.'

'And it's great.'

Dan drained his glass. 'Thanks for telling me.'

'I don't usually,' said Ash.

'I guess I'm lucky to have Cordelia, even if she is going away for a while.'

Ash nodded.

'And I guess I shouldn't resent her caring so much about her job.'

'Lots of women care about their jobs. I care about mine,' said Ash.

'I must be totally old-fashioned at heart.' Dan sighed. 'And selfish. She's the first person I've ever wanted to marry and I just went for it without thinking about how she felt.'

'You obviously thought that she loved you,' said Ash. 'And you were right. She does.'

Dan nodded. 'I suppose I thought that once I'd asked her, it would be the most important thing in her life. Because asking her was the most important thing in mine.'

'I'm sure it is,' said Ash. 'And you'll be really happy together.'

'You think so?'

'Absolutely.' Ash tilted her head to one side. 'I think I hear a taxi.'

'I don't,' said Dan.

'Definitely,' said Ash. She stood up and gathered her belongings together. 'Sorry for boring you with my life history.'

'It was interesting,' said Dan.

'Only when you hear it the first time,' Ash told him. 'And when you live it it's especially not interesting.'

'Thanks again for tonight,' said Dan.

'Anytime! Don't forget to buy that ring.'

He laughed. 'I won't.'

He watched her as she walked down the steps and got into the taxi. He waited until she'd pulled away and then he went back into the house and drained the glass of unfinished Baileys she'd left behind.

Chapter 7

Cajun Cobbler
Spring onions, red pepper, mushrooms, tuna, prawns, stock,
tomatoes, lemon juice, green chillies, Tabasco, coriander
Sauté vegetables, add remaining ingredients and bring to
boil. Top with scone mixture of flour, herbs, margarine and
yoghurt. Bake at 220°C until golden brown

Ash hadn't intended to go out the following weekend. She was still punishing herself for hurting Brendan by splitting up with him the way she had, but Jodie insisted that she come to the restaurant and check out the food. They'd employed a new chef, Jodie told her, and he was great. 'You might get some fresh ideas,' Jodie told her and Ash tried not to appear annoyed with the younger girl. As far as she was concerned she was perfectly capable of coming up with her own ideas and she resented the fact that Jodie apparently thought that she'd learn something from another chef. But she hadn't been out since she'd split up with Brendan and, much as she enjoyed curling up on the sofa with a tub of her favourite ice cream and

Bagel at her feet, she knew that she should make some kind of effort. This is my time, she told herself as she rummaged through her wardrobe and selected her most comfortable jeans. I'm a single woman under thirty. I'm *supposed* to be out there having fun every night. Even if I don't feel like it right now. And tonight might be the night that changes my life for ever!

Bagel sat on her neatly made futon as she dabbed Maybelline onto her face. His green eyes stared solemnly at her in the mirror, as though appraising her looks. Every so often he yawned widely.

'Stop it, Bagel!' Ash twisted her hair into a loose coil. 'You're looking at me as though you're my guardian or something who thinks it's too late to be up! No wonder I spend so much time sitting on the sofa. I'm only going out with Jodie. And I won't be late.'

She pulled on her loose-fitting jeans and a long-sleeved T-shirt in a dusky rose that brought out the pink in her cheeks and the brown in her eyes. Then she pulled on her warmest fleece and her favourite pair of Timberland boots.

As always, she did her paranoia check before she left the house. The central heating. The taps. The sockets. The worktop surfaces. And, finally, the alarm.

She walked quickly because it was cold and she could feel the tip of her nose beginning to freeze. Ash hated the cold – once she began to feel it, it took ages for her to warm up again. Power-walk, she told herself as she swung her arms in rhythm with her step and almost collided with a man power-walking in the opposite direction. He growled at her and she made a face as she continued her twenty-minute walk to the restaurant. She breathed a sigh of relief as she pushed open the door and a rush of warm air carried the aroma of garlic to her.

Jodie had asked half a dozen people to come along that night. As always, her guest list was eclectic. Ash already knew Seamus and Margaret, both of whom worked for her from time to time while they studied at college. But she hadn't met Gene who was a production assistant at TV3, or Stefanie, a physiotherapist, who had moved into Jodie's apartment a couple of weeks ago, or Alistair who'd recently made a fortune by selling most of his shares in the technology company he'd founded but who'd known Jodie since they were children.

Ash wondered how on earth Jodie managed to collect such a diverse range of friends. She sat down between Alistair and Gene and thought, rather gloomily, that she'd never be able to muster up a gathering of people who weren't mainly her clients. She could, she supposed, muster up a gathering of her ex-boyfriends although she didn't know where most of them were any more. People said that Dublin was a small city and that no matter where you were you could bump into someone you knew, but Ash had never found it like that. But then the men that she'd gone out with rarely became friendly with the people she was closest to.

'What do you think?' Jodie was sitting with them until her stint began in half an hour's time. 'That roasted plum and tomato soup is gorgeous.'

'Sounds nice.' Ash mentally skimmed through the

probable ingredients. 'But the sardine pâté must be disgusting.'

'That's just because you don't like them,' objected Jodie. 'The customers love it.'

Ash wrinkled up her nose. 'Well, not for me, thanks. But I'll try the soup, I think, and the Cajun Cobbler.'

Jodie grinned at her. 'It's hot.'

'Good,' said Ash.

'You like hot food?' Alistair turned to look at her and she nodded. 'Me too,' he said. 'But it's never hot enough for me here. I lived in Thailand for a few years, got used to really spicy food there.'

'I've always found Thai food more aromatic than hot,' said Ash.

He shrugged. 'Depends on how many chillies you throw in, I guess.'

The restaurant was crowded. Ash liked the buzz, the sound of glasses clinking, the waiters and waitresses hurrying around. It wasn't an expensive restaurant because the ones in Temple Bar rarely were; they catered for tourists and people who wanted activity, not subdued conversation, and Ash preferred that atmosphere.

'You cook.' It was more a statement than a question from Alistair.

'Yes,' said Ash. 'And I do hot and spicy as well as aromatic.'

He laughed at her. They ordered wine and Margaret launched into a story about a dinner party she'd been at where the host had fallen asleep at the table. Seamus topped it with his tale of a chef and a waitress getting it together in the kitchen pantry. Jodie glanced at her watch from time to time and sucked throat pastilles.

Eventually she got up to sing. Whenever Ash listened to Jodie sing she was amazed that so strong a voice came from such a small person. Jodie was like a little pixie tonight, she thought, in deep red velvet and with a bright green hair slide holding back her jet-black hair.

'More wine?' Alistair refilled her glass. Ash hadn't realised that she'd almost finished her wine – the soup hadn't even arrived!

But when it did she had to admit that it was excellent. As was her nicely spicy Cajun dish. She didn't bother with dessert but the others drooled over the honey and almond ice cream and lemon mallow pies.

Alistair refilled Ash's glass again. She realised that she was getting drunk but she didn't care. She was relaxed, more relaxed than she'd felt in ages, and it was nice to have eaten food that she hadn't prepared herself. She was enjoying Alistair's company too; he was witty and amusing and didn't seem to care that he could have afforded to buy the restaurant, let alone the meal.

'So what have you done with the money you got for your shares?' she asked eventually. 'I remember reading about the deal in the papers.'

'Are you interested in business?' he asked.

She shook her head. 'Not really. But the sale of Archangel got a lot of publicity. And so did you!'

'I know.' He looked at her ruefully. 'It's been a curse rather than a blessing. But fortunately there's been so many more interesting stories since then they've kind of forgotten about me and my money.'

'So what have you spent it on?' she asked again.

'Not a lot yet,' he told her. 'Invested some in the stock market. Paid off my mortgage. Bought a car.'

'What sort of car?'

He grinned. 'An Audi TT. Not the flashiest I could have afforded but I like it.'

She laughed. 'My cousin really, really wants one of those. He says it's a babe magnet.'

'Men might think they're babe magnets,' said Alistair. 'The question is, do women?'

'I think so,' she said seriously. 'Although I was at a function a few weeks ago and the wife said that there was no point in her husband buying one for her because there wasn't enough room in the boot for her shopping.'

Alistair laughed. 'Glad she's not my wife. Although she's right, I guess, it's not exactly a huge boot.'

'And it's totally impractical,' Ash told him. 'No back seats.'

'Very impractical if you've magnetised a babe,' agreed Alistair.

'Where do you live?' she asked.

'Islandbridge,' he told her. 'Not too far.'

'Did you drive here tonight?'

He shook his head. 'I knew I'd be swigging back a few bottles of wine so I thought I'd better not. You know yourself, driving a sports car means you're twice as likely to get stopped and, even if I'd only had a glass, I'd hate to have to blow into that Breathalyser thing.'

'Pity,' said Ash. 'I'd have let you drive me home.'

'Another time perhaps?' said Alistair.

'Maybe.' He was fun to be with tonight but she wasn't sure about another time.

Jodie came back to the table, smiling broadly. 'What did you think?'

'You were fantastic,' Ash told her. 'Brilliant, as always.'

'Thanks,' said Jodie.

'Utterly wonderful,' said Stefanie. 'I wish I could sing but I can't keep a tune in my head.'

'Me neither,' said Ash who poured Jodie a glass of wine. 'Cheers.'

'Cheers!'

It was then that Ash saw Cordelia Carroll. She couldn't place her at first, recognising the face without remembering who she was, but then she realised that she was looking at the woman Dan Morland was going to marry. Always supposing that they'd got further than the preliminary engagement discussions. Poor Dan, she thought. He'd wanted it all to be so perfect. She watched Cordelia laughing and joking with the two men in her company and wondered when she was supposed to be going to the States. Then she saw Cordelia reach for a bottle of wine and the light in the restaurant caught the ring on the third finger of her left hand. It had a large dark stone surrounded by diamonds which glittered and sparkled under the light.

They obviously did get past the preliminary engagement discussion, thought Ash. She was glad for Dan but couldn't help wondering if he really had done the right thing. He clearly thought so. And so did Cordelia, no matter what she said about her career. Maybe a time came in your life when you should really work at a relationship, at turning it into the one for ever, no matter what. She could see why Dan would want to do that with Cordelia who was absolutely stunning. Ash would have loved those thick, chestnut locks and grey-green eyes instead of her own colour hair. She truly believed that blonde was the most boring hair colour in the world, not to mention the fact that people were perfectly prepared to label you thick as two planks just because you weren't a brunette. She patted the back of her head.

'I'd love to pull that clip out,' Alistair whispered.

'Pardon?' She looked at him in surprise.

'I'd like to pull the clip out of your hair and let it loose,' he said. 'I'm sure it looks lovely.'

'It looks like hair,' she said shortly. Then she smiled at him. 'I'm sorry, I didn't mean to snap.'

'That's OK.' Alistair refilled her glass and his hand brushed against hers. Maybe it's him, she thought suddenly. Maybe he's the one I should make it work with. He's attractive, he seems nice and he's loaded! What more could anyone ask for? She sighed. Had Julia thought like that? When she met Dene or Will or Greg or Tyke? Had she thought that they were attractive, nice and loaded?

'What are you doing for Christmas, Ash?' Jodie suddenly broke in on her thoughts.

'Going to Molly's as usual,' Ash told her. 'She's a Christmas person, loves having us all around. What about you?'

'We're going for a charity swim at the Forty Foot,' said Jodie. 'And the restaurant is going to open for soup and sandwiches afterwards. You're welcome to join us if you like.'

'I like the thought of the soup and sandwiches.' Ash grinned. 'But not diving into the sea on Christmas Day. I don't know how you do it.'

'Will you sponsor me?' asked Jodie. 'A pound a minute for every minute I stay in the water?'

'Sure, no problem. I prefer giving you the money than freezing to death.'

It was another hour and another couple of glasses later before they left the restaurant and spilled onto the street. Seamus and Margaret were holding each other up, giggling like children as they tried to flag down a taxi. Stefanie was almost asleep on Gene's shoulder. Alistair seemed sober enough but his eyes were glazed. Ash felt extremely light-headed. Only Jodie, who'd drunk very little, seemed OK.

'Come on, Steff.' She pulled the other girl's arm. 'Time to go home.' Stefanie moaned gently but followed Jodie obediently. 'See you Monday, Ash,' said Jodie. 'Butler's, isn't it?'

Ash yawned and nodded. Gene, without Stefanie, seemed to have sobered up completely and said goodnight to everyone.

'Want to see the car?' Alistair turned to Ash.

'What?'

'The TT. Would you like to see it?'

'I thought you said you'd left it at home,' said Ash.

127

'I have,' said Alistair. 'Doesn't mean you can't come and look at it.'

'What's the point if you can't drive it?'

'I just thought you might like to sit in it anyway,' he told her. 'It's very nice to sit in.'

'Thanks,' said Ash, 'but I don't think so.'

'How about coming back to the apartment for a coffee?' suggested Alistair.

She shook her head.

'A nightclub then?' he asked.

'Really, Alistair, no thanks.'

'Am I that terrible?' he asked.

She sighed. 'Of course not. But I want to go home.'

'That's a shame,' said Alistair. 'I want to do something madly impulsive.'

'I don't do impulsive,' said Ash. 'Anyone will tell you that.'

'Why not?'

'I like to plan my impulsive moments.' She shivered in a sudden blast of cold air and pulled her jacket more tightly round her. 'I've got to go.'

'Will I walk back with you?' he asked.

'No.' It sounded sharper than she'd intended. 'No,' she said again, more gently. 'I like walking by myself.' And, she thought suddenly, if you're trying to be nicer to men, trying to get to know this one because he might be The One, because he's attractive and nice and loaded, you're going the wrong way about it.

'It must be a good mile,' said Alistair. 'And at this time of night . . .'

'At this time of night, nothing,' said Ash. 'The streets are crowded. I'm fine. Thanks, Alistair, but I want to be on my own.' She might or might not want to know him better. But not tonight.

'Can I call you?' asked Alistair.

'Sure.'

'Then you'd better give me your number.'

'Oh, right.' Ash took a business card out of her bag and handed it to him.

'Aisling O'Halloran, Celtic Dream Food,' he read. 'And is it?'

'What?'

'Dream food?'

'Some people think so.'

'Maybe I'll get you to cook for me,' said Alistair.

'I charge top rates,' said Ash.

'I can afford to pay them,' Alistair told her and waved at a passing taxi which pulled in a few yards down the road. 'I'll be in touch,' he said as he climbed into the cab.

'Yes. Right.' Ash watched as the taxi drove off then turned eastwards back towards her apartment and her futon and her cat.

Chapter 8

Hangover Cures
Lovage cordial. Chilled Perrier. Fructose. Chicken soup.
Hair of the dog

Dan reached out and pressed the off button on the alarm clock. Just five more minutes, he thought, as he pulled the duvet round his shoulders. Five more minutes and I'll happily get up and go to work.

But a lot more than five minutes had elapsed before he opened his eyes again. This time he was instantly alert and he sat up in shock because he vaguely remembered switching the alarm off earlier. His head was pounding and his tongue felt as though it was stuck to the roof of his mouth. He groaned as he turned gingerly to look at the clock.

'Shit,' he said out loud. 'I don't believe it.'

Normally Dan got up before seven so that the absolute latest he was at his desk was eight. Quite often he made it in to the office before half seven. But not this morning. It was already half past eight and the idea of getting out of bed was gruesome. He rubbed his face vigorously with his hands but only succeeded in making himself feel worse.

I shouldn't have gone out with Peter and Donie last night, he told himself. Both of them worked from home and it didn't matter that they hadn't got in from the nightclub until three in the morning. But it was different for someone who was supposed to be at his desk a mere five hours later. Dan knew that he couldn't survive on less than six hours' sleep at the very least.

He pushed the duvet off the bed and staggered into the bathroom. His dark hair was sticking up in every direction and there were black bags under his eyes. He opened the bathroom cabinet and took out a couple of Solpadeine. I can't do this any more, he realised. I can't go to clubs on a weekday – especially early in the week – and wake up feeling OK. I feel like shit. I look like shit. And, he remembered in horror, he had a meeting with Ross Fearon at nine o'clock! Jesus wept! He swallowed the tablets without water. Dan had once read a James Bond novel in which 007 had taken painkillers without water and he'd decided that this was a particularly macho thing to do. Also, because they tasted so foul, he reckoned that it might put him off getting stupidly drunk again. It didn't, of course. And, he told himself as he stood under the shower, taking tablets without water when his body was already dehydrated was ridiculous. Still, they worked. Usually. Somehow he felt that today's headache might need more than a couple of pills to shift.

What had they been thinking of? Well, what had *he* been thinking of, because the whole damn night had been his idea. Cordelia had left for the States on Saturday. He'd spent the rest of the day feeling alone and sorry for himself. Sunday had been worse. He tried to tell himself that he didn't always meet Cordelia on Sundays anyway so why should he feel alone today? But it hadn't made any difference. He'd thought of her in the States, doing things without him, and he'd hated it. Eventually he'd called his two best friends and suggested that they go for a few beers together. A couple of drinks would sort him out, he reckoned, stop him feeling like such a wimp to be missing his damned girlfriend. His damned fiancée, of course! The sapphire and diamond engagement ring she'd chosen had cost a fortune.

Donie and Peter had thought that a night of drinking was a great idea and they'd met in McDaid's, ready for action. Dan couldn't remember how much he'd had to drink in the pub before they'd been almost forcibly ejected because it was closing time. And then they'd gone to the nightclub.

It had worked, he admitted. His mind was so off things that he'd forgotten about Cordelia, forgotten about this morning's meeting, forgotten about every-thing except the complete pleasure of getting absolutely rat-arsed.

He squeezed Aquafresh onto his toothbrush. The minty smell made him feel sick. He stood, undecided, beside the sink and then jack-knifed towards the toilet where he threw up the night's drinking plus the doner kebab he'd bought on the way home.

You absolute idiot, he thought as he leaned his head

on the cool ceramic of the cistern. What in God's name did you think you were doing?

When he knew that he wasn't going to throw up again he rinsed his toothbrush and cleaned his teeth without toothpaste. Then he hurried back into the bedroom and got dressed. He wore his Armani suit, on the basis that if his clothes looked good Ross mightn't notice that his face was ghostly white and that his eyes were bloodshot. He grabbed his wool coat from the banister where he'd flung it the night before and hurried to his car.

He was late. And the traffic into the city was dreadful. He pressed the speed dial on his mobile and called the office.

'I'm really sorry, Ross.' He winced as he spoke to the managing director. 'I'll be in as soon as I can. I'm just stuck in the most awful jam here right now.'

'Why weren't you in earlier?' demanded Ross. 'I have another meeting at ten, you know.'

'I'm sorry,' repeated Dan. 'My bloody alarm didn't go off.' He made a face at the obviously transparent lie.

'Oh, all right. But I need you in my office as soon as you get in.'

'Sure. Absolutely.' Dan realised that he was sweating. It wasn't from nerves at talking to Ross – he might be the managing director but they were actually good friends – the beads of perspiration (pure alcohol, he supposed) were reaction to the night before. And the sudden memory of the girl the night before. He couldn't remember her name. Maybe she hadn't told him her name but he was pretty sure that she had. She'd been tall and blonde and the proud possessor of a surgically enhanced chest, reminding him of the Barbie doll that his twin sister, Bronwyn, had once owned. In his head he'd thought of her as Barbie no matter what her name was. She'd been wearing a short black Lycra dress that had clung to every curve of her unbelievable body and, from what he vaguely remembered her saying, she hadn't been wearing anything else – other than a pair of fur-trimmed black ankle boots. He remembered dancing with her – no, dancing was completely the wrong word. Music had been playing, the nightclub was alive with the beat and he'd been beside her and moving in some kind of disjointed rhythm but you couldn't, he reckoned, by any stretch of the imagination have called it dancing. And then she'd put her arms round his neck and he'd been overcome by her perfume, one that he didn't recognise but it was sweet and cloying. And she'd kissed him, long and hard, and he'd put his arms round her then because he couldn't think of what else to do and, quite frankly, he liked the idea that a tall blonde woman with the kind of body you normally only saw on the cinema screen had decided that she wanted to kiss him, Daniel Morland, whose fiancée had hightailed it to America to cut it with the big boys.

Barbie had broken away from him eventually and murmured something into his ear. And he'd finally come to his senses even though he hadn't the faintest idea what she'd said. Despite the encouraging looks from Donie and Peter, he'd disentangled himself from Barbie and come home alone.

He heaved a sigh of relief that he'd made it home alone.

He simply could not remember what had happened to the girl and how he'd left her; he was just grateful that he had and that he hadn't done anything he'd really and truly regret later.

He rubbed his forehead as he turned onto the canal and joined another snaking line of traffic.

God, he thought, what if Cordelia ever found out about it? He couldn't imagine any way that Cordelia would find out that he'd been in a clinch with a blonde bombshell (even if her roots had needed a bit of a touch-up) but he couldn't see her understanding it. When girls were feeling alone and hurt they went out with other girls and talked about it. Dan knew this because that was what Bronwyn did. Whereas whenever he felt hurt he went out with the guys, got drunk and tried his luck with any girl he could. Which was awful, when you thought about it in the cold light of day. He shook his head and the pain bounced around his skull. Well, he was being punished for it now.

Traffic in Pearse Street was appalling as usual. He fumed as he sat behind a container lorry and in front of a Hiace van and wished that he lived nearer the office. In fact, he didn't live that far away and if he could be bothered to do the things he sometimes promised himself, like buy a bike and cycle into work, he'd be in in less than half the time. But I'm soft, he muttered as he slid the Saab convertible into gear. Soft and lazy and thirty-three years old with a hangover.

Eventually he crossed the bridge and turned along the River Liffey. He glanced back at the southside of the city and thought, unaccountably, of Ash O'Halloran, the chef with the amazing past, who'd been so nice and understanding after his engagement dinner and who was probably asleep in her apartment which was so bloody convenient for the financial services centre when she didn't even work there!

Actually, Ash had been awake since six o'clock. She'd woken with a jump, her heart thudding in her chest, convinced that there was someone in the apartment, and she'd lain rigid in the bed, frozen with fear. Then she heard a scratching noise and realised that Bagel was outside her bedroom door trying to get in.

She slid out of bed and wrapped her towelling robe round her. 'You wretch, you scared me half to death.'

Bagel took no notice as he leaped gracefully onto the futon and rolled onto his back. 'You needn't think I'm going to scratch under your chin,' she informed him, nevertheless sitting beside him and rubbing his head. The cat purred furiously and Ash sneezed. 'And I'm becoming allergic to you,' she told him.

She pulled the duvet over her and lay down again, comforted by the purring but feeling guilty that she'd let Bagel into the bedroom. She had a rule that he shouldn't be there when she was sleeping but it was a rule that she regularly broke then felt bad about breaking. Molly hadn't believed in allowing pets into the house and Ash hadn't quite managed to bring herself to believe that it was OK to do what she liked in her own apartment.

'I've got a lunch for ten today,' she told Bagel. 'Thank

God Jodie's wrist is better.' She went over the menu again in her head. It was a nice menu for the time of year, she thought. Roasted tomato soup (a recipe she'd used long before calling into Jodie's restaurant and tasting the tomato and plum!), Spanish pork with olives served with ratatouille and, for dessert, warm poached pears. The lunch was in one of the banks where she wasn't the regular chef so she was especially pleased to have got the opportunity to cook for them. And tomorrow she had another lunch in Chatham's – it wasn't a partners' lunch, it was a lunch for a client who was (she gathered from the gossip) about to float a company on the stock market. She yawned as she thought of Chatham's and particularly of Dan Morland. She'd spoken to him once or twice since his dinner with Cordelia and he'd been particularly warm and friendly. More than likely embarrassed, she reckoned, given how drunk he'd been and how the engagement dinner had ultimately turned out. Cordelia was probably right to go to the States, Ash thought, but she couldn't help feeling a little sorry for Dan who had been left behind.

The rest of the week was busy too, out tonight with Alistair which was her only free evening this week because she was catering for a dinner on Thursday evening and both a lunch and a dinner on Friday. Then more party food on Saturday. She'd done some of the cooking already and had frozen it, but there was still lots to do. November and December were always hectic as the party season hotted up.

Bagel rolled over beside her and started to snore very

gently. Ash grinned as she listened to him. Better than some bloke, she laughed to herself, who I'd have to roll onto his side to make him stop. Better than Alistair Brannigan? She smiled to herself. Since she'd met him at the restaurant with Jodie he'd phoned her twice to ask her out. But she'd been busy both nights he suggested and he'd been busy on her alternatives. He'd said not to worry, they might manage to get it together sometime and she hadn't heard from him for a couple of weeks. But on Friday he'd sent her an e-mail inviting her to the premiere of, as he'd put it, a movie that might be another walk down the lane of having a miserable Irish childhood. The movie had been described as a cross between *The Commitments* and *Angela's Ashes* and was supposed to be quite funny. One way or another, thought Ash, people seemed to enjoy hearing about miserable Irish childhoods. Or maybe it was just miserable childhoods full stop. Maybe you always wanted to think that someone had had a worse life than you.

She'd agreed to go to the premiere because she'd never been to one before and because Alistair's e-mail had been funny and because she suddenly felt like going out. The feeling that she never wanted to go out with another man again (which she always had when she'd split up with someone) had subsided and she was in the mood to lighten up a little. So she'd phoned Alistair and he'd told her that after the movie they would be going to dinner at the Tea Rooms in the Clarence which would give her plenty of opportunity to spy on the competition.

'Why does everyone think I spend my time spying on

the competition?' she asked him. 'I don't compete. And I don't need the Clarence's menu ideas either!' (Although, she admitted privately to herself, they did a wonderful mushroom risotto.)

He'd laughed at that and told her she didn't have to eat anything if she didn't want to – the dinner was being sponsored by one of the firms that had advised him during the sale of his technology company so he wasn't paying and he wouldn't be insulted if she pushed the plate away.

It might be fun tonight, thought Ash. She moved Bagel out of the way and got up. It was a good idea to get out and about before the stress of November and December took its toll.

After having a shower and getting dressed she logged on to her computer and checked her e-mails. There were two from clients confirming numbers for dinners the following week and one from Alistair.

'Hi there,' she read. 'Hope you haven't forgotten about our date tonight. Will collect you – taxi not TT, I'm afraid – at seven outside your apartment. Am looking forward to seeing you again. Much more than spending time in cinema watching the effects of miserable Irish childhood on individual psyche. Wondering if we should skip movie and just have dinner instead. What do you think? Alistair.'

She grinned. 'Do not think skipping movie would go down well with your corporate hosts (who is it, by the way?). Also, impossible to book dinner somewhere else at this late stage. Besides, am looking forward to hobnobbing with the glitterati.'

She sent the message. She was definitely looking forward to tonight. Alistair seemed to be a really nice person. She twisted her fingers through her hair. Maybe it was OK to get involved with a really nice person. Maybe Alistair would be the one she'd last the pace with. And she bit her lip because she'd never even got close to lasting the pace with anyone. No matter how nice they were. She was better at breaking up with a boyfriend than any other girl she knew. She could write articles on how to say goodbye to them – *One Hundred and Fifty Ways to Leave Your Lover* by Ash O'Halloran. She sometimes wondered would there ever be a day when she'd manage not to say it.

The sound of Bagel mewing made her switch off the computer and go into the kitchen where he was sitting on the windowsill anxious to go out. She opened the window and watched him scurry up to the roof in one fluid movement then disappear behind the parapet.

She buttered a slice of Ryvita and ate it while she waited for her coffee to brew. She liked this time of the morning when it was still peaceful and she could look forward to the day ahead.

She drank her coffee quickly then did her usual check before she left the apartment. But when she reached the ground floor she couldn't remember having turned the computer off. She stood indecisively beside the front door. It wouldn't matter if the computer was on all day – computers were designed to be on all day. All the same, she didn't like to think of it. She chewed her lip for a moment then took the lift back upstairs again.

Of course she'd turned off the computer. It was second nature. But she felt better for having checked.

'You look like shit,' said Ross when Dan finally arrived at the office. 'Where were you last night?'

'Met some mates,' Dan told him. 'Bit of a late night.'

'How late?'

'Late enough.'

'Can't hack them any more?'

Dan sighed. 'Obviously not. Sorry, Ross.'

'Oh, it doesn't really matter. I only wanted to go through Mrs Mullen's account with you. She's coming in to see me this afternoon and I noticed she's got a couple of dog stocks.' Dog stocks weren't anything to do with dogs. They were shares that were losing money badly.

'I know.' Dan shook his head. 'She insisted on buying those pharmaceuticals even though I told her that the drugs didn't look like they'd get FDA approval. I think she got a so-called hot tip from someone.'

Ross nodded. 'If only people would just go for decent growth stocks instead of wanting instant riches!'

'Everyone wants instant riches,' said Dan. 'You'll never change that.'

'I know.' Ross turned over a page in the file. 'What about this one?'

'Evvervescent?'

'Yes.'

'She asked me to find a small company in that sector to invest in. She's looking for a spectacular growth share. I picked this because it has a reasonably good product. The reason it's down is because there was a story about someone bringing out a faster, better version of their bestselling software programme. But I talked to one of the guys in New York and apparently not. So I'm expecting this to go up again – she might even make some money out of it before the bottom really drops out of the market!'

Ross laughed. 'Still waiting for that to happen?'

'Maybe.' Dan shrugged. 'I hold some crazy stocks myself so it really doesn't suit me to think that the market might collapse. But you know how it is – when you're least expecting it . . .' He rubbed his temples. The Solpadeine was taking its time about working. His head still felt as though it was in a vice.

'You really do look awful,' said Ross. 'Maybe you should go home.'

'Not now that I've made the effort to get here,' objected Dan. 'And I'll be OK after a cup of coffee.'

'Hope you'll be OK by this evening.'

Dan stared at him. 'Why should I be?'

'The corporate event? The premiere?'

'What prem— oh, hell, that bloody movie thing.'

'Yes,' said Ross. 'And you're not meant to think of it as a bloody movie thing. It's an opportunity for us to entertain our best clients.'

Dan groaned. 'I hate our best clients.'

'Better not say that to them,' said Ross. 'You're supposed to care about them.'

'Right now the only thing I care about is staying awake.' Dan couldn't believe he'd forgotten about the movie premiere. It was one of their big entertainment events in the year. And I'll have to sit through the bloody movie and be nice to people when all I want to do is go to bed, he thought bleakly.

'Why don't you get a bottle of Lucozade? Or Red Bull,' suggested Ross. 'That'll get you up and running again. Much more effective than coffee. And take some bloody Solpadeine or something.'

'Good idea.' Dan stood up. 'I'll talk to you later.'

Ross was right about the liquids even if he was a bit late in suggesting the drugs, he thought as he walked back to his desk. He definitely needed something to rehydrate him and give him energy. Right now, he felt as weak as a kitten.

'Hey, Debbie!' He waved at one of the administrative assistants.

She came over to him and sat on the edge of his desk. 'You look like shit,' she told him.

'I feel like it.'

'And there's the premiere tonight.'

'I know. I know.'

She laughed. 'Take something for it.'

'I chewed a couple of Solpadeine earlier,' he said. 'I'll be all right. But I desperately need something to drink. Can you be a real pal and nip out for me? Get me something that's meant to invigorate you?'

'Not my job.' But her eyes twinkled at him.

'Oh, please?'

'For you, Dan Morland,' she said. 'But only because I like you.'

'Thanks,' he said as he slouched over his desk.

Chapter 9

Lamb with Caper Sauce
Lamb chops, salt, pepper, lemon juice, flour, chopped parsley,
chopped capers, new potatoes
Simmer chops and potatoes in saucepan with water and
salt. Remove when cooked and keep warm. Blend flour
and cold water, add to cooking liquid. Bring to boil and
simmer. Add capers, lemon juice and parsley. Spoon over
chops. Serve with potatoes

Ash was late getting back to the apartment. The lunch had gone on much longer than she'd expected, partly because the diners were nearly an hour late sitting down at the table and partly because they lingered over everything. She'd sent Jodie out to clear away the plates as quickly as she could to try to hurry them up, but it was only marginally effective. And she didn't want to appear too pushy because it was a new account and she wanted to make a good impression.

Which she had, she knew. The woman who'd booked her on behalf of the bank had thanked her profusely as she'd handed her the cheque and had promised her more work in the future. The real problem, though, was that the lunch had been held in offices on the other side of the city and there hadn't been a free taxi to be found for love or money because it had started to rain. She'd eventually got a bus into the city and had half run, half walked along the quays to the apartment, cursing under her breath all the while.

Her feet were wet and she had a blister on her little toe but at least she was home, she thought, as she sprinted up the stairs. Bagel appeared at the kitchen window almost immediately and she let him in.

'I've got some duck for you,' she told him as he rubbed his head against her ankles. 'Hope you like the flavour, it's a bit smoky.'

She emptied some of the meat into his bowl and left the cat purring and eating at the same time while she went upstairs to shower and change. The worst thing about cooking, she thought as she pulled her T-shirt over her head, was that your clothes always stank of food. She threw the garment into her laundry basket and headed for the shower.

Given her limited wardrobe, the decision on what to wear tonight had been easy and she'd selected her fuchsia silk dress with its sugar pink detail before she'd left for work. In the summer, when she'd first bought the dress, she'd worn it with delicate pink kitten-heel sandals. But, since the temperature was hovering around zero outside, she'd decided to wear her only pair of boots – slate-grey suede – this evening.

She sat in front of the mirror and blow-dried her hair, wishing that she'd time to do her nails but knowing that, even with so-called fast-drying varnish, she'd only end up smudging it. And tonight wasn't a night for smudged nail varnish. She tied her hair back, securing it with silver and pink clips shaped like butterflies, then she opened her jewellery box and took out her fake diamond necklace and earrings. One day, she told herself as she fastened the necklace round her throat, one day I'll buy myself the real thing.

Suddenly she thought that Alistair Brannigan was probably rich enough to buy her the real thing if he wanted to. It was, she had to admit, an appealing thought.

Ash was scared of having no money at all; her life with Julia had been one in which possessions didn't matter very much but it had also been a life where they'd sometimes struggled to get by. Ash hated struggling to get by, which was why she saved more than she spent and why she always had something put away for the rainy day that she dreaded would one day come. It would be nice, she mused, as she slipped the earrings into her ears, to have an obscenely rich boyfriend. Maybe if his way of giving her a surprise was to load her with jewellery she might change her views on things a little.

She began to close the jewellery box and then stopped. Julia's pearls nestled on the blue velvet padding of the box. Ash bit her lip. Julia had loved the pearls, she had been given them by the boyfriend before Tyke. Julia had been madly in love with Greg and when he'd left her she'd hurled the pearls out of the bathroom window and cried that they were unlucky. Julia was a great believer in things being lucky or unlucky. If something bad happened to her when she was wearing a particular skirt or dress or pair of shoes, she'd never wear them again, consigning them to her unlucky pile. Sometimes Julia's unlucky pile of clothes was higher than her lucky pile. She'd had lucky and unlucky jewellery before too, but never real pearls. She'd wished for them, she told Ash as they'd spun through the air, but she shouldn't have because they'd brought nothing but bad luck.

That night, when Julia sat unseeingly in front of the TV, Ash had gone out into the garden and retrieved them. It was one thing throwing fake pearls away but Greg had insisted these were real and Ash thought that they might need real pearls one day.

Later, after Julia was killed, Ash thought that maybe her mother had been right after all. But she'd kept the pearls anyway even though she'd always been afraid to wear them herself. Just in case it was true. Just in case they really were unlucky. She looked at her watch. Almost time. She took her grey woollen coat out of the wardrobe, picked up her bag and went to see what Bagel was doing. He was sleeping, curled up on the sofa, his eyes covered by his paws.

'Be good,' she told him as she did her appliances check.

She waited in the foyer of the apartment building for ten minutes before Alistair arrived.

'Why did you wait here?' he asked as she opened the door of the taxi. 'I would have come in for you. And I'm sorry I'm late, but it was only five minutes.'

'I know.' She'd been five minutes early herself, in the end. 'And I wasn't waiting long. Just thought it'd be easier if you didn't have to come and get me.'

'It should be a good night.' Alistair moved closer to her. 'And both the stars are coming along, which is great.'

'What's it in aid of?' asked Ash.

'Oh, some children's charity.' Alistair looked embarrassed. 'I don't know. I didn't ask. But I suppose I'll bid at the auction afterwards.'

'There's an auction?'

'Yes.' He nodded. 'Memorabilia from the movie. Like Brad Pitt's underpants or something.'

'You're joking.' Ash wasn't sure whether he was pulling her leg.

'Well, I don't know the specifics. More likely a couple of signed programmes. But still, all in some good cause. And if I bid the highest I'll end up getting a good profile in the newspapers, which'll be excellent for the company.'

Ash shot a glance at him. 'I thought you'd sold the company.'

'Only the controlling interest. I'm still the managing director. They pay me a huge, huge salary to keep the show on the road.'

'Really?' she asked.

'Absolutely,' he assured her. 'And I still care about what happens to it.'

The taxi pulled up outside the cinema where a crowd had already gathered to celebrity-watch.

'We've got to be here ages in advance of the celebs,'

Alistair told her. 'I suppose that means we'll be sitting around eating popcorn for hours before the movie actually starts.'

Ash giggled. 'So we end up fat and bloated and they look skinnier than ever.'

'Quite possibly,' said Alistair.

Ash looked around the cinema and furrowed her brow. She'd just seen Chatham's managing director take a seat in the aisle opposite her, followed by his personal assistant, Kate. She turned to Alistair. 'Who's sponsoring tonight?' she asked.

'My stockbrokers,' he replied.

'Chatham's?'

He turned to her in surprise. 'Yes, Chatham's.'

'I thought I recognised the managing director,' she said.

'You know Ross Fearon?'

She nodded. 'I have an account with Chatham's. And they're a client of mine.'

'You have an account?' Again, he looked surprised.

'There's no need to say it like that,' she said sharply. 'As though I'm too much of a moron to have an account with a stockbroking company. Lots of people have shares these days, not just millionaires like you!'

'I didn't mean it like that at all,' he assured her. 'I was just surprised at the coincidence.'

'Obviously my account is nothing like yours,' she said. 'Otherwise I'd have received my own personal invitation. I have a few shares. They're the only thing I ever gamble with.'

149

'Interesting gamble,' said Alistair.

'Not really,' she shrugged. 'I don't own enough to make a big difference. But it is interesting all the same. It means I know what people are talking about when I cater for different companies.'

'You probably pick up all sorts of useful tips. And they should've asked you to do the catering.'

'I don't think so.' She smiled at him. 'I don't cater for groups this size.' She glanced around the cinema again and saw a couple more of Chatham's staff. And Dan Morland who should have looked well in a tux, she thought, but actually looked dreadful. His face was shockingly pale and his eyes were puffy. Pining for Cordelia? She shook her head. Surely not. He probably talked to her every day anyway.

The movie was enjoyable although not as funny as the hype. But there were lots of shots of stunning Donegal scenery and the haunting tunes of Enya to go with the misty backgrounds. As Ash watched the final credits roll she wondered what a movie of her childhood from the age of eleven in the Rourke household would be like. They could play up the scene where Michelle had tried to flush the tiny teddy bear she brought everywhere with her down the toilet and had flooded the house. Molly had gone berserk, Ash remembered, and had screamed at Michelle until her cousin had burst into uncontrollable tears. And then Molly had put her arms round her and told her that it wasn't worth crying over, while Ash had hugged the sodden teddy who'd emerged from his immersion in Bloo Loo somewhat the worse for wear.

She frowned. Sometimes her childhood seemed so long ago, as though everything that had happened then had happened to somebody else. Sometimes it was hard to believe that she'd been conceived on a crazy hippie commune and she didn't have a clue as to the identity of her father. She'd asked Julia, of course, but Julia had always been vague about it and Ash really didn't care any more. She knew that some people went through everything to find out about their parents but she didn't want to know. What was the point in knowing that her father was a loser like Julia? Or that he'd eventually married a nice Californian girl with white teeth, a wide smile and they now had a couple of blonde, suntanned children of their own?

Her childhood hadn't actually been all that bad, she told herself. It was a pity she could hardly remember the States and, of course, a lot of her time in England had been spent worrying about Julia, but she hadn't been unhappy or unloved. Even when she'd moved to the Rourkes and she'd embarked on a life of constant arguments with Michelle she'd known that Molly loved her.

'Ash? You OK?'

She turned to Alistair who had been watching her curiously.

'Sorry,' she said as she slipped into her coat. 'I was daydreaming. I'm fine.'

The dining room in the Clarence looked fabulous. Ash liked the freshly starched brilliant white tablecloths, the modern cutlery and the stark floral displays. It was her kind of room.

'Ash!' Kate Coleman looked at her in surprise. 'What are you doing here?'

'Gate-crashing,' said Ash solemnly.

Kate looked at her in confusion.

'I'm with someone.' Ash nodded towards Alistair.

'Alistair Brannigan!' This time Kate looked at her with envy. 'You're going out with Alistair Brannigan! You know he's worth millions.'

Ash grinned. 'Yes.'

'You dark horse,' said Kate. 'I never knew. You'll be giving up the job, I suppose, and allowing him to keep you in the lap of luxury.'

'I don't know him that well,' said Ash.

'He's gorgeous.' Kate sighed. 'He used to come into the office a lot when the company was being bought out. We all fancied him like mad.'

'He seems a nice guy,' said Ash.

'Nice!' Kate looked at her in disgust. 'How can you say that! He's wonderful. Much sexier than the so-called Hollywood heart-throb in the movie.'

'Goodness, Kate, I didn't realise you were so infatuated! And I thought you were involved already.'

'Hey, doesn't stop me from looking.' Kate laughed. 'Anyway, you'd better go, he's waving at you. And, Ash, please don't feel bad because we didn't invite you – it's a kind of select group of our biggest customers, you know?'

Ash smiled. 'I understand. Don't worry. Just tell Ross that he'll never know the day or the hour when I put an extra hot chilli in his dinner for revenge.'

She left Kate and joined Alistair who was sitting at the table with a man Ash didn't know.

'Curtis Walsh,' he said as she sat down beside Alistair. 'I'm one of the analysts.'

'Oh, Curtis.' She nodded. 'I've read some of your research.'

'Really?'

'I have an account,' explained Ash while Alistair grinned at her and turned towards the new arrivals, a well-known building contractor and his wife. Curtis glanced at Ash again as he got up to greet them but was sidelined by Maeve Heaney who hugged Ash. 'Nice to see you, Ash,' she said.

'And you, Maeve,' said Ash. 'How are you keeping?'

'Very well, thanks. You haven't forgotten our dinner party on December the eighth?'

'Of course not,' said Ash.

'And this is . . . ?' Maeve turned to Alistair.

'Alistair Brannigan,' he told her.

'Oh, of course!' She beamed at him. 'I was a shareholder in your company. I made a lot of money when it was taken over.'

'I'm glad to hear it,' he said.

'I hope you did too, Ash,' said Maeve.

Ash smiled noncommittally.

'Did you?' asked Alistair.

'What?'

'Have shares in my company?'

'Regretfully no,' she said. 'Anyway, my two hundred pounds wouldn't have made much difference.'

'You would have made a great profit even on two hundred pounds,' Alistair told her.

She shrugged. 'Oh well, better luck next time.'

'Hi, everyone.' Dan Morland arrived at the table and looked at Ash in surprise. 'What are you doing here?'

'Really, Dan!' Curtis hissed at his colleague. 'She's a client!'

Ash stifled a giggle.

'She's also the cook!' said Dan shortly.

'Not tonight,' she told him. 'Tonight I'm the guest.'

'She's with me,' said Alistair.

'Alistair. Nice to meet you.' Dan held out his hand and looked at both of them in surprise. 'I didn't realise you and Ash – oh, Ash, I'm sorry.'

'Neither did we,' said Maeve Heaney. 'Good catch, Ash.'

'Good catch, Alistair,' said John Heaney.

'We're not caught,' said Ash hastily. 'Just friends.'

'What a shame,' murmured Alistair as they all sat down again.

Ash looked at Dan Morland covertly. The man looked absolutely wretched, she thought. He couldn't possibly look like that because of Cordelia, could he? He might be missing her but the way he looked now you'd think she'd dumped him for ever, not just gone away for a few months. His face was positively ashen and she could see now that his eyes were bloodshot.

The waiter arrived with appetisers. Ash saw Dan pale even more as he looked at the delicate anchovy creation that was placed in front of him. She wondered if he was going to faint. She felt sorry for him. It would be dreadful, just dreadful, to collapse in such a public setting. It was the one thing that she feared above all else. Whenever she panicked in public herself her terror was always that of fainting in front of everyone. She would imagine them crowding around her, wondering who she was and what had happened to her and she would fight to keep herself under control. She watched Dan as he kept his eyes open with the greatest of difficulty.

'How are the markets, Dan?' she asked conversation-ally. 'I heard all sorts of things on the news before I came out.'

He opened his eyes properly and looked across the table at her. 'Had a bit of a rough ride today,' he told her. 'But they're OK.'

'And how are things going in the States?' She dipped saffron bread into the flavoured olive oil.

'The Dow traded well.'

She saw him swallow with difficulty and wondered if he was actually sick. Maybe it would be better not to say anything else to him, to let him mark time until he could go home. If he wasn't feeling well then he wouldn't want to talk. She smiled vaguely at him and turned back to Alistair.

Dan couldn't remember ever feeling so bad in his life. Despite popping more Solpadeine later in the day (and this time drinking gallons of water at the same time) his headache hadn't gone away. If anything, it was worse and it hadn't been helped by sitting in that bloody cinema for nearly three hours. He'd nodded off once or twice during the movie but every time he'd fallen asleep a loud noise or shriek on screen would jolt him awake again. It had been miserable. Never again, he thought, never again will I go out with a bunch of blokes and get pissed out of my brains. It's just not worth it.

He glanced up and caught Ash O'Halloran looking at him again, her dark brown eyes huge in her cream complexioned face. She gave him a half-smile then quickly looked away and began speaking to John Heaney.

He hadn't expected to see Ash here. He was astonished to realise that she was Alistair Brannigan's girlfriend. He hadn't thought of her as being anyone's girlfriend, which, he supposed, was silly. But she was the cook. Even on the occasions when he talked to her about her shares he still thought of her as the cook. You didn't think of the cook in terms of having a life of her own. And she was the cook who had sat and listened to him ranting the night of his dinner with Cordelia.

He couldn't believe that he'd gone on and on at the poor girl about his feelings and how unhappy he was about her going to the States. My God, she was there as a business person giving a service, it wasn't as though she was a close personal friend or anything. And he'd talked about his parents, which he never did, although she hadn't picked up on that too much, thank God.

When he'd sobered up the following day he'd thought about phoning her to apologise but that would probably have made things even worse. The only saving grace in the entire affair was that she'd also told him some very un-cook-like things about herself, which she probably regretted too.

He'd spoken to her very little since then, although he'd tried to be as friendly as possible whenever he did, to defuse any embarrassment and at the same time to make her realise that their relationship was completely businesslike and that his drunken ramblings on the night of his preliminary engagement discussions had been the exception rather than the rule. Although, he thought ruefully, she'll think I'm a complete lush if she realises that I'm hungover tonight as well. And he really ought to make amends for that ridiculous comment earlier about her just being the cook. Crass beyond belief, he muttered to himself as he recalled it.

He dragged his attention back to the conversation around the table but didn't take part. In any event Curtis was doing a great job of keeping them amused, telling stories of company presentations that had gone wrong and making them laugh. Dan tried to laugh at one of his colleague's stories himself but he knew his laughter was forced. Ash was laughing, though, leaning her head to one side, showing her even white teeth and a dimple in her chin.

She was pretty, thought Dan. He'd never noticed that before; he'd only ever seen her wearing a white top and black trousers – her chef's uniform. And she'd always had her hair scraped back from her face instead of piled into that soft arrangement on the top of her head which made her look so very different from the rather more severe person he was used to. But it was a very girlish prettiness, quite unlike Cordelia's strong good looks. He wondered how old Ash was.

This time it was Ash who caught Dan staring at her. Although, she thought as he glanced away, perhaps he wasn't staring at anything. He actually looked as though he was in some kind of trance.

The food was excellent – the daube of beef just fell apart at the touch of her knife.

'So, what did you think?' asked Alistair once the coffees were served. 'Up to your exacting standards?'

'Almost.' She looked at her watch. 'But I'll never be able to sleep tonight – it's after midnight and far too late to be eating rich food.'

'That late?'

She nodded.

'At least you don't have to get up too early,' said Alistair.

'I have a lunch tomorrow,' she told him. 'I have to get up and buy my produce.'

'Surely you don't buy everything the morning you cook?'

'It depends,' she told him. 'But vegetables almost always.'

He shuddered. 'It's one thing being at your desk at six, it's quite another walking around smelly markets.'

'Much more real to be around the markets,' said Ash.

Alistair nudged her as Ross Fearon got up and thanked them all for coming. He told them that he had a number of items of memorabilia from the movie to auction and, since it was for a very worthy cause, he hoped they'd be extremely generous.

'What would you like?' asked Alistair.

Ash shook her head. 'Nothing.'

'Come on,' he said. 'The leather jacket as worn by our hero? The gold necklace worn by the heroine? The original script? Some of the stills?'

Ash shrugged. 'I'm not a great movie-goer and I really don't care who owned any of it. Sorry.'

'The necklace might be nice,' mused Alistair. 'Plus, if this film wins an Oscar or something it could be valuable.'

'This film will never win an Oscar,' said Ash. 'And the necklace is probably a fake.'

But Alistair bid for it anyway. And Dan, briefly entering into the spirit of things, bid a little higher. Alistair upped his bid. So did Dan. The other guests were amused at the battle between the two men as Alistair bid higher again. And Dan topped it again.

Ash looked from one to the other. It was for charity, she reminded herself, they were donating money to charity. But it was extraordinary to see them outbidding each other for a necklace which was probably worth less than the opening bid to start with.

They bid against each other again. Finally Alistair raised his bid by five thousand pounds and there was an awed murmur around the room. Dan grinned at him and suddenly looked a lot less ashen-faced. He certainly couldn't have afforded to spend such a ridiculous amount of money on a gold necklace.

'Sold!' said Ross Fearon. 'To Mr Alistair Brannigan.'

Alistair went to collect the necklace and Ash looked at Dan. 'Why on earth did you bid so much?' she asked. 'I know it's for a good cause but—'

'Oh, Brannigan's loaded,' said Dan easily. 'He can afford it. Why let him away too cheaply?'

When Alistair returned to the table he handed the necklace to Ash.

'Are you out of your mind?' she said. 'After what Dan forced you to pay! You should be putting it in the bank.'

'I bought it for you,' said Alistair. 'It wouldn't look much good in the bank.'

She turned it over in her hand. It was a plain necklace with solid gold links. Even if the gold was real it still wasn't worth what Alistair had paid for it, no matter what movie star had worn it.

'I really can't,' she said. 'You spent thousands on it. There must be someone else who—'

'Oh, for heaven's sake, Ash, take it,' said Dan. 'If I'd bought it I'd have given it to you too.'

She looked up at him in surprise. Alistair smiled. 'Would you?' he asked.

'Sure,' said Dan carelessly. 'It wouldn't look much good in my bank either.'

Ash looked at Dan and then at Alistair. 'Well, thank you both,' she said. 'But—'

'Oh, Ash, take it!' Maeve Heaney grinned at her. 'I wish I was young enough and pretty enough to have two men fighting over me.'

'They're not fighting over me!' cried Ash.

'Not at all.' Dan got up from the table. 'I was just trying to make Mr Brannigan spend some of his money!'

With the conclusion of the auction, people began to leave the restaurant.

'Do you want to go?' asked Alistair and she nodded.

'We'd better be off too,' said John Heaney. 'I've a meeting in the morning myself.'

They all got up from the table and shook hands. Alistair walked through the restaurant with John and Maeve while Dan returned to the table, a glass of water in his hand.

'Are you going now?' Ash asked him.

He nodded and rubbed his temple. His headache, which had gone into temporary abeyance during the auction, had come back with a vengeance.

'Are you OK?' she asked. 'You seemed awfully intense there for a while. Not to mention looking pretty terrible.'

'I was out late last night,' he said. 'Self-inflicted illness.'

'I see.' So maybe he was missing Cordelia, she thought, but it wasn't stopping him from having a good night out. What was it about blokes, she wondered, that made them able to forget their girlfriends so easily?

'I didn't realise you were Alistair's girlfriend.'

'I hardly know him,' she said lightly.

'It didn't seem that way.'

'I beg your pardon?'

'He desperately wanted that necklace for you. And you were right. He paid way over the odds for it. Flash bastard!'

'We're friends,' said Ash. 'And you and he were both silly about the necklace. Besides, you would have kept it for Cordelia, not given it to me.'

'Sure.' Dan's smile was faint. 'But he didn't know that.'

'It was good for the charity,' said Ash. 'But silly all the same.'

'You must know by now that most blokes are very silly. We do stupid things all the time.'

'Oh, Dan, only some of the time!'

He sighed. 'I feel particularly stupid tonight. But Brannigan certainly isn't. He fancies you like mad, doesn't he?'

'No!'

Dan looked surprised at the vehemence of Ash's exclamation. 'It looked like it to me.'

Ash stared at him. 'Maybe, maybe not. You mightn't exactly be the best judge when it comes to personal relationships.' And I shouldn't have said that, she thought as she saw a shadow cross Dan's face.

'I know. I'm sorry.' He massaged the back of his neck. 'I'm putting my foot in it. I'm not thinking straight. And I was rude to you earlier, wasn't I?'

'Wondering what I was doing here in the first place? It was the way you said it that was rude. But I made allowances because you looked so awful.'

'Thanks,' he said wryly.

'Go home and get some sleep,' advised Ash. 'All these late nights aren't good for you.'

He smiled suddenly, a crooked smile. 'I don't have that many late nights. This was a one off.'

'Was it?'

He nodded and shuddered. 'I went out with some mates. Cordelia went to the States this weekend. It was stupid.'

'Maybe not.' This time there was more sympathy in her gaze. 'But I have to say, Dan, that you look wretched.'

'I feel awful,' he admitted. 'But I couldn't back out of tonight, Ross would've freaked out. And he was already mad at me for being late in this morning.'

'Ash?' Alistair Brannigan appeared at her side again. 'I thought you were ready to go.'

'I am.' She smiled at Dan. 'Look after yourself.'

'I will,' he said, although she wasn't sure she believed him.

Alistair took a taxi back to the apartment with her even though she'd insisted that she could get one on her own.

'I don't like the idea,' he'd said as he got in beside her. 'I picked you up, I'll leave you home.'

When the taxi arrived at the apartment she leaned towards him and kissed him on the cheek. 'Thanks for a lovely evening,' she said. 'I really enjoyed myself.'

'I did too.'

'And thank you for the necklace.' She'd fastened it round her neck before leaving the restaurant.

'It looks wonderful on you,' said Alistair.

'I'm half afraid to wear it,' she said. 'It must be the most expensive plain gold necklace in the world.'

He laughed. 'I can afford it.'

'It doesn't mean you should throw money away. And you really shouldn't have given it to me, Alistair. If you want it back—'

'I wanted to buy it for you, Ash. So did Dan Morland.'

'He would never have bought it,' said Ash. 'All he did was make you spend more money.'

'That's his job, I suppose.' Alistair grinned at her.

'And I'd better go in and get some sleep,' said Ash. 'Otherwise I won't be able to do my job tomorrow.'

She half expected Alistair to ask her if he could join her for a nightcap. And she didn't know what she'd say to that because it was really late, she was very tired and she didn't bring men home to her apartment. But he'd spent so much money on the necklace that she felt obliged to ask him. Before she could say anything, Alistair yawned.

'I need to go home myself,' he said. 'I have an early start tomorrow too and I'm exhausted. But next time, perhaps we'll have a nightcap.'

'Next time,' said Ash with relief as she slid out of the taxi.

Chapter 10

Soured Cream Waffles
Eggs, caster sugar, plain flour, baking soda, cardamom,
soured cream, butter
Beat eggs and sugar, sift dry ingredients, fold in half the
flour, cream, remaining flour. Melt butter. Stir in lightly.
Stand for 10 minutes before using. Serve with maple syrup

Cordelia rubbed her eyes. They were tired from twelve hours staring at her computer, working on her part of the strategy for saving one of their clients from a hostile takeover bid. Having spent the day looking at the company's balance sheet and profit and loss statements, Cordelia couldn't help feeling that they deserved to be taken over, and as hostilely as possible. As far as she could see the management was completely inept! But she wasn't paid to decide that the people running the company were useless, she was paid to come up with a way to help them keep control of it.

She yawned, just as DeVere Bassett walked past her desk.

'Tired?' he asked.

She smiled and shook her head. 'Just having a quick time out.'

'I'm exhausted.' DeVere massaged the back of his neck. 'At this point I feel that most of the directors of UpperCut don't deserve their jobs.'

Cordelia muttered something noncommittal. DeVere was the same rank as she was within the bank – an assistant vice president – but you never knew when somebody might be testing you for loyalty. Or trying to put one over on you in some other way. You couldn't trust any of your colleagues, even someone like DeVere with his wide smile and friendly eyes. Probably especially not somebody with a wide smile and friendly eyes!

'So what part are you working on?' he asked her.

'The sale of some of the smaller subsidiaries,' she told him. 'I think it'll work.'

He nodded. 'And I'm looking at cost-cutting in a whole range of areas. They're so overstaffed it's unreal. People duplicating each other's work all over the place.'

'I agree,' said Cordelia. 'It's like every time they decided to do anything new they hired a dozen people to make it happen, even if they didn't need to.'

'That's the problem with some of these places,' DeVere told her. 'They equate stature with size. The bigger the company, the better. They haven't realised that the best, most profitable corporations are ones without spare employees all over the place.'

'Well, there won't be any spare left by the time we've finished,' Cordelia promised him and he laughed. But for a brief moment Cordelia felt sorry for all the people who'd lose their jobs simply because the directors of the company couldn't do theirs properly.

She watched DeVere as he walked across the room. Despite their equal rank, he had more authority. Not in fact, but in personality. Whenever DeVere talked, people listened. He had a way of instilling belief, of making people trust him. Cordelia knew that she needed to be more like DeVere, more confident and outgoing.

She sighed. In Ireland she'd been considered particularly outgoing. But it was different in the States. At home people expected a level of humility or at least some false modesty. Here they expected you to go for it. Cordelia had every intention of going for it. She had six months in which to prove herself, six months to move from an assistant vice president to a vice president, which was exactly what she was going to do. Although she still hadn't worked out how. And when she was vice president she'd move DeVere out of the department because she knew that he'd always be snapping at her heels.

She doodled on the edge of her notepad. Dream on, she told herself. The much more likely outcome is that it'll be DeVere who gets promoted. But you never knew and she was going to give him a run for his money.

It was nice to think of being promoted and doing well. It would mean a lot more money and a lot more prestige and, unfortunately, a lot more late nights in the bank because they really knew how to work you over here. Twelve-hour days were common, sometimes they were much longer. But, in the end, you got the rewards and Cordelia really, really wanted the rewards.

She flexed her fingers and the light hit off the diamonds in her engagement ring so that it sparkled and glittered in a rainbow of colours. Dan wouldn't be all that happy if she got the rewards, she thought. Dan would feel threatened by her success, she felt sure of it. But there was no need for him to feel threatened, she did love him. She just wanted him to know that her career was as important as his. And maybe, she mused, as she twirled the ring on her finger, maybe if I am a vice president in six months Dan will get a job over here and we can live in New York for a few years. Much better than Dublin, for all that people liked to compare it to the most sophisticated capital cities in the world. She'd like to go back there, of course, but she wanted a few years at the real cutting edge first. And this assignment was just the start of it. If things went as she hoped and she was offered something else in New York she knew that she could persuade Dan to move to the States to be with her. He loved her so much that he'd agree to anything. All she had to do was to put it to him the right way.

She was still twirling her ring on her finger when Melissa Kravich dumped yet another file on her desk.

'I need the figures on the Cordoba production line,' said Melissa. 'As soon as you can, Cordelia. Sooner.'

Cordelia nodded and pulled the file towards her as Melissa strode assuredly across the floor.

It was Melissa's job that Cordelia coveted. The vice president had a great salary, great options, spent her life at meetings with household-name companies and even got to fly to meetings in the company jet. Cordelia would know that she'd made it when she got to use the company jet! It wasn't something you'd give up so that you could sit in Rathgar and watch the nine o'clock news with Dan Morland, no matter how attractive he was.

She looked at her watch. Seven o'clock. And she'd been in the office since six thirty this morning. No wonder her mind was beginning to wander. She got up from her desk and walked over to the coffee machine. She selected an espresso. If that didn't keep her concentrated, she didn't know what would.

Although it was midnight, Irish time, Dan couldn't sleep. Today had been a busy day in the markets, with stock prices taking a sharp fall following an interest rate hike in Europe. He'd had a number of anxious clients on the phone throughout the afternoon checking to see exactly what was going on. It had been a bad day for it to happen because two of the other dealers had been out – Steve Proctor was sick and Jim Dwyer was away. Which meant that Dan had been on the phone constantly and now his head hurt.

Dan had noticed that, in recent years, constant telephone conversations left him with a pain in the ear – and not just because he often had to listen to the most awful bullshit from his clients. Of course the ones with the largest portfolios were usually the most relaxed – they could ride out the ups and downs of the markets. It was people with smaller holdings who needed constant reassurance and who took up far too much time. Sometimes Dan would tell them to sell their shares because he knew that neither he nor they would have any peace until they did. Many times he talked them out of selling and usually that was the right move. All the same, he was a little more anxious himself these days. Markets had done so well for so long – even with rate rises in the past – that he felt there was a greater chance of a real fall than ever before.

So he tossed and turned as he weighed up the pros and cons of selling some shares himself and putting some cash into his bank account. Dan was comfortable but not extremely wealthy. Nevertheless, he'd made a nice sum of money over the last year and he really didn't want to lose it all. He'd earmarked it for doing up the bathroom which desperately needed professional attention. Cordelia had muttered grimly about the bathroom last time she'd stayed the night.

He'd sell some of the riskier stocks, he decided, even though those were the ones that had fallen the most. But he'd still made a good profit on them and, as he often said to his clients, knowing when to take the profit was the best skill of all. But nobody liked to sell at a price lower than the highest price they'd seen. They felt as though it was a personal affront. Sometimes he had to force people to let their stock go.

Alistair Brannigan's company, Archangel, was one that had come under a lot of selling pressure, as had Transys, the company that had bought a majority of the shares. Dan had spent a lot of time talking to Archangel holders during the day. He hoped, suddenly, that Ash O'Halloran had been telling the truth when she'd said that she didn't own any and that she wasn't sitting at home looking at a huge loss. He didn't think that Ash could afford to lose money.

He wondered how long she'd known Alistair Brannigan. He'd done a double take when he'd seen her with him at the movie premiere and he knew that he'd been abrupt despite trying to salvage the situation afterwards. She'd been incredibly nice, he remembered, for someone who'd been described somewhat disparagingly by him as the cook. As soon as the words were out of his mouth he'd regretted them and he knew that he'd never have said anything at all if he hadn't been so bloody tired and hungover.

He'd phoned Cordelia when he got home from the Clarence and she'd sounded tired and hungover too even though it was only nine in the evening there. But she was still at her desk in the bank working, she said, on advising a company on a hostile takeover. He'd told her that he missed her and she said that she missed him too and that she wished she was back in Dublin with him. Then she'd laughed and said, well, maybe not just yet because her first day had been incredibly busy even though she was dog tired. And he'd laughed too and told her he was quite happy for her to be dog tired because it meant that she didn't have time to be chasing other men. At which point she'd told him that the only man in her life at the moment was the one walking towards her with a computer printout and she'd better go.

He'd felt better after talking to her and more secure about things. And he felt proud of her too, which surprised him. Dan admired dynamic people even if he had to admit to himself that sometimes he wished Cordelia was slightly less dynamic. But he liked to think of her as someone who could hold her own in any circumstances and he knew that she would. All the same, he mused, the idea of a more compliant fiancée wasn't a bad one either!

He thought about Alistair Brannigan and Ash O'Halloran again. They'd looked good together, Ash's fairness contrasting with Alistair's almost ink-black hair and blue eyes. Dan couldn't help envying Alistair's rather piratical good looks as well as his stellar success. Would Cordelia really have wanted to go to the States to enhance her career if he, Dan, had sold part of a company for around ten million dollars?

He wondered if Ash knew how rich Alistair was. Obviously she did, he told himself, since there had been extensive newspaper coverage of the Archangel deal. But she'd seemed truly concerned about the amount he'd bid for the necklace at the auction and embarrassed afterwards when he'd given it to her. Dan smiled to himself as he remembered the auction. He'd driven the price up because nobody else had wanted to lock horns with Alistair and somebody had to push up the price. For a moment he'd wanted to top Alistair's last bid too – the man had looked impossibly smug when he'd bid the extra five thousand pounds. But then he'd had the horrible thought that Alistair mightn't have bid any

172

higher and Dan couldn't have afforded a gold necklace at ten times what it was worth, even if it had been worn by Gwyneth Paltrow or Nicole Kidman or whoever it had been in the movie.

Alistair Brannigan checked the price of his shares on the Internet. It didn't matter, of course, that the market had plunged, he was still worth a hell of a lot of money but it was somewhat less today than it had been yesterday. He wondered whether or not things would steady up during the week. With a bit of luck, he thought, they would. Archangel was a good company and he was proud of it. And proud of the fact that he'd made a lot of money from it, even if he hadn't had time to spend it yet. But he would soon. He'd looked over a few properties in the last couple of weeks – one in Naas, close to where he'd grown up, one in Dalkey, which was already populated by rock stars and other celebrities, and one in Clonskeagh, which was more modern and boring but much more convenient for the office. He might buy something in the country, he thought, and the house in Clonskeagh for town living. He laughed out loud at the thought. And there was the new car to buy as well – he'd bought the TT as soon as he'd sold the company and, although he liked it, he felt that he should have something more befitting a man who'd made a bucket load of money. He wished, very briefly, that he'd held out for more. He reckoned that there'd been the possibility of a higher bid but Chatham's had advised him to go with the Transys offer. Maybe they'd been right but, in retrospect, maybe they'd been a little conservative. It was a whole new world out there and he wanted to grab as much of it as he could.

He called up his e-mails on the chance that someone might have sent a message about the stock to him. His in-box was full of messages but they were ones that he couldn't be bothered to read.

He clicked on the 'new message' icon and began to type to Ash O'Halloran. 'How are you? You didn't call back yesterday – too busy or don't you find me attractive any more??? Wondered would you like to go to dinner at the weekend? I know you're busy – I remember all that stuff about November and December being your busiest time of the year. However, I will double whatever you're being paid for Friday night if you'll cook for me. (Or even if you don't!) Talk soon. Love, Alistair.'

Ash was too tired to sleep. She'd had a busy day with a big lunch party which hadn't ended for ages. And when she came home she'd needed to go through a few menus for the rush of lunches and dinners she had for the rest of the week. She was taking on too much work again, she knew she was, but she couldn't help herself. She wasn't able to say no. And she enjoyed the feeling of being stressed all the time, of working to her absolute limits.

But now she desperately wanted to sleep because she was catering for a breakfast meeting in the morning and she had to be up early. And despite an early night she was wide awake, her thoughts spinning round in her head, while she tried really hard not to think.

Of course it was impossible not to think, especially

about Molly and Michelle and the Christmas holidays ahead. Molly had phoned earlier. Ash had been soaking in a bath scented with lavender oil and had missed the call so she'd listened to Molly's message afterwards. Her aunt had wanted to know if there'd been a row between Michelle and Ash because, for the first time in a few weeks, Michelle had been to Sunday dinner and had been particularly scathing about her cousin. What, Molly wanted to know, had they argued about now? Michelle had simply said that Ash was being Ash again and Molly wanted to know exactly what that meant. Had Ash found and dumped another boyfriend? Or had she simply irritated Michelle by making some unthinking remark about Michelle's weight since Shay junior had been born? Michelle, Molly told Ash, hadn't ever forgiven her for referring to her as hefty following Shay's arrival. Which, Molly added, had been particularly insensitive of Ash when poor Michelle's hormones were undoubtedly all over the place.

Ash had listened to Molly's questions and Molly's own answers and had sighed in frustration. Why did they get at her all the time? And what the hell would it be like at Christmas if they continued to nag her all over the holidays? She wasn't looking forward to it although she knew that she had to spend Christmas with them because that was what she always did. And even though Molly always asked her if she was going to come, Ash knew that her aunt would be horrified if she ever said no. She wished that the Christmas holidays weren't such a big thing in Ireland – a couple of days off like they had in the States would have been much more appropriate.

The sound of a door banging startled her. She knew that it was the apartment next door but it started her heart racing all the same. She strained to hear the murmur of conversation and was rewarded by the sound of the TV suddenly blaring and then being hastily turned down.

She was even more awake now and she knew that it would be ages before she'd sleep. She pushed the quilt away from her and got out of bed, wrapping her robe around her. She padded down the wooden stairs and into the kitchen where she filled the kettle and spooned some hot chocolate into a mug. She jumped as she saw Bagel on the windowsill, his green eyes reflecting into the kitchen. She opened the window and the cat jumped lightly over the kitchen sink and stalked past her into the living room where he curled up on the back of the sofa.

Ash opened a packet of marshmallows and dropped a pink one into the drink before carrying the steaming mug into the living room after him. She put the mug on the small table and switched on her computer. Her home page told her that the European markets had ended down while the US was still falling. She made a face. That meant the value of her shares had gone down and she hated it when that happened.

She read through a few of her favourite recipe pages, too, then her horoscope for the day ahead. Ash didn't believe in astrology but whenever she surfed the net she checked her stars all the same. They never said anything she wanted to hear. According to the prediction, she would be feeling tired tomorrow. Not very surprising, she thought, as she glanced at the clock at the top of the page and realised that it was nearly one o'clock.

Finally she checked her e-mail. She hadn't expected any and was surprised when she realised that she had two. One was spam which she immediately trashed, the other was from Alistair Brannigan. She wrinkled her nose as she read his message.

She hoped that he thought he was being funny because otherwise who did he think he was, offering to pay her to cook for just him? Or not, which was even worse! She'd never gone out with anyone who was loaded before; usually her boyfriends were more than happy for her to pay her own way, and it was a strange feeling to think that, with Alistair, she could go into any restaurant and not feel bad about ordering the most expensive thing on the menu. If she let the relationship with him develop, she might never have to worry about money again.

He would be Julia's choice, she thought suddenly. Rich but a bit flaky because all those technology people were a bit flaky. So that would have suited her mother and maybe it would suit her too.

She'd enjoyed going to the premiere with him even though she'd been embarrassed when he'd bought the necklace. But he'd been nice afterwards and she'd liked the way he hadn't tried to insist on coming into her apartment. He was, she thought, more mature than some of the men she'd gone out with in the past.

She closed her eyes and thought of some of them. David. Lorcan. Conor. Kieran. Brendan. The goodbye guys. And, despite what she sometimes told herself, probably perfect for her. But she pushed them all away because (and she hated admitting this even to herself) she was afraid of getting close to them. Afraid that she'd grow to care for them. And afraid that they'd stop caring for her. Then one of them would end it. Not her. And that terrified her more than anything.

But I can't go on like this for ever, she told herself. Molly and Michelle are right. It would be nice to have someone to share things with. Someone to curl up with in the evenings and rest my head on his shoulder. Someone who'll comfort me when things go wrong and cheer me when things go right. Someone who matters to me. It would be nice to have someone who matters.

She sat down at the computer and began to type. 'Not necessary to pay me double time for cooking, my rates are the same for everyone. But would rather go out as cooking is something of busman's holiday. Would prefer pizza and beer. Friday sounds good.' She reread the message then added 'Love, Ash' before she sent it.

Chapter 11

Cookies and Cream
Milk, egg yolks, caster sugar, double cream, dark biscuits,
vanilla essence
Heat milk, beat egg yolks and sugar, pour over milk. Cook
over gentle heat. Leave to cool. Whisk cream and vanilla
essence into cold mixture. Freeze for 2 hours. Turn into
bowl and beat again. Add dark broken biscuits. Refreeze
overnight

D an Morland gazed around the office and wondered where Debbie was. He'd noticed, in passing, that she hadn't been around yesterday although it hadn't really registered with him as being important. But it was important today because she was supposed to be accompanying him to a charity Christmas ball tonight. He'd accepted the invitation to the ball months ago and Cordelia had said that she'd come. It was the fact that she'd been so enthusiastic about coming with him even though it was so far in the future that had made him feel that their relationship had grown. Otherwise she'd have hedged her bets, told him that she didn't know what she was doing in December. But she'd been enthusiastic and he'd sent back his reply with Cordelia's name on it as his partner. But her trip to the States had changed everything. Of course he'd forgotten all about the ball until the reminder had popped up on his office computer, causing him to swear under his breath and wish that he wasn't the sort of guy who accepted invitations months in advance.

The ball was an annual event held by Honor Carmody, the wife of a leading industrialist. She had a significant portfolio of her own and had been dealing with Dan since he'd started as a stockbroker ten years ago. Honor considered Dan to be one of her most eligible bachelors and she'd been devastated when he told her that he was in a long-term relationship with Cordelia. If he turned up without her now, Honor would put two and two together, come up with five and start inviting him to all her functions as a spare man, despite what he might say. He found it very difficult to turn down any of Honor's invitations because she was a good client and, even more than that, one of the most determined people he'd ever met. There was no way he was going to the ball on his own, which was why, when he'd seen the reminder, he'd asked Debbie, one of the administrators who knew Honor. Debbie had been delighted, which had cheered Dan. He hoped she was still looking forward to it.

He caught sight of Kate Coleman standing by the photocopier, a bundle of documents in her hands. 'Hey, Kate!'

She turned round at his call. 'What? I'm not bloody copying a pile of stuff for you, Dan Morland, this is for Ross and it takes precedence.'

'I wasn't going to ask you to copy anything,' said Dan peevishly. 'I just wanted to know if you'd seen Debbie today.'

'Debbie?' Kate looked at him as though he'd grown two heads. 'Have you been going around with your head in the sand, Dan? Debbie is in hospital.'

'What!'

'Everyone was talking about it yesterday! Appendicitis. She was brought in screaming in the middle of the night apparently.'

'I didn't hear,' said Dan. 'But I was out for a lot of yesterday.'

'You just weren't listening,' said Kate. 'You haven't been with it the last few weeks at all.' She grinned. 'Missing your fiancée?'

Dan made a face at her. 'So how long will she be in hospital?' he asked.

'I don't know,' replied Kate. 'But a few more days at least. Why? You going to visit her?'

'She was supposed to come to Honor Carmody's do with me tonight,' explained Dan.

'So she was. She'll be raging she's missed it, she even bought a new dress!'

'I'm raging she's missing it too. I don't want to go to Honor's on my own. You know what she's like and she'll stick to me like glue all night. Not to mention marking me down again as her favourite spare man.' Dan looked at Kate hopefully. 'I suppose you wouldn't like to come instead, would you?' He hadn't the nerve to ring Honor and say he wouldn't be there at all.

'I'd love to,' Kate told him. 'You know I would – it's in the K Club, isn't it?'

Dan nodded. 'Great—'

'I said I'd love to,' Kate continued, 'but I really can't, Dan. I'm out with Pat tonight and I can't not turn up – it's his work party.'

'Surely you don't have to go to his office party?' asked Dan.

'I don't have to go,' said Kate, 'but I promised I'd be there. He wants me there. He'd probably break off the engagement if I didn't turn up.'

Another dodgy engagement! Dan sighed deeply. 'Anyone else in the office free tonight?' he asked.

Kate laughed. 'I don't know. Why don't you send around an e-mail?'

'You know what would happen.' Dan frowned at her. 'Someone I've never even met would say yes.'

'And that'd be a bad thing?' asked Kate. 'You need to meet a few more people in the company, Dan. You're stuck at your desk most of the time. Be good for you to see a few of the other girls.'

'Maybe.' Dan looked doubtful.

'Or else you just go on your own,' Kate's eyes gleamed wickedly, 'and allow Honor to put her arms around you and say, "This is Dan, my most eligible man friend."'

'Please don't,' said Dan. 'Remember her at the tennis tournament last summer?'

'Do I what?' asked Kate as she began to remove the collated documents from the photocopier.

It was very unusual for Ash to be catering for two lunches in Chatham's in the same week. She'd had the scheduled Monday lunch and now, on Friday, Dan Morland's lunch for six. Although Kate had booked her for it a couple of weeks earlier, Dan himself had come into the kitchen on Monday to remind her. She hadn't seen him since the movie premiere and she was glad to see that he looked healthy again.

'It's a group of men,' he told her. 'Nothing fancy, Ash, more quantity, less decorative stuff if you know what I mean.'

'Sure,' she said easily. 'How about fish and chips?'

'Fish and chips? I know I want basic but isn't that oversimplifying things somewhat?'

'I can do you some really nice Dover sole, or some ray wings – they're good at the moment – plus some decent home-cooked chips. It's very popular.'

'Sounds good,' Dan conceded.

'It is good,' she promised him. 'They'll love it. Are they important clients?'

'Every client thinks that they're the most important in the universe,' said Dan gloomily.

Ash smiled at him. 'I must remember that next time I'm on to buy something.'

'Thinking of investing some more?' asked Dan.

'I'm still paying off the painter and decorator,' Ash told him. 'And I'm cautious at heart really; this is my one flirtation with danger.'

'You don't live dangerously in any other way?' asked Dan.

'Not really.' She sighed. 'When you've had a – a less conventional upbringing, your rebellion is the wrong way round. Most kids become mad and bad. I'm the complete opposite.'

Dan nodded. 'I can see how that might happen.'

Ash replaced some bottles of wine in the cooler.

'The necklace looks nice,' said Dan.

Her hand flew to her throat and she touched the gold chain. 'It was stupid of him to buy it,' she said.

'But it suits you.'

'Gold suits everyone,' said Ash. She put some pats of butter in the fridge. 'How's Cordelia getting on?'

'Great,' Dan told her. 'Loves it. She's doing well, they're working on some kind of rescue plan for a company at the moment. She seems to be in the office all hours, which is good and bad – good because she can't go out enticing all sorts of men, bad because she's working side by side with some guy called DeVere who seems to be interesting, clever and attractive.'

Ash smiled. 'But not you. And she's engaged to you.'

'I know,' said Dan. 'I just wish she was back home, that's all.' He looked at his watch. 'Better go,' he said. 'I've a few orders to do in New York time myself. And I might just give her a call beforehand.'

'Fine,' said Ash as she locked the cupboard doors. 'See you Friday.'

Now it was Friday and she was seasoning the fish while Jodie set the table.

'I went to see that movie last night,' said Jodie when she'd finished. 'The one you went to the premiere of with my ex-friend Alistair Brannigan.'

'Ex-friend?'

'I wasn't expecting you to snare him, Ash.'

'I didn't snare him,' Ash told her. 'I've gone out with him a couple of times but it's nothing serious, Jodie.'

'It never is with you,' said Jodie waspishly. 'But that doesn't mean that the bloke concerned doesn't take it far more seriously.'

'Alistair is young, single and rolling in it,' said Ash. 'He doesn't need to take it seriously.'

'He takes a lot of things seriously,' said Jodie. 'How do you think he built up that company?'

'True,' conceded Ash. 'But I'm sure he has hordes of girls ready to throw themselves at him. He doesn't need me.'

Jodie raised an eyebrow at her. 'Would you like him to?'

'Oh, give it a rest, Jodie! Did you enjoy the movie?' Ash changed the subject.

Jodie knew by her tone that Ash didn't want to talk about Alistair any more but she decided to give it one more try.

'A bit stagey, I thought. But enjoyable all the same. Would have been nicer with a slap-up meal in the Clarence afterwards! And somebody buying me a gold necklace.' She looked at Ash knowingly.

'It was for charity,' said Ash. 'Nothing else. And

although it was an enjoyable night I didn't sleep for ages because we ate so late.'

Jodie decided not to push it any more. 'I didn't sleep for ages afterwards myself. But that was because Chris came back to the apartment . . .'

'Well, no messing around with baby oil again,' said Ash firmly. 'I can't afford to have you off with another sprained wrist in December.'

Jodie laughed and Ash started to chip the potatoes.

'I think I hear them arriving,' said Ash. 'Time to get going.'

Jodie headed into the dining room and began handing out drinks.

'No women,' she said when she came back into the kitchen. 'Six men and no women! You know what the conversation will be like.'

'You're not there to listen to their conversation,' said Ash sternly.

'I know. But when they get drunk they start telling the most awful jokes and making lunges at my bum,' complained Jodie.

'Who says they're going to get drunk?' asked Ash. 'Just because it's a bunch of men doesn't mean that they have to get drunk.'

'Oh, doesn't it?' Jodie said darkly.

'No, it doesn't,' said Ash. 'And this is a business lunch, Jodie, not a piss-up.'

'Come on, Ash!' Jodie laughed. 'It's a couple of weeks to Christmas. You're not seriously thinking that they're just going to eat the food, have a glass of wine and leave, are you?'

'I was hoping so,' said Ash.

Jodie giggled and went back to check on their progress while Ash continued to prepare the food.

Jodie was more accurate in her assessment of the clients than Ash. She was topping up the wine glasses with monotonous regularity except, she told Ash, Dan Morland's glass.

'Something's bothering him,' she told Ash when she brought back the empty starter dishes. 'He's not with it at all. Doesn't really matter because the others are having a whale of a time.'

'Once his clients are happy it doesn't much matter, I suppose.' Ash slid ray wings onto six plates and poured a little sauce over them.

'Smells good,' said Jodie.

'I like this myself,' admitted Ash. She watched Jodie take the plates into the dining room. Then she leaned against the kitchen wall and closed her eyes. She'd been up late the previous night icing Christmas cakes. Ash preferred cooking to baking and wasn't interested in cake decoration at all, but she did it every Christmas and Molly and Michelle, as well as the two sisters-in-law Irina and Nancy, expected her to bake and ice cakes for them. She'd done the cakes ages ago but always left icing them until as late as possible. Once, she'd done Michelle's cake on Christmas Eve. It still hadn't set properly by the time she'd brought it to Molly's later that night.

I should say no, she thought. I should tell them to bake their own cakes. Or even buy them. But she knew that she could never do that. It had become a tradition that she did the Christmas cakes – and the puddings. Everyone laughed and joked that there was no point in having a cook in the family if she couldn't turn out a few cakes and puddings for Christmas. And, when it came to Christmas dinner, they were happy to let her do everything because none of them enjoyed cooking the way she did. They didn't see it as hard work for her, and she didn't mind. She knew that she'd only interfere if someone else did it anyway. It was just the cakes and puddings that irritated her.

She still hadn't spoken to Michelle since their latest row. But she knew, from experience, that Michelle would act as though nothing had happened the next time they met. Especially since that would be when they called in to collect stuff from her on Christmas Eve before setting off to Molly's. Ash would follow later by train as she always did.

Molly had very rigid views about Christmas. It was a time for them to be together. A time for them to realise that they were family and that families stuck together no matter what. A time for them to remember Christmases in the past and realise how lucky they were to have each other. Molly was a marketing man's Christmas dream.

Ash and Julia had spent their last Christmas together in the Dominican Republic. Julia had always hated the cold, damp weather of England in the wintertime and she hated Christmas too. So she'd booked two weeks in the sun even though Ash had wanted to stay at home.

Ash remembered sitting on the beach on Christmas Day while Julia buried her feet in the soft white sand and sang 'American Pie' to her. Later, they'd had burgers and Coke while they watched the sun go down. I didn't appreciate it at the time, thought Ash, as she got ready for action again. Christmas on a sunny island sounds damned nice just now!

'They're ready for desserts.' Jodie pushed open the kitchen door. 'They've eaten everything!'

Ash smiled. 'That's good. I hate it when people leave food.' She placed slices of key lime pie onto dessert plates. 'Here you go. Keep them stuffed with food. Might curtail their alcohol consumption.'

'I doubt that,' said Jodie. 'I've never been able to curtail Chris's consumption when he's drinking free drink.'

'These people get free drink all the time,' said Ash impatiently. 'You'd imagine they'd be tired of it by now.'

'No one ever gets tired of something that's free,' Jodie told her. 'Sometimes I think you're terribly naïve, Ash.'

'Hand out the desserts and hold the philosophy.' Ash grinned as Jodie disappeared out of the door again.

The sound of laughter from the dining room was becoming ever more raucous. Jodie was probably right, thought Ash despondently. Whenever something is free people just lash in. Which would mean that they'd be late finishing up today. Oh well, Ash mused, Chatham's can afford to pay the overtime.

But she was wrong. At half past two she realised that the men next door were beginning to leave. She looked at Jodie in surprise.

'I thought they'd be later too,' said Jodie in answer to Ash's look. 'Maybe they've all got things to do tonight. Perhaps that's why they're leaving promptly.'

'Good for us,' said Ash. 'Means we won't be hanging around.'

There was a tap on the kitchen door and the girls exchanged glances as Dan Morland walked in.

'Hi, Ash,' he said. 'Thanks for a great lunch.'

'Anytime.'

He looked from Ash to Jodie and back again. 'I was wondering if I could have a word.'

'Sure,' said Ash.

'With you,' he said.

Jodie looked at him. 'Do you want me to leave?' she asked brightly.

'Well, I—'

'Don't worry, I've things to do inside,' she said. She left the kitchen and went into the dining room, casting a backward glance at Ash as she went.

'Is something wrong?' asked Ash.

'No. Nothing.' Dan looked incredibly uncomfortable.

'What?' asked Ash anxiously. 'If there's a problem, say so.'

'It's not a problem at all.' Dan rubbed his chin anxiously.

'So?'

'I know this sounds mad, Ash. I don't know you that well and yet we've met a lot lately and you've seen me at my absolute worst . . .'

'That's a good thing?' asked Ash.

'And we know a bit about each other – especially that I'm engaged and you're seeing someone who could probably buy you a small island or something if he wanted.'

'I don't—'

'Please don't get the wrong end of the stick here or anything. I wanted to ask you a favour.'

'Me personally?'

He nodded. 'And if you can't, I understand completely. But I was thinking of it during lunch and suddenly I thought that maybe you could . . .'

'Could what?'

'It's like this,' he said quickly. 'I accepted an invitation to go to a ball tonight. Cordelia was meant to come with me, of course – we were invited ages ago. Obviously she can't come to a ball in Ireland while she's working her butt off in the States. For a whole variety of reasons I didn't want to go on my own and I'd asked one of the girls in the office to come with me. But she's ended up in hospital with appendicitis and neither of the two others I rang today can come at such short notice. I know that it's extremely short notice for you too and if you can't come that's fine but I've run out of people to ask! If it's a problem I quite understand. I know that you and Alistair are an item and I don't want to do anything to upset you or him but I reckoned he'd realise that it was just you doing me a favour, nothing more than that.'

'You want me to go out with you tonight?' she asked.

'As a favour,' he said. 'If you can. That's all. No strings or anything. To help me out.'

'To a ball?'

'Well, that's what it's called,' said Dan dismissively. 'It's something one of my clients organises every year. About fifty people, I think – not a huge affair by any means.'

'Why don't you simply go on your own?' asked Ash. 'What are your variety of reasons?'

'Mainly because it's a couples thing,' said Dan. 'And if I go on my own the damned woman who's organising it will spend the whole evening trying to persuade me to come to other damn events that she's involved in. Which is all very well but she'll ask me as an unattached man and start hitching me up with women I've no interest in whatsoever.'

'But if she knows you're engaged to Cordelia, why would she bother?' asked Ash.

'Because that's the kind of woman she is,' said Dan.

'Why don't you say you can't go?' asked Ash. 'After all, if she knows Cordelia is in the States then she'll hardly expect you to turn up.'

'I have to turn up,' said Dan. 'I never miss it and I can't miss it this year. She's an important client and, despite everything I'm saying about her, she's a decent woman. I don't want to bow out at this stage. It's just that this is the kind of thing where I need moral support.'

Ash laughed.

'It's no laughing matter,' said Dan glumly. 'Really it isn't.'

'So you want me to come out with you tonight to be your – what, exactly?'

'Old friend?' suggested Dan. 'I feel as though we are

at this stage. You've seen me drunk, hungover and at my rudest. It can only improve from here!'

Ash looked at him helplessly.

'I know you're probably busy,' said Dan. 'And if you're off to Paris for the weekend with Brannigan or something, I understand completely. I know that you've got your own life and this isn't a date or anything, it's just – just . . .'

He reminded her of her cousin Charlie, who looked just like that when he was trying to make you do something for him.

Ash pushed a stray hair out of her eyes. She wasn't busy tonight – Alistair was in London this weekend so she'd scheduled this evening as a 'cookies and cream' night with Bagel at her feet and a tub of their favourite ice cream at the ready. Both she and Bagel loved cookies and cream. She'd leave the lid on the sofa beside her and plop the occasional spoonful of ice cream on it for Bagel, who also licked out the tub when she was finished. Dan's request meant an unexpected change of plans and Ash hated the unexpected. Which was why she so rarely did anything herself without having planned it in great detail first.

'When?' she asked finally.

'Eight o'clock,' said Dan.

She looked at him uneasily.

'It's not a problem if you can't,' said Dan. 'It was just an idea.'

'I suppose I could,' Ash said doubtfully. 'If you're really stuck.'

'I'm really stuck,' said Dan. 'And I'd consider it a real favour, Ash. I truly would.'

'I'm sure there are other people you could ask,' she told him. 'It's not that I wouldn't if you really need someone but if you've only asked three people – Dan, I'm sure you know more than three people!'

'Not that I can haul out at such short notice,' he said ruefully. 'And not people who wouldn't think that I was asking them out for some ulterior motive.'

'I'm glad you think I wouldn't expect you to have an ulterior motive. And that I lead such an uneventful life that I have nothing to do on a Friday night.' She grinned suddenly and her brown eyes were full of mischief.

'You were a long shot,' Dan told her. 'I thought you'd probably be out with Brannigan, to be honest. If you want to think about it . . .'

'That's not much good to you,' said Ash.

'I know.'

'Oh, OK.' She shrugged. 'I don't have anything else on, Dan, and if you really need someone . . .'

'You're a pet!' His face showed his relief. 'Thanks a million, Ash. How about I pick you up around seven?'

'I thought you said eight,' she objected.

'It'll take us an hour to get to the K Club,' said Dan.

'The K Club!' Ash looked at him in horror.

'Don't you like it?' His voice was full of surprise. 'It's a great place, Ash. The clients always love it.'

'It's bloody expensive,' she said. 'And I don't know if I have anything to wear. How dressed up is this event?'

194

He shrugged. 'Cocktail dress. Really, Ash, you don't need to worry. Anything will do. Honestly.'

She sighed. She had a horrible feeling that she'd just walked into something that she'd regret. The K Club was a very exclusive country house just outside Dublin. Ash really didn't think she could wear just anything to the K Club. People would be wearing all sorts of expensive dresses and she'd look completely out of place in her so-called glad rags. She hadn't bought a new dress in ages.

Dan watched her, unable to read the expression on her face. 'Is it OK?' he asked. 'Have you changed your mind?'

She shook her head. 'No. It's OK. I'll go.'

'Great.' Dan smiled at her. 'Which apartment?'

'Four A,' said Ash. 'Just buzz, I'll be ready.'

'Great,' repeated Dan. He left the kitchen by the main door as Jodie came in through the dining-room door.

'What did he want?' asked Jodie.

Ash made a face. 'For me to go to a ball with him tonight.'

'Oh, Cinderella! You're joking!'

'No.' Ash shook her head. 'That's exactly what he wanted.'

'Come on! And what did you say? That you were busy?'

'Actually, I said yes,' Ash told her.

'You didn't!' Jodie stared at her. 'Somebody asked you out and you didn't say that you were supposed to be at home with your cat tonight?'

'He's stuck for someone,' said Ash. 'And, eventually, I said yes.'

'Stuck for someone my arse,' said Jodie. 'He fancies you, Ash.' She looked at her admiringly. 'I have to hand it to you, you're on a roll. First Alistair, now Dan and you haven't even dumped Alistair yet, have you?'

'It's not like that at all.' Ash began to put away the condiments. 'He really is stuck. And his company is a good client. So it's kind of in my interest to keep him happy. It's not a date, Jodie. Nothing like it.'

Jodie looked at her sceptically. 'Come on, Ash. You believe all that?'

'Yes,' said Ash. 'I really am just helping him out, Jodie.'

'I suppose it never occurred to you that I could help him out? If it's not a date. If he's just stuck for someone. If you'd really prefer to be at home with your cat.'

Ash looked at her in surprise. 'No, I didn't think. But maybe that's a good idea, Jodie. I mean, it's not going to matter to Dan Morland whether you or I go with him and if you'd like to go, I certainly don't mind!'

'Don't be so bloody silly!' Jodie looked at her in disgust. 'He doesn't want to go with me.'

'He doesn't want to go with me,' said Ash. 'He really wants to go with his fiancée.'

'His fiancée?' squeaked Jodie. 'I didn't know he had a fiancée! He's bloody two-timing his fiancée?'

'Oh, don't be ridiculous,' said Ash in exasperation. 'She can't go so I really am just helping him out.'

'Where's the fiancée?' asked Jodie. 'Why can't she go?'

Ash shrugged. She didn't want to discuss Dan's private life with Jodie but she didn't feel as though she had much option. 'Working in the States,' she told her.

'So you'll get him while he's feeling lost and unwanted.' Jodie shook her head. 'Do me a favour, Ash. Let Alistair down gently, will you? I'm fond of him.'

'Oh, for heaven's sake!' Ash looked at Jodie. 'I've only gone out with Alistair a few times. And we get on well but that's all. He hasn't tried to jump into bed with me yet, Jodie, so if anyone needs letting down gently it's me! And Dan Morland doesn't fancy me either – he's crazy about Cordelia. So I'm a stopgap, nothing more. The same way that I'm probably a stopgap for your friend Alistair too before he decides to run off with a skinny supermodel or someone else more suited to the lifestyles of the rich and famous.'

'I can't decide whether you truly are naïve or just a femme fatale,' said Jodie.

'Neither!' Ash spoke impatiently. 'So you get on with what you're meant to be doing. And let me think about what on earth I'm going to wear.'

Chapter 12

Seafood Pilaf
Onion, green pepper, pimiento, mushrooms, butter, brown
rice, saffron, stock, cooked smoked haddock, prawns, almonds,
tomatoes
Prepare vegetables. Melt butter, add onion then rice, sauté,
then turn into casserole, add pepper, pimiento and mush-
rooms. Mix saffron in water, pour over, add stock. Cook
until tender. When rice is cooked, fork in flaked haddock
and some prawns. Tip rice onto serving dish, decorate
with reserved mushrooms, peppers, pimiento and prawns.
Sprinkle with chopped almonds, garnish with tomatoes

I must have been mad, thought Ash as she surveyed the contents of her wardrobe, which were now strewn across the bed. Just because I felt sorry for him. Just because he looked at me with those dark blue eyes and made me feel as though I couldn't say no. And because he treated me, somehow, as if I was a friend who could help him when nobody else could and I felt kind of flattered. Flattered! When he'd already been turned down by all of the other girls he'd asked! And I should have said no too because I don't usually say yes to someone who asks me out on the spur of the moment.

Only he hasn't asked me out, he's simply asked me to help him out. Except that I don't move in the kind of circles where I have suitable clothes for one of the poshest places in the city just lying around at home, and helping him out is turning into a bloody nightmare. She sighed as she looked at her three best dresses and then frowned. The fuchsia pink which she'd worn to the movie premiere was out of the question. It was bright and cheery and very young-looking – all of the things that she didn't want to appear tonight. She wanted to be cool and smart and sophisticated. The soft grey jersey, while suitable in a nondescript sort of way, really didn't fit the bill. Which left the plain black three-year-old – neither cool nor smart, although vaguely sophisticated. But hardly, thought Ash bleakly, at the cutting edge of fashion. It had a rounded neckline, no sleeves and came to just above her knee. However, it had a short, matching jacket which made it look more dressy and it went well with her only pair of really high-heeled shoes. It was also the most expensive piece of clothing in her wardrobe and Ash felt that an evening at the K Club deserved her most expensive piece of clothing no matter how old it was. She hoped that she'd still fit into it – she hadn't worn it since last March. I obviously don't do enough socialising, she murmured as she did her make-up and coiled her hair. Maybe Jodie is right when she says I spend too much time at home with Bagel!

She slipped into the dress and gazed at her reflection in the mirror. It fitted her, which was something, although she'd had to give the zip more of a tug than she would have liked. And the spun gold of her hair contrasted with the starkness of the black, which, she remembered, was why she'd bought it in the first place. But she wouldn't exactly be winning prizes as the most glamorous person there. She opened the small jewellery box and gazed at Julia's pearls. She knew that they'd go well with the dress, their soft sheen would be enhanced by the black fabric. She took the string out of the box and held them to her neck. Then she shivered. Not Julia's pearls. The unlucky pearls. Instead she took out the gold necklace and fastened it round her neck. She had to admit that it was a surprisingly useful piece of jewellery. And more appropriate than the narrow silver chain or gold locket that she normally wore.

Perfectly acceptable, she murmured as she sprayed herself with Chloë and checked herself in the mirror again. As befits the old friend called on at the last minute to help out! She glanced at her watch. A quarter to seven. Excellent timing despite the rush.

She went into the kitchen and opened the window. Bagel hadn't come home yet today, probably because it had been cold and bright all day and he liked to spend cold bright days stalking round the nearby buildings. Ash didn't like to go out without seeing him, without telling him to look after himself. She whistled softly but there was no sign of him.

'Come on, cat,' she muttered but she knew she was

wasting her time. If he was on some kind of hunt he wouldn't come home no matter how much she called him. Even though she would have preferred him to come home, it was the very fact that he did his own thing that endeared him to her. Cats didn't expect much from you other than regular food and a lap to sit on. They didn't need to be taken for walks, they didn't need to be told that you loved them, they didn't make unreasonable demands.

She closed the window again and checked that everything was switched off. She moved the tea towel over the chrome rail so that it hung evenly and then she wiped the worktop with kitchen paper. She went into the bathroom, washed her hands and rubbed some Boots apricot hand cream into them.

She'd expected Dan to be late but his car pulled up outside the apartment block just as she arrived in the foyer. He opened the driver's door then closed it again as she let herself out of the building. She hurried round to the passenger side and got into the car.

'Punctual,' said Dan.

'Always,' she told him.

He put the car into gear and moved away. 'Thanks again,' he said. 'I really do appreciate this.'

She shrugged. 'No problem.'

He glanced at her as he drove round the block and into the Friday-night traffic. She really was quite pretty, he thought, if you liked that sort of thing. Not striking, like Cordelia, but still good-looking. He wondered what her mother, the incredibly daft-sounding Julia, had looked like. And whether Ash resembled her or her unknown father.

He glanced at her again, surprised that she hadn't begun a conversation with him. In his experience women weren't good at travelling silently in a car. They wanted to talk to you, find out about you, share their thoughts. Maybe she didn't have any thoughts, he mused. And after all, what did he want her to talk about? Maybe asking her along tonight had been a bad idea, even though it had seemed such a great one at lunch. Maybe his judgement had been impaired by the one glass of Chateauneuf du Pape he'd drunk. But he'd suddenly thought of Ash – a girl who had no interest in him whatsoever, who knew all about Cordelia and, usefully, who had a boyfriend of her own so that she couldn't by any stretch of the imagination get the wrong end of the stick about his request. Of course she'd said they were just friends, but what girl could just be friends with Alistair Brannigan? Surely his money alone would be a powerful aphrodisiac even if he wasn't young and good-looking. Lucky bastard, thought Dan, as he sped through amber lights.

'Alistair didn't mind?' He felt as though he should make some conversation.

'Sorry?' Ash had been looking out of the window, wondering if they'd be late because the traffic in the city, even at this hour, was very heavy.

'Alistair? He didn't mind you coming along with me tonight?' repeated Dan.

'I didn't ask him,' said Ash. 'But there's no reason for him to mind.'

'I know you told me you were just friends. But afterwards I thought that maybe he'd be annoyed and maybe I'd put you in an awkward position.'

She shook her head. 'Not at all. And the only awkward position you put me in was in finding something decent to wear.'

He hadn't seen what she was wearing beneath her big woollen coat.

'All girls complain about having nothing to wear,' he told her. 'Even when their wardrobes are bursting at the seams with clothes.'

Ash thought about her wardrobe, bursting at the seams with jeans, and her pathetic collection of dresses. I'm so bad at girlie things, she thought helplessly. And I really don't know why.

'But I take it that, out of the hundred or so dresses which you probably have, you managed to find something suitable?' asked Dan.

'Cordelia might have hundreds of dresses but not me,' Ash told him. 'I'm hopeless at clothes.'

'You can't be.' He changed lanes rapidly to get in front of a slow-moving truck. 'It's an inbuilt thing with women. And you wore a very pretty dress to the movie premiere.'

'You remember it?'

'Not a lot, I have to admit. That night is something of a blur. But it was a nice dress.'

'But not for tonight,' said Ash.

'You see!' he exclaimed triumphantly, running another amber light. 'You don't think you're the same as every other woman on the planet but you are. A perfectly good dress in the wardrobe but you still have nothing to wear!'

Ash giggled. She couldn't help it.

'I rest my case,' said Dan complacently.

They drove in companionable silence until a couple of miles outside Straffan where a fox ran across the road, his eyes gleaming in the lights of the car, and Dan had to brake hard to avoid hitting him.

'Oh my God!' Ash's hands flew to her face as the car skidded on some loose gravel.

'Don't worry, you're quite all right,' Dan assured her. 'Even if I'd gone into the ditch, this car has side impact bars and goodness knows what else as safety equipment.'

'I was thinking more of the fox,' said Ash.

'Oh.'

Dan drove a little more slowly until he turned through the gates of the K Club. There, the ramps on the road prevented him from going above twenty miles an hour anyway.

'Perfect timing,' he said in satisfaction as he pulled into the car park.

Ash looked at her watch. It was exactly eight o'clock.

She opened the car door and shivered as she stepped outside. The temperature was freezing and her breath hung in little clouds in front of her.

'Come on,' said Dan. 'Let's get inside before we turn into blocks of ice.'

She followed him out of the car park and up the steps

into the imposing country house. She'd never set foot inside the K Club before – it wasn't her type of place and it wasn't frequented by her type of people. And she didn't play golf either – one of the club's claims to fame was its selection to host a Ryder Cup competition. All the same, thought Ash as she gazed around the foyer, it was certainly impressive with its elegant marble and luxurious thick blue carpets.

'Dan, darling! So good to see you!' A perfectly groomed woman in her mid-forties swept from one of the corridors and gathered Dan into a fulsome embrace. Ash smiled to herself as she saw the uncomfortable look on Dan's face.

'And this must be the wonderful – Cordelia?' Her voice faltered at the end, taking in Ash's fairness against the description she'd been given of Cordelia Carroll.

'Actually, no, Honor. This is Ash.'

'Ash?' Honor looked at Dan, then at Ash.

'Aisling O'Halloran.' Ash held out her hand and the other woman grasped it firmly.

'Ash is a very old friend of mine,' said Dan.

'So old I've never even heard of her?' Honor raised her eyebrows at him. 'I thought I knew all of your girlfriends, Dan.'

'I'm an old *friend*.' Ash emphasised the last word.

'But where's Cordelia?' asked Honor. 'I thought I was going to meet Cordelia tonight.'

'She's in the States, Honor,' said Dan. 'Working.'

'What foul luck.' Honor smiled sympathetically at him. 'So you had to trawl through your address book, did you?'

'Not quite,' said Dan.

'He was going to come alone but then he thought I might like to come too,' said Ash easily. Dan glanced at her and she saw the twitch of his mouth as he hid a grin.

'I see.' Honor smiled at them both although there was still curiosity in her eyes. 'Well, you'd better come through. So many people here already! We're the second room on the left and we have the dining room to ourselves tonight.'

'Great,' said Dan. 'Talk to you later, Honor.'

She kissed him on the cheek and then turned to some new arrivals.

'You did that terribly well,' Dan murmured to Ash. 'You'd almost think that we'd known each other from the cradle.'

'She's a formidable woman!' Ash followed Dan down the corridor. 'No wonder you didn't want to come on your own.'

'She's very nice,' said Dan, 'just overpowering.'

'I can see that.'

'She's involved in lots of charity work and she's on the board of directors of a number of companies,' he added.

'They're probably afraid not to have her,' said Ash wryly as they entered the room. Once again it was effortlessly elegant, the walls hung with oil paintings, silver candelabra on the imposing fireplace and a round rosewood table in the centre. Almost immediately a waiter offered them champagne while another took their coats. Ash felt underdressed in her plain black when she looked at some of the creations that were being sported by other women. One girl was wearing a dark blue gown with a flared skirt which took up a sizeable corner of the room, while huge diamonds (Ash was certain they were real) glittered round her neck and dangled from her ears. Ash was very glad she hadn't worn her own fake diamond necklace. In this crowd it would have stood out like a sore thumb. She was sure that every woman here could tell fake from genuine from forty paces. She sipped her drink and envied the dresses and the jewellery while Dan was greeted by yet another friend.

'Ash.' He gestured to her. 'This is Gerry Casey, an old business pal of mine. Ash O'Halloran.'

She hadn't realised how many people Dan knew. It seemed to Ash that he was on intimate terms with almost everyone there, both male and female. She found herself being greeted by people as though she, too, were an old friend, as though by knowing Dan she was automatically accepted as someone worth knowing also. Would it be like this with Alistair? she wondered. With the exception of the movie premiere, she hadn't gone to a big social event with him. They usually settled for cosy informality although the last time they'd gone out he'd insisted on something a little more upmarket and had brought her to Guilbaud's. The food had been wonderful but Ash preferred the atmosphere of Il Vignardo's or Wagamama's. She also preferred to eat the sort of food she didn't cook much herself.

Where did Dan and Cordelia go when they ate out? she wondered. Obviously Dan, despite only being able to renovate one room at a time, was reasonably well off. Did he prefer starched tablecloths and shining cutlery to scrubbed tables and a pint of beer? And what about Cordelia? Was she a grape or grain kind of girl at heart?

'OK?' asked Dan when they were temporarily alone together.

'Fine,' she replied. 'But I never realised before what a popular person you were!'

He laughed. 'Not really. I just know a lot of these people.'

'Are they all incredibly rich?' asked Ash. 'I mean, some of the sparklers on those women are absolute rocks! I can't help thinking I could swipe a necklace here and be set up for life.'

'You might get life,' said Dan, 'which is a totally different thing.'

Ash laughed. 'It's a bit breathtaking, all this conspicuous wealth. I see it sometimes, you know, when I do functions for people but this is different.'

'Is it?'

She nodded. 'I get the feeling that these people live this sort of life all the time. Not like my clients who do it occasionally. I find it hard to imagine what it would be like to be filthy stinking rich like them.'

'But are they happy?' asked Dan solemnly.

She looked at him. 'Is that a serious question?'

'Partly, I suppose. I know I work in an industry where money is everything, but it isn't, you know.'

'Easy to say when you have it,' said Ash dryly.

'Maybe. But if you're unhappy, having loads of money won't change things.'

'Helps, though,' said Ash.

'Of course now that you're hitched up with Brannigan it's a moot point for you,' said Dan. 'He's rolling in it.'

'I'm not exactly hitched up,' said Ash. 'I told you, we're friends.'

'That's why I asked you tonight. Because we're just friends, Ash. But Alistair wants to be more than that with you.'

She laughed. 'You've got a great imagination.'

'No imagination,' said Dan. 'Maybe he's a slow worker.'

Alistair certainly hadn't tried to rush her. And Ash was more than happy to take things slowly.

'And how long-term does he want this hitching-up to be?' she asked. 'Since you seem to know so much about it.'

'Ah, well, there you have me!' Dan grinned. 'You know us men, fickle creatures.' He drained his glass just as the waiter appeared with more champagne. As he refilled their glasses they were joined by Michael and Stella Watts, another couple with whom Dan was friendly.

'Where's Cordelia?' asked Stella after they'd been introduced. 'Don't tell me you dumped her, Dan. You really are a serial lover, aren't you?'

Ash was surprised at Stella mentioning Cordelia in front of her, given that she could have been Dan's latest girlfriend, but amused by the fact that Dan had obviously had so many girlfriends in the past. Which was clearly why he was so worried about Cordelia being away. He probably couldn't imagine that she didn't have scores of blokes flocking around her. Oh well, thought Ash, do him good to worry. She excused herself before he answered and disappeared to the Ladies where she surveyed herself in the full-length mirror.

She knew she looked OK, she'd thought that at home, but she wished fervently that she had the glow about her that other women here tonight had. The glow of being loaded. Her pathetic little portfolio (her nest egg, her security as she always thought of it) wouldn't keep any of these people for a week! She thought about Alistair Brannigan again and wondered what he was doing in London tonight and what motivated him to work at the weekends when he'd made so much bloody money already.

A girl in her early twenties pushed open the door and Ash jumped out of the way. For all the extravagance of the building, thought Ash as she made room for the other girl, the Ladies was a little on the small side.

'Oops, sorry!' The girl smiled at her.

'It's OK,' said Ash.

The girl flicked her long black hair behind her shoulders and looked quizzically at Ash. 'You're with Dan Morland, aren't you?'

'Is Dan some kind of famous person?' asked Ash. 'It seems as though everyone knows him.'

'Infamous, more like!' The girl laughed.

'Why infamous?'

'Honor has hosted this event every year for the past six

years. And every year Dan has brought someone different.'
She grinned at Ash. 'Last year he brought me.'

'Oh.'

'I'm Thea.' She said it as though her name should mean
something.

'Ash,' said Ash.

'Have you been going out with him long?' Thea took
a compact out of her bag and dabbed at her face.

'I've known him a long time.' Ash didn't want to say
anything that would land Dan in hot water.

'We've all known him a long time,' said Thea wryly.
'Not that it does us much good.'

'How long did you go out with him for?'

'Three months.' Thea sighed. 'I was mad about him,
you know, but he thought I was too young and silly.
Which is bloody stupid, if you ask me. I'm twenty-two!
But Dan told me that he couldn't see himself settling
down with me and that it was better if we split up.'

'That sounds a bit heartless,' said Ash, although she
understood the sentiment perfectly well.

'It was my fault really,' Thea conceded cheerfully. 'I
asked him to marry me.'

'Really?'

She nodded. 'He's such a nice bloke and I'd gone out
with a real shit before him. But it was no go with Dan
and I was gutted for ages afterwards. Then I heard he was
seriously involved with another girl. Cordelia.' Thea's big
blue eyes glittered. 'I heard he was bringing her tonight.
I heard they'd got engaged.'

'She's in the States,' said Ash easily. 'And you're right,

they did get engaged. I'm just an old friend he dragged along for company.'

Thea looked at her speculatively. 'But I've never heard of you.'

'Perhaps he didn't tell you everything.' Ash was tired of this girl with her perfect skin and her perfect clothes and her desire to glean information that she didn't need to have. She snapped her bag closed and opened the door. 'See you later,' she said and slipped outside again.

People were moving towards the ornate dining room. Ash looked around for Dan but couldn't see him. If what Thea said was true he was probably chatting up some other ex-girlfriend, she thought waspishly, and he should have asked one of them instead of me and I could be at home with Bagel and my tub of ice cream.

She saw their names listed at one of the tables and walked over to it. The girl with the huge blue dress stood beside her.

'Derbhla Hislop.' She smiled at Ash.

'Ash O'Halloran,' she said.

Derbhla looked round her. 'I seem to have lost my date.'

'Me too,' said Ash.

'I mean, where do they get to?' Derbhla raised an eyebrow. 'It's not that there's even a big bar in this place, you couldn't lose a pin in it, but they somehow manage to disappear. Maybe mine's gone to the room.'

'The room? You're staying overnight?'

'Oh, absolutely,' said Derbhla. 'I couldn't face driving back to town tonight and I wouldn't let Maurice drive me anyway. He's hopeless when he gets a few drinks on him. Oh, look, there he is!' She waved at a tall man who'd just walked into the dining room. 'Over here, darling.'

Ash grimaced. She wished Dan was here, she felt completely out of place. It was one thing catering for business people or rich people, it was quite another socialising with them.

Then Dan did appear and Derbhla went through the same litany as Thea had before her, asking Dan how it was that he always brought different women to Honor's ball and where was the lovely Cordelia that they'd all heard so much about. Although, Derbhla added archly, it would hardly be surprising if Dan had dumped Cordelia for Ash who was terribly, terribly nice, wasn't she?

Ash thought about hitting her but didn't. She glanced at Dan whose jaw was clenched and who made the usual comment about Ash being nothing more than an old friend. Ash was getting quite tired of being dismissed as Dan's old friend. She didn't mind being his stand-in date for the night, but it was irritating to feel as though she was someone he'd dragged out of the back of the wardrobe for the occasion. She toyed with the idea of throwing her arms round him and kissing him passionately on the lips. That would shock them all. Especially Dan! She hid a smile at the thought. She often had thoughts like that – of doing the most outrageous, impulsive things – but she knew she'd never actually do them. Which was why imagining them was fun.

She sat beside him but didn't bother taking part in the conversation which ebbed and flowed around the table. She didn't know most of the people they were talking about anyway, so she didn't care that Emilie and Patrick's divorce had finally come through, or that Dominic had built a wonderful new house near Bantry while Leonard had just bought his second villa in Spain. But she stored up the conversations so that she could relate them to Molly and Shay at Christmas when they could all laugh at the antics of the people whose names appeared in glossy magazines.

Then one of the company, a striking redhead named Lisa, said that she'd heard that Alistair Brannigan had a new squeeze and she was, according to gossip, absolutely stunning.

'Gorgeous,' said Lisa. 'A natural blonde, so I'm told. He's a quick worker to have found that out already!'

Ash said nothing but her heart was beating faster.

'I believe there's a technology company almost ready to float on the market,' said Dan abruptly. 'Might be almost as good an opportunity as Archangel.'

'I hope so,' said Lisa. 'I made a nice few bob out of that one. But I'm a little disappointed in Alistair. I knew him at college, and he was such a down-to-earth kind of guy then. I didn't think that he'd fall for the blonde bimbo approach so quickly.'

'I'm sure he hasn't fallen for anything.' Dan glanced at Ash who was buttering a warm bread roll.

'Oh, Dan, don't be so bloody naïve!' Lisa giggled. 'You know how these women come out of the woodwork as soon as a man makes a few bob. Then they get as many baubles as they can before moving on to someone else!'

I'm sure she doesn't give a jot about him, only his bank balance. Goodness knows, you've seen it yourself. Remember you and Jennifer Lennon?'

'I remember,' said Dan flatly. 'That was completely different.'

'I don't see how,' said Lisa.

'I'm a friend of Alistair Brannigan too,' Ash cut into the conversation. 'And I don't think he's the type to be duped by a woman, natural blonde or otherwise.'

The others looked at her with new interest.

'How well do you know him?' asked one of the other girls, whose name Ash thought was Lillian.

'Well enough,' said Ash.

'Maybe you could get me an introduction.' The girl swept her fair hair out of her eyes. 'Lisa's always saying that she'll introduce me but she never does. And Seb here is all very well,' she leaned against her boyfriend's shoulder, 'but he's only worth a few hundred thousand. He can't possibly keep me in the style to which I desperately want to become accustomed. And although I'm not a natural blonde I'm sure I'll do him just as well.'

'I'm sure he'd love to meet you,' said Ash insincerely.

'Tell us about the other company, Dan.' One of the men looked at him. 'You really think there's another opportunity?'

The conversation moved away from Alistair Brannigan and back into a more general discussion. Ash concentrated on the food which was excellent and the wine which was superb. And she continued to store up nuggets of gossip for Molly – that the wife of a TD was supposedly having an affair with a political affairs correspondent in RTÉ; that a well-known pop-star's wife was leaving him to live with her lesbian girlfriend; that there was a murky fraud scandal about to erupt about a prominent church dignitary.

Quite often when she was catering for dinner parties she'd hear equally lurid stories and Molly loved listening to them even though most of them were probably completely untrue. Ash never told stories to anyone other than Molly or, when they were speaking, to Michelle.

The dinner seemed to go on for ever. Then Honor Carmody made a speech about this being her favourite time of the year and about looking after people less fortunate than themselves and requesting that everyone donate what they could to help alleviate the suffering of those who couldn't afford to have lavish evenings like this evening. To her dismay, Ash realised that people were putting hundred pound notes into large John Rocha vases in the centre of the tables – apparently this was the price of the raffle ticket which might win you an overnight stay in the K Club at a time of your choosing.

Ash knew that an overnight stay in such luxurious surroundings would certainly cost much more than a hundred pounds but she hadn't bargained on having to donate quite that much this evening. She had less than a hundred pounds on her.

She opened her bag and looked into its depths indecisively.

'I'll put it in for you,' said Dan.

She looked at him and bit her lip. 'I'll pay you back,'

she said. 'I don't have that much with me. I brought my credit card and some cash but—'

'Please,' said Dan. 'I asked you along. I don't expect you to shell out money.'

'It's for a good cause. I truly don't mind only I don't have the cash.'

'I'd prefer if you let me do it.'

'I *will* pay you back,' she said determinedly. It would be ironic, she thought, if she won the prize, but very untypical. She never won raffles. If I won, she mused, maybe I could take Alistair here. It'd be the sort of place where he'd feel right at home!

Her luck held. The raffle was won by a girl at Honor's table amid amused cries of 'Fix, fix'.

'Never mind,' said Dan as they got up to allow the tables to be rearranged so that the dancing could start. 'You can always come back another time.'

He might not be rolling in cash like Alistair, thought Ash, but he's clearly living in another world if he thinks I can wander down here for the odd night whenever the mood takes me!

While Dan chatted to another of the guests, Ash wandered out of the dining room and into the entrance hall where a huge fire burned brightly in the grate and there were deep seats designed for comfort. She sat down opposite the fire and picked up a copy of *Harpers* although she didn't bother looking through it. It was quiet and peaceful by the fire and she had to fight the urge to tuck her legs beneath her and close her eyes for a while. Bagel would like it, she thought. She imagined sitting here with him curled up beside her in a cookies and cream moment.

'Here you are!' It was about ten minutes later when Dan found her still gazing into the flames. 'Aren't you coming back inside?'

'Oh, I just wanted some peace and quiet,' said Ash. 'I'll be back in a minute.'

Dan sat down beside her. 'Did the girls upset you with their comments about Alistair?'

Ash shook her head. 'Not a bit. How were they to know that I knew him anyway? But they're not exactly the most tactful bunch, are they?'

'Not really.'

She looked at him, amusement in her eyes. 'And how many of them have you gone out with?'

'Sorry?'

'I met a girl in the loo who said you'd brought her to this event last year. And everyone seems to be devastated at the thought of you and Cordelia. I thought you'd scoured your little black book before asking me tonight. I got the impression that there was nobody you could ask but as far as I can see there are hundreds!'

'Not quite,' said Dan.

'How many of them have you gone out with?' she asked again.

'A few,' he admitted, 'but you're making it sound as if I went through them like a dose of salts. It was over a very long period, you know.'

'They're all complete airheads,' she told him.

'I know.'

'But Cordelia isn't?'

'That's why I liked her so much.' He shifted on the seat. 'I'm not really good with women, Ash. But it's different with Cordelia.'

'What on earth do you mean, you're not good with women?' she demanded. 'They positively flock around you.'

'That crew would flock around anything,' he said disparagingly. 'And goodness knows why they flock around me, I'm nowhere near the Alistair Brannigan class when it comes to cash.'

'But you're well off,' said Ash. 'You've a lovely house and a nice car . . .'

'I'm OK,' Dan conceded. 'Thing is, Ash, there's always someone richer than you. You think, oh, if only I had ten grand in the bank I'd be fine. Then you have ten and you want twenty. When you have a hundred grand you want two hundred. And you start meeting people who have stables of cars and private jets and suddenly you think you're poor.'

'That's ridiculous,' she said.

'Relative to Alistair Brannigan, I'm very poor.'

'Relative to Alistair Brannigan everyone is poor.' Ash grinned. 'It must be fantastic to have all that money but probably a bit scary too.'

'So you'd turn it down?'

'Are you joking!' She laughed and gazed into the flames again.

'Thinking of how you could spend it?' asked Dan.

She smiled at him. 'It'd be interesting to try.'

'And will you?'

'I don't know.' She shrugged. 'I like him but we honestly are just friends at the moment. And I don't know if . . .' She didn't finish the sentence.

'Is there any such thing?' asked Dan.

'As what?'

'Friends. Men and women? I don't think so.'

'You're probably right,' conceded Ash. 'I do have some male friends that are pretty much just friends. But not close friends.'

'Exactly,' said Dan.

'We're old friends,' she reminded him. 'I've been introduced so many times tonight as your old friend that I feel I've known you for ever.'

He laughed. 'Sorry. It makes you sound like an old boot.'

'I know,' she said wryly. 'And all of your old girlfriends are suspicious of me because they've never heard of me before. Why did you go out with so many of them?'

'Practice,' he said.

'Dan!'

'I've never been good at the girlfriend thing,' he told her. 'To be honest I find a lot of women intimidating, especially girls like Lisa, all teeth and hair and gold jewellery. I'm a bit superficial, really. I meet someone and I think she's gorgeous and suddenly I ask her out and then I'm completely thrown when she says yes.'

Ash's eyes twinkled at him. 'So you ask them out expecting them to say no?'

'I'm not sure,' he said. 'I usually ask them to couples' things. Like tonight. Only not you,' he added hastily. 'I didn't – you know – I'm not trying to – with Cordelia away or anything, obviously.'

'Obviously,' said Ash. 'And you're forgetting that we've been friends practically since we could walk, Dan, or you wouldn't have needed to tell me that.'

He smiled at her. 'Sure, I'd forgotten. Anyway, truth is, I go out with lots of girls but, until now, I've been totally unable to last the pace with any of them. Cordelia is the only one I've felt comfortable with. Maybe because she's in the same business, we have things in common, you know?'

Ash nodded.

'The others, well, they all do PR and interior design and media work, that sort of thing. It's all glitzy and glamorous but it's not real life.'

'You think what goes on in Chatham's is real life?' asked Ash. 'Or even what Alistair does?'

'It's more real life than worrying what Prada are doing this spring,' he said forcefully.

'You might be right,' she said. 'But it's less real life than cooking!'

'So what about you and Alistair?' asked Dan. 'Techno-king and techno-cook. I told you he was positively drooling over you at the premiere. And he would have paid anything for that necklace. He was quite determined to get it for you.'

'That was just a stupid macho thing. Besides, you were practically drooling yourself, only in your case because you were suffering from an alcohol-related speech impediment.'

'I hope it works out with him, if that's what you want,' said Dan.

'I've no idea what I want.' She looked at him. 'I'm not very good at relationships either.'

'Why not?'

She gazed into the dancing flames of the fire and thought about it for a moment. She didn't want to be flippant and she didn't want to bare her soul to someone who, despite being flagged as her old friend, she hardly knew. But he was incredibly easy to talk to and she found herself telling him things that surprised her afterwards.

'I get panicky about men,' she said eventually. 'I get panicky about maybe falling for them and about getting hurt.'

'We all get hurt,' said Dan. 'You have to get over it.'

'I know,' said Ash. 'But I don't want to get hurt.'

'Occupational hazard in dating,' he said.

'Not if you're the one who does the breaking up,' she told him.

'Not on those occasions,' he agreed. 'But when someone else dumps you, even if you weren't that mad about them anyway, you feel hurt.'

Ash pulled at the gold necklace round her neck. 'Nobody's ever dumped me.'

Dan stared at her. 'Ever?'

She shook her head. 'I'm the dumper, not the dumpee. The world is supposed to be full of twentysomething girls who are nursing broken hearts because they've been dumped and I just don't want to be one of them.'

'But—'

'If it gets too serious, I dump them,' said Ash baldly. 'I can't help myself.'

'Even if you like them?'

'Especially if I like them.' She bit her lip. 'I'm worse with the ones I like.'

'Gosh.' Dan whistled beneath his breath. 'I guess I'm glad we're old friends and not old lovers. I can't imagine being dumped by you is much fun.'

'It's not fun for me either.' Her voice was brittle.

'I'm sorry. I didn't mean to make a joke out of it.'

'No, I'm sorry. I'm – my aunt and my cousin keep telling me that I should settle down with one person. But I'm – I'm not ready for that yet.' She turned her brown eyes to him and he was struck by how dark they were in her oval face, framed by her golden hair. 'I envy you and Cordelia, I really do.'

'I thought you were laughing at me,' said Dan.

'Laughing at you?'

'That night. I thought you went home and laughed that I'd proposed to a girl who was heading off to a new important job a couple of weeks later. I thought you reckoned I was a fool.'

'No,' she said. 'I didn't.'

'You'll find someone that you want to settle down with,' Dan assured her. 'And you won't want to dump him.'

'He'll be the one who dumps me.' Ash's voice wobbled. 'And I don't know if I could take that.'

'Of course you could,' said Dan. 'Everyone gets hurt, Ash. But they get over it.'

The clock on the mantelpiece chimed the hour and Ash looked at it in surprise. 'We'd better go back inside,' she said. 'Otherwise they'll start asking questions about us, think of you as the complete shit and Cordelia might ultimately get to hear about it!'

'That might be a good thing,' said Dan. 'Get her nice and jealous! But you're right, let's rejoin the madding crowd.'

It wasn't really a madding crowd. The small band was playing waltz music and a number of couples had taken to the floor.

'Do you dance?' asked Dan.

'Yes,' she said.

'Then you'll probably be better than me.' He sighed. 'My mother tells me that I have two left feet, but we can give it a go.'

Actually, he was a very good dancer. Ash felt confident as he spun her around the room to 'Tales From the Vienna Woods'. Afterwards, they sat down at their table and Ash drank more champagne while Dan switched to mineral water. She danced with Nigel, one of the other people at their table, while Dan got up with Derbhla, then Lillian, and was finally claimed by Lisa who held him a little too closely and, Ash was amused to see, whispered more often than she was sure was strictly necessary into his ear.

Eventually he got back to the table and danced with

her again. And, at almost three in the morning, he looked at his watch and asked her if she'd had enough.

'I'm knackered,' she said honestly.

'In that case let's hit the road,' he said. 'These things can go on for ever even when the band has finished. Last year there were people lying around the place at six a.m.'

'I can't afford for that to happen,' said Ash. 'I'm cooking tomorrow.'

'In the morning?' Dan looked horrified.

She shook her head. 'Thankfully no. But I've to do things for a party tomorrow night. I'll be delivering the food and then going but there's a lot to be done.'

'I'm sorry to have kept you out so late,' he said. 'I didn't think you might have something to do on a Saturday.'

'I enjoyed it,' she told him as they went in search of their coats. 'I didn't think I would but I did. Tell you the truth, Dan, it was nice to be out with a bloke and for it to be so – so platonic. Just like we really were old friends!'

'I've never been called platonic before,' he said.

'I like the idea of knowing a guy platonically,' said Ash. 'It's a great weight off your mind to know that he isn't going to make a lunge at you because he's interested in lunging at someone else!'

Dan laughed. 'Don't worry. I won't lunge.'

They said goodbye to Honor who kissed Dan warmly on both cheeks and told him to bring Cordelia next year. Although, she said as she kissed Ash more lightly, Ash had been a good substitute. And rather too pretty, didn't Dan think, for an old friend? He told Honor not to be

225

a troublemaker, promised to invite her to his wedding and steered Ash down the steps and back out to the car park.

It was freezing outside and he had to scrape a light covering of ice from the windscreen before getting into the car. Ash sat in the passenger seat and watched him, suddenly too tired to help and wanting desperately to sleep. So that when Dan opened the driver's door he saw her leaning against the seat, her eyes closed and her hair tumbling around her shoulders.

'Ash?' he whispered. He leaned across her and fastened her seat belt.

'I'm awake,' she murmured. 'Don't worry. I won't go to sleep on you.'

She really wanted to sleep. But she stayed awake by reciting recipes in her head until Dan pulled up outside her apartment where she yawned so widely that she thought she'd dislocated her jaw.

'Goodnight, Ash,' he said.

'Goodnight, Dan.' She got out of the car. 'I enjoyed it. It was fun being your old friend.'

'Thanks for coming,' he said. 'I'll see you Monday, at lunch.'

'It's baked cod on Monday.' She slammed the car door closed, opened the door of the apartment block and almost broke her ankle as she tripped over Bagel who'd appeared as if by magic as soon as she'd arrived home.

Chapter 13

Rich Fruit Cake
Mixed fruit, glacé cherries, almonds, candied peel, flour,
mixed spice, nutmeg, almonds, dark brown sugar, eggs,
margarine or butter
Place all ingredients together in large mixing bowl and
beat with wooden spoon until well mixed. Bake for 3.5/4.5
hours

Emmet and Michelle called to Ash's apartment to collect her luggage and the supply of cakes and puddings before setting off to Molly's on Christmas Eve. As expected, Michelle behaved as if she had forgotten the anger of their last meeting. Ash herself had felt a surge of rage when Michelle had phoned bright and breezy to say that they'd pick up her stuff as usual, around lunchtime. And sorry that they didn't have room for Ash in the car, too, it was a pain that she'd have to travel by train but maybe next year they'd buy a bigger car. You said that last year, thought Ash sourly.

Emmet took her case from the apartment while Michelle

looked around inquisitively. 'Why did you redecorate?' she asked. 'It was lovely the way it was. Mam said that you'd redone it and I couldn't believe it.'

'It was too dark,' said Ash. 'I like this better.'

'It's brighter,' agreed Michelle. 'Although I prefer darker colours. But I do like your view, Ash, even though I couldn't bear not to have curtains on my windows.'

'You get used to it,' said Ash.

'I suppose so.' Michelle sighed. 'It's easy seeing you don't have kids, they'd have the place destroyed in five minutes.'

They almost have already, thought Ash. She'd fought the urge to scream at Lucy who'd picked up a delicate porcelain figure and almost dropped it, while Brian, who was entranced by the decorations on Ash's miniature Christmas tree, had come perilously close to knocking the whole thing over as he grabbed at them.

'Do you want to take your cake now or pick it up on your way home?' asked Ash.

'Did you ice it with Happy New Year like I asked?'

'Of course,' said Ash.

'I'll get it on the way home,' said Michelle. 'No point in taking up more space in the car.'

'No,' said Ash.

'It's jammed with presents,' said Michelle. 'I swear to God those kids have far too much. When I think of what we used to get at Christmas . . .'

'I suppose every generation thinks the next one is doing a hell of a lot better,' said Ash.

'But we didn't have much money.' Michelle sighed.

228

'Lots of kids and Dad's work was so seasonal . . .'

'Building isn't that seasonal,' said Ash. 'Look at Emmet – he's busy all the time.'

'It's different now,' said Michelle.

'Maybe,' murmured Ash.

Emmet pushed open the apartment door. 'OK,' he said. 'Let's go.' He kissed Ash on the cheek. 'See you later. You'll ring from the station, won't you, and I'll pick you up.'

Ash nodded. 'Thanks, Emmet. Oh, don't forget the ice-cream puddings. They're in the freezer box. Here you are.'

'You'd swear we were going on a three-month expedition,' said Emmet as he looked at all the boxes, 'not just a few days with the mother-in-law.'

'See you later,' said Michelle. 'Kids, say goodbye to Ash.'

The children yelled their goodbyes and clattered out of the apartment while Ash heaved a sigh of relief that her home was unscathed. Which was very unfair of her, she told herself, because they were good kids and they'd never break anything deliberately.

Bagel reappeared at the kitchen window after they'd gone. Ash's neighbours from across the hall, a couple in their mid-twenties, had offered to feed him while she was away but she felt guilty about leaving him. She took a piece of smoked salmon which she'd kept specially for him out of the fridge and dropped it into his bowl. Then she filled his drinking bowl with water and opened a pot of Petit Filou which she put beside it.

And if all that doesn't let you know that I'm away for a few days, nothing will, she thought.

She still had a couple of hours before her train. So she scrubbed the kitchen sink and worktops, did the same to the bathroom and swept the rest of the apartment. She tidied up the newspapers that were in the corner of the living room and then she straightened the Christmas cards that were on the sideboard and which Michelle had rearranged as she picked them up to look at them. She'd inspected every one of the cards but, unusually, hadn't asked who the senders were which surprised Ash. As well as all of her corporate cards there were new names this year – Janice and James Butler, who'd married during the summer and who'd had a breakfast in their garden which Ash had really enjoyed doing despite the fact that she hardly ever catered for weddings; Peter Hammill – he'd been a guest at the wedding breakfast and then she'd done a birthday dinner for his eighty-year-old mother; Alistair Brannigan – Ash was grateful that Alistair's signature was such a scrawl that Michelle would have found it hard to decipher; and Dan Morland who had gone to Cancun in Mexico for Christmas. Lucky him, she thought as she replaced his card in the right place. None of the hassle of a loving family Christmas for Dan. The Monday after the ball in the K Club he'd dropped into the kitchen and told her that Cordelia wasn't coming back to Ireland over the holiday because it was such a short one in the States and she was so frantically busy, but she'd be home in January and she was counting the days. She'd sounded a bit frazzled, Dan told her, but pleased that the project she was working on had almost been completed. He thought that Cordelia might be under more pressure than she'd expected and wishing that she had someone to share things with. She'd talked to him for ages on the phone whereas normally their conversations were shorter and, he had to admit, more like business conversations than those between people who were going to get married.

Ash was pleased that things might be working out for Dan who, she felt, nearly *was* an old friend at this point. And who had reached a time in his life which maybe she'd reach herself someday. A time when you were ready to trust yourself to someone and able to put up with the hurt that they could cause you. She shook her head at the idea. Nothing was worth the hurt people could cause you. Nothing.

Connolly Station was jammed with people. Ash had left plenty of time to catch her train but it was already half full by the time she boarded it and she counted herself lucky to have got a seat. It was an old diesel train, noisy and uncomfortable, with dirt-caked windows and threadbare upholstery. She opened her magazine and tried not to notice her surroundings and the fact that, as it pulled out of the station, there were more people standing than sitting and the carriage seemed perilously overcrowded.

She hated crowds. She hated being in places where she was pressed up against a stranger's shoulder or where she could be face to face with someone she'd never seen before. The last time she'd been to London she'd been on the tube during the rush hour and she'd had to get off after one stop and practically sprint back up the escalators and out into Tottenham Court Road because she'd thought that she was going to faint with the crush of unknown people.

Even now, thinking about it brought her out in a sweat so she turned the pages of the magazine and forced herself not to look around her. But she could feel her heart racing and her breath coming in fast mouthfuls and she had to start counting to calm herself down.

It's so stupid, she thought, when she'd managed to bring her breathing under control. I know that nothing awful is going to happen. I know that I'm really OK. So why can't I stop myself feeling like this?

A few years after she'd come back to Ireland following Julia's death, Molly had arranged for her to see a therapist because she was worried about Ash who still didn't like to sleep in the dark and who panicked over the silliest of things. Ash hadn't wanted to talk to anyone but eventually had given in to Molly's demands. The therapist or counsellor or whatever the damned woman had been had talked about the responsibility Ash had felt towards Julia and the feeling of helplessness that she'd encountered after Julia's death and had suggested that her panic attacks were due to that. And, she said, maybe Ash's desire to have everything so neat and tidy in the house that she drove Molly to distraction was a way of exerting some personal control over her life, which had been so lacking before. Ash had tried to agree that there might be something in it and she supposed that the therapist had a point, but she was never a hundred per cent convinced that she wasn't just plain flaky.

Michelle had called her flaky on more than one occasion. Most specifically on the day that she'd refused to go out with Michael McCormack, the sexiest bloke in the neighbourhood.

'Any girl would kill to go out with him,' Michelle had told her.

'Then any girl would be out of her mind,' retorted the fifteen-year-old Ash.

'It's you that are out of your mind,' Michelle said. 'You're a complete flake, Ash. Everyone says so. And you're seeing a shrink! Nobody in Ireland sees shrinks – d'you think you're some kind of Hollywood film star or something?'

Maybe she was right. Ash burrowed into her seat and turned a page in the magazine. With a jolt she saw that they'd devoted an entire article to Alistair Brannigan. 'The Net-Worker!' screamed the banner headline over a flattering photograph of Alistair standing beside his Audi TT. 'Too Hot To Handle?' asked another shout-line.

Her mouth twitched as she read about how wonderful and talented Alistair was and how he'd built his company up from nothing and how he was now young, rich and incredibly desirable. He was all of those things, Ash agreed, but it seemed funny to read them in print, as though she were reading about a person she didn't know at all. The piece made him sound like some kind of superman while, in reality, he was quite an ordinary sort of bloke. Mind you, he hadn't told her that his favourite item of clothing was a pair of silk boxer shorts! She'd bet any money that he wished he hadn't told the journalist that either.

The train picked up speed as it passed through Howth Junction and out towards the coast. Ash put down the magazine and looked out of the window as the housing developments petered out into a more rural landscape. Alistair had asked her to spend Christmas with him. He told her he was taking some family and friends for a week in a Spanish parador – one of the historic buildings now turned into an upmarket hotel. It was at the foot of the Pyrenees – guaranteed snow and skiing if that was what she was into. It had sounded wonderful and part of her had wanted to say yes. But she said no. She explained to Alistair that she always went to Molly's for Christmas, that Molly would be incredibly hurt if she didn't show up because she was big into the whole family aspect of the holidays. Which Alistair would understand since he was taking his away and, to be honest, she'd feel a bit awkward about butting in on a family occasion even if there were other friends around. Oh, and she couldn't ski anyway.

He'd shrugged, said it didn't matter only he thought she might have enjoyed it. And for the first time she thought that he was impatient with her. She'd told him that she knew that she would have enjoyed it very much but he knew how people were about Christmas and it just wasn't worth the hassle, was it? He'd smiled then and told her that she was absolutely sweet, that most girls would have decided that a week in the Pyrenees was much more enticing than a week with their family and he was glad that they meant so much to her. And she'd thought that, if he really knew her, he'd know that she was dreading a week with Michelle and the extended Rourke family and she'd almost changed her mind and agreed to go with him.

She rang Emmet ten minutes before the train arrived in Drogheda and he told her he'd be there to pick her up. Which he was, dependable as always.

She got into the seat beside him and fastened her seat belt.

'How are things at Molly's?' she asked.

'Oh, you know.' He turned to her and smiled. 'Rob and Charlie are lounging around the place being no help whatsoever while Shay keeps muttering about going to the pub for a drink. I haven't seen Mick yet. Molly is locked in her bedroom wrapping presents. The kids are running wild and I'm trying to keep out of the way while Michelle pokes around trying to decide what's changed since the last time we were here.'

Ash giggled.

'Oh, and they've all decided that you'll be making the stuffing et cetera for the turkey as per usual but that, this year, they'd prefer plain Brussels sprouts.'

Ash wrinkled her brow. 'What did they get last year?'

'You did them in a kind of sauce,' Emmet reminded her. 'I thought it was quite nice myself.'

'I did them with almonds,' remembered Ash. 'And I thought they were nice too – I hate sprouts!'

'So does Michelle.' Emmet turned up the narrow road

that led to the Rourke household. 'But she has them every year anyway. Your family are real tradition freaks.'

Brian and Lucy hurled themselves at her as though they hadn't seen her in years rather than hours. Charlie, the eldest of the Rourke sons, kissed her on the cheek and told her that it was far too long since she'd visited. Rob, the youngest, kissed her too, on the back of the head as he disappeared out the door. 'Meeting some mates,' he mouthed. 'Back soon.'

Molly and Michelle were in the kitchen, unstacking Molly's best dinner service from the dishwasher.

'Ash, darling, it's lovely to see you again.' Molly straightened up and hugged her.

'You too, Molly. Happy Christmas,' said Ash who remembered, guiltily, that she'd promised to visit her aunt and uncle before now.

'Was the train late?' asked Michelle. 'I thought you'd be here sooner.'

'No, it was on time,' Ash told her. 'Crowded, though, the trip is a nightmare.'

'Why don't you go inside and pour yourself a drink,' suggested Molly. 'Michelle and I are nearly finished here and we'll join you.'

'Sure there isn't anything I can do to help?' asked Ash.

'Well, actually, you could wipe the cutlery,' Michelle told her. 'It's supposed to be dry but it never is and it stains if you don't rub it.'

Ash smiled wryly as she picked up the tea towel. She was surprised that Michelle had decided on something as easy as drying cutlery – she was certain her cousin would rather she was emptying the bins or something.

'I was telling Mam that your flat looks completely different since you redecorated again.'

'I like it,' said Molly.

'It's surprising how much brighter it makes the place feel.' Ash put the knives in the cutlery tray.

'It must be very wearing to change the paintwork every time you change a boyfriend, though.' Michelle carried some cups over to the table. 'Hard on the bank balance, I'd have thought.'

'I don't change it every time I change a boyfriend,' said Ash mildly.

'I suppose not.' Michelle made a face at her. 'You'd never have the decorators out of the place.'

'Give it a rest, Michelle,' said Ash.

'I just—'

'Nora Maguire's girl had a baby boy last week,' Molly interrupted them. 'After three girls she must have been delighted.'

'I suppose you were when you had me after your crop of boys,' said Michelle.

'Of course.' Molly smiled at her. 'But I wouldn't have cared even if you had been a boy. At the final moment, all you want is a healthy baby.'

'That's true.' Michelle smiled back at her mother in complete understanding. 'And it's such a powerful bond, isn't it, between mother and baby.'

'Very,' said Molly.

'Nothing could replace it,' said Michelle.

'Perhaps not,' Molly acknowledged placidly. 'But the most important thing is knowing that you're loved. And loving in return.'

Ash clattered some spoons into the drawer and dropped a fork onto the flagstone floor. 'Sorry,' she said as she bent down to pick it up. 'I'm getting careless in my old age.'

By ten o'clock that evening Molly and her husband Shay, Michelle and her family, Ash and Charlie and Rob were all sitting around the fire in the living room. Ash was surprised Rob had come back from the pub and even more surprised that Shay and Charlie hadn't gone out to join him, but Molly had managed to ensure that they were all together as she handed out sausage rolls and glasses of beer or port before they went to Midnight Mass.

When they'd been younger they'd all gone together, but now the two married Rourke sons went to church with their families on Christmas morning. This was the first year in a while that they would all have dinner in Molly's, although they always called round to her on Christmas Day at some point. Ash often wondered how their wives, Irina and Nancy, felt about the closeness of the Rourkes.

'What do you think of this?' Michelle, who'd been flicking through Ash's magazine, held open the page with the article about Alistair. 'Filthy rich, good-looking and only thirty! What a combination!' She sighed. 'He's probably gay.'

'No, he's not.' Ash didn't mean to say anything but

the words spilled out of her mouth before she could stop them.

'How do you know?' Michelle looked at her cousin curiously. 'He's not one of your millions of filthy rich clients is he?'

'I don't have filthy rich clients,' said Ash. 'Most of my clients are companies and the others just want to make a good impression. And, no, Alistair isn't a client.'

'But do you really know him, Ash?' Charlie Rourke looked at her with interest. 'I applied for a job with his company before the takeover. Didn't get it unfortunately. I would have made some money on the share options!'

'I know him,' said Ash.

'How?' demanded Michelle.

'I was at a dinner and he was there,' said Ash.

'So you don't actually know him personally.' Michelle sounded satisfied.

Ash eyed her cousin speculatively. 'I went to the premiere of *Donegal Stoned* with him,' she said.

'You what!' Michelle's eyes were wide in her face.

'We had dinner in the Tea Rooms afterwards. It was fun.' Ash kept her tone as bland as possible. She really hadn't intended to mention Alistair to them at all and she knew that she was just storing up trouble by talking about him now, but really and truly Michelle had been pissing her off ever since she arrived and she just couldn't help herself.

'Don't tell me he's your latest boyfriend!' Molly looked at Ash in amazement.

'You had a Christmas card from an Alistair,' said

Michelle accusingly. 'At least that's what it looked like. Was it him?'

Ash nodded.

'Bloody hell, Ash.' Rob's eyes were almost as wide as Michelle's. 'He's loaded. According to the papers he made millions out of selling his company.'

'I know. He did,' said Ash calmly.

'What did he buy you for Christmas?' asked Michelle.

'Nothing, I hope,' said Ash. 'I didn't buy him anything.'

'But if you're going out with him . . .'

Ash shrugged. 'I've gone out with him once or twice,' she said. 'It doesn't—'

'Mean anything,' finished Michelle.

Ash flushed. 'I like him. That's as far as it's gone.'

'Ash O'Halloran, if you let this bloke slip through your fingers you're madder than I thought you were!' Michelle waved the magazine in front of Ash. 'Look at him – he's gorgeous. And rich!'

'Rich isn't everything,' said Ash.

'That's great coming from you.' Michelle looked at her knowingly. 'The girl who opened a Post Office savings account with her pocket money. The girl who always knew exactly how much everything cost and who saved – saved! – half of the measly amount that we got. The girl who can afford the mortgage on those trendy quayside apartments without having someone to stay with her – don't tell me that you don't think rich isn't everything.'

'I'm careful,' said Ash. 'Not rich.'

'You'd like to be, though,' said Michelle shrewdly. 'I know you, Ash. You'd like to think that you had all the money in the world so that you didn't have to work. Then you'd probably work anyway.'

Ash moved uncomfortably in her armchair while the rest of the family looked at her with interest.

'Do you like him, Ash?' asked Molly gently.

'Of course I do,' said Ash. 'But I still don't know him that well and – well, he probably has loads of girlfriends.'

'You're bound to be the best looking,' said Charlie. 'I reckon you can snare him with your looks, Ash.'

'Charlie!'

'More likely with her cooking,' said Rob. 'A bloke like that will like to think that there's someone working in the kitchen for him. Ash, if you cook that duck with plum sauce thing you used to do for us on Sundays, he'll never be able to let you go.'

'It's irrelevant at this point,' said Ash uneasily. 'We've had a few dates, nothing much.'

'But we could do with a squillionaire in the family,' wailed Michelle. 'If there's nothing else that can get Ash to settle down, surely the promise of a six-, seven- or eight-figure bank account might.'

'Don't be stupid, Michelle.' Ash drained her glass of port.

'What's stupid?' asked her cousin. 'You've proved yourself totally incapable of sustaining a relationship with a bloke because you love him, but surely you could manage it because you love his cash?'

'That's rubbish,' said Ash hotly. 'I can sustain whatever I want with whoever I want.'

'Yeah, right.'

'Oh, why don't you grow up!' Ash was getting more annoyed by the minute.

'You're forever saying that to me,' said Michelle angrily. 'And, as I've told you a hundred times before, I am the grown-up one. I am the one with the husband and the kids and the house and the car.'

'Fine,' said Ash. 'Just don't keep wishing them all on me.'

'Girls, girls!' Charlie looked from one to the other. 'Keep the gloves on.'

'Oh, shut up, Charlie,' snapped Michelle.

'I'm going upstairs to change,' said Ash. 'Call me when you're going to Mass.'

The church looked the same as always. The same crib at the right-hand side of the altar. The same banner proclaiming Alleluia hung to the left. The same – well, obviously not the exact same, thought Ash – but the usual wreaths of holly were fixed to the pillars. And Fr Moran gave his standard rambling Midnight Mass sermon while at the entrance to the church some late arrivals direct from the pub around the corner tried to stay awake.

Ash liked Midnight Mass. She liked the very sameness of it, the well-known hymns, the familiar readings. Julia hadn't gone to Mass, of course; Julia had been an agnostic and had railed against the beliefs of her childhood. When Molly realised that Ash hadn't even been baptised she'd nearly had a fit and had called the parish priest around to the house straightaway. Ash had been baptised even though she wasn't sure she'd wanted to be. But she hadn't wanted to be different, and while she was a child and lived with Molly she did what everyone else did. Now she only went to Mass at Christmas. But she liked it. It was peaceful and serene. Though not tonight, Ash realised, as she watched some people she didn't know walk up the aisle with offertory gifts. Tonight she didn't feel peaceful, just angry that she'd mentioned Alistair Brannigan to the family even though she hadn't wanted to.

And listening to them talk, it seemed as though they'd all decided that he was the right man for her. Again, she told herself. There'd been a couple of other boyfriends who had been marked down as potential husband material by Michelle and Molly, and they'd been mad at her for dumping them. They'd lock her up if she dumped Alistair Brannigan!

She sighed. Maybe she'd deserve to be locked up if she dumped Alistair Brannigan. She liked him. He was easy to get on with. He didn't push her too much. So perhaps he was The One. And maybe she was getting upset over nothing and annoyed with the Rourkes simply because that was what she always did. Maybe Michelle was right and it was time for her to grow up and settle down. And, if she had to do that, wasn't it better that she should settle down with someone with £5 million in the bank rather than £5?

She shook her head. Why on earth would Alistair want to settle down? Surely he'd want to have a good time with his money? Live it up a little? Which wouldn't mean sticking with her.

And that might mean him breaking it off with her. She chewed on the inside of her lip as she thought about him breaking it off with her. She didn't want that to happen. She'd been cool enough with him and, so far, that had seemed to make him even more interested in her. She sighed. All this guessing and second-guessing was stupid. Surely she should just know what was right?

'You know she's quite cracked,' Michelle told Molly on Christmas morning as they ate an early breakfast together while the children attacked the presents under the tree.

'Ash?'

'Why even ask!' Michelle spooned sugar into her coffee and stirred it vigorously. 'I do my best to be like a sister to her. I do my best to advise her. I tell her often enough that she doesn't need to be alone. That she can visit me any time she wants. And I try to make her understand that she can have a relationship with a bloke without it all ending in tears. But she doesn't seem to believe me.'

'She does her best,' said Molly.

'Oh, Mam, you can't believe that.' Michelle's voice was scathing.

'She's different,' said Molly. 'She's Julia's child.'

'That shouldn't make her a nutcase,' said Michelle.

'Julia did her own thing,' said Molly. 'Ash likes to do her own thing too.'

'And see where doing her own thing got Julia,' said Michelle. 'Ash should think about the rest of her life.'

244

'Ash is only twenty-nine,' Molly told her daughter. 'She doesn't have to settle down.'

'But don't you think it would help her?' demanded Michelle. 'Don't you think she needs to get over this bloody commitment problem? I mean, what about Alistair Brannigan! If she can't commit to him, who the hell can she commit to?'

'Leave her be,' said Molly. 'Don't worry about her. What worked for you doesn't necessarily work for her.'

'You mean, I got married and had kids too soon, don't you?'

'Of course not,' said Molly. 'That's what you wanted, wasn't it? Same as being on her own is what Ash wants.'

'I might have known you'd take her side.' Michelle looked angry. 'You always did.'

Molly took another slice of toast from the pile in front of them and buttered it slowly. She didn't look at Michelle who was pulling at her own toast, ripping it into small pieces.

'I never take anyone's side,' said Molly eventually. 'Never. I never did and I never will. You are two different people and you look at things in two different ways. I'd like to see her settle down but there's no point if she's not ready.'

'You always make allowances for her.' Michelle tried not to sound pettish.

'Maybe I used to,' said Molly. 'God knows, Michelle, she had a hard time—'

'Yes, but she can't trade on that for ever!'

'I don't think she does.'

'Huh,' Michelle snorted.

'I wish you didn't resent her,' said Molly.

'Resent her!'

'You seem to.'

'I don't resent her. I feel sorry for her.'

'Don't feel anything for her for a while,' suggested Molly. 'Live your life, Michelle. Let her live hers.'

'I never understood her,' said Michelle. 'I tried, but I didn't.' She pushed her plate away. 'I never understood why someone who's the daughter of the flightiest woman in our family should turn out to be such a damn cool stick.'

'She only tries to be cool,' said Molly. 'She's not really.'

'And I only try to give her advice.' Michelle yawned. 'But I'm not going to try again.'

'What aren't you going to try again?' asked Ash as she pushed open the kitchen door. 'Morning, Molly. Morning, Michelle. Happy Christmas.'

Chapter 14

Ham Baked in Guinness
Cooked ham, Guinness, sugar, mustard, ginger, carda-
mom
Peel skin off ham, discard, and place ham, fat side up,
in roasting tin. Pour Guinness over meat and bake in
moderate oven for three hours, basting occasionally. Score
fat, mix sugar, mustard, ginger and cardamom, add some
liquid to form a paste and spread over ham. Bake for
further 15 minutes at 200°C

Cordelia didn't wake up until almost eleven on Christmas Day. She'd been in the office until nine the previous night, having arrived at her desk at six in the morning. The rest of the bank's staff were scattered around the building at various departmental drinks parties, but Cordelia's division was still hard at work. Every so often she'd look up from the numbers she was working on and notice the huge Christmas tree in the corner of the extensive open-plan office and she'd be surprised because it didn't feel like Christmas. How could it, when she hadn't had time to go shopping? Just as well she wasn't going home, she thought gloomily, because everyone would have expected designer gear, knowing that it was so much cheaper in the States.

She hadn't realised it would be such hard work. She liked it, no doubt about that, but it was difficult to haul yourself in every morning when you didn't feel as though you'd even slept the night before. Maybe that was a good thing, though, because it meant that she wasn't lonely or homesick or missing Dan. Actually, she'd admitted to herself on Christmas Eve, she was missing Dan more than she'd expected. He'd called her – from Cancun where he was holidaying, the lucky bastard! She'd felt just a little bit put out that Dan was having a great time in Mexico while she was slaving away in New York because she was too busy even to take a few days off so she'd told him not to bother coming to New York to see her. And when he'd wished her a Happy Christmas she'd almost cried because then, for the first time, she'd felt homesick. So far, in the melting pot of the city, people had wished her Happy Holidays, not Happy Christmas. And much bloody holiday I'm getting, she'd mutter under her breath. She knew that it was simply a matter of bad luck that she was working so hard at the moment (though she also knew that she should consider it good luck because the busier they were, the more likely it would be that she'd get herself noticed and promoted), but she did wish that it felt like Christmas. Right now it was just an inconvenient day off because they still had more work to do on the rescue plan and she wanted to get it over and done with.

She pulled the covers over her head. She was too tired to get up even though the phone was ringing for the second time that morning. The machine could answer it, she thought. Nobody in the office would ring today, no matter how awful things were. She'd be back in two days and probably, by the look of things, be working right through the weekend as well. As far as she was concerned the best present in the world right now was uninterrupted sleep for another couple of hours until it was time to get dressed and go to Shayla's for dinner.

Shayla Kroenig worked in the same department as Cordelia but was merely a graduate trainee. Cordelia wasn't sure whether or not Shayla had invited her to spend Christmas with her family because she thought that Cordelia might be someone worth being friendly with, or whether Shayla had genuinely felt that she wanted her to be there. It was hard to judge, thought Cordelia, more awake now than she wanted to be. Shayla, like DeVere, was incredibly friendly but Cordelia wasn't convinced that it was friendship without strings. All the same, it was nice to spend Christmas with someone and Cordelia had been grateful for Shayla's invitation.

Her eyes opened. She was awake now and there was no chance of getting back to sleep. She shivered in the cold air of the apartment and wrapped her heavy, towelling robe round her before turning on the heat. The red light on the answering machine blinked three times, indicating three messages. Three, thought Cordelia, I was obviously out of it for the first!

According to the machine the first message had been

left at seven in the morning. No wonder I didn't hear the phone ring, Cordelia murmured as she pressed playback. Why on earth would someone want to ring me at seven in the morning today?

'Hello, Cordelia. It's me. Mum. Sorry, you're probably still asleep. It's later here, of course. I'll call you back. But Happy Christmas!'

Bloody hell, Mum, Cordelia muttered. You'd think you'd have copped on to the time difference by now.

'Hi, Cordelia, it's me again. Were you out late last night or don't you want to talk to me? Ring me when you get up. Happy Christmas!'

She knew that the third message would be from her mother too.

'Cordelia, it's Dad. Your mother is now convinced something terrible has happened to you. Phone us as soon as you can. Happy Christmas.'

Cordelia picked up the phone and pressed speed dial for her parents' house. She wished that she wasn't their only child, wished that they didn't feel as though they had to keep track of her no matter where she was.

'Hi, Mum, it's me.'

'Cordelia! How typical of you to ring back just because your dad phoned.'

'Not at all,' said Cordelia. 'I was asleep. It's only eleven o'clock here.'

'Eleven o'clock on Christmas morning,' said Linda Carroll. 'You should be up and about before now.'

'Why?' asked Cordelia. 'There's no one else here.'

'What about your flatmate?' asked Linda.

'Alicia has gone away with her folks for the holiday,' said Cordelia. 'And I was using the time to catch up on some sleep.'

'Why? Partying like crazy?'

'I wish! Working like crazy. Though it's good, Mum, I'm doing well.'

'But what about today? What are you doing for Christmas? I thought you were spending it with friends.'

'I am,' said Cordelia. 'One of the girls in the office invited me to her home and I'm going there a little later. Don't panic, Mum. I've things to do.'

'I hate to think of you on your own out there without me.' Linda's voice trembled. 'I know you're doing well but Christmas is a time when you should really be with your family. And as for Dan – well, I just don't know how he feels about it.'

'Dan has been extremely supportive.'

'Well, tell me to mind my own business if you like but I think it's insane for a girl who's just got engaged to head off to another country for six months. Anything can happen in six months.'

'Anything like what?' asked Cordelia.

'Like he might meet someone else,' said Linda.

'He loves me,' Cordelia told her. 'He didn't want me to leave.'

'Of course he didn't!' exclaimed Linda. 'He wanted to get married to you. Cordelia, he's a great bloke and I'm sure he loves you, why wouldn't he, but he won't wait for ever.'

'Mum, he knows the score,' said Cordelia firmly. 'We

agreed on it. So don't worry. And I was talking to him last night. He misses me. He told me so.'

'I don't like to think that he'll miss you so much he'll end up in the arms of someone else,' said Linda darkly.

Cordelia laughed. 'You don't know Dan. And you don't know me. I'll be back in a few months, we'll get married and we'll live happily ever after.'

'You always were an optimist,' said Linda.

'And aren't I always right?'

'I suppose so,' conceded her mother. 'Just – you know – be careful.'

'I will.'

'And I do wish you were back home.'

'There's no way I was passing up this opportunity,' said Cordelia. 'It's what I've always wanted.'

Linda sighed. 'I know it's what you want to do and I know you're doing really well. I'd just like it better if you were doing it here.'

Which is why I'm not, said Cordelia silently, as she listened to her mother talking. Linda's conversations were always the same, always full of pride in Cordelia's achievements while still wondering if she couldn't have fulfilled them all without having to leave the family home.

She couldn't, of course. Much as she loved both her parents she found it stifling to be at home with them. It was impossible to be cool and businesslike around people who still treated her as though she was ten years old. They'd hated it when she'd first gone to the States and had been thrilled when she came back to Ireland although they'd have preferred her to have landed a job in Wexford rather than Dublin. Though what sort of job they thought she'd get in a tourist town with her brilliant financial qualifications Cordelia couldn't imagine. They're a different generation, she reminded herself. They didn't realise how important her independence was. Or how important her success was either.

'Anyway, Gran sends her love too, darling, and we all hope you'll be home soon.'

'I will,' promised Cordelia. 'As soon as I've finished the project I'm working on now.'

'How is it going?' Linda knew nothing about banking and finance, nor did she want to. She asked because she loved hearing Cordelia talk with authority even though she hadn't a clue what her daughter was talking about.

'I think we've put a good package together,' Cordelia said. 'Hopefully, we'll prevent the hostile takeover.'

'And they'll recognise that you were responsible?' asked Linda.

Cordelia didn't want to burst her bubble by telling her that she was just one of a crowd all trying to save the incompetent management. 'Not responsible exactly,' she compromised. 'But I've made a good contribution.'

'Oh, well, once you're happy,' said Linda. 'And once you don't forget us.'

'How could I forget you?' asked Cordelia dryly. 'You ring me every week. And three times at Christmas!'

'I'm sorry,' said Linda. 'But I worried when you didn't answer the second call.'

'I'm up now anyway,' Cordelia told her. 'And I'll

be with Shayla's folks all day. But I'm glad you rang, honestly. And Happy Christmas to both of you.'

'Hold on, I'll get your dad.'

She wished her father a Happy Christmas too, spoke to her mother again and finally hung up. At least the apartment was warmer by now. She thought about ringing Dan. It would be nice to talk to Dan again. She picked up the phone and dialled his number. But she got his message minder instead.

Glad you're sitting around pining, she thought wryly, and then chided herself for being unfair. He was probably on the beach, pining there. And she knew Dan, he wouldn't bring his phone to the beach. Much as she loved him she felt that Dan sometimes lacked ambition. DeVere brought his phone everywhere! She yawned. A cup of coffee, she decided, and then she'd get ready to go out and spend Christmas with people she hardly knew.

The extended Rourke family sat down to dinner at four thirty in the afternoon. Ash, mindful of the exhortations of the family that they wanted absolutely traditional, hadn't done anything to the vegetables other than steam them. And everyone agreed, when they'd finally worked their way through turkey, ham, roast potatoes, Brussels sprouts, carrots, cauliflower, as well as half a dozen bottles of wine, that it was the best meal they'd ever had.

'You didn't have to do the cooking, Ash.' Molly sat back in her chair feeling absolutely bloated.

'I like it.' Ash shrugged. 'I'd feel odd if I didn't do it.'

'I wish you'd stay with us and cook for a while.' Irina, Mick's wife, sighed. 'I hate it, I really do.'

'I like cooking.' Michelle finished her fourth glass of wine. 'But it's not a passion.'

'What is your passion?' asked Irina.

'My family,' said Michelle. 'They're the most important thing in the world to me.' She beamed at Emmet and glanced blearily at the two children who were dismantling a toy truck that Brian had received from Santa.

'Mine is keeping fit.' Rob patted his rotund stomach while the rest of the family dissolved into laughter. Then Shay made them pull the silver and gold foil crackers and insisted they wore the party hats too.

Nancy and Irina laughed and joked with each other while the male Rourkes read out the awful mottoes inside the crackers. Molly and Shay looked at them indulgently as Michelle bounced Shay junior on her knee and Emmet helped the children reassemble the truck. Then Charlie refilled their wine glasses. Why do I feel detached from them all? Ash wondered. Why can't I laugh at the jokes or think that Mick's imitation of a dying walrus is even remotely funny? What's wrong with me that I look at them all and I want to be home on my own? Or is it simply that I'm drunk? Though usually I'm just silly when I'm drunk.

'Are you OK, Ash?' Molly turned to her.

'Absolutely.' Ash smiled. 'I was just wondering whether or not people would be up for the Christmas pudding ice cream I made, or whether you'd like to leave it until later.'

'Oh, bring on the food,' said Rob. 'No point in giving up now!'

Ash went into the kitchen where the individual frozen puddings had been softening. She upturned them each into a bowl, pleased that they looked so authentic. This was her break-with-tradition moment – usually the Rourkes had real pudding after their meal but last year Shay had wondered if there wasn't something else they could try because he was always too full to really enjoy the pudding. And Molly, typically, had said that you couldn't not have pudding. Pudding was part of the whole day. So Ash had suggested the ice-cream puddings and there'd been a general consensus that it might be a good thing. Well, she thought as she carried them into the dining room, the proof of the pudding . . .

'Oh, Ash, you are so bloody talented you make me want to weep!' Irina beamed as she tasted the pudding – chocolate and rum with fruit and candied peel. 'This is better than the real thing.'

'How do you do it?' asked Nancy. 'How do you manage to come up with such good food every single time?'

'I like doing it,' said Ash. 'It's a creative thing.'

'You wouldn't if you were doing it for a ravenous family that wants to pack in as much as possible at every available opportunity,' said Michelle. 'Cooking in my household isn't creative, it's a necessity.'

'But you can enjoy it as well,' said Ash.

'Sure, when it' s your job and you're getting paid for it,' Michelle said dismissively.

'It wasn't my job today,' Ash told her.

'Oh, it was.' Michelle put her spoon beside her bowl. 'You have to do it because you don't want anyone else to do it. You like feeling as though there's something you're better at than anyone else.'

An uncomfortable silence developed around the table as Ash ate the last of her pudding and said nothing.

'Every Christmas is the same.' Though Michelle's words were slurred, her bitterness was evident. 'Every bloody year you come in and take over the kitchen and we all have to say how great your food is. Fine, Ash, it's fantastic, no doubts about that at all. But it can get a bit tiring having to tell you that all the time.'

'You don't have to tell me anything,' said Ash tightly. 'You don't even have to eat the damn food if you don't want to. I thought I was contributing something but sorry, I didn't realise you didn't want me to. Next year I won't bother. I won't bother with the Christmas cake for you either.'

Molly tried to smooth things over. 'Ash, Michelle didn't mean—'

'Of course she did,' said Ash, feeling the floodgates open. 'Just like she always does. Just like she always points out to me that I was damned lucky to be taken in by you and damned lucky to have shared your home. And just like she likes to say that I'm a hopeless neurotic because I didn't marry the first man who asked me. Michelle and I have had this conversation over and over again and it won't change until Michelle realises that she never liked me, that she always resented me and that she has big problems about me. Which

257

pretending that she's looking after my interests won't solve.'

This time the silence around the table was horrified. The Rourke brothers busied themselves with scraping their already empty bowls. Emmet looked from Ash to Michelle. Molly's lower lip trembled. Nancy and Irina exchanged uncomfortable glances.

Shay Rourke got up from the table. 'I'm going to make coffee,' he said. 'Anyone who wants to behave in an adult way can have some.'

'I made the coffee earlier.' There was a note of defiance in Ash's tone. 'It's a special Christmas blend that all my clients like.' She pushed back her chair. 'But I won't bother with it myself, thanks, Shay. I won't hang around where I'm not wanted.'

'Ash, sit down and don't be so silly,' said Shay. 'Michelle, apologise to Ash.'

'For what?' asked Michelle. 'I simply said it like it is. She doesn't bother her arse to come here any other time of the year but Christmas and then she breezes in and takes over everything and we're all supposed to be grateful to her. If it wasn't for us she'd be on her own.'

'Actually, I wouldn't.' Ash hadn't sat down again; she stood with her hand on the back of her chair. 'Alistair Brannigan asked me to spend Christmas with him in the Pyrenees this year but I didn't because I know what a big thing the whole family Christmas stuff is for Molly and for the rest of you so I came here.'

'Hah!' Michelle's face was flushed. 'But you'd rather have gone with him! Just like I thought – you only put up with us or you come here to show off. And all that posturing about his money meaning nothing to you was just that – I knew that the day someone turned up with a few bob in his pocket it'd be very different.'

'Michelle!' Molly's voice was hard. 'There is absolutely no need for this.'

'Because it's true,' said Michelle wildly.

'Give it a rest, girls.' Mick looked annoyed. 'We've all had a lot to eat and maybe a bit too much to drink. And so we say things we don't mean.'

'She means every word,' said Ash spiritedly. 'And she'd say it even if she hadn't guzzled an entire bottle of Côtes du Rhone.'

'There's a pair of you in it,' Charlie told them. 'There always was and there always will be.'

'I don't go round insulting her at every available opportunity,' snapped Ash. 'I don't walk into her house and comment on the décor. I don't criticise her food or her husband or her children or her clothes but she does to me. And I'm sick of it.'

'I don't see why you two can't get on,' said Molly. 'And I don't see why you're acting like children!'

'Because she's still locked in some kiddy time warp,' Ash said angrily. 'Where she's the queen of the castle, the only girl in a family of boys, and I'm some interloper.'

Nobody said anything then Michelle began to cry.

'And that's her other trick,' said Ash. 'Waterworks.'

'Ash!' Shay's voice was harsh. 'Stop it.'

'OK,' said Ash. 'You know and I know that I can't go home today. But I'll stay out of your way and get back as soon as I can. And then Michelle can be the little fairy princess that she wants to be.'

'Ash, you're being even more childish than Michelle,' said Molly.

'I'm glad you realise how childish she's being,' said Ash.

'For goodness' sake!' Irina threw her napkin onto the table. 'Neither of you realise how lucky you are. You have a big family, you're loved, you're wanted and people care about you. The pair of you need to grow up.'

Ash said nothing but walked out of the room and climbed the stairs. The guest room, the one she was staying in, used to be Mick and Rob's room. When Ash had lived there the walls had been covered with pictures of football stars and motorbikes. Now it was decorated prettily in soft blues and pinks.

Ash sat on the bed and began to count. Her heart was racing in her chest and her hands trembled.

Ten, eleven, twelve, she counted. I should be used to it by now. I shouldn't rise to Michelle's bait. But I can't help myself. Twenty, twenty-one, twenty-two. She was supposed to think of a peaceful place when she was counting but she couldn't get the scene downstairs out of her mind. Michelle's face had been flushed with anger. Molly's had been white. And Emmet had looked first at Ash and then at Michelle with increasing despair.

I've never fitted in, thought Ash. I'm not the kind of person they wanted me to be. I'm sure Molly thought that I'd be a friend for Michelle but Michelle never wanted me to be her friend. And Michelle never wanted Molly to know that. Forty, forty-one, forty-two. Her fingers tingled and she felt light-headed. Maybe I should have looked for my father. Even though I don't care who he is and what he's like. Either an ageing hippie still wandering around in jeans and a tie-dyed T-shirt. Or a groomed corporate businessman who'd blanked out his past. Maybe I should care who he is. Maybe *he'd* care about me.

Sixty-nine, seventy. But I don't care. And he doesn't even know I exist. And it's better that way.

Eighty, eighty-one.

The shaking was beginning to ease. She could feel her heart rate slowing down.

There had been lots of days like this when she was smaller. Only then, sometimes, she'd fainted and Molly had brought her to the local doctor who'd said that physically she was in great shape. Which was when they'd got her to see someone to talk it all through. She shook her head. She was past talking things through. And arguing with people.

And the next time a multimillionaire asked her to spend Christmas in the Pyrenees that was exactly what she was going to do.

Chapter 15

Thai Red Chicken Curry
Chicken breasts, coconut milk, red Thai curry paste, soy
sauce, caster sugar, bamboo shoots, aubergine, lime, basil
leaves, grated coconut
Boil coconut milk and curry paste in saucepan. Add chicken
pieces to sauce, bring back to boil, simmer. Stir in soy sauce
and sugar. Dice bamboo shoots and aubergine. Add to pan.
Boil, then simmer. Stir in remaining coconut milk, lime
juice and shredded basil leaves. Spoon into serving dish,
sprinkle with basil leaves and grated coconut

Ash was glad to be back in Dublin. She sat at the computer and looked at her schedule of bookings – January was usually a light month and this one was no exception. It was because of the light months that she took as many bookings as she could whenever they presented themselves. Which actually meant that most months weren't light at all. She was flicking through the list of menus and wines when her phone rang. She looked at the instrument warily. Molly had called at least half a

262

dozen times since Christmas, each time to tell her that Michelle was really upset that they'd argued and that she wanted to talk to Ash but she was afraid that Ash would be cool and dismissive and Michelle couldn't stand that. And, Molly told Ash, she wouldn't be being fair if she didn't say that Ash hadn't been especially nice to Michelle either. In fact, Ash had been bloody rude to Michelle and Ash should really apologise too. But Michelle knew that she'd been the one to start it and she wanted to be the one to extend an olive branch. Ash had told Molly on each occasion that Michelle was perfectly welcome to phone and that she had no problem about talking to Michelle but that she wasn't going to pretend that Michelle hadn't said some pretty awful things and meant them.

The remainder of Christmas had been a nightmare. Although nothing more had been said between the cousins while they stayed in Molly's, the atmosphere had been glacial and Ash had come home after two days instead of staying for New Year like she normally did. Molly had begged her not to go home early and she'd urged both Ash and Michelle to sit down and talk but neither of them wanted to. When Ash arrived home at the apartment she'd indulged in a frenzy of unnecessary cleaning that had left every surface dust-free and shining. She'd rearranged her kitchen cupboards (already, as Michelle would have told her, pathologically tidy) so that each tin and each jar was perfectly placed in order of size and contents. She'd taken down her Christmas decorations and packed them neatly away and she'd thrown out all of her Christmas cards. Much to

Bagel's disgust, she'd washed the cushion in his basket so that it was no longer a mass of comfortable cat hair and she'd bought him a new food dish which he had yet to break in. By the time she'd finished she felt good about herself again. But she was still edgy every time the phone rang.

She sighed and picked it up. She'd been practising what she would say to Michelle if she called but she wasn't sure that she'd actually manage to be as calm when and if she heard her cousin at the other end of the line.

'Hello, stranger,' said Alistair.

Ash was surprised at how glad she was to hear his voice again.

'Hi,' she said warmly. 'How was the skiing?'

'Wonderful,' he told her. 'The snow was perfect and the weather was great. And the place we stayed was utterly fantastic.'

Ash laughed. 'Sounds like you had a good time.'

'We did. I'm sorry you couldn't come.'

'Me too,' she said ruefully. 'Christmas at Molly's was the nightmare it always is. Only each year I forget how it was the year before.'

'Why is it a nightmare?' asked Alistair.

'Oh, we fight,' Ash told him. 'My cousin and I don't get along all that well and there's always some barbed comment floating around the place. Only this year she really pissed me off and I came home early.'

'Were you lonely?' asked Alistair.

'I don't get lonely,' said Ash honestly. 'I quite like being on my own. But I was so mad at her. She rubs me up the wrong way, she knows she's doing it. I know she's doing it. She knows that I know—'

Alistair laughed. 'Never mind,' he said. 'How about you come to dinner with me tonight and forget about it?'

'Where to?' asked Ash.

'You mean you'll come?' He sounded surprised. 'On the same day I ask you?'

'I'll come,' said Ash. 'I truly was very busy in November and December but January is my slack month.'

'Good old January,' said Alistair. 'Will I pick you up around eight?'

Ash hesitated.

'Is that a problem?'

'No,' she said. 'It's just – well, I could meet you. There's no point in picking me up if we're going to be in the city.'

Alistair sighed. Ash never wanted him to pick her up at the flat. It seemed odd, but he couldn't let it bother him. 'Oh, OK. If you like. Any preferences?'

'Something spicy,' said Ash. 'I'm so fed up with meat and two vegetables sort of stuff that I'd throw it back at whoever gave it to me.'

'Diep le Shaker?' suggested Alistair. 'Only if we go there I should pick you up, it's a bit of a distance.'

'Don't be ridiculous, it's a fifteen-minute walk,' said Ash, although she knew it would take her longer than that. 'I'll see you there at eight.'

'Great,' said Alistair.

'Fine,' said Ash.

Her heart was thumping when she put down the phone.

She wanted to see Alistair again. She liked him – and not just because he happened to have a few million in loose change rattling around in his pockets, no matter what Michelle might think.

Bagel jumped onto the table beside her, sending a sheaf of papers fluttering around the room.

'You bloody nuisance,' she said crossly and the cat looked at her with injured innocence. 'You're always doing that.' She picked up the papers and glanced through them. The top sheet was a printout of her share portfolio at the end of the year. Chatham's had e-mailed it to her while she was away. She hadn't bothered to look at markets since she'd come back – she'd heard on the news that they were trading higher but not spectacularly so. I'll ring Steve Proctor tomorrow and ask him how things are going, she thought. Or maybe I'll ring Dan instead.

She wondered how he'd got on over Christmas and whether he'd had a good time in Mexico. Lucky Dan, she thought. Mexico sounded lovely at this time of the year. She wondered whether Cordelia had come back for her visit yet. Perhaps she would look at handsome, tanned Dan and wish she'd never gone away! Ash hadn't seen Dan but she was pretty sure that he'd be tanned and he was quite good-looking even if he did have some grey flecks in his hair. It was funny, she thought, how proprietorial she felt about Cordelia and Dan's relationship. It was as though, having been there when they decided to get married, she had a vested interested in seeing that it all went off without a hitch. The first

Chatham lunch of the year was on Monday. Maybe he'd have time to talk to her afterwards and let her know how things were with Cordelia. She'd planned a pasta dish for lunch – anything to get away from turkey and ham.

Ash arrived at the trendy Thai restaurant at exactly eight o'clock and thought about walking round the block so that she would be a little late. It seemed positively over-eager to be on time and it might send Alistair Brannigan the wrong sort of signals completely for her to be sitting at the table before him. I should live in Germany, she thought wryly, they understand the meaning of punctuality.

But when she pushed open the door of the restaurant Alistair was already there, sipping a gin and tonic. He smiled as he saw her and stood up to greet her.

'Happy New Year,' he said and kissed her on each cheek. 'You look lovely tonight, Ash.'

'Thank you.' After intense deliberation, she'd bought a suit in the Brown Thomas winter sale the day she'd come back to Dublin – silver-grey trousers and jacket and a rose-coloured top to go with it. It had been expensive even in the sales (she'd tried to shop at the quietest possible time) but Ash knew that it was worth it, especially since December's profits had been so good. She'd bought a soft red cocktail dress in the sales too on the off chance that she might spend an evening in the K Club or somewhere equally sophisticated again. She'd felt at a complete disadvantage that night with Dan Morland. It was one thing not being bothered about spending too much money on clothes yourself, it was quite another if you were in the company of people who did bother.

'Would you like a drink?' A waiter hovered nearby.

Ash ordered a mineral water.

'Don't you want something else?' asked Alistair.

'I'll have wine later,' said Ash. 'But mineral water is fine for now.'

She looked around the restaurant, decorated in shades of yellow and red, which made good use of the available space. It was half full which she supposed was reasonably OK for a week night in early January.

'Hungry?' asked Alistair.

She picked up her menu. 'Starving,' she said.

They ordered dim sum to start with and Ash decided on red curry while Alistair ordered fish cooked in banana leaves.

'One thing I like about you,' said Alistair as she spooned the dim sum onto her lettuce leaf, 'is that you eat your food.'

'Of course I do.' She looked surprised.

'You'd be surprised how many girls just pick,' he said. 'The first time I saw you I thought you'd be a picker.'

She grinned. 'Why?'

'Because you look like a picker.'

'Thanks,' she said.

'But you're not. You're a real trencherwoman,' he said admiringly as she stuffed food into her mouth.

'Did you ask me out because you hoped I wouldn't eat that much?' she demanded after she'd swallowed it.

'No,' he said. 'I asked you out because I like you.'

268

'Thanks,' she said. 'After the magazine article I was kind of surprised you'd ask anyone out.'

Alistair groaned. 'That bloody, bloody article. My life has been a misery since. People believe every word, which is such a pain!'

'You mean the bit where you said you like to work hard and play harder is a joke?' asked Ash innocently. 'And the boxer shorts? What about the boxer shorts?'

Alistair covered his eyes with his hands as he shook his head. 'Actually, I did say that. Only it didn't sound so awfully pretentious at the time. And I won't even comment on my underwear!'

She laughed. 'You sounded like a complete dick.'

'I know,' he said.

'But is the rest true?' she asked as she loaded up another lettuce leaf. 'About being nearly broke this time last year and having problems getting additional financing? About giving up a pretty good job to start up Archangel?'

'Oh yes.' He nodded. 'I could see there was a gap in the market and I went for it. The problem with companies like mine is that everyone's so nervy about technology stuff and I don't blame them. Nobody wants to think that they've bought into the companies that will go wallop and I agree that loads of them will. You know, back when they started manufacturing cars, there were about two hundred car companies in the States. Now there's only three. Gets it all into perspective, doesn't it?'

'I suppose so.'

'And how's your share portfolio doing?' asked Alistair.

'OK, I guess. It's my top-up pension plan, really, I don't actually trade them. Whenever I have spare money I buy some and sometimes, if I need the money, I sell them.'

'What else do you spend your money on?' asked Alistair.

She scratched the back of her head. 'My apartment, I suppose. And my cat – he eats me out of house and home!'

'Holidays?' asked Alistair. 'Clothes? Cars?'

'Hang on, I'm not you.' She laughed. 'I don't go on that many holidays. Weekends away usually, down to Cork or Kerry, which I like. But I'm a city person, I like where I live and I'm happy there. Clothes – I wear lots of T-shirts and jeans. Cars – I don't need one.'

'Ash, I hope you don't mind me saying this but maybe you should cut loose and live a little.'

'I don't mind.' She sipped her water. 'People say that to me all the time but I like my life the way it is, thank you.'

'What about your family?' asked Alistair.

She shrugged. 'They do their thing, I do mine.'

He looked at her curiously for a moment but said nothing.

'Anyway, you're far more interesting,' said Ash. 'Everyone tells me that the numbers quoted in the papers are true. If that's the case then the bit about you being one of Ireland's most eligible bachelors is deadly accurate.'

'I'm very rich,' said Alistair solemnly. 'Which is utterly fantastic. I spent an absolute fortune at Christmas and it didn't even make a dent in my bank balance.'

Ash laughed. 'Good. I hated the thought that it all might be a lie and I'd end up washing the dishes to pay for dinner tonight.'

He asked her to come back to his apartment after their meal and she agreed. There was no need to keep him at arm's length, she told herself. She liked him. He liked her. And, even if she wasn't head over heels in love with him yet, she cared about him.

She'd expected a huge place but Alistair's apartment was an average two-bedroomed one, although it had spectacular views over the Phoenix Park. Ash stood on the balcony and looked across the huge expanse of green which made you feel as though you were in the country instead of in the city.

'It's lovely,' she told Alistair as he joined her with a mug of steaming coffee.

'I like it,' he said. 'I'll move, of course. Doesn't do the image any good to be holed up here and I suppose one does have to live up to one's image. I've been looking at a few places.' He glanced at her. 'Maybe you'd like to help me?'

'Perhaps.' Ash sipped her coffee. 'What'll you do when the money runs out?'

'It won't,' said Alistair. 'I'm still working, you know. The technology we've developed is only the tip of the iceberg. You think Archangel's done well now – all I say is wait until next year. I'm going to be the most successful businessman in Europe.'

'Really?'

'Oh, absolutely,' he told her. 'I know exactly what I want and I'm going to get it.'

'It must be nice to be so certain.'

'Hard work,' he said. 'And a love of good things.'

'I told my – my family that I was seeing you. They reckon I should put handcuffs on you and keep you for ever.'

'That might not be the worst thing in the world,' said Alistair lightly.

'With me it probably would,' said Ash. She sipped her coffee again then shivered in the cold night air.

'Come back inside,' said Alistair. 'The media wouldn't be too pleased if they heard that my girlfriend died of pneumonia because I made her stand on my balcony for a few hours.'

'Girlfriend?' She raised an eyebrow.

'That's what you are, isn't it?'

'Probably.'

'I know we haven't done a lot of the things that couples do,' he told her as he led her inside.

'Like what?'

'This.' He kissed her full on the lips. She tasted coffee and, more faintly, lemon grass. He held her closely to him and she allowed herself to be moulded into his arms.

'I have something for you.' He let her go quite suddenly and she looked at him in surprise.

'Pardon?'

'I have something for you.'

'I would have thought you'd given me quite enough, thank you,' she said and smiled.

'Something for Christmas.'

'A present?' She looked at him doubtfully. 'Alistair, I don't want a Christmas present from you and not for any stupid reason but I didn't get you one and you already gave me the necklace and—'

'Oh, be quiet, Ash,' he told her. 'I picked this up in Spain and it's really nice. I thought you'd like it.' He got up from the sofa and padded across the room. The gold-wrapped package was hanging from the branches of his small Christmas tree. 'Here you are,' he said.

'Thank you.' Ash felt very uncomfortable about accepting the gift from him. She unwrapped it and opened the box inside. Pearl earrings nestled in soft cotton wool. They'd go really well, she thought, with Julia's pearl necklace. But they might be equally unlucky.

'They're beautiful,' she told him.

'Try them on.'

She didn't want to. She knew that she was being really stupid and that there was no reason not to wear the pearl earrings. She squeezed her eyes closed and tried to blot out the memory of Julia flinging her necklace out of the bedroom window. She undid the tiny gold hoops in her ears and put on the pearls in their place.

'I've always had a fantasy,' said Alistair as he looked at her, 'of making love to a girl who was wearing nothing but pearl earrings. And, of course, a horrendously expensive gold necklace as already worn by Gwyneth Paltrow.'

'Really?' asked Ash.

He nodded.

'I guess that's me then,' she said as she put the gold hoops on the table beside them.

Chapter 16

Strawberry Snow
Ripe strawberries, egg whites, sugar, double cream, vanilla
essence
Purée strawberries, combine with egg whites and sugar, beat
vigorously until stiff and glossy. Whip cream and flavour
with vanilla. Fold gently into strawberry mixture. Chill or
serve at once

Ash looked at her watch and frowned. It was unlike
Jodie to be late but she hadn't arrived at Chatham's
yet and Ash was getting worried. The two new partners
who had been appointed at the end of the previous year
would be attending lunch today, which meant a total of
eight people. Ash couldn't cater for eight people without
a waitress. She could feel the flutter of panic in the pit of
her stomach and she forced herself to be calm. Jodie had
been delayed but she would turn up. If there was any
chance that she wouldn't be able to make it, she would
have called before now.

So don't worry, she commanded herself as she picked

up a green pepper and began to slice it into even pieces.

She heard the kitchen door opening. 'About time,' she said without looking up. 'I was beginning to think you weren't going to show.'

'Me?'

'Ouch!' Ash sucked on the tip of the finger she'd nicked with the knife with the surprise of hearing Dan Morland's voice. She turned round. 'No, I wasn't expecting you.'

'Are you all right?'

She nodded. 'Barely scratched it.'

'Sorry if I startled you. I suppose I shouldn't creep up on people with kitchen knives in their hands.'

She smiled. 'Not a good idea. I might have used it as a weapon if I was really worried. Did you ever see *Under Siege*?'

'Steven Segal?' Dan nodded. 'I hope you're not a bloody martial arts expert as well as a cook.'

'Regretfully not.' Ash wrapped a piece of kitchen towel round her finger which was still bleeding. 'But that movie raised the stock of cooks everywhere.'

'Bloodthirsty lot, aren't you?' Dan smiled.

'We cut up meat, of course we are,' said Ash. 'Was there something you wanted?'

'Not especially,' said Dan. 'A gossip thing really.'

'Gossip!' Ash laughed. 'I didn't think serious stock-brokers gossiped. And I'm sure you should be at your desk doing the buying and selling stuff, not up here with me gossiping.'

'Old friends gossip,' Dan assured her. 'And the markets are doing nothing today. I just thought I'd tell you,

276

because I know you want to know, that Cordelia is coming home for her holiday next week.'

'Great,' said Ash.

'And she says she can't wait,' said Dan. 'That she's utterly exhausted and that the rescue has finally gone through and that everyone in the department is getting whacking great bonuses because of it.'

'Excellent,' said Ash. 'How long will she be home for?'

'At least a week.'

'And will she stay with you?' Ash opened the cupboard door and took out a green first aid box.

'Here, let me.' Dan opened the box and selected a plaster. 'That's a more serious cut than I thought!'

'It's not that bad really. They just bleed a lot.' Ash waited while he took the dressing out of its paper seal and then held out her finger. Dan grimaced as he wrapped the plaster round it.

'Are you OK?' asked Ash. 'You've gone rather pale.'

'I don't like blood,' he told her. 'Makes me feel queasy.'

'For heaven's sake!' But her eyes twinkled at him. 'Don't keel over on me and create another medical emergency.'

'I won't.' Dan took a glass from the rack and poured himself some water. 'I'm fine. And yes, Cordelia will be staying with me. For some of the time anyway. She's got to spend a few days with her folks. She's an only child and they dote on her. Drives her mad. But I've another little bit of gossip for you.'

'Oh?'

Ash picked up the knife again and Dan watched her warily.

'Remember I went to Mexico at Christmas?'

'How could I forget?' asked Ash feelingly. She'd thought of Dan's sunshine Christmas just as she'd thought of Alistair's snow-filled Christmas while she sat in the icy atmosphere that Michelle and herself had managed to create in Molly's.

'I met a really nice girl there,' he told her.

'God in heaven!' Ash glanced at him. 'Is there no end to your seductive powers? Do girls everywhere simply fall at your feet?'

'No,' said Dan.

'Only I'm remembering the night in the K Club and the fact that the place was littered with girls you'd once dated.'

Dan grinned. 'It seems more when they're all gathered in one place.'

Ash laughed. 'Maybe.'

'Anyway, this girl's name was Alicia and she was staying at the same hotel as me. Have you ever been to Cancun, Ash?'

'Nope.'

'Wonderful place,' said Dan feelingly. 'Gorgeous beaches, absolutely azure skies, warm sea—'

'I get the drift.' Ash took some oregano from the shelf.

'Anyway, I met Alicia at one of the beach bars. Stunning-looking girl – Latin American descent herself

278

I think – long black hair, dark eyes – a real cracker.'

Ash made a face at him.

'So we got talking,' Dan continued. 'And guess what?'

'What?' asked Ash dryly.

'She's Cordelia's flatmate.'

'Not really?' Ash opened the fridge.

'Absolutely.' Dan beamed at her. 'Once we got chatting we both realised who the other person was.'

'Oh.'

'And she said that Cordelia was up to her tits – her words not mine, Ash, don't look so disapproving – in work and that she'd been moaning that maybe she should have stayed in Ireland and married me straightaway instead of working eighteen-hour days in the bank.'

'Really?' Ash rinsed her hands.

'So I reckon it all looks pretty good. I told Alicia to say that she'd met me and give me a good review, so to speak.'

Ash laughed. 'And did she?'

'I don't know. But Cordelia phoned me every single day over the holidays!'

'You've probably made Cordelia jealous,' said Ash. 'There she is slaving away over a hot computer while you and her flatmate cavort on the beach – I'd be pretty jealous myself.'

'Do you think so?'

'Absolutely,' she said. 'I know that whenever I meet a bloke I've gone out with and he's with someone else I feel a bit jealous. Even if I haven't got the slightest bit of interest in him. And Cordelia has a significant interest in you, Dan, since you're getting married this year.'

'I know. But given the way things went I suppose I need reassurance.'

Ash smiled. 'God knows why, Dan. She's going to marry you. She loves you. And, even if she didn't, every other woman on the planet seems to!'

'You are so good for my ego!' said Dan and kissed her on the forehead.

'I hope I'm not interrupting anything.' Jodie stood at the kitchen door and looked at Ash and Dan.

'I'd better get back to the desk,' Dan said. 'I'll let you know how things go.'

'Great.' Ash knew that her cheeks were pink. She was embarrassed that Jodie had caught her being so light-hearted with one of the clients. 'See you later,' she added as Dan disappeared out of the door.

'What was all that about?' Jodie looked at Ash quizzically. 'I thought you were just friends. I thought you simply "helped him out" at the K Club. I thought he was engaged.'

'You're getting the wrong end of the stick.' Ash was recovering her composure. 'That was nothing, Jodie. We were talking about his fiancée coming home.'

'And he felt the need to kiss you?' asked Jodie archly.

'It wasn't that sort of kiss,' said Ash. 'You saw it, for goodness' sake. It didn't—'

'Mean anything,' finished Jodie dryly. 'I know.'

It was Emmet rather than Molly who rang Ash that evening. She was making soup when he called, whirring the ingredients in her blender so that at first she didn't hear the phone. She was unenthusiastic when she heard Emmet's voice.

'What can I do for you?' she asked.

'Don't talk to me as though I was one of your clients,' said Emmet. 'I'm your brother-in-law.'

'Not exactly,' said Ash. 'You're my cousin's husband. I'm not quite sure what that makes you in the legal sense.'

'Oh, for heaven's sake, Ash, it doesn't matter what I am.' Emmet was irritated by her. 'I'm ringing because of you and Michelle.'

'Is Michelle totally unable to speak herself?' asked Ash. 'I've had phone calls nearly every day from Molly asking me to be nice to Michelle. If Michelle wants to talk to me she can bloody well ring me herself.'

'She's upset, Ash.'

'Oh, and I'm not?'

'Come on, everyone knows that you're a much less emotional person than Michelle. She talks before she thinks, Ash. You know that. She was just lashing out. You knew exactly what you were saying.'

'Did I?'

'You lived with her for long enough.' Emmet's voice was pleading. 'She truly is upset. She didn't mean to get at you.'

'Yes she did,' said Ash. 'She's been getting at me for the best part of nineteen years and she'll be getting at me for ever. It's in her damn nature to get at me.'

'You got at her too, Ash. And she doesn't mean it.'

'So when I'm nasty I mean it and when she is she

doesn't? You're her husband and I'd expect you to think like that. But I'll tell you something, she resented me from the moment I moved into that house and she hasn't stopped resenting me ever since.'

'That's not true, Ash.'

'What makes you say that? Because Michelle says so?'

'She loves you. You're family.'

'Huh.'

'She knows if she rings you'll pretend everything is OK but you won't have forgiven her.'

'Emmet, she's the one who pretends everything is OK. We had a row last time I was in your house but she just sailed into my apartment on Christmas Eve as though nothing had happened. Every time we argue, that's the way it works out. But she festers and it keeps nagging at her and so, of course, the next time we meet we have a row again. I'm tired of rowing with her but just because she wants to draw some line in the sand this time doesn't mean I want to.'

'So you want to keep rowing with her?'

'No. But I don't want us to kiss and make up and for it all to be just a façade either. Because I know and you know that sooner or later she'll start up all over again and I'm bloody well tired of it, Emmet. I know she's your wife and you love her but she drives me insane. Besides which she says some pretty cutting things and I'm tired of her thinking that I don't care.' Ash was horrified to hear her voice tremble.

'I know,' said Emmet gently. 'She doesn't mean to be cutting or cruel, Ash. You have to make allowances for her.'

'Oh, I have to make allowances for her and she has to make allowances for me – so in the end we both tiptoe around making allowances for each other and what good does that do?'

'That's what families do, Ash,' said Emmet. 'You grow up with people and you get to know what makes them tick and you do make allowances for them.'

Ash said nothing.

'Look, why don't you drop over at the weekend?' suggested Emmet. 'We'll have a few drinks, strictly no cooking, and you and Michelle can mend broken fences. The kids would love to see you too.'

'They saw me at Christmas,' muttered Ash.

'It doesn't have to be a special occasion for you to see them,' Emmet told her. 'And you know that Lucy adores you.'

'Stop soft-soaping me,' said Ash irritably.

'I'm trying to be a peacemaker,' admitted Emmet. 'Michelle is unhappy and you must be too and life's too damn short, Ash.'

'I know.'

'I'm sorry,' said Emmet. 'Maybe that wasn't the best thing to say to you.'

'Maybe it was.' Ash sighed. 'All right, I'll come over on Saturday, I'm working Friday night.'

'Great, Michelle will be pleased.'

'She should have phoned me herself,' said Ash.

'You wouldn't have agreed if she'd phoned you herself,' Emmet said. 'The two of you would've had another bloody argument and she would have spent the night in a huff again. And I have better things to do than spend the night beside someone in a huff.'

Ash smiled weakly. 'For your sake, then.'

'Absolutely,' said Emmet. 'And we look forward to seeing you.'

'Right,' said Ash as she hung up the phone.

She poured the curried parsnip and apple purée out of the blender and into a saucepan then heated it gently. Almost perfect, she thought, as she tasted it. She ground a little more pepper into it and tasted it again. 'Absolutely perfect,' she said out loud.

She brought a bottle of St Emilion as well as Michelle's uncollected New Year's cake to their house. She walked up the pathway and thought about the last time she'd come here and wondered was there any time she met Michelle when they didn't have a row. And she sighed because they'd done the apologising thing to each other a hundred times before only it didn't make any difference and, sooner or later, they fought again.

She rang the bell and, as always, Emmet answered the door. Lucy was with him and she flung her arms round Ash.

'Hiya, Lucy.' Ash hugged her. 'How are you keeping?'

'Fine, thanks.' Lucy always spoke to Ash as though they were both adults. 'And you?'

Ash smothered a grin. 'I'm fine too. Have you been playing with your Christmas presents?'

'Yes.' Lucy nodded. 'But I'm back to school now so I'm doing homework too.'

'Homework?' asked Ash. 'What sort of homework?'

'Art,' said Lucy.

'Making necklaces out of pasta pieces,' said Emmet as they walked into the living room. 'And thereby robbing all the food in the house.'

'You don't like pasta,' said Lucy severely. 'I'm doing you a favour really.'

Ash and Emmet both laughed.

'Hello, Ash.' Michelle got up from the armchair where she'd been sitting, Shay junior asleep on her shoulder. 'It's nice to see you again.'

'Is it?' asked Ash.

'Don't start already,' begged Emmet. 'Can't you two just talk without having all sorts of hidden agendas?'

'I don't have any hidden agendas.' Ash handed him the bottle of wine.

'Neither do I,' said Michelle warily.

The cousins sat down, Michelle in her armchair and Ash on the sofa opposite. Emmet went into the kitchen followed by Lucy and Brian.

'How's Shay?' Ash nodded at the baby.

'Fine,' said Michelle.

There was silence, broken only by the faint sound of the baby snoring.

'This is silly,' said Ash finally. 'Sitting opposite each other like adversaries.'

'Is that what we've become?' asked Michelle.

Ash shook her head. 'I don't want us to be.'

'Neither do I,' said Michelle. 'But we seem to spark off each other the wrong way, don't we?'

'Why?' asked Ash.

Michelle shrugged. 'You don't like me.'

'That's rubbish,' said Ash.

'You think I was stupid to have married Emmet and had the kids.'

'No, I don't.'

'You think we've nothing at all in common.'

'We've lots in common,' said Ash. 'And according to Molly we're practically sisters – we're the same family, aren't we? We should get on with each other, no problem.'

'Molly lives in a fantasy world,' said Michelle, 'where everybody loves everybody else and there are no arguments.'

'She's easygoing all right,' admitted Ash.

'That's why she wanted you when you were a kid,' said Michelle. 'She said that it'd be easy enough to look after you, you were only another mouth, after all.'

'Charming.' But Ash smiled slightly.

'But it wasn't like that, was it?' asked Michelle. 'Because you weren't like us. You didn't like climbing in the fields or playing football or helping Charlie with his bike.'

'Well, I—'

Michelle was really getting into her stride.

'You were the pretty one. The delicate one. The exotic one who'd lived in America and England and who'd had tragedy in her life.'

Ash could hear the bitterness in Michelle's voice. 'I wouldn't recommend tragedy,' she said, determined to keep calm.

286

'Of course not.' Michelle looked straight at her. 'But you used it to get what you wanted.'

'Michelle, I didn't!'

'Anytime things weren't going your way you'd look at Mam and you'd open those brown eyes really wide and flick back your blonde hair and she wouldn't be able to resist you.'

Ash shifted uncomfortably on the sofa. 'I never meant—'

'But me – I used to come straight out with what I wanted and if I didn't get it I'd have a row with her and then I certainly wouldn't get it!'

'I know but—'

'And in the meantime she'd go off and buy you a new dress or something because, of course, you liked pastel pinks and blues and socks with lace on them while I preferred jeans.'

Ash sighed. 'I liked jeans too. They're practically all I ever wear nowadays. It was Molly who picked out the other stuff. I didn't think I could say no.'

'And then all this cooking malarkey,' continued Michelle as though Ash hadn't spoken. '"Oh, Aunt Molly, let me try that. Let me do the cookies. Let me bake the cakes. Let me try and cook Sunday lunch."'

'Michelle, I like cooking. I really do.'

'But you're not supposed to like it when you're four-teen,' snapped Michelle. 'You're supposed to be out meeting blokes and drinking cider and smoking behind the shed. Not cooking for a family of seven. Or tidying our bedroom – God, our bedroom was always so bloody tidy! All I wanted was a normal teenage room, one that looked like it had been hit by a stray meteorite or something but no, we had one where I used to be afraid to drop anything on the floor instead of putting it in a specially labelled drawer!'

'I can't stand things being untidy,' said Ash. 'And you didn't drink cider behind the shed.'

Michelle sighed. 'I did drink cider. Only once though, it made me feel sick.'

'I did too,' said Ash.

Michelle stared at her.

'Not behind the bicycle shed, obviously,' Ash told her. 'I bought a can of Taunton's for the ham I was cooking and I drank it instead. In the bathroom.'

'Ash!'

She shrugged. 'Actually, I quite liked the taste. But I felt terribly woozy afterwards. Not sick though.'

'I never knew.'

'I didn't see any point in shattering your illusions about me being a neatness freak who cooked.'

Michelle smiled faintly at her. 'That's exactly how I'll always see you.'

'I know,' said Ash.

'But I don't understand it,' Michelle said. 'How could you have lived the kind of life you lived with Julia and ended up as neat and tidy as you did?'

'How could I not?' demanded Ash. 'We spent our lives wandering around, Michelle. Packing and unpacking and always meeting new people. All I wanted was to have somewhere neat and tidy that nobody could come into and mess up.'

288

Michelle was quiet for a moment. 'I never thought of it like that before,' she said eventually.

'Why would you?' asked Ash.

Michelle shifted baby Shay in her arms. 'But you don't have to go on being like that,' she said. 'Once you know why you do what you do, surely you can change.'

'Why would I want to change?' Ash looked at Michelle in surprise. 'I like my life the way it is. I like my apartment. I like my job. I don't want to change.'

'But you can't like keeping people at a distance, Ash.'

'I don't.'

'You do. You don't get involved.'

'Of course I do!' retorted Ash. 'And, if you remember, when I get involved, like at Christmas, all I do is piss you off.'

Michelle smiled wryly. 'That's different.'

'No it's not.'

'I'm sorry about Christmas,' said Michelle. 'I really am.'

'Christmas was just an extension of how it usually is,' Ash told her.

'Well, I'm sorry about that too.'

Ash stared at Michelle. Her cousin had never apologised to her in two consecutive sentences before.

'Oh, I suppose I sometimes feel envious of you,' Michelle continued. 'What with the apartment and the boyfriends and the kind of life you lead . . .'

'My life is ordinary,' said Ash. 'The apartment is nice but it comes at a price – working my butt off! Which I'm lucky that I like, I suppose, but I still have to do it. And if

I don't work I don't get paid and if I don't get paid I can't pay the mortgage – it's not starry stuff, Michelle. And as for the boyfriends, don't you think you're happier with Emmet than you would be with a string of boyfriends – even if I had a string, which I don't!'

'I love Emmet,' said Michelle. 'I always have and I always will.' She shrugged, almost embarrassed. 'But I sometimes think that it was a mistake to marry him so quickly. I feel like my whole life was mapped out by the time I left school. Emmet was always part of it and so was having a home and a family – I don't regret it, I just sometimes wish I'd waited.' She smiled wryly at Ash. 'I think I would've liked a couple of years on my own in an apartment.'

'Well, sometimes I wonder what it'd be like to be married with kids,' said Ash. 'I suppose the grass always is greener!'

'You don't really think that, do you?' asked Michelle.

She grimaced. 'It's just that the whole family thing is such a grown-up thing to do,' she told her cousin. 'And I'm not sure I'll ever be grown-up enough to do it.'

Michelle laughed. 'You're grown-up enough, Ash.'

The door opened and Emmet peered around. 'Just checking,' he said, 'to make sure you haven't decapitated each other yet.'

'Not yet,' said Michelle easily. 'But give it time.'

Emmet looked worried.

'We're fine,' said Ash. 'Really.'

'Will I get you a drink?' he asked. 'A beer or wine, Ash?'

Ash glanced at her cousin.

'No thanks,' said Michelle. 'I can't hold my drink at the moment, as you might have already guessed. I suppose things sometimes get a bit out of proportion, what with coping with Shay and everything.' She twisted towards the door. 'Tea'd be nice, Emmet.'

'Beer for me,' said Ash.

'I had a horrible hangover on Christmas Day,' said Michelle. 'I haven't touched drink since.'

'I wasn't the best myself,' admitted Ash.

'Wait until you have a baby screaming at you when your head is pounding,' Michelle told her. 'Then you'll know what suffering for your family is all about!'

'But you love it,' said Ash. 'You love the whole family thing.'

Michelle nodded. 'I know. Which is why I only envy you sometimes.'

'Don't envy me,' said Ash. 'There's nothing to envy.'

'What about the squillionaire?' asked Michelle. 'Now that's what I call enviable!'

Ash fiddled with the gold necklace round her neck. 'He's OK,' she said cautiously.

'Ash, he's worth millions! Surely that's better than OK!'

'Money isn't everything,' said Ash.

'But it can help.'

'I know.' She sighed. 'I do like him, Michelle. And he did ask me to spend Christmas with him – although he took a gang of people away so maybe it wasn't quite the intimate candlelit dinner for two scenario you might want to imagine. All the same, I don't know whether I could spend the rest of my life with him.'

'Why not?' asked Michelle.

'I don't know. He's fun to be with. He's good-looking—'

'Bloody good-looking,' Michelle interrupted her, 'if those pics in the magazine are anything to go by.'

'Very good-looking, then,' amended Ash. 'It's just – oh, I don't know, Michelle. Maybe I'm just not the one man, one relationship type.'

'You could be,' said Michelle, 'if you allowed yourself to care once in a while.'

The door opened again and Emmet appeared carrying a tray with tea and biscuits as well as a tin of Miller for Ash.

'Beer and biscuits,' she said. 'Great combination!'

'I'll get you some crisps,' said Emmet.

Ash laughed. 'No, don't. I'm not hungry and if I start eating crisps I won't stop.'

'You're not fat, Ash,' objected Michelle. 'You should eat a few cholesterol-laden crisps from time to time.'

'I eat lots of fat-laden things,' said Ash. 'Hot chocolate with extra chocolate squares, or marshmallows for example. But I try to be moderate. Only with crisps it's impossible.'

'Tell you what,' said Michelle as she handed the baby to Emmet. 'You eat the crisps and I won't get at you again for at least three months.'

Ash giggled. 'Don't be so silly.'

'Seriously,' said Michelle and her face was very serious.

'Do it, Ash. Do something kind of spontaneous like eating a whole tube of Pringles and I swear that I won't call you anally retentive or an arrested developer or anything like that for ages.'

'You mean it.' Ash stared at her.

'Yes.'

'But that's silly.'

'Indulge me,' said Michelle.

'OK,' said Ash eventually. 'But I won't eat a whole tube. I can't sleep if I eat a whole tube. I'll eat some, though.'

'Three-quarters,' insisted Michelle.

'You two are quite insane,' said Emmet but he brought a tube of spring onion crisps into the living room anyway.

'So are you seeing him again?' asked Michelle as she poured tea into her mug.

'Alistair?' Ash pulled the ring on her tin.

Michelle nodded.

'If he calls me.' Ash smiled and took some crisps from the tube. 'We're talking as though it's me who has any control over how this relationship might develop but it's him that calls me.'

'Nothing stopping you calling him,' said Michelle.

'I know.' Ash spoke through a mouthful of crisps. 'But I don't want to.'

'Because it'd make you look needy.'

'That's not why!'

'Why then?'

Ash made a face. 'Because it'd make me look needy?'

Michelle laughed.

'I don't know, Michelle.' Ash drank some beer to wash down the crisps. 'Maybe it'll develop, maybe not.'

'You have to work at it,' Michelle told her. 'Don't just wait for it to develop. Be proactive. Suggest places you want to go. Let him know that you care.'

'You didn't do all that with Emmet,' Ash objected. 'It just sort of developed between you, didn't it?'

'Are you mad?' Michelle looked at her as though she might be. 'I had my Emmet Somers campaign clearly defined from the start.'

'Really?'

'Really,' said Michelle. 'Which is why I can't complain that I landed him!'

'You're much better at this kind of thing than me,' said Ash.

'Not really,' Michelle said. 'But I like it, which is definitely different to you. You see blokes as some sort of threat, Ash, when they should be a challenge.'

'Oh, God, not a challenge.'

'And yours is to get the squillionaire to propose,' Michelle told her.

'But what if I don't want him to?'

'Ash, every girl wants a man loaded with money to propose to her. You don't have to accept! Although,' she added, 'I would be very, very disappointed in you if you didn't.'

'It's not just money,' said Ash. 'It's supposed to be for life.'

'I know,' said Michelle. 'But given your track record, Ash, I truly think that you need someone with money behind him. You're afraid of not having any. You're afraid that someone will one day grab everything you have away from you. You'd never be able to relax with someone who just earned a decent wage. You *need* a multimillionaire!'

Ash laughed. 'You're mad, you know that?'

Michelle nodded. 'And you were always flaky.'

This time they both laughed and Ash offered Michelle some crisps.

Chapter 17

Chocolate Fudge
Butter, icing sugar, evaporated milk, plain chocolate
Melt butter, remove from heat, stir in icing sugar and evap-
orated milk. Return to heat and bring slowly to boil. Reduce
heat and cook for 20/30 minutes. Add melted chocolate and
mix well. Pour into prepared tin and leave to cool

Cordelia looked for Dan the moment she stepped into the arrivals hall at Dublin airport. She hoped he was looking out for her too; the terminal was, as always, crowded and she couldn't see anyone she knew. She pulled her case wearily towards the meeting point, feeling peeved that he hadn't immediately rushed from the mass of people to throw his arms round her and welcome her. That was how she'd imagined it on the long, tiring and very full flight from New York. She'd been sandwiched between two beefy businessmen who, like her, were not flying business class. Whenever she flew on business for the bank the company paid the extra money but Cordelia didn't think she was rich enough yet to pay another couple of thousand pounds for a wider seat, complimentary drinks and an overnight pack. All the same, she thought as she continued to scan the crowd for Dan's face, the extra room would've meant that she'd have been able to sleep. It had been impossible to doze off in the main cabin even though she was exhausted. She'd watched the movie which had almost been restful and had thought of Dan who'd told her about his night at the premiere of the same movie, where he'd been hungover because he'd gone drinking out of loneliness for her.

Well, he wasn't too damn lonely now, was he? she thought as she tapped her foot impatiently. If he'd missed her all that much then surely he'd be here waiting for her. She glanced at her watch. The flight had been on time so he shouldn't have been caught out. Unless he'd factored in the possibility that, like most flights and despite what the airlines tried to tell you, it would be late. She looked around the crowd again but there was still no sign of him. I'll give him ten minutes, she decided, then I'm getting a taxi home and he can come and get me. And he'd better be bloody apologetic when he does!

'Cordelia!'

She turned round and saw him at the edge of the swirl of people, waving to her.

'Cordelia!'

She acknowledged him with a slight wave and then pulled her case towards him, almost taking the ankles off a bearded tourist checking a map of Dublin.

'I'm so sorry,' Dan said as she reached him. 'There was

an accident on the motorway and the traffic was backed up to Santry. I thought I'd never get here.'

'That's OK.' She supposed she could forgive a pile-up. 'Was there anyone hurt?'

'I don't know.' Dan took her case and began to lead her out of the terminal building. 'They were clearing it away by the time I passed by. One of the cars looked pretty flattened.'

'I thought you'd forgotten me,' she said.

'Don't be stupid.' He stopped opposite the pay machines for the car park. 'How the hell could I forget you when I've been thinking of nobody else for the last three months?'

She smiled at him and he kissed her. She held him tightly, surprised at how pleased she was to be back in his arms again. 'I missed you,' she murmured.

'Did you?'

'Of course I did.' She moved her head so that she could look at him. 'I'm glad to be back.'

'That's good.' He squeezed her close to him and kissed her again.

He slid his ticket into the machine and paid the fee. 'Up a couple of levels,' he told Cordelia. 'I reckon that unless you're here at six in the morning you'll always end up miles from the terminal.'

'Doesn't matter.' She yawned.

'Tired?'

'Didn't sleep,' she told him.

'You can sleep when we get back to the house,' Dan promised her.

She grinned. 'I thought you'd have something else on the agenda!'

'Well, I have,' he said. 'But I've been without you for so long that another few hours won't matter. And I don't want you falling asleep in the middle of my performance.'

'Not likely!' She laughed at him. 'And thinking of you was the only thing that kept me going on that damned flight.'

'I'm glad,' said Dan. 'I thought of you on it too.'

She followed Dan through the car park until they arrived at the Saab. He heaved her suitcase into the boot and turned to her.

'I thought about you all the time.' His hand slid beneath the camel-coloured coat she was wearing.

'Dan!'

'I don't know if I can wait to get you home.'

'I don't know if I want you to,' said Cordelia as she opened the car door.

Alistair Brannigan sat in his Blackrock office and gazed across Dublin Bay at the two ESB chimneys at Poolbeg. They stretched high into the sky, disappearing into the low grey clouds like two red and white needles pushing through kapok. Alistair liked the chimneys even though they really did spoil the skyline. But they'd always been there and he found them restful and, somehow, inspiring. They reached higher than anything around them, he thought, as he leaned back in his black leather chair. Just as he wanted to do.

He thought about the new protocol his company was developing. If they got the technology right it would mean quicker, speedier and, importantly, more secure Internet transactions. Alistair knew that some people were still nervous about supplying financial details over the net. Hell, he thought, some people are scared about providing them over the phone. ChainMail, the working name for his new product, looked like being a winner. Which would propel Archangel's share price even higher and make him even richer. Maybe, he thought, instead of buying a car he should think about a company jet. Transys, the company that had bought the controlling interest in Archangel, had a company jet. But it would be nice to have one for himself. Save all that hanging around in airports – Christmas had been a nightmare what with delayed flights out of Dublin and Barcelona. Not to mention having to share the plane with a crowd of strangers, any of whom could be a psycho or infected with a fatal disease. Get a grip, he muttered, as he spun back to his desk. For a start, you're not in the company-jet league yet. And who the hell do you think you are worrying about getting on a plane full of people? Eighteen months ago you could hardly afford Ryanair's cheapest flight to meet with the Transys people! He grinned to himself. He'd come a long way since then and he was proud of it. He was proud at how quickly things had gone right for Archangel, how he'd managed to catch the right wave in an industry where he knew that many companies would one day fail. But Archangel wouldn't. And he wouldn't. Because he was determined to make it succeed.

His phone buzzed and Natascha, his Russian PA, told him that he had a call.

'Take a message would you?' he asked her. 'I'm thinking and I don't want to be disturbed.'

He leaned back in the chair again. No matter what happened now he was set up. Even if the unthinkable happened and both Transys and Archangel went down the tubes he had five million pounds in hard cash as well as his shares and share options. So worst-case scenario – well, there wasn't really a worst-case scenario for Alistair Brannigan. And ChainMail was going to be another blinding success which would mean he was going to be worth twice as much by this time next year. This time next month, perhaps, he thought. All he had to do was put out a couple of stories about some mind-boggling new technology and the markets would love it!

Maybe I should walk away, he thought idly. Take the money and hide out on a desert island for a few months. Chill out completely. But Alistair knew that he wasn't the chilling out sort. Last year he'd gone to Ibiza for a week with four of his mates and he'd spent half the time messing with his laptop while the others went lap-dancing. When they'd eventually managed to drag him to Manumission, he'd been bored out of his mind by the noise and the lights and the sex that was going on all round him. Which had worried him until he reminded himself that he was working on something that would change his life much more dramatically than a quick shag in the sun. And the sale of Archangel had been much, much better than sex!

301

Best not say that out loud, he told himself, or people will begin to wonder about you. And about the fact that the last time you had sex with anyone it was with the lovely Ash O'Halloran who was, as he'd suspected, a very natural blonde. And almost great in bed although he couldn't help feeling that part of her was somewhere else. Oh, she'd moaned in the right places and groaned in the right places and she'd done one or two surprising things to him in exactly the right places, but he still felt as though he hadn't managed to break down her reserve and that, in the end, she'd faked it. He'd never thought that any of his girlfriends had faked it before.

She was a challenge, thought Alistair. He wanted to make her love him and want to be with him all the time and he wanted to know that it wasn't because of the money. He sighed. The money was great, there was no way he'd do without it, but it had changed everything. Now when girls looked at him he could see them thinking share options before they even uttered a word.

Ash didn't seem to care about the money but it was impossible to tell. She was more intriguing than anyone he'd ever met before. Capable of being ice-cool and yet other times brimming with fun and laughter until some invisible switch seemed to click in her and the shutters would come down again. And sometimes she would look at him and it was as though it was from somewhere deep inside her soul. The brown eyes did it, he decided. Those huge brown eyes in that clear-skinned face surrounded by that mass of pale gold hair. He sat up straight and tried not to think about Ash because what was happening to him was not what he wanted to happen at three o'clock on a Wednesday afternoon. Not when he was supposed to be thinking about ChainMail.

Ash in chains, he thought, unable to put her completely out of his mind. Wearing a dress made out of chains. Nothing else. He groaned softly. Ash as she had been in his apartment. Gloriously naked except for the pearl earrings and the gold necklace.

He smiled to himself as he remembered the auction and Dan Morland bidding up the price. There had been a moment when he thought of backing out and letting Morland take the strain of paying over the odds for a very ordinary necklace. But he'd wanted to make a gesture to Ash because it was their first date and he knew that his final bid, which had blitzed Morland, had been a very grand gesture indeed. He chuckled to himself. It had worked and Ash had gone out with him again. The next task, thought Alistair, was to make her be the one to call him. He'd know that he'd gotten to her if she was the one to call him!

The phone buzzed again and he dragged himself back to the present.

'Herr Hoffman for you,' said Natascha in her almost unaccented English. 'He wishes to speak about the new project. He says that it is most important.'

'Tell Herr Hoffman that I am working on the new project,' said Alistair. 'And that I will call him later this afternoon. And, Natascha, when I say that I'm busy and don't want to be disturbed, that includes Herr Hoffman.'

'Yes, Mr Brannigan,' she said stiffly. 'I apologise.'

'Oh, that's OK.' Alistair didn't like to think of his lovely PA getting upset with him. 'And don't call me Mr Brannigan. You know it terrifies me.'

'OK, Alistair,' she said and her voice was noticeably warmer. 'By the way, your other call was from Ash O'Halloran. She wanted to know if you were free for a drink this evening.'

Ash stood at the window of her apartment and looked across the river towards the docklands office buildings which had changed the riverside views for ever. She noticed that the sky was lighter now than it had been at four o'clock in the afternoon a few weeks ago, even with the clouds that had formed around the bay, and she could feel herself begin to warm to the idea of longer days, shorter nights and milder weather. She especially liked the idea of shorter nights. Ash had never quite overcome her fear of the dark and though she sometimes deliberately made herself sit in an unlit room, she preferred to know that the light switch was to hand. Her fear was part of the reason why she didn't have drapes or blinds of any kind on her floor-to-ceiling windows – even with all the lights out, Ash's apartment was never completely dark.

Bagel padded across the room towards her and wove around her legs.

'I wish you wouldn't do that,' she said absently. 'Every time you do you deposit at least a pound of fur on me.'

Bagel mewed.

'And how could you possibly be hungry?' she asked. 'I

gave you chopped liver for lunch. A cat who's been fed chopped liver can't possibly be hungry.'

Bagel disagreed. He mewed at her again then trotted towards the kitchen. Ash followed him. His bowl was empty and he was sitting in front of the fridge, looking at it expectantly.

'What?' she asked him.

He mewed again.

She opened the fridge and took out some milk which she poured into his bowl. Bagel sniffed the milk and walked back to the fridge.

'Oh, come on!' she cried. 'You can't want anything else.' She looked at the shelves, then had a sudden thought. She opened the freezer and took out one of the tubs of ice cream. 'You normally don't start this until I'm eating it,' she told him, scooping some of the creamy mixture and dropping it into his bowl. Bagel mewed again and began to lick the ice cream. 'Mad,' said Ash. 'This is chocolate fudge, Bagel. Cats aren't supposed to like chocolate fudge ice cream!'

She replaced the lid on the tub and put it back in the freezer. If Michelle could see me now, thought Ash, she'd think I was even more barmy than she probably still thinks I am already.

Ash didn't consider that she and Michelle had suddenly become great friends after her last visit to her cousin's house. She was realistic enough to know that you didn't get rid of eighteen years' worth of prejudices in one evening. But it had been cathartic and she'd left Michelle's feeling happier than she'd done in ages. She'd also left Michelle's feeling that maybe her cousin was right on the subject of men and her relationship with them. Particularly in her view about Alistair Brannigan.

Ash knew that she was afraid of being poor. She had been poor and she hadn't liked it. So it made sense that, if she really was committed to a man, he'd have to be a man who had something behind him. Mind you, she'd thought as she came home on the DART that evening, even she hadn't visualised someone with a few million in cash and shares behind them, but why not reach for the stars? She hadn't felt quite the same way the following day, thinking that it was ridiculous to be nice to Alistair simply because he was wealthy. All the money in the world wouldn't make any difference if she didn't love him. But she liked him. And she knew that he liked her. Maybe, she decided, it was possible for them to love each other.

She hadn't told Michelle that she'd slept with Alistair. She didn't want her cousin to think it was that serious. Besides which, Alistair had said that he'd call and he had, the following day, but she'd been out and so he'd left a message on her machine. She'd been unwilling, then, to call him back. And he hadn't called again. So, in a rush of humiliation, she'd thought that it had just been a sex thing with Alistair after all and that having got her into bed he'd lost interest in her. But the following night, when she'd checked her e-mails before going to bed, there was one from Alistair.

'Yo, Ash,' it said, 'Don't think I'm ignoring you! Am currently in Frankfurt having talks with parent company about new technology. Sudden visit. Very boring. Would much rather be talking to you about the value of pearls. Miss you – will message you again. Love, Alistair.'

He'd sent one more message, very brief, just saying that he was busy but should be home soon. Message him, he said. She'd decided to ring him instead. She wanted to hear his voice. But he'd been busy, as the husky PA had told her, and unavailable to take calls. Ash hadn't known whether to leave a message or not. Part of her had wanted to say that it didn't matter, she'd call him back. And then she thought that Michelle would tell her that she'd wimped out and so she'd left the message after all.

Why is it so complicated? she wondered as she watched Bagel lick the last scrap of chocolate fudge out of his bowl. Why isn't everything simple?

Cordelia's eyes flickered open and it took her a minute or two to figure out where she was. She turned her head but the bed beside her was empty. She yawned and stretched beneath the covers. She didn't know how long she'd been asleep but she felt a lot better. She'd almost fallen into the bed when she arrived back at Dan's house and he'd immediately got in beside her and put his arms round her. He'd kissed her on the shoulder and – she'd fallen asleep! Poor Dan, she thought, as she swung herself out of the bed. He'd think that she didn't care. But she'd been so, so tired and surely, she reasoned, he'd think of it as a compliment that she'd been so relaxed with him she could fall asleep. Or maybe not. She looked around the bedroom and robbed his black and white striped dressing gown from the hook on the back of the door. She tied it tightly round her waist then went in search of him.

Dan was sitting at the counter in the breakfast room just off his ultra-modern kitchen. He was reading the *Financial Times* and sipping coffee but he folded the paper when Cordelia pushed open the door and smiled at her.

'Sleeping Beauty awakes!'

'Not so much Beauty,' she told him. 'More like the Beast the way I felt. I'm sorry I fell asleep.'

'I was surprised you stayed awake as long as you did. I'm always knackered when I come back from the States.'

'Truly?'

'Absolutely. What would you like to do now?' He glanced at his watch. It was almost six o'clock in the evening.

'Have a shower,' said Cordelia. 'Freshen up. And then get something to eat, I'm utterly starving.'

'Do you want to go out or send out?' asked Dan.

'Oh, let's go out!' She smiled. 'I know I haven't been away that long but it feels like ages and I want to get the atmosphere of Dublin back in my veins.'

'I've never heard anyone put it like that before,' said Dan. 'I'd have thought that New York was a great city to have fizzing around you.'

'It is,' said Cordelia. 'But I won't feel like I'm home until I go out.'

'OK,' said Dan. 'Let me get you some towels and you can have a shower.'

'Thanks.' She followed him up the stairs. She was glad

he hadn't tried to kiss her or make love to her. She still hadn't quite woken up enough to enjoy the idea.

'Hello, Ash?'

'Alistair?' Ash shifted on the sofa and Bagel jumped down. He looked at her in annoyance at having been disturbed then turned his back on her and began to wash.

'How are things?'

'Fine,' she said. 'And you? How was Germany?'

'Boring,' said Alistair. 'The trouble with being bought out by a conglomerate like Transys is that there are loads of people you have to talk to who haven't the faintest idea what you're talking about. They just want to discuss the balance sheet and growth prospects while I want to tell them that the new technology is going to be brilliant.'

'I'd have thought they'd like to hear that.'

'They do. But they don't like "going to be". They want "already is".'

Ash laughed. 'Just like cooking. People don't want to know that the food will be ready in an hour, they want it now.'

'I can understand that,' said Alistair with feeling. 'When I'm hungry I don't like to mess about waiting. I want to eat straightaway.'

'Philistine!' But she laughed.

'Anyway, I was really glad to get your call,' said Alistair. 'I'm sorry I had to rush off and I know it's not the kind of thing that women really like—'

'It was OK,' said Ash. 'I didn't mind.'

'Most do.' Alistair sighed. 'Thing is, when it's work I forget everything else.'

'I'm gutted to think you forgot me,' said Ash. 'But I'm glad the work is going well.'

'So the least I can do is be the one to ask you to dinner,' said Alistair.

'I asked you first,' Ash told him.

'You said drinks.'

'Drinks, food, whatever.'

'How about we go to Jodie's restaurant?' asked Alistair. 'I like it there.'

'Fine by me,' said Ash. 'What time will I meet you there?'

'I'll pick you up.'

'Now that is particularly silly,' said Ash. 'You'd have to come past it to get to me. I'll meet you there.' She glanced at her watch. 'Say around seven thirty?'

'Why do you make me feel like a child?' asked Alistair. 'I'm an important business executive in this town and the way you told me I was silly reminded me of my teacher in primary school.'

'Sorry!' Ash giggled.

'So you should be. OK, see you there at half past.'

'Great,' said Ash and replaced the receiver.

Chapter 18

Lemon Sorbet
Sugar, lemon rind and juice, egg white, water
Heat sugar and water until dissolved. Add lemon rind,
boil for 10 minutes. Cool. Stir in lemon juice and strain
into container. Freeze for about three hours. Turn into
bowl, beat gently. Whisk egg white and fold in. Freeze
overnight

Ash was already sitting down at a window table, sipping a glass of white wine and gazing across at the illuminated river, when Alistair arrived. She noticed that the waitress made a big fuss of him as he entered, smiling hugely at him as she took his soft black leather jacket, and joking as she led him to the table.

'Hi,' he said as he sat down. 'Sorry I'm late. Couldn't get a cab.'

It was nearly ten to eight. 'No problem,' said Ash.

'Sure?' he looked at her with amusement in his eyes. 'Jodie told me that you were a punctuality freak. That's why I always try to be on time when I meet you.'

'What else did Jodie tell you about me?' Ash unwrapped a breadstick and snapped it in half. 'And how well do you know her?'

'Quite well.' Alistair answered her second question first. 'Her family lived close to mine in Naas where we grew up. I was pally with Jodie's older brother, Kevin, so I used to see her a lot. Went to her debs ball with her, as a matter of fact. And a couple of dates afterwards. But we're more like brother and sister ourselves. No spark.'

Ash nodded.

'I still see her a lot,' Alistair continued. 'We get on well and it's nice to be able to talk to someone who knew you when you were a scabby-kneed five-year-old. Especially now, because since Archangel, people treat me as though I'm some kind of celebrity which is so bloody silly. Jodie still treats me like a nuisance.'

'So you're just friends,' said Ash.

'Absolutely.'

'I had a conversation about that with someone quite recently.' Ash thought of Dan Morland. 'We were debating whether or not men and women could really be friends.'

'I know that debate.' Alistair took two breadsticks and unwrapped them. 'And I don't really know the answer. But, in case you're worried, there's nothing between Jodie and me.'

'I'm not worried,' Ash told him. 'I didn't think there was.'

'Don't you get jealous?' he asked. 'Don't you want to know about all my past girlfriends and stuff?'

'Why?' asked Ash. 'I'm not going to tell you about my past boyfriends.'

'Fair enough, I suppose.' Alistair sighed and picked up the laminated menus which the waitress had left with them. 'I was hoping that I'd have to tell you about Suzannagh, the girl with the luscious lips and very large breasts, but I guess it'll have to wait.'

'I guess it will.' Ash grinned as she opened her menu.

The restaurant was almost full by the time Dan and Cordelia arrived. I'll go mad if we don't get a table, Dan thought, as he looked around the large candlelit room. He'd wanted to book Guilbaud's or Peacock Alley or somewhere equally upmarket to celebrate their first night back together. But Cordelia had wanted to come here – she'd liked it a lot, she said, the last time she'd come with some clients, it was noisy and fun and full of life. The one thing, she told Dan, that she actively disliked about corporate entertaining was the fact that she usually took people to boring but expensive places where you were supposed to worship at the shrine of the cooking. Shaun and Doug, the guys she'd taken to the Temple Bar restaurant, had wanted cheap and cheerful and had enjoyed it as much as she had. So, unless she had to, she told Dan, she wasn't going to go for upmarket when she could go for fun instead. He'd said fine, he'd book it, could she remember the number? Of course she couldn't, but she insisted that they go there anyway. They'd had a nightmare looking for parking and now it seemed unlikely they'd even get a table. Dan exhaled slowly as

313

he gazed around. It wouldn't matter, he told himself. There were hundreds of restaurants around Temple Bar. They wouldn't exactly starve.

A waitress looked at them pityingly when he said that they hadn't booked. She consulted a list and then smiled brightly at them.

'You're in luck. But I only have a table for an hour,' she told him.

'That's OK,' said Cordelia before Dan had the chance to respond.

'Great.' The waitress threaded her way through the already occupied tables and towards the back of the restaurant. 'For two,' she said.

'Thanks,' said Dan.

The tables were closely packed together. It irked Dan who preferred space, although he had to admit that this place had lots of atmosphere as well as a smoky, garlicky aroma which was making his mouth water.

He glanced at the table nearest them and opened his eyes wide in surprise. Ash O'Halloran and Alistair Brannigan were sitting opposite each other, oblivious of anyone else in their vicinity. She was laughing at whatever he was saying, her brown eyes dancing with merriment as she pushed her fingers through her hair. And Brannigan was looking at her in a way that Dan knew meant that he hoped to get her into bed very, very soon. The way he'd looked at her the night of the movie premiere when Ash had said they were just friends.

'Dan?' Cordelia touched him on the arm. 'You're staring!'

'What? Sorry.' He turned away from Ash and Alistair and looked at Cordelia. 'I was distracted.'

'So I see. Why?'

'Don't you recognise them?' asked Dan.

'No. Are they famous?'

'He is,' said Dan. 'And I'm surprised you don't recognise him since I know you owned a chunk of his stock.'

'Did I?' She looked at Dan, her eyes puzzled.

'Archangel,' he said. 'I remember you buying Archangel.'

'Oh, yes,' she breathed. 'Good old Archangel. I made a lot of money out of that company.'

'That's Alistair Brannigan, the former owner and now the managing director,' said Dan.

'And who's the bimbo with him?'

'You don't recognise her either?' asked Dan.

'No. Don't tell me she's the MD of the company that bought them or I'll puke. It's bad enough knowing that people the same age as me are making fortunes out of technology without them being good-looking too.'

Dan laughed. 'That's the chef,' he said.

'The chef?'

'Remember the night of our engagement dinner? Or what turned out to be our preliminary engagement discussion?'

'Of course!' Cordelia looked at Ash and back to Dan. 'She cooked for us. I remember now.' She raised her eyebrows. 'She looks better in civilian clothes.'

Dan grinned. 'I'll tell her you said so.'

'I wonder where the power lies in that relationship.'

315

'What do you mean?'

'Is she with him because he's rich and famous? Or is he with her because she's easy on the eye and can rustle up a mean steak and chips?'

'Cordelia!'

'It's a valid question,' she said. 'Give and take in relationships, that's what I always say.'

'And who's giving and taking in ours?' asked Dan.

'Oh, it's evenly balanced.' She leaned across the table and kissed him on the nose. 'Absolutely evenly balanced.'

It was when Cordelia leaned across the table that Ash noticed her. She was distracted by the movement and glanced towards the other table to see what was going on.

She recognised Cordelia immediately and her heart jumped because at first she didn't see Dan and the thought whizzed through her mind that maybe Cordelia was back in Dublin and she was without him and Ash wondered what that meant for his engagement. But she saw Dan as Cordelia settled back into her chair and Dan was able to see Ash looking at him. He nodded in recognition to her and raised his hand in a half-wave.

'Who's that?' asked Alistair, following her gaze.

'Dan Morland,' replied Ash. 'And his fiancée.'

'Dan? From Chatham's?'

Ash nodded.

'I didn't realise he was hitched.' Alistair ate his last

garlic mushroom. 'I got the impression he was single and happy about it.'

'How wrong those impressions can be.'

'She's not bad looking, is she?' asked Alistair. 'Very striking, in fact.'

'I think she's gorgeous.' Ash tried and failed to keep the envy out of her voice and Alistair laughed.

'What is it about women?' he asked. 'Here you are, a perfectly attractive woman with a natural hair colour that half of your so-called sisters would love to have, and you're wishing you looked like someone else.'

Ash made a face. 'People think you're thick when you're blonde,' she said. 'And I've always wanted to have masses of curly hair instead of this fine, straight stuff.'

'Never satisfied, that's your problem,' said Alistair. 'You don't see blokes worrying like that, do you?'

'That's because you all obviously think you're God's gift,' said Ash. 'Even though somewhere deep down in your psyche you're probably equally worried.'

'I'm perfectly happy with how I look.' Alistair patted his chest and Ash couldn't help smiling.

'That's because you look pretty good,' she told him. 'Much as it pains me to say it.'

He smiled too. 'Thank God! I was beginning to worry a bit but I couldn't let it show.'

What were they laughing about? wondered Dan. He didn't seem to laugh and joke with Cordelia the way Ash and Alistair were laughing and joking. Somehow his relationship with Cordelia was more – well, more mature, he supposed, although he wasn't certain that he liked the idea. It made him sound middle-aged and boring and he didn't want to be middle-aged and boring. Especially since Cordelia was young and not boring at all. She'd hate to think he was musing about the maturity of their relationship!

'He's very attractive, isn't he?' asked Cordelia.

'What?'

'Alistair. Very hunky.'

'Hunkier than me?'

'Younger than you, I'd say.'

'Gee, thanks.'

Cordelia giggled. 'Be still, my wounded heart! He is younger than you, isn't he?'

'Not much,' Dan protested. 'Three years, four years.'

'Really?' Cordelia looked surprised. 'Maybe it's just the way he dresses.'

'What about the way he dresses?'

'Very modern. Very stylish.'

'And I'm not?'

She giggled again. 'Dan, you're stylish in a stockbroker kind of way. He's stylish in a techno kind of way.'

'Why don't I think that's a good thing?' asked Dan.

'Don't be silly,' said Cordelia. 'I like the stockbroker kind of way.'

'Do you?'

'Of course,' she said as the waitress appeared with their food. 'I'm in financial services myself, aren't I?'

God, but she was sensational looking, thought Ash

enviously as she covertly observed Cordelia. She knew that Alistair didn't understand what she meant about Cordelia's good looks; to Alistair, good-looking women were pretty, and someone like Cordelia, with her strong features and piercing eyes, wasn't conventionally pretty. But she had a strength of character and determination in her face that Ash would have loved. As well as the tumbling chestnut locks.

'Wake up!' Alistair clicked his fingers under her nose as he sat down in his seat again following his visit to the men's room.

'Sorry,' said Ash. 'I was miles away.'

'Thinking about?'

She shook her head. 'Nothing really. Is Jodie singing tonight?'

'I don't know,' said Alistair. 'She has a wonderful voice, doesn't she?'

'Superb,' said Ash. 'It's such a shame that she hasn't been signed up yet.'

'That becomes more a matter of luck than anything else,' Alistair told her. 'It's rotten but true. Think of all those talentless people making heaps of money who can hardly hold a note but they were in the right place at the right time.'

'I know,' said Ash. 'When it comes down to it, a lot of life is about luck, one way or another. I mean, you think you're in control of things but you're not really.'

Alistair nodded. 'Selling Archangel was luck. At least, selling it when I did and how I did. Liking technology was luck too – now people feel they have to be involved even if they'd much rather be doing something else. It used to be fun to say you couldn't programme the video, now you'd be embarrassed to admit it.'

'I can programme the video,' Ash told him. 'Although I managed to delete one of my menu files on my computer the other day and I don't know how.'

'It's probably still there somewhere,' said Alistair. 'I'll look for it if you like.'

'Maybe.' Ash took a sachet of brown sugar and tore the strip off the top. Alistair watched her. She poured half the sachet into her coffee then propped it up against the narrow glass vase on the table.

'You don't want me to come to your apartment, do you?' he said.

She stirred the coffee. 'Not yet.'

'You've been in mine.'

Their eyes met, both remembering the pleasure that they'd given and received when she'd been in his apartment. Less pleasure for me, I think, Ash thought as she placed the spoon on the edge of her saucer. Less pleasure because I really wasn't ready to sleep with him even though I felt that the time was right.

'Did you fake it?' he asked.

She looked up at him, startled.

'You were good,' he said. 'I enjoyed it. But I wasn't sure about you.'

He was such a nice person, she thought. She liked him more than anyone else she'd ever gone out with. He was kind and he was thoughtful and there was something about him that made you care about him.

'Of course I didn't fake it,' she said. 'Why would I do that?'

'Who knows?'

'It was great,' she told him. 'Really it was.'

'And tonight?' he asked.

'What about tonight?'

'Would you like to come back to my apartment tonight? Given that you're obviously wary of me coming to yours.' He looked at her, his eyes twinkling with amusement.

'I'm not wary . . .' Her voice petered out. 'I just don't have people in my apartment very much. It's private space. You know.'

'Sure,' said Alistair lightly. 'So you'll come back to mine.'

She thought of Bagel curled up on the sofa at home. There was food in his bowl. He was OK.

'Great,' she said.

Dan scribbled his name on the credit card docket and added more than he meant to for the tip. But the food had been good and Cordelia had been right about the atmosphere so it was almost worth it. Except that their hour was nearly up and they had to give up the table. And he'd sworn that he'd reduce the tip because of having to give up the table.

They walked past Ash and Alistair who were both drinking brandies. He smiled at Ash and she smiled back at him. Then Alistair stood up and shook his hand.

'Nice to see you,' said Alistair. 'Meant to give you a call, Dan. I believe there's a company called Rodotronics about to come to the market. Know anything about it?'

Dan frowned. 'I haven't heard of it,' he admitted. 'But so many of them are launching these days—'

'It's an American company,' Cordelia interrupted. 'Well-run, well-managed. But it won't be launching until after the summer.'

Alistair turned towards her.

'Cordelia Carroll.' She extended her hand. 'I work for Harrison's in the US myself.'

'So you're really the one I should be talking to,' said Alistair. 'Do you know much about Rodotronics?'

'Actually very little,' admitted Cordelia. 'But I do know that their offering won't be before August. Which means it's likely to be September because nobody does anything in August.'

'Fair enough,' said Alistair. 'I'm interested in them.'

'I'll let you know if I hear anything,' said Cordelia. 'Although if my firm gets involved I can't talk about it.'

'No problem.' Alistair fished in the pocket of his jacket. 'Here's my card. Call me anytime.'

'Great, will do,' said Cordelia and smiled broadly at him.

'And how are you, Dan?' asked Ash.

'Fine,' he said. 'No change.'

'Doing any cooking in that kitchen of yours?'

He shook his head.

'Such a waste,' said Ash.

'It's bloody frightening if you ask me.' Cordelia turned

from Alistair to look at Ash. 'All that steel. All those cupboards.'

Ash laughed. 'All those empty cupboards. Or ones with tins of spice with best before nineteen ninety-five labels on them.'

'Really?' Cordelia looked at Dan.

'Probably,' Dan admitted.

'You've been in Dan's kitchen?' Alistair looked from Dan to Ash, puzzlement in his face.

'I cooked for him,' said Ash.

'At home?'

'For me,' Cordelia explained. 'The night Dan and I got engaged.'

'Ash told me that you two were engaged!' Alistair gripped Dan's arm and pumped his hand. 'Although,' he added as he kissed Cordelia on the cheek, 'it's a bit of a disappointment to see such a lovely girl as you hitch up to a reprobate like him.'

'Oh, we suit each other,' said Cordelia.

'Maybe.' Alistair sighed. 'But it's a shame all the same.'

'How about you and . . .'

'Ash,' said Ash.

'Oh, yes. Any chance of anything?'

'Cordelia!' Dan looked at her warningly.

'Oh, be quiet, Dan. I like finding out about people. Well?' she asked. 'Any chance of you two tying the knot? Multimillionaire and cook?'

Ash flushed. She didn't like the way Cordelia said the word 'cook' as though it was an insult. As if Cordelia would know anything about it. Ash got the impression that those stainless steel units in Dan's house would stay very much unused when Cordelia took up residence there.

'No,' she said flatly.

'We don't know each other that well yet,' said Alistair. 'But you never know, Cordelia. When Cupid's arrow strikes and all that sort of thing.'

'Oh, I wasn't even talking about love!' Cordelia laughed. 'I was talking about the suitability of the whole match. That's my job, you know. Putting companies that suit each other together. Synergy – you know that terrible word?'

Alistair laughed. 'And your company training tells you that Ash and I would make a good couple?'

'I think so.' She looked at him consideringly. 'Although you could always hitch up with me instead.'

'Cordelia!' This time Dan's voice held more of an edge but Cordelia simply smiled at him. 'I'm talking about it in a business sense, Dan,' she said. 'First option was multimillionaire and cook. But option two, multimillionaire and corporate banker – businesswise a much better opportunity.'

'You might be joking,' said Dan, 'but I don't think it's very funny.'

'Narky old sod.' Cordelia squeezed his arm.

'I'm sure you'd make a great couple whoever you were with,' Ash told Cordelia. 'I think you have the knack of being part of a couple.'

Cordelia narrowed her eyes and looked at Ash. 'I probably have,' she said. 'But you?' She furrowed her brow. 'Why do I think that you're more of a go-it-alone type of person?'

'Probably because I am,' admitted Ash.

'You see!' Cordelia beamed at them all.

'We'd better get going,' said Dan. 'You're tired from the flight, Cordelia. She got in from the States earlier,' he explained.

'You don't have to make excuses for me,' complained Cordelia. 'I'm perfectly all right.'

'You've had a bottle of wine and it's starting to catch up with you,' said Dan.

'I'm not drunk and I'm not tired,' said Cordelia.

'Anyway, we'd better get going.' Dan put his arm round her. 'Nice to see you again, Alistair. You too, Ash.'

'See you next week,' she told him. 'Partners' lunch.'

He nodded. 'See you then.'

'I'm not drunk and I'm not tired,' repeated Cordelia as they got outside and Dan steered her towards the car.

'It wasn't very tactful of you to start asking Ash and Alistair if they were getting engaged,' said Dan.

'Why not?'

'It's not the sort of thing you ask people,' said Dan.

'Oh, lighten up!' Cordelia yawned. 'He's nice, isn't he? But she's – there's something a little odd about her, don't you think?'

'Odd?' Dan glanced at Cordelia. 'What do you mean, odd?'

'As though she's looking right through you. As though she's not really listening to you. As though – oops.'

'Careful!' cried Dan as he grabbed Cordelia's arm. 'You nearly fell off the pavement, Cordelia. The wine is certainly catching up with you.'

'Maybe,' she admitted. 'I'm sorry, did I annoy you by talking to them in the restaurant?'

'Of course not,' said Dan.

'But you don't like the fact that I don't like the cook.'

'I don't care whether you like her or not,' said Dan.

Cordelia looked at him out of the corner of her eye. 'Sure you're not a bit taken by her yourself?' she asked. 'That pretty as a picture face? That helpless little me look?'

'She's not helpless,' said Dan.

'How do you know?'

'I've seen her in a kitchen with a meat cleaver,' he told her. 'It doesn't leave a helpless impression.'

'Maybe not.' But Cordelia didn't sound convinced.

Ash lay in Alistair's bed, her eyes open. He was asleep, his breathing slow and even. Their lovemaking had been fierce tonight, unlike the first time when Alistair had been slow and patient and had teased her and tortured her in a way that she'd quite enjoyed. But tonight he'd been rougher and quicker and afterwards he'd looked at her quizzically and asked her if she'd preferred it that way or the other way. And she hadn't been sure what to say because she hadn't bothered to fake it this time. She'd been wrong to fake it the last time.

She sighed deeply. How did you know, she wondered, when you truly loved someone? It was so easy for people and magazines to say that you just would, and maybe when you were twenty or twenty-one you'd experience a 'just would' kind of feeling. But by twenty-nine you'd experienced lots of different emotions and it was almost unbelievable to imagine that there was one that 'just was'. She cared about Alistair. She couldn't help caring about Alistair. She wanted to love him. But she didn't know what being in love was supposed to feel like. And if she loved him and he didn't love her then she'd get hurt, wouldn't she? And she was scared of being hurt, scared that she wouldn't be able to get over it.

But if I don't love him, she said to herself as she stared at the ceiling, but just care about him, wouldn't that be a better relationship? That way, neither of us would get hurt.

The magazines really didn't tell you much about not being in love. They were good with unrequited love, with how to make someone love you, with how to turn yourself into an irresistible sex goddess, but they didn't tell you how to be twenty-nine and not be afraid any more.

Chapter 19

Antipasti
Tuna in oil, Italian salami, prosciutto, anchovy fillets,
artichoke hearts, green and black olives, pimientos, toma-
toes, peppers

Spring came in April. One morning when Ash woke
up she realised that the city breezes were from the
south, the air was warmer and the clouds in the skies
were soft white puffs rather than grim grey blocks. The
smell from the river was stronger and more pungent too
but she could put up with that. She liked the city when it
was warm, even when the diesel fumes of the buses hung
in the atmosphere.

It wasn't warm enough for that yet, she thought as she
opened the kitchen window and Bagel jumped through,
but maybe it would be another hot summer. Two in a
row! Almost unheard of.

Bagel purred as he ate, his body a round mass of quivering
silver-grey fur. Ash watched him for a moment then she
went into the living room and switched on her computer.

Today was a free day even though it was Wednesday. She liked having the occasional free day during the week, although if it happened too often she began to panic and wonder whether or not she was losing her touch, whether anyone would ever book her again. Usually when that happened she took far too many bookings for the following weeks until she could hardly wait for a free day again. Although she wasn't cooking today she did have some work to do because she was calling over to Dan Morland's house this evening to discuss plans for his wedding reception. He'd insisted that she come despite the fact that she'd already told him that she didn't think she'd be able to help. She'd repeated to him that the occasional weddings she'd catered for in the past had been extremely low-key with a small number of guests. Even with the backup of other chefs she knew, Ash didn't have the resources to deal with big events and she didn't really enjoy them. She preferred things smaller and more intimate. She'd been surprised when Dan asked her about it because she'd felt certain that Cordelia would have wanted a huge bash with an extensive guest list in an upmarket hotel. But Dan said no, that Cordelia wasn't interested in huge traditional weddings and that she wanted something more understated but meaningful.

It was usually when both couples were in their thirties that they wanted understated and meaningful, thought Ash as she looked through her menus. From what she knew, couples in their twenties wanted the day to be fun and they didn't much care about the food once there was plenty of it and plenty of drink to go round too. When they got past twenty-nine, things were different. Then they were more into antipasti, selected poetry readings and thoughtful quotes on the menus. What would Cordelia consider a thoughtful quote? Ash wondered. Happy Ever After would probably be the most appropriate. Despite the rocky start to their engagement and the fact that Cordelia had spent most of it on the other side of the Atlantic, it had clearly worked out for her.

And for me? She sat back in her chair. What's the quote for me and Alistair?

They were an official couple these days, she supposed, because they went out every week together and they'd been invited, as a couple, to the Seniors Tennis Tour which had taken place in Dublin the previous month. Chatham's had issued the invitations and she'd been placed beside Ross Fearon, which demonstrated that her status with the stockbroking company had changed. Ash noticed that people were somehow respectful of her when she was with Alistair, something that was both amusing and annoying. Kate Coleman had practically fawned over both of them in a way that she had never fawned over Ash before. Dan Morland hadn't been at the tennis. He'd gone to New York to spend a long weekend with Cordelia.

The day had been fun, John McEnroe had lost his temper (as hoped), much to the enjoyment of the crowd and the irritation of his opponent, and afterwards about twenty of them had gone to Señor Sassis for something to eat. Alistair had kept them entertained with scary stories about technology that didn't work and was never going to work and the companies that were keeping it a secret.

He was fun to be with. Sometimes Ash went back to his house after an evening out (he'd sold the apartment and bought a five-bedroomed detached home in Clonskeagh for a breathtaking amount of money after she'd given it her seal of approval), sometimes they went their separate ways. But he'd always leave an e-mail for her the following morning telling her what a good night it had been, and she felt that he cared about her.

She cared about him too. She was concerned when he was anxious about his business because she understood his anxiety. She was happy when things were going well for him because she understood that too. And she was getting used to going out with him almost every Friday night. It wasn't as stifling as it had been with Brendan or as intense as it had been with Kieran or as boring as it had been with any of the others. But he hadn't been to her apartment yet and he'd stopped asking. He probably thinks I have some dark secret hidden here, which I'm terrified of him discovering. And, she thought as Bagel jumped up onto her lap and scratched her thighs with his claws, he might be right.

She printed out some menus and flicked through her contacts list to see who might be available later in the summer to help her if she did agree to get involved in the reception. Then she closed the list again because it would all depend on how many people Dan and Cordelia were inviting to their understated and meaningful wedding and there was no point in worrying

331

about it until she had a better idea of what their plans were.

She stood up and Bagel leaped from her lap with an accusing look.

'I'm sorry,' she told him. 'But I have to go out.' He jumped onto the back of the sofa and began to wash his face. 'And you're in charge,' she told him as she checked that the computer was properly powered-down and that the sockets were switched off.

There was a part of her that now felt these rituals were even sillier than before. A part of her that knew that nothing terrible would happen if she accidentally left the immersion heater on or the tap dripping or – horror of horrors – the towels crumpled up in a heap on the floor. But the thought always nagged her that if she didn't do these things and something terrible did happen then it would be all her own fault. And it was easier to follow them and feel confident than not follow them and spend the whole time worrying.

She took her pale cream gilet from the wardrobe and slipped it on over her long-sleeved T-shirt. Today she wasn't going to worry about anything. She wanted to check out some of the kitchenware shops in the city to buy a few bits and pieces. Kitchenware shops were the only ones that Ash actively enjoyed wandering around and spending money in, which she knew that most people would think was particularly pathetic.

She thought about her job situation as she walked along the quays. Jodie had shown her an advertisement the previous week for a chef to work on a cruise ship.

'Wouldn't it be fantastic?' Jodie had asked, her eyes shining. 'Spending your time in the Med or the Caribbean and doing something you really enjoy?'

But Ash had shaken her head. She couldn't think of anything more awful than being in a steaming kitchen in a hot climate feeding hordes of hungry tourists. And she'd heard that life on board those cruise liners wasn't so great for the staff – all the decent accommodation went to the paying guests. I couldn't, she thought, sleep in a crummy little bunk even if I was cruising around the West Indies.

She walked around by Trinity College and up Grafton Street. A pavement artist was outlining a picture of the college in chalk while a juggler threw some glittering silver clubs into the air and a young man, dressed in jeans and T-shirt, offered to give tarot readings to passers-by for a mere fiver.

A fiver to know what the future held. Ash was almost tempted but walked by. She didn't want to know about the future, the idea was too scary. If the future was something she didn't like, she certainly didn't want to know about it now. She bought a new zester and some stainless steel napkin holders as well as a dozen scented candles. She couldn't understand how it was that she could happily spend time browsing in kitchen shops but got the shakes in clothes shops. All the same, she gritted her teeth and bought a couple of summer tops and a contrasting wraparound skirt in Vero Moda on her way back down Grafton Street. Then she went into Bewley's for a cup of frothy coffee and a sticky bun.

She hadn't breakfasted much in Bewley's since her break-up with Brendan. The last few times she'd sat in the café she'd just felt guilty about him and inadequate about herself. She'd looked at the couples around her and wondered if she'd ever manage to get her act together enough to be like them. And she'd remembered her panic attack afterwards and had almost panicked again. Now, though, she was beginning to feel better. In fact, she thought, it was a while since she'd really panicked and had one of those moments when she was sure that her heart would burst because it was beating so quickly or felt certain that she would faint because her head was so light. Maybe she was turning into a normal person. One with a steady boyfriend who loved her and whom she loved too. Maybe.

She finished her coffee and bun then strolled back to her apartment and sat by the window while she browsed through a recipe book she'd picked up in the Dublin Bookshop. She didn't really need yet another recipe book but this one was all about cooking vegetables and, with more and more of her clients giving up meat, Ash felt that she could do with some new vegetable ideas.

At six o'clock she stepped under the shower for a quick splash and changed into the new plum-coloured top and wraparound skirt. She dusted some bronzer onto her face and some tinted lip balm on her lips, gathered up her notebook and menu cards and went outside to hail a cab. She'd told Dan that she'd be at his house sometime between six thirty and seven. She knew that, in off-peak times, a car could get to Rathgar from her apartment in less than ten minutes. But it was hard to judge what was off-peak in the city any more.

She arrived at exactly a quarter to seven which she was comfortable with. She paid the driver, slung her camel-coloured bag over her shoulder and walked up the footpath.

'Hi, Ash.' Dan smiled at her as he opened the door, a bottle of Miller in his hand. 'I was just sitting in the conservatory grabbing the last of the sun.'

'I missed the conservatory last time I was here,' said Ash.

'It's off the living room at the back,' Dan explained. 'Like lots of things in this house, it needs to be replaced, really, but it catches the evening rays brilliantly. Want a drink?'

'Why not?' she asked as she followed him.

'Through that door.' He pointed the way to her. 'I'll just get you a beer. Beer is OK, isn't it? Or would you prefer something else?'

She shook her head. 'Beer's fine.'

The conservatory was small and didn't have many flowers. Ash supposed that Dan wasn't a flower person – how could he be when he was a city suit. She sat in one of the old wicker chairs and looked out over the garden which was long and narrow and rather overgrown. It didn't have very many flowers either. She thought of Alistair's garden in Clonskeagh where he'd hired a landscape gardener to transform it into a show garden almost overnight.

'Needs to be tidied up a bit.' Dan nodded at the garden

as he walked into the room and handed her a bottle. 'Cheers.'

'Cheers.' She took a sip of the beer. 'I think it's nice. Not too fussy.'

'Thanks. But I know it needs a lot more work.'

'Not much.' Ash shrugged. 'As they say – it has loads of potential.'

'Oh, God.' Dan grinned at her. 'They said that about the house too. Potential always means borrowing huge amounts of money to make somewhere barely habitable.'

Ash giggled. 'It's more than barely habitable now. It's lovely. And Cordelia is very lucky to be marrying you and moving in here.'

'Thanks again,' said Dan. 'I keep telling her that but she doesn't believe me.'

'I'm sure she does.'

'So what do you think?' asked Dan.

'Of what?' she looked at him in puzzlement.

'Of here. For the reception.'

'Oh, right.' Ash looked round her again.

'I thought we could have it in the garden and people could come in here if they were cold. You know.'

'If you really want an outdoor thing in Ireland you have to think of cold being the more likely weather scenario,' Ash told him. 'If people are cold it doesn't matter how nice everything else is, they're totally miserable.'

'You're right.' Dan nodded. 'I remember we had a do out in Powerscourt one year. The day before was beautiful but the day we held it was cloudy and chilly. I hated it.'

'How many people?' asked Ash.

'That's the thing,' said Dan. 'We don't want anything over the top. Say sixty or seventy. I don't think I could cope with more here anyway.'

Ash rubbed her forehead. 'Then I definitely don't think I can help you, Dan. That's way too many for me. I'm not a caterer, you see. I'm a chef. There's a lot of work involved in weddings – flowers and place settings and all that sort of thing and it's really not what I do best.'

'Rubbish,' said Dan. 'You did a brilliant job of the dining room the night I proposed to Cordelia. If proposed was the right word for the way it turned out.'

Ash smiled. 'It turned out fine. And the room was good but that was because I knew what I was doing and it was, after all, for only two people. Seventy is a different thing altogether.'

'It's just . . .' Dan frowned. 'I'd like you to do it. I feel as though we're friends and I like to give business to friends.'

'You'd be handing me a nightmare,' she told him frankly. 'I wouldn't be much of a friend if I said I could do all this for you when I couldn't.'

'But I thought you said you had people who helped you for bigger events.'

'I do,' said Ash. 'But it depends on what those events are. Sometimes we do food after presentations – you know, where people have a splash of chilli or Stroganoff and some rice – but this is too much, Dan, and I don't want to be responsible for wrecking your big day.' She took a mouthful of beer. 'To be honest I guessed it'd be too big for me but I didn't like to say no before talking to you.'

'I understand. And you did say so before.' Dan sighed. 'I suppose I was trying to do things the easy way.'

'Doesn't Cordelia have preferences?' asked Ash.

'She's left it all up to me,' said Dan. 'And don't tell me how bloody unusual that is because I know. Even with the massive amount of role reversals going on in business and family life these days I still always thought women were the ones who were meant to go demented over their big day. I didn't realise I was marrying someone who'd just swan in at the last minute to say I do.'

Ash laughed. 'I think it's great! No fuss, no bother, just turn up looking good.'

Dan sighed. 'Just so long as she does turn up.'

'Of course she will!' cried Ash.

'I know,' said Dan. 'I just get nervous about it sometimes.'

'She probably went to the States to get out of all the work,' said Ash.

'Maybe.' Dan smiled at her.

'Sure she did,' said Ash. 'She's a smart lady.'

'So smart she terrorises me sometimes.'

'I can't see anyone terrorising you.'

'You don't know me very well,' said Dan darkly. 'Lots of people terrorise me.'

'Me too,' confessed Ash.

'Just as well we're both with strong partners, I guess.' He drained his bottle of Miller. 'Will you have another with me?'

'OK.'

'Come into the house,' he said. 'It's getting a bit cool out here.'

They went to the living room and Ash sat down on the deep sofa.

'Do you think it's odd?' Dan handed her another Miller.

'What?'

'Me and Cordelia and our long-distance engagement.'

'Not really,' said Ash. 'I suppose it's a bit unusual but she probably got a shock when you asked her – she obviously hadn't thought about it, especially if she'd been considering the States. But I think it's all worked out well for you. She gets her six months, comes home, gets married – everything according to plan!'

'As you might have gathered, she'll be there longer than six months,' said Dan gloomily. 'Because of the project she was working on. She's only just started the training course she was actually meant to start before Christmas. So she'll only arrive home in time for the damned wedding. July is the earliest she'll get home and it might even be August.'

'Does that bother you?' asked Ash.

He shrugged. 'It did but not now. I've come around to the idea.'

'Well, she's getting what she wants and she'll be happier

339

as a result,' said Ash. 'And it's such a short time in the whole scheme of things.'

'I know,' said Dan. 'I see that now but I didn't before.' He smiled. 'Will you just decide to run up the aisle one day in between doing lunches?'

'I don't know if I'll ever get married,' said Ash.

'Not even to the Technology King?' Dan looked surprised. 'I thought you and he were a permanent fixture on the social circuit these days.'

Ash wrinkled her nose. 'You saw that picture of us in the *Irish Times* I suppose?'

He laughed. 'Looked good.'

'They only wanted photos of him,' said Ash. 'And I truly didn't want to go to the opening of whatever wine bar it was. It's not really my sort of thing. But Alistair knew the owner and he'd promised.'

'He'll be setting you up in a place of your own soon.'

'No,' said Ash.

'Wouldn't you like it? Your own restaurant? Isn't that what all chefs want?'

Ash shook her head. 'Not me.'

'What do you want?' he asked.

'I've no idea.'

They sat in silence while she played with the ends of her plait and Dan sipped his beer. She wasn't going to break the silence, he realised. She was the sort of girl who could sit without speaking for as long as it took.

'Do you mind if I ask you a personal question?' he asked eventually.

'No.'

'Do you ever wonder about your father?'

Ash looked at him in surprise. 'That's a *very* personal question.'

'I know,' he said. 'Don't answer if you don't want to. I was thinking about families before you arrived – I guess you do when you're about to get married. And I just wondered about you.'

'I don't think about him at all,' said Ash. 'To me, he's a biological incident in my past.'

'I thought that everyone needed to know.'

'It depends.' Ash shrugged. 'I don't.' She laughed suddenly. 'I have enough trouble with Julia's side of the family without discovering anyone else!'

Dan laughed too and the tension that had grown between them suddenly disappeared again. 'I suppose if you've lived with your aunt and uncle and cousins since you were a kid they are your family.'

She nodded. 'Although, to be honest, I've never grown really close to any of the Rourkes. I thought I would but, in a lot of ways, they're quite different to me.'

'How many of them?'

'Four other kids. It seemed like hordes to me.'

'It'd be difficult moving into that when you were an only child yourself.'

'Julia's only child,' corrected Ash. 'God only knows who else was sired by my biological father.'

'And how do they feel about you and the Technology King?'

'They want me to rush him up the aisle as quickly as possible.' Ash grinned at him.

'But you don't want to?'

'I'm not that good with relationships.' Ash drank some more beer and pulled at her plait again. 'It takes me time. I get flustered by them. I don't like being too involved with anyone too quickly.'

'I know exactly how you feel,' said Dan. 'It's how I felt myself.'

'Which is why the K Club was strewn with former girlfriends?'

'Something like that,' he said. 'And is the rest of Dublin strewn with your former boyfriends?'

'Strewn is probably too strong a word,' said Ash. 'But there's a few of them about.'

'Do you think that you might settle down with Alistair?' Dan asked.

'Perhaps.'

'And, if he offers to buy a restaurant for you, you might even say yes?'

'Do you know something I don't?' asked Ash. 'What's with the restaurant thing? I haven't discussed restaurants with him.'

'No, I just thought you might like it. Get some recognition for yourself.'

She shook her head. 'Maybe I'll write a cookbook or something instead.'

'Great idea!'

'Actually, not,' she said. 'I could never be precise enough for a cookbook. You have to measure things out for recipes and I tend not to. I look at them and make adjustments by throwing my own stuff in.'

Dan leaned back in his chair and put his hands behind his head. 'You know, that's not how I think of you.'

'What do you mean?'

'Throwing things into the cooking. I think of you as being precise. Organised. Exact.'

She smiled. 'Mostly, that's how I am.'

'You see!' He grinned. 'I bet you arrange the towels neatly on the towel rail in the mornings. And I bet your bathroom cabinet never has any stray hairs lurking in it, or any best before last year bottles of cough syrup congealing on the shelves.'

Ash squirmed uncomfortably and Dan watched her in amusement.

'You look so neat,' he told her. 'It had to be the case.'

'Oh, well . . .'

'Your form of rebellion,' he reminded her.

She pulled at the label on the beer bottle. 'I know.'

'When my parents split up I used to spend my days tidying the house,' said Dan.

Ash looked at him in surprise.

'One day my mother yelled at my father that she couldn't live in the kind of house he lived in, in the state he lived in, the way he lived.' Dan shrugged. 'She left him and took us with her.'

'Us?'

'Me and Bronwyn. My twin. We were nine.'

'Oh.'

'Of course a messy house wasn't the reason she left at all. But I thought that if the house became untidy she'd

343

leave us too.' Dan's mouth twisted. 'It seemed logical at the time.'

'It was perfectly logical,' said Ash. She drained the bottle of Miller and Dan got out of the chair.

'One for the road?' he asked.

She glanced at her watch. After eight o'clock. But she'd nothing to do, she might as well be here. She nodded.

'What did your father work at?' she asked when he returned with the beer. 'Was he a DIY person or something that the place was untidy?'

Dan sighed. 'No. Not DIY. You might have heard of my father.'

'Really?' Ash looked surprised.

'Joss Morland.' Dan said it with the air of someone who was bored with the name.

'Joss Morland! The writer?' Ash looked at him in amazement. 'The one who writes about that female detective? The Italian one?'

Dan nodded. 'Vanna Savino.'

'They've made a TV series out of those books!' cried Ash. 'I watched them every Sunday during the winter.'

Dan nodded again.

'He's mega successful.'

'I know,' said Dan. 'But he was a shit father and a shit husband. Which is probably why I was so bloody wary of the whole thing.'

Ash bit her lip.

'He didn't mean to be, of course,' said Dan. 'But he lived in a world of his own. He was obsessed with that bloody Savino woman. To him, she was more real than me, or Bronwyn or my mother. Everything in the day depended on how Vanna was feeling, how Vanna was getting on. We all lived according to Vanna.'

'I never made the connection,' said Ash.

'Why would you?'

'I like Vanna Savino books.' Ash looked defensively at him. 'They're clever.'

'Of course they are,' said Dan. 'They're quite brilliant. I like them too. But that wasn't much use to us then.'

'And now?' asked Ash.

'I see him more now. I understand him more. Sometimes my mother understands him too.'

'What does she do?'

'She's works for an estate agent,' said Dan. 'Most of the time she's happy.'

Ash smiled. 'That's good.'

'But Dad wasn't good for her. He believed he could do anything because he was an "artist". Other women, for starters!' Dan snorted. 'Just because he did some brilliant stuff didn't mean that he was exempt from the normal rules of behaviour although he reckoned he was. Mum had to leave him in the end. She's had some men in her life since then but it's like she's connected to Dad by some kind of invisible thread. He can still upset her.'

'Does she see him that often?'

'A couple of times a year. Actually . . .' Dan looked at Ash speculatively. 'I've just had an idea. Since you can't do the wedding there's something else that you could do instead and I think it would be great.'

'What?' she asked warily.

'You could do the end-of-book dinner.'

'The end-of-book dinner?'

'When Dad finishes a book we all get together and celebrate. We did it after his third book and it was his breakthrough. So now it's a tradition for good luck. Our one and only family tradition! Until the third book, Vanna Savino was an OK seller but *Antipasti* was huge.'

'Hadn't you left him by then?' asked Ash. 'Surely after three books . . .'

Dan nodded. 'Yes, but after the third, Mum and Dad were going through their sophisticated separation period. They were speaking to each other and it was all terribly civilised. It hasn't always been as civilised since then but Dad feels that it's something he has to do now. He's dreadfully superstitious about things like that. And Mum keeps up the tradition because it makes him happy. And, after all, he still pays her alimony. Guilt money, as she likes to call it.'

'Your dad should've known my mother,' said Ash. 'Julia was terribly superstitious too. She had piles of lucky and unlucky things.'

'Don't you have anything lucky?'

'No,' said Ash. She certainly wasn't going to tell Dan about her insane rituals before she left the apartment every day. They weren't lucky, it was just that not to fulfil them was unlucky. Quite, quite different, she thought.

'Oh, well, Dad likes to do this. It's the one time we all get together.'

'Well, I – when d'you think it would be?' she asked.

'Soon,' Dan said. 'I was talking to him a couple of

weeks ago and he reckons by the end of May.' His face fell. 'I suppose that means it's unlikely Cordelia will be there because I can't see her getting the time off. I'm going over to visit her again soon, though. Maybe I can persuade her.' He smiled again. 'You will do it, won't you?'

Ash frowned. 'I suppose—'

'It'll be great fun!' Dan was full of enthusiasm. 'We're always talking about having it at the villa instead of going out to a restaurant and this time we can.'

'The villa?' Ash looked at him inquiringly. 'Where does he live? Not in Spain, surely. You wouldn't bring me to Spain simply to cook dinner, would you?'

Dan shook his head. 'No. Of course not. Dad hates Spain. Anyway, he goes there for the atmosphere and Spain would be the wrong atmosphere. Obviously.'

'And where is *there*, exactly?' asked Ash.

'Sorry. I thought you'd realised.' Dan grinned at her. 'It's in Sicily. Vanna Savino is actually Sicilian. He thought that would make her more interesting.'

Chapter 20

Garlic Mushrooms in Filo Pastry
Olive oil, chopped onion, garlic cloves, button mushrooms,
pepper, soft cheese, melted butter, filo pastry
Cook onion and garlic in oil, add mushrooms and pepper.
Drain excess juice, add cheese and stir until cheese has
melted. Allow to cool. Place cooked filling into corner of
pastry and fold into triangle. Brush with melted butter.
Bake until golden brown

Cordelia went to the Nail Bar Express at lunchtime. When she'd first come to the States she was surprised at how perfectly manicured so many of the women were. Nobody seemed to have short nails or broken nails or nails with chipped varnish. It was only later that she realised that most of them were sporting false nails. They were a good idea for women like her, Cordelia realised, because when she was worried or thinking about a problem in the office she would pick at her natural nails and break them and then have to file them down to almost nothing. There was no point, she knew, in looking glamorous yet businesslike and having bitten nails. So it was very convenient to drop into the Nail Bar and have someone kit her out with a perfect set whenever she needed them.

She needed them tonight because the bank was having celebration cocktails following the successful rescue of UpperCut. It would be the first time that Cordelia had been on the thirty-third floor and she was looking forward to it. Since most of the senior staff would be there it was important that she made a good impression. It certainly justified a full manicure, she thought, as she pushed open the glass door. She'd also blown almost a month's salary on her newest Calvin Klein suit.

'Oh, sorry!' She almost collided with the woman coming out and then stepped back in surprise as she realised that it was her boss, Melissa.

'Hi, Cordelia.' Melissa smiled at her. 'Getting ready for tonight?'

'Yes,' Cordelia replied.

Melissa glanced at her watch. 'You do know that we have a meeting at two fifteen?'

'Absolutely,' said Cordelia. 'I'll be there.'

'Fine.' Melissa waved her scarlet-tipped fingers at Cordelia and disappeared up the street.

Cordelia looked at her watch. It was only twelve thirty and she had plenty of time to get her nails done. Melissa was just staking out her territory, letting Cordelia know who was in charge. Melissa was good at that, she thought ruefully. Despite the fact that she tried not to be intimidated by her, Cordelia was in awe of the older, very successful, woman.

She sat down at one of the little tables and held out her hand while the Vietnamese manicurist took an emery board from the stack beside her and began to file Cordelia's nails. She felt her mind shifting from a work mentality to a rest mentality. It was difficult to think of mergers and acquisitions while someone was working on your hands.

She'd make sure she had a nice set of extra long nails for the wedding. Dan was utterly entranced with the idea of marrying during the late summer and having the reception in his garden. Cordelia liked the idea too – although she'd suggested to Dan that he buy some tubs of flowers to brighten it up. And cut the grass. And trim the hedges.

He'd e-mailed her his revised guest list that morning which had brought the numbers up a little bit more. They'd originally talked of about fifty people but suddenly old friends and family were appearing out of the woodwork and it was difficult to keep numbers low. It would be hard to keep the event as sophisticated and elegant as she wanted if there were hordes of people milling around the place. They had seventy-eight on the list at the moment and Cordelia felt that it was more than enough.

Very fortunately, Dan's favourite chef had refused to do the catering. Cordelia was extremely relieved at that; she hadn't been in the slightest bit enthusiastic about the idea that Ash would be involved. The girl might be a professional chef, but that didn't mean she could do a spectacular meal for seventy-eight people. At least she'd had the decency to say no, thought Cordelia, as she watched the manicurist dab some of the acrylic mixture for the new nails onto her old ones. There was no way one person could deal with a wedding for nearly eighty and she'd said that to Dan herself but he hadn't listened.

He seemed to have a soft spot for the blonde-haired brown-eyed cook. Cordelia didn't know why because Ash wasn't the sort of person that she thought Dan would normally be attracted to. At the thought that he might actually be attracted to Ash, she jerked her hand and the manicurist clicked her tongue in irritation while she repaired the damage that the movement had caused.

'Sorry,' said Cordelia.

'Keep your hand still,' the other girl told her.

'Sure.'

He wasn't attracted to Ash O'Halloran, Cordelia knew that. She'd asked him about her the day after they'd met Ash and Alistair in the Temple Bar restaurant.

'I like her,' Dan had said. 'She's so cool and efficient but she's had a difficult childhood and I think she's kind of a softie at heart.'

'You're the softie,' she said. 'Worrying about the cook's childhood!'

'It's not like that.' He kissed her.

'Besides,' Cordelia smiled up at him, 'she's going out with a multimillionaire.'

'Indeed she is.'

And he'd sighed then, as though he was somehow disappointed in Ash for going out with a multimillionaire.

351

She'd said that to him and he'd laughed and told her, no, he was simply disappointed that he wasn't a multimillionaire himself. And then she'd told him not to worry, that she would be the multimillionaire in the family.

Which she might be, she told herself. If she worked hard and stayed alert to the opportunities around her there was no reason for her not to climb the corporate ladder and knock Melissa Kravich and any of the others off their perches. It wouldn't exactly be easy to knock Melissa anywhere, she admitted. The older woman had a good network of friends and colleagues. Cordelia doubted that anyone actually liked Melissa although she had a reputation for being fair. Cordelia wondered how the other woman had managed to build up such a reputation when she herself knew that Melissa could sometimes be incredibly unfair. Like the time when the invitations to the Knicks versus Boston Celtics game at Madison Square Garden had come onto Cordelia's desk and Melissa had spotted them and nabbed them for herself.

'You don't mind, do you?' she'd asked Cordelia. 'It's just that Al is such a Knicks fan.'

She didn't mind but that wasn't the point. Melissa and Al had gone to the game with some clients that Cordelia had wanted to meet. And Cordelia didn't think that was fair even though the only basketball team she'd ever heard of was the Harlem Globetrotters, and that only because of the cartoon show on TV.

The lights from the overhead rail caught her engagement ring as the manicurist turned her attention to Cordelia's left hand.

'Lovely ring,' she said.

'Thank you.'

'When are you getting married?'

'Later in the summer.'

'It will be very hot.' The girl looked up from Cordelia's nails.

'I'll be marrying at home,' Cordelia told her. 'In Ireland. It won't be hot there.'

'I have some family in Ireland,' said the manicurist. 'They moved there when we left Vietnam. They live in Clare. Do you know it?'

Cordelia nodded. 'It's a nice place.'

'They say so.' The girl tapped Cordelia's nails with the thin handle of the fine brush to check if the false nails had hardened properly. 'Is your fiancé American or Irish?'

'Irish,' said Cordelia.

'He works here?'

She shook her head. 'Back home.'

'You miss him?'

'I don't have time.' Cordelia smiled. 'I've been really busy.'

'I'd miss him,' said the manicurist. 'I wouldn't like to be away from my boyfriend.'

'We love each other,' said Cordelia. 'It doesn't matter how far apart we are.'

The manicurist looked at her sceptically.

'Really,' said Cordelia.

'Which colour?' The girl pointed to a row of bottles. Cordelia looked at the varnishes. Not scarlet, she thought, since Melissa had gone for scarlet. And not pink because it was a pale and insipid shade. There was a rather nice green which Cordelia thought would look very dramatic but she wasn't sure that she should be too dramatic on her first visit to the upper echelons of the bank. So she chose a less vibrant red than Melissa, even though she would have preferred the scarlet.

'You going anywhere nice tonight?' The manicurist shook the bottle vigorously.

'Work do,' said Cordelia.

'You work in Harrison's, don't you?'

Cordelia nodded.

'I have shares in Harrison's.' The manicurist smiled. 'It's a good bank.'

'I'm glad you think so.'

'Oh, absolutely. Lots of nice people work there. You'll do well.'

'I hope so,' said Cordelia.

'You will.' She deftly painted Cordelia's nails with the red varnish while Cordelia wondered if the girl told everyone the same story. There were hundreds of banks around Wall Street. If the manicurist had shares in them all she was a very wealthy lady!

She sat and waited for the varnish to dry although it was difficult for her to sit still once the job had been done. Cordelia knew that she was an impatient person but experience had told her that you couldn't be patient in business. You had to close the deal and get the job done as quickly as you could. Which was why she was so pleased that the UpperCut deal had worked out. She'd cut a few corners to bring her part of it to fruition and she'd been worried that it would all go horribly wrong but it had worked perfectly in the end. It had renewed her confidence in herself and her career with Harrison's and meant that she felt good about meeting the head honchos on the thirty-third floor tonight.

As she stood in the lift (elevator, she reminded herself) she hoped that she'd manage to meet the important people in the bank and not a crowd of middle-management wannabes. It was sometimes difficult to get talking to the right people at this sort of event and there was nothing worse than being stuck in a group of no-hopers while someone else chatted with the people who really mattered.

'Nervous?' DeVere's brown eyes twinkled at her.

'Nope.'

'You should be,' said Shayla Kroenig. 'Our esteemed CEO will be there today and he's not an easy man to get on with.'

'I can get along with anyone,' said Cordelia, 'but he's not likely to talk to us, is he?'

'He'll talk to me,' said DeVere. 'My aunt delivered his daughter.'

Cordelia raised her eyebrows. 'Does he know that?'

'Not yet.' DeVere grinned. 'But he will.'

Typical, thought Cordelia bitterly, DeVere always seemed to have some kind of advantage over her.

The lift sighed its way up through the building. Cordelia watched the floor numbers tick away. Her department, mergers and acquisitions, was on the twelfth floor.

'I like your nails,' Shayla remarked. 'They look good. I wish I'd had time to pop out myself.'

'Thanks.' Cordelia extended her left hand where her sapphire and diamond ring glowed under the lights of the elevator.

'Did you see Melissa's?' asked DeVere. 'Absolute talons!'

'She was leaving the Nail Bar when I arrived,' said Cordelia. 'She warned me not to be late for our meeting at two fifteen.'

DeVere laughed. 'No way Melissa's going to pass up the opportunity to make you nervous!'

'She doesn't make me nervous,' said Cordelia as the lift stopped at the thirty-third floor and she stepped out.

The thirty-third floor was quite unlike the rest of the bank's offices which were comfortable but utilitarian. The lobby area in front of the lift was square, with light wood panelling and a thick pale-green carpet flecked with a gold motif. The lighting was subdued and came from occasional lamps beside leather armchairs. A huge glass coffee table took up a large portion of the space – on it were various banking magazines. In addition there were two leatherbound books, one the history of the bank, the other the biography of its founder, Arthur J. Harrison. A security man, dressed in navy uniform, pointed them in the direction of the boardroom. As they walked along the short corridor even DeVere was suddenly reduced to silence by the opulence of his surroundings. I want to be part of this, thought Cordelia. I want an office on the thirty-third floor.

A waiter stood outside the boardroom. He opened the door and allowed them inside.

There were more people there than Cordelia had expected. The room was more than three-quarters full, making it difficult to cross it and stand at the windows to look over the city that never sleeps. Cordelia took a glass of red wine from one of the waitresses who were standing around with laden trays.

'Cordelia!' Melissa Kravich waved at her. 'Cordelia, this is Earl Winter, he's one of our executive vice presidents.'

'Hi, Earl.' Cordelia shook his hand.

'Earl looks after our private client department,' said Melissa who almost immediately waved at someone else and left Cordelia and Earl standing together.

Bitch, thought Cordelia. Private clients wasn't a department that Cordelia was interested in. And Earl wasn't someone who was important enough for her to waste her time talking to. Which was why Melissa had dumped him on her so expertly.

She wasted almost ten minutes with Earl before murmuring an excuse and walking away from him. Ten minutes was enough, she reckoned, not to appear incredibly rude just in case Earl ever did amount to much in Harrison's scheme of things.

She grabbed another glass of wine from one of the passing waitresses and deliberately caught Melissa's eye again. The other woman was talking to a tall, well-dressed (but weren't they all) man who Cordelia reckoned was in his late thirties or early forties. His brown hair was flecked with grey and he wore large-rimmed glasses which had been fashionable about a year earlier but were now a little passé.

'Hello again, Melissa,' she said as she joined them and was rewarded by a flicker of irritation in Melissa's eyes.

'Cordelia. This is Mike Fuller.' Melissa made the introduction. 'He's one of our executive VPs.'

The same rank as Earl, thought Cordelia as she shook Mike's hand, but she knew instantly that he was more important and more powerful.

'He's a very influential person on the board, aren't you, Mike?' Melissa echoed her thoughts while smiling at Mike. Cordelia was astonished to see that her smile was almost flirtatious. Cordelia had never considered Melissa to be a flirtatious woman. Mike grinned at Melissa. 'As you will be one day, Mel, I'm sure of it.'

'Why, thank you.' She smiled at him again.

Was this how she did it? wondered Cordelia. Did she rant and rave and order people around on the twelfth floor only to become this sultry seductress on the thirty-third? Cordelia knew that she wasn't above a little flirting with people herself but there was a difference between smiling at them and positively leering at them which was what Melissa was doing!

'Oh, look, there's Henry!' Melissa pecked Mike on the cheek. 'I just have to go and speak to him for a moment.' She threaded her way through the crowd, leaving Mike and Cordelia together.

'She's a whirlwind,' said Mike. 'She really is. And, of course, Henry is even more important than me.'

Cordelia smiled at him in tacit understanding.

'So what do you do, Cordelia?'

'I work with Melissa. I'm an analyst.'

'And you were part of the UpperCut team?'

Cordelia nodded.

'Great work,' said Mike.

'Thanks.'

'No, really. It was a difficult one for us to advise on. I'm on the legal team myself.'

'Oh.' Cordelia nodded again and tried to think of something interesting to say to him about the bank or about the UpperCut deal. But she couldn't and she didn't want to appear banal or stupid so she said nothing and sipped her wine instead.

Mike grinned at her. 'Am I making you nervous?'

'No,' said Cordelia quickly. 'Should you?'

'I shouldn't but I often do,' Mike told her. 'That's because I'm actually pretty senior in Harrison's despite what people call my youthful good looks.'

'I hope to be pretty senior myself some time,' Cordelia said lightly, feeling suddenly more relaxed. She was rewarded by Mike's smile. This is good, she thought, I'm making the right impression on him.

But then they were joined by some other people that Cordelia didn't know. She tried to remember their names, assessing whether or not they were likely to be of use to her in her future career, but they were a blur of dark suits, light shirts and similar hairstyles. They didn't matter too much, she decided, they were senior to her but not senior enough and they were trying to make a good impression on Mike Fuller too.

'There you are.' DeVere sidled up beside her just as Mike finished talking to the group of men. Cordelia was irritated by DeVere's arrival. She'd wanted a little more time on her own with Mike. Now DeVere was going to monopolise the conversation as he always did, tell stories that would show him in a good corporate light and overshadow her completely.

Cordelia had improved at turning stories to her own benefit these days but she knew that she still couldn't better DeVere. I can stay here and fume, she thought, or I can mingle and try to find someone even more important than Mike. Mingle, she thought. You never knew who else you might meet.

'I was just going to freshen up,' she told DeVere. 'This is Mike. He's an important person, so he tells me. You might like to give him the benefit of your hard sell.'

She had the satisfaction of seeing a flash of annoyance in DeVere's eyes and a flash of amusement in Mike's. She walked slowly across the room, pausing from time to time to catch the nuances of conversations, wondering whether there was a group of people worthy of interrupting.

'Cordelia!' Melissa, standing on her own, beckoned her.

'What?' asked Cordelia.

'Will you do me a favour? I absolutely need to talk to Bill Dreyfuss for a moment and he's just finishing up a conversation. Will you give my home a call for me and find out exactly what's going on?'

'Pardon?' Cordelia looked at her in confusion.

'My nanny sent me a text message.' Melissa showed her

phone to Cordelia who read, 'Ham OK but hurt earlier.' Cordelia looked at Melissa in confusion.

'Ham's my son,' explained Melissa.

'Your son?' Cordelia knew that Americans sometimes thrust the strangest of names on their children, but calling him after a side of meat seemed somewhat over the top.

'His name's Ervin,' said Melissa, 'but we call him Ham because he's always acting.'

'Oh.'

'Which is probably what this message is all about but can you call and find out?'

'Call your house?'

'Call the nanny's mobile,' said Melissa. 'It's here, under N. I just want to check things out.'

Cordelia was irritated. Why the hell didn't Melissa check out her own domestic arrangements and leave her to talk to Bill? But Melissa had thrust the phone in her hand and was striding towards the portly figure of the CEO, a wide beam slashed across her mouth as she extended a hand to him.

'Cow,' muttered Cordelia as she took the phone out of the boardroom where it was impossible to hear anything over the buzz of conversation.

'Mrs Kravich?' The nanny sounded young.

'No,' said Cordelia. 'I work with Melissa. She asked me to call.'

'I sent her a message,' said the nanny.

'I know.' Was the girl thick? Cordelia asked herself. Why else would she be calling?

'Ham fell down the stairs,' the nanny said.

'Oh God! Is he all right?'

'He's in the hospital. They're keeping him in for observation because he knocked himself out. But he's OK now, he's conscious and he seems fine.'

'I'll tell Mrs Kravich,' said Cordelia. 'I'm sure she'll get there as soon as she can.'

'They'll let him home in the morning,' the nanny told her.

'Are you at the hospital now?' asked Cordelia.

'Of course. It's my job. I live with them, you know.'

The girl sounded frazzled, as well she might, Cordelia reckoned. Obviously Ham had taken a tumble while she was supposed to be looking after him. In the circus that was the US courts, the girl was probably terrified of losing her job and being sued by the irate Kraviches.

'I'll tell Mrs Kravich,' said Cordelia. 'What about Mr Kravich?'

The nanny laughed shortly. 'He's in Puerto Rico.'

'Mrs Kravich it is then,' said Cordelia. She ended the call and went in search of Melissa.

Her boss was still talking to Bill Dreyfuss, her face animated as she emphasised a point to him. Cordelia walked up to them.

'Can I have a word, Melissa?'

Melissa turned to her. 'Is it really important?'

'What?'

'This word? Can it wait for a couple of minutes?' There was a wealth of meaning in her question.

'I suppose so,' said Cordelia uncertainly.

'Then give me a moment,' said Melissa. 'I'm having a

private conversation with Bill.' She glanced at the CEO. 'Bill Dreyfuss, Cordelia Carroll, who works with me. But is a little inclined to fuss.'

'I'm not fussing,' said Cordelia sharply.

'I'll be back to you.' Melissa's voice was firm. 'Momentarily.'

'OK.' Cordelia walked away from them and over to the corner of the room. The lights of the city were spread out around her and beneath her. This was one of the most vibrant places in the world to work, she thought. Vibrant and exciting and businesslike and it had just come home to her how damned businesslike it was. Melissa Kravich had decided that it was more important to talk to Bill Dreyfuss than to find out about her son. Cordelia pictured little Ham in hospital with his nanny, crying for his mother who was eating hors d'oeuvres and drinking champagne.

Maybe not, she thought wryly. Maybe Ham was happier with the nanny whom he probably knew better than his mother anyway. Maybe he couldn't have cared less whether Melissa was there or not.

She leaned against the window and thought of what it would be like to be standing here and know that somewhere, out there, her own child was in hospital, wanting her. Just as well, she thought, that children were a long way down her personal agenda at the moment. She might be able to be hard-hearted when she wanted but she wasn't sure that she'd manage to leave her kid in hospital while she chatted to the CEO. Would Dan abandon a Chatham's party to be with an injured son?

Of course he would. Dan was a complete marshmallow, for all he tried to appear hard-headed. But she knew that Dan sometimes felt that the business was too cutthroat, too people-unfriendly.

He needed people, thought Cordelia. He hadn't grown up in a loving family as she had done. Sure, her parents were overprotective of their only child and certainly they drove her crazy from time to time, but Cordelia knew that she was the most important person in their lives. Dan hadn't felt like that. He'd told her that his parents had split up when he was younger and that, although they got on OK now, they hadn't for a long time. He hadn't said any more than that but Cordelia could see that he ached to have a stable family unit for himself. Which was why he was going to make such a good husband, she thought. He wouldn't risk his family. And he was truly supportive of her career.

'Well?' Melissa stood beside her and jolted her back to reality.

'Your son fell downstairs and was taken to hospital,' Cordelia told her. 'They're keeping him in overnight to be certain but he appears to be fine.'

'And what about Simone?' asked Melissa.

'Simone?'

'The so-called nanny. What has she to say for herself?'

'Not much. I didn't ask. I just checked that Ham was OK.'

'I suppose I'd better ring myself.' Melissa seemed more irritated than upset. 'I can call a delivery service and get them to send around some balloons or something to him.'

'Don't you want to see him?' Cordelia looked at her in surprise.

'Of course,' said Melissa. 'But it's nine o'clock. He's probably asleep. It doesn't matter whether I call in now or in another hour.'

Cordelia stared at her in complete amazement.

'Look, Cordelia,' said Melissa patiently. 'You might not realise it but this is an important event tonight. It's the one opportunity for me to do a bit of networking on a social footing. It won't make any difference to Ham whether I rush off now or see him on my way home.'

'I know,' said Cordelia.

'But you don't approve.'

'It's not that.' Cordelia looked at her uncomfortably. 'It's just – I thought you'd *want* to leave.'

'I do want to leave,' said Melissa. 'But not until it's over. Which is going to be within half an hour or so anyway.' She patted Cordelia on the shoulder. 'The glass ceiling is still there,' she told her. 'We may have put a few cracks in it, and one or two of us may have broken through it, but it's self-repairing and we have to keep banging and banging to get rid of it for ever. If I go before anyone else it looks bad for me.'

'I suppose so.'

'I know so,' said Melissa. 'And it's something you'll have to know too if you want to stay here.'

Cordelia watched her as she walked across the room and put her arm round Ethan Blake, another of the senior management team. She knew them all, thought Cordelia, and she's working them all too! She deserves to be successful. And it's not fair that she feels she can't go and see her son. But it's frightening to know that she can distance herself from her worry all the same.

She admired Melissa. She feared Melissa. She respected Melissa. And, as she smiled at Mike who'd looked in her direction, she wondered if she would one day become like Melissa herself. And if it would all be worth it.

Chapter 21

Dauphinois Potatoes
Large waxy potatoes, garlic, butter, double cream, grated
Gruyère cheese, grated Parmesan cheese, grated nutmeg,
salt and pepper
Peel and cut potatoes into thin slices. Rinse. Cut garlic
clove in half and rub cut surface over shallow dish. Rub
butter over dish too. Place potatoes, cream, Gruyère cheese,
Parmesan cheese, nutmeg and seasoning in layers in dish.
Finish with layer of Gruyère then Parmesan. Cover with
foil and bake for 1½ hours (remove foil for last 20 mins)

Ash knew that she was asleep and she knew that she was dreaming. She'd woken earlier at around five o'clock when she'd heard Alistair getting out of the bed. He often got up at that time, he told her, because when he woke in the early morning ideas would come to him and if he didn't get up and think about them he'd fall asleep again and forget about them. She'd heard him pull on his tracksuit and stub his toe at the end of the bed which made him swear softly under his breath. Then she'd heard him walk quietly down the stairs so as not to disturb her. She hadn't moved in the bed, hadn't let him know that she was awake. She'd lain on her back for a while and then found herself drifting into the zone between sleep and wakefulness when she knew exactly where she was but where images she couldn't control played in her mind.

Images of Julia. Like a badly tracking video she could see her mother standing by the garden gate, wearing her black T-shirt, faded blue jeans and black leather jacket. She was laughing, her dark curly hair blowing across her face in the wind as she waved at Ash. Ash was wearing her pale pink leotard and her hair was held back in a neat ponytail, secured by a pink ribbon. And she was begging Julia not to go, knowing that Julia was going to go anyway. She could feel the warmth of the day, the sky milk-white with morning haze, the air humid and laden with scent from the flowering bush which bordered the garden.

And then she heard the sound of the bike as Tyke started it up, she could smell the oil and the diesel, and although she couldn't see him at all, she knew that everything was going to go wrong and that, no matter what she did, she couldn't stop it.

She woke suddenly and properly, her heart racing and her body drenched with sweat. I should have stopped her somehow, she thought wildly, as her eyes snapped open. I could have stopped her if I'd tried hard enough. I could have thrown a tantrum or pretended to be sick or anything at all but I could have stopped her. Only I didn't because I knew that her face would fall and her eyes would brim with tears and she'd have to explain to Tyke, whom she loved, that her selfish bitch daughter whom she looked after so well wouldn't let her do anything. Ash sat up in the bed and felt her pulse which was hammering her wrist. This time might be the time, she thought, as she felt her whole body tremble. This might be the time when it really *was* a heart attack and she'd die here, in Alistair's bed, but alone.

One, she thought, making herself count. Two. It wasn't my fault. Everyone says it wasn't my fault and they're right. I was only a kid! Three. Four. Five. But I was a kid who was much more sensible than my mother. I knew that Tyke was trouble. I knew it would never work out in the long term. And I didn't protect her. Six. Seven. Eight. Nine. Ten. I should have protected her. I was the sensible one. I was supposed to look after her.

She wrapped her arms round her knees and rested her head on them while hot tears flooded her eyes. She remembered the neighbour, Jeannie, who rushed out of her house when she heard the squeal of brakes and the sound of the crash and who had, almost immediately, gathered Ash to her and told her to go inside and stay inside. Everyone on the road had known instantly that it was Julia who was involved in whatever accident had taken place because most people believed that Julia was an accident waiting to happen.

And I knew that too, thought Ash as she hugged her knees. I always knew that someday something terrible would happen because Julia seemed to wrap disaster around her the same way other people shrugged on a new coat.

She heard the creak of the stairs as Alistair walked up and she glanced at the clock. Almost eight. She should get up, she had a lunch to do today and she didn't have time for a heart attack. Which she knew she wasn't having after all because already her heartbeat was beginning to slow down and the trembling had eased and Alistair would never find out that she was a complete basket case. She wiped her eyes with the edge of the sheet.

'Awake?' he asked as he came into the room.

She looked up at him. 'Just now.'

'I thought I'd better get you up,' he said. 'You told me you had a lunch booking today.'

She nodded. 'Thanks.'

'Are you all right?' He looked at her curiously. 'You look awful.'

'Yes.' She yawned. 'Bit of a bad dream. But I'm OK now.'

'Sure?' asked Alistair.

'Oh, yes.'

He sat beside her and put his arm round her. Then he pushed her gently back onto the bed. 'I have a cure for nightmares,' he told her.

'Really?'

'Of course.' He traced his finger around her face, along the side of her neck and between her breasts. 'A surefire cure.'

She smiled at him. 'And a great cure it is too. But not this morning, Alistair.'

'I've got the time,' he said. 'And so have you. You panic about being somewhere but you know you've loads of time really.'

'I know.' She shivered as he brushed the tip of her nipple with his lips.

'You see,' he told her. 'Much better.'

'Maybe.' She lay on her back and closed her eyes.

He pushed the sheets away from her. 'I love your body,' he said as he took off his jogging pants. 'I love the way your breasts are just round enough for me to hold. The way your stomach falls in and then rises. I love the golden triangle between your legs and I love your legs and your ankles and your toes too.'

'Thank you.' She opened her eyes again.

He lay on top of her and kissed her on the forehead. And on the tip of her nose. And her shoulder. And then each breast.

'Alistair – not this morning.'

He didn't hear her.

'Please,' she said more loudly.

He looked up. 'What's the matter.'

'Not this morning,' she said. 'I – I just can't this morning.'

'Don't be silly.' He bent over her breast again.

'I mean it!' Her voice was sharper, tinged with anger, and he sat up again.

'What the hell is wrong with you?' he asked.

'It was the dream,' she told him. 'It upset me. I don't feel like it.'

'Ash, whatever it was, it was only a dream,' said Alistair.

'And you're awake now. So forget what's not real and think about what is.'

'I am thinking about it.'

'Come on.' He stroked her stomach gently which he knew she liked. 'Relax.'

'I'm sorry.' She sat up. 'I can't relax. Not today I can't.'

'Ash!'

'Really.' She scrambled out of the bed. 'I just can't, Alistair.' She stood on the opposite side of the bed, her eyes dark and worried, her hair loose around her shoulders. 'Don't touch me,' she said.

'I'm not going to touch you.' He was angry now. 'What kind of person do you think I am?'

'I don't know, Alistair,' she said quickly.

He stared at her and she could see his jaw clench. 'Great, Ash, thanks. We've known each other since before Christmas, we've been going out together for the last few months and now you say you don't know me. That's just wonderful.'

'I'm sorry.' She pulled her T-shirt over her head. 'I didn't mean to upset you.'

'Oh, really. That's all right then, isn't it?' There was controlled fury in his voice. 'You practically accuse me of being about to rape you but you didn't mean to upset me!'

Ash was horrified at the hurt in his voice. 'I'm sorry,' she said again. 'I really, really am, Alistair. I just lost it there for a minute. It was a horrible dream and I . . . You know I wouldn't say anything, wouldn't do anything to hurt you. I'm sorry.'

'It's too late to be sorry,' said Alistair hotly. 'You know, Ash, I've been really patient with you. I haven't rushed you or pressurised you or anything. Plenty of guys in my position would have dumped you before now – a girl who won't even let her boyfriend into her apartment! But you said that you had "issues" about it and I respected that. You said it was very personal. And I respected that too. You made me feel as though I'd be some kind of monster if I pushed you. So I didn't push you. But this is too much, Ash. Way too much.'

'But—'

'You know, I could have any woman I wanted. Any woman. And don't think that I haven't had a few chances since we started going out together. But I didn't take advantage of any of them. Because I cared about you. Even with all of your damn stupid obsessions.'

'I don't have stupid obsessions,' said Ash tautly.

'Yes you do,' snapped Alistair. 'What about the fact that you always have to have just one lump of ice in your drink. Or that you won't drink tea if someone has put milk in the cup first? And this stupid, stupid need to have a clean towel every time you take a shower. Christ, Ash, every time you stay with me my laundry basket fills to overflowing with your used towels!'

'I like one lump of ice,' she said.

'And the drinking? And the towels?'

'I told you those things so that you'd understand me,' she said defensively. 'I've never told anyone else. Surely that means something to you?'

'I can't cope with it any more,' said Alistair. 'I just want a normal relationship with someone who has fun, gets drunk, and doesn't spend all her time switching things off. Someone who isn't a complete flake.'

She shivered. She hated anyone calling her flaky. 'I said I was sorry.' She liked Alistair. She liked him a lot. She didn't want to fight with him.

'It's not enough, Ash,' he said firmly. 'You had your chance and you blew it. This half-vulnerable, half-confident act works for a while but then people get tired of it. And I'm tired of it.'

She stared at him, her brown eyes huge in her face. And then she realised that this was it. He was about to break up with her. The thing she'd been protecting herself from all of her life was finally happening. Her worst nightmare. And she couldn't do anything to stop it.

She felt her mouth go dry and she thought she was going to be sick. 'You're making too much of this,' she croaked. 'Really you are.'

'No, I'm not.' Alistair's jaw was set. 'I'm not some kind of accessory, Ash. I'm a person, with feelings. And, as far as you're concerned, I'm all feelinged-out right now.'

'I had a nightmare,' she said again. 'It scared me. That's all it was.'

'Ash, when you care about someone and they come to comfort you after a nightmare the proper response isn't to jump away from them and tell them not to come near you,' said Alistair. 'You need to grow up. And I need to move on.'

If I let him break up with me I'll be hurt, thought Ash frantically. I won't be able to cope with it. I'll cry for nights and nights on end. And I won't be able to work properly. He can't break up with me. He just can't.

'Alistair—'

He sighed. 'It's over. It really is. So the best thing for you to do now is to get dressed and to leave.'

She pulled at the hem of her T-shirt. 'No,' she said. 'You can't do this to me. You can't break up with me.'

'I just have,' Alistair told her baldly.

He turned and walked out of the room. Ash stood, frozen, by the side of the bed. He can't mean it, she said to herself. He can't. He loves me. He told me that he loved me.

She reached out for her jeans and pulled them on. Maybe he'd change his mind. If he changed his mind then they could go out together again and next time she could be the one to call it a day. She could do it the way she always did it, coolly and calmly. Not in an angry confrontation. Not shouting at each other. She could do it in a way that made him understand that it hurt her to do it. And she'd know how she was supposed to feel about it then.

She finished dressing and walked downstairs. Alistair was sitting in the kitchen, his laptop open on the table in front of him.

'I like you a lot,' said Ash.

He looked up at her. 'I'm supposed to be grateful for that?'

'I didn't ask you out,' she said. 'You asked me.'

'So what?'

'So you were the one that wanted me. I didn't want you.'

'Ash, you really are incredibly silly. It's not about wanting or not wanting. It's not about who asks who out. It's about being friends. About sharing.'

'We could share,' she said.

He shook his head. 'I thought so too. But I know that we can't. You need to change, Ash, and I don't think you ever will.'

Why did they all think she should change? What was wrong with her the way she was?

'You don't love me?' she asked.

'No.' He looked at her regretfully. 'I thought I did. But I don't. I'm sorry.'

She picked up her bag and put it over her shoulder.

'Goodbye, Ash,' said Alistair.

But she wasn't able to say anything more.

She stood in the kitchen of Barnes and Little and realised that she'd forgotten to buy half of the ingredients she needed for lunch. She'd never forgotten to buy ingredients before. They were all carefully listed on her menu cards and she bought them in the same order each time, checking them off as she went. But she hadn't done that today. She'd walked around the shops in a daze, her heart thumping so loudly in her chest that she was sure that the other shoppers could hear it. She'd kept visualising herself keeling over and fainting. And she'd thought of the Barnes and Little people waiting for their lunch and how they'd feel when she didn't show up.

Alistair was right, she admitted, as she poked around the plastic bag and wondered why on earth she'd bought half a dozen mangoes and no Gruyère cheese for the Dauphinois potatoes. She was actually quite crazy. Michelle was right too. She'd been a flake when she was a kid and she was a flake now. She'd treated the one man she really liked as though he was some escaped convict. No wonder he was upset. No wonder he'd broken up with her.

But I'm still standing, she told herself, as she hastily rearranged the menu in her mind. And I didn't faint. I didn't collapse. I didn't have a heart attack. But I made a terrible fool of myself and I never make a fool of myself. She couldn't believe that she'd practically grovelled to him. She may not have collapsed but she felt pretty pathetic all the same.

Alistair sat at his computer and punched the keys angrily. He'd wasted six months of his life on Ash O'Halloran. On someone who hadn't treated him with the respect he deserved. On someone who'd managed to get close enough to him to actually hurt him. He'd allowed her to get close because she hadn't treated him as though he was the kind of bloke who could walk into a shop and buy whatever he wanted without even knowing what the price was. She hadn't treated him the way the girls he'd met at product launches treated him, smiling at him, putting their hands on his shoulder, brushing against him and laughing at his jokes. Well, he thought, as he scanned through his e-mails, he'd had it with girls that didn't think it was a privilege to go out with a man who had just ordered a top-of-the-range Mercedes convertible to go with his Audi TT. Next girl he went out with wouldn't push him away if she'd had a nightmare. And the next girl he went out with certainly wouldn't fake it on their first night together.

Bagel had vomited on the living-room floor. Whenever he had a furball or ate something disgusting from outside the apartment (and Ash never really wanted to know what the something disgusting might be) he would be sick. He'd vomited in a neat pile beside her computer terminal, followed by another smaller sickie at the entrance to the kitchen.

Ash wrinkled up her nose, put on her yellow rubber household gloves and proceeded to clean up after him. The one great advantage of having a natural wood floor when you had a cat was that at least you could clean up properly whenever he threw up.

'Are you OK?' she asked him. He trotted to his bowl and looked at her expectantly. She spooned a small portion of cat food into the bowl. Bagel purred happily as he wolfed down the food. She hoped he wouldn't be sick again. Alistair wouldn't have liked Bagel, she thought. And Bagel wouldn't have liked Alistair. She knew he wouldn't.

She leaned against the worktop and realised that she felt lonely. She'd never felt lonely before. She'd felt sick and scared and nervous for a while and she'd occasionally had to resort to the brown paper bag but she'd never felt lonely. I'm twenty-nine, she thought. I should have copped on by now. Why can't I just go with the flow like Jodie? Why can't I be as sure about things as Michelle is?

She opened the window and Bagel jumped onto the sill and she suddenly wished that she'd been able to live a zany, cluttered, disorganised, Bridget Jones kind of life. That she'd been more like the girls who spent their time trying to get and keep the man of their dreams and whose main occupations were flicking through magazines and moaning about spots and diets and stayfast foundation to their very best girlfriends, all of whom shared a pigsty of an apartment. She should have had the kind of life where she had to search through a mound of unwashed T-shirts to find something to wear on a Friday night. Where she tottered home blind drunk from raucous nights out with her friends and collapsed in a heap on the bed still wearing her party clothes. Where she had lots of party clothes! Where she hated her job and hated her boss and spent all her time in the office surfing the net and finding astrological pages to tell her that she was caring, warm-hearted and lovable and ideally compatible with a Taurean man. And where everything always came right in the end. Because that was how women lived these days, wasn't it? And that was what men really wanted.

But instead, she thought furiously, I'm a psycho relationship freak who lives with a cat, takes off all of the tiny amount of make-up I wear every night, and has massive problems with the idea that the one really nice bloke I ever met in my life might make me want to do something I don't want to!

And, she realised, she didn't have the slightest idea how to make it all come right in the end.

Chapter 22

Minestrone Soup
Fresh cannellini beans, onions, olive oil, Parma ham,
diced carrots, diced leeks, diced potatoes, peas, tomatoes,
cabbage, bay leaves, basil leaves, small pasta tubes, salt and
pepper, broth
Sweat onion and garlic in olive oil. Add Parma ham,
vegetables and herbs (except basil). Cover with strained
broth, bring to boil, cook for an hour. Add basil, cook for
another 10 minutes. Season to taste

Jodie was in the bathroom singing her own version of 'I Will Always Love You' when the phone rang. She hurried into the tiny living room and pulled cushions off the sofa as she tried to locate the handset which, as usual, she'd dropped where she'd last used it. She screwed up her nose as she tried to remember where she'd been the last time someone had called. Then she went over to the laundry basket in the corner of the room and rummaged around her collection of underwear.

'Gotcha!' She picked it up and pressed a key. 'Hi, it's me.'

'Hello, Jodie.'

'Alistair! How are you, stranger – it's been ages since you called.'

'I know. I'm sorry.'

'Huh!' But Jodie grinned. 'Far too caught up in my boss to worry about me these days.'

'No,' he said. 'I'm caught up in developing a new system which'll blitz everything else that's out there and propel me into a league that'll make Bill Gates look like a positive pauper.'

'I've got to hand it to you.' Jodie caught sight of the wire poking out of her favourite white underwired bra and frowned. 'You certainly don't aim low.'

'You know me,' said Alistair. 'Always reaching too high.'

'It's worked up till now.' Jodie wedged the phone between her shoulder and her ear and picked up the bra. How the hell had that happened? she wondered. If that was because Chris insisted on practically ripping it off me the other night I'll kill him!

'Actually, I did want to talk to you about your boss,' said Alistair.

'Hah!'

'Hah?'

'I knew you weren't really calling me to talk about network protocols and stuff like that,' said Jodie. 'It had to be sex after all.'

'It's not sex,' Alistair told her. 'Honestly, Jodie!'

'What then?' She pulled at the wire of the bra and

382

sighed as it slid out of the fabric. One perfectly good bra ruined, she thought bitterly. I'll murder Chris. Then she remembered what it had been like and she smiled. Maybe not.

'I wanted to warn you,' said Alistair.

'Warn me?'

'We've split up.'

'Oh, Alistair!' Jodie drew her legs up underneath her and prepared for a longer conversation. 'How the hell did that happen? What did she say to you? That she really cared about you but that she wasn't ready for commitment? Apparently that's one of her favourites. Or did she simply say that it really wasn't working out and that you didn't have enough in common?'

'She didn't break up with me,' said Alistair, 'I broke up with her.'

'Alistair!' Jodie's voice was practically a shriek. 'Nobody breaks up with Ash.'

'You think?' he said. 'What's so fucking wonderful about her that nobody breaks up with her?'

'Actually nothing,' admitted Jodie. 'It's just that she never lets anyone break up with her. She always makes her move first.'

'Well, not this time,' said Alistair. 'I've just about had enough of her.'

'Just about?'

'No,' he said definitely, 'I've had enough of her. God, Jodie, she was so bloody difficult. It was as though she was kind of watching us together rather than being part of it.'

'What?'

'You know. Like it was planned by her all the time. She'd laugh and she'd smile and she'd make love but I always had this feeling that she didn't mean half of it.'

'I think you're being a bit hard on her,' said Jodie.

'I don't think I am.' Alistair sighed.

'So what happened?' asked Jodie.

'Oh, she threw a wobbler this morning when I tried to make love to her.'

Jodie giggled. 'So did I when you tried it with me.'

'You were only eighteen then,' said Alistair. 'And it was just a bit of fun.'

'Thanks,' said Jodie dryly.

'Oh, come on.' Alistair groaned. 'You're my friend, Jodie. Please don't go all girlie on me. It was years ago.'

'All right,' she said. 'But only because I'm in a long-term serious relationship myself.'

'Lucky you,' said Alistair bitterly.

'Maybe it was the wrong time of the month or something for Ash,' said Jodie. 'I mean, I know you do have a fatal animal charm and everything, Alistair, but maybe she just didn't feel like it.'

'Not feeling like it is one thing,' said Alistair. 'But leaping out of the bed and yelling at me not to touch her is something else altogether.'

'You're joking!'

'Nope.' Alistair rubbed the back of his neck. 'She said she'd had a nightmare and that was why she was so tense but that was an excuse, Jodie. She doesn't really love me. She doesn't love anyone but herself.'

'Oh, Alistair, she's not that bad.'

'You weren't there,' said Alistair.

'It'd be definitely kinky if I was,' said Jodie.

'She never really loved me,' said Alistair. 'I *know* that she's faked it a few times in bed.'

'Alistair!'

'She's the only one,' said Alistair hastily.

'And how do you know?'

'The times she fakes it are the times when she moans and groans the most,' said Alistair.

Jodie laughed. 'Are you sure?'

'Not sure,' he admitted. 'But almost certain.'

'I'm sorry,' said Jodie. 'I really thought you two were working.'

'I thought so too,' said Alistair. 'But, in retrospect, maybe it's a good thing. I have a life, Jodie. A busy life. And she was complicating it. Now I can go ahead and push on with the business and not have to worry about her.'

'It's still a shame,' Jodie said.

'Yes, well.' Alistair laughed shortly. 'Easy come, easy go.'

'Do you want to call over?' asked Jodie.

'Thanks but no,' said Alistair. 'I'm in the kind of mood where I might try jumping on you again, Jodie. I'm going to have a night in tonight and concentrate on my work for a few days. Then maybe I'll go to Paris or somewhere. Lose myself in a few fast girls with fake blonde hair.'

Jodie laughed. 'Your heart isn't broken then?'

'No,' said Alistair. 'But it hasn't exactly been a great day.'

'I understand,' said Jodie. 'And thanks for telling me.'

'Oh, well, thought I'd better,' said Alistair. 'I wanted you to be aware that she might be a bit mean with the carving knife next time you see her.'

'Suicidal?' squeaked Jodie.

'No, you nut, just – mean!'

'You'll find someone,' said Jodie. 'Someone a lot better than Ash.'

'Probably,' said Alistair. 'Eventually. But, you know, Jodie, what was good about her was that she didn't seem to give a toss about the money and the company and anything like that. She just treated me like a normal person.'

'You *are* a normal person,' said Jodie. 'She's the idiot. And I wouldn't say that she didn't care about the money. She's a canny sort of person when it comes to hoarding the pennies. It wouldn't surprise me to know that she's sitting at home now cursing herself for having let the Brannigan millions slip through her fingertips.'

'You say the nicest things,' said Alistair.

'I do my best,' Jodie told him.

Ash stood in her kitchen and peered into the pots on the hob. There were four of them, contents simmering, and the aroma of tomatoes, mushrooms and herbs filled the kitchen. She was making soup. She always made soup when she was upset and she was upset today. She wasn't sure exactly how upset she was, but she'd never been upset enough to make four pots of soup before. She lifted the lid on the minestrone and wondered whether or not she had enough containers to freeze it all when she'd finished. It was particularly stupid, she told herself, to make soup when the weather was warm. She never served soup in the summer. If she'd been thinking straight she would have made a chilled soup. But she wasn't thinking straight. It was a weird feeling, not being able to think straight. Usually she could. But tonight was different. Tonight she was a girl whose boyfriend had broken up with her.

Dan was lying on the sofa, his legs hanging over the arm rest, when the doorbell rang. He groaned. It had been a hard day, he'd stayed late in the office and he was just beginning to chill out. He wasn't expecting anyone and he didn't want to get up from the very comfortable position he was in. He waited for a moment, hoping that whoever it was would give up and go away.

But the doorbell rang again, more insistently this time. Dan sighed deeply and got up from the sofa. He walked, barefoot, into the hall and opened the door.

'Cordelia!' He stared at her in surprise and was aware of an uncomfortable feeling in the pit of his stomach. Why was she here now, looking tired and serious? What was wrong? He opened the door a little wider and saw that she had a small suitcase with her. 'Are you home?' he asked.

'Don't be daft.' She grinned at him and the uncomfortable feeling in his stomach eased straightaway. 'Mike needed someone to come to the Dublin office for a couple of days so I volunteered.'

'You never said anything!'

'I only found out yesterday. So I thought I'd surprise you.'

'You did.' He hugged her fiercely. 'It's the best surprise I've had in months.'

'You must be leading a dreary life in that case.' She put her arms round him and began to kiss the side of his neck.

'Very dreary,' he assured her. 'So dreary you wouldn't believe.' He reached for her suitcase and, still with one arm round her, carried it into the hall.

'Miss me?' she asked.

'What do *you* think?'

It was everything about her, he decided, as he led her into the living room. It was her looks and her presence and the perfume she wore. It was the way she was so decisive about everything and the way that she made him feel decisive too. And the way that she moved her hands so gently along his body so that he felt an explosion of desire. 'God, *how* I've missed you,' he said.

They didn't bother going upstairs. She led him into the living room and she stood in front of the fireplace.

'Miss this?' she asked as she slid her cotton top over her head.

He nodded.

'And this?' She unhooked her bra.

'I missed it all.' He interrupted her and pulled her fiercely to him. And he thought that never in his life had he made love to someone in the way he made love to Cordelia Carroll. Never had he known anyone more inventive and more demanding, who enjoyed it as much as she did and whose very enjoyment made him enjoy it all the more too.

Later that night, as they lay in bed together, her head resting on his arm, he wondered how he had ever doubted her. Because sometimes he did. Sometimes he wondered whether or not Harrison's and Mike Fuller, Melissa Kravich and DeVere Bassett meant more to her than he did.

'Don't be silly,' she said lazily when he asked her. 'It means a lot to me, Dan. But not everything.' She grinned. 'I don't get off on mergers and acquisitions the same way I do with you. It's close, sometimes, but not quite the same!'

'Will you be able to leave it all and come home to me?'

'Of course,' she said.

'What about the end-of-book dinner?' He turned to look at her. 'Will you make it to Sicily for that?'

She sighed. 'I honestly don't think so, Dan. I'd love to come, you know I would. But I'm terribly busy and . . .'

'I understand.' He kissed her gently. 'But I'd love you to be there.'

'And be needled by your bloody sister,' said Cordelia waspishly.

'She doesn't mean it,' Dan told her.

'Yes she does,' said Cordelia. 'She doesn't like me, Dan.'

'She—' Dan broke off, unable to finish the sentence

because he knew that Bronwyn and Cordelia didn't click and he didn't know why. But then his twin rarely liked any of his girlfriends.

Cordelia giggled. 'It doesn't matter. I won't be living with her.'

'I've asked Ash O'Halloran to do the meal for us,' said Dan.

'You've what?' Cordelia sat up in the bed beside him.

'Asked Ash,' he told her. 'I felt bad about her not doing the wedding and I thought—'

'For heaven's sake, Dan!' Cordelia's eyes were angry. 'She's a cook. She couldn't deal with the wedding. That's hardly your fault. I don't see why on earth you now want her to do the dinner for you. Besides, how does she plan to get there?'

'She's flying over,' said Dan.

'And who's paying?'

'Well, I am.'

'Dan!'

'What's the problem?' he asked.

'What the fuck is your relationship with this woman?' demanded Cordelia. 'Why the hell do you want her to do this dinner for you? What's the attraction, Dan?'

'No attraction.' He looked at her in amazement. 'I like her, of course I do, but – there's nothing between her and me, Cordelia, if that's what you're thinking.'

'The whole thing is damned odd is what I'm thinking.' Cordelia pushed her fingers through her thick hair and stared at Dan. 'She's supposed to be a professional woman and you treat her like a friend.'

'I do think of her as a friend,' said Dan.

'I'd like to have a friend that'd fly me to Sicily for a holiday,' said Cordelia.

'It's not a holiday,' Dan assured her. 'She's only over to cook.'

'I still don't see why you couldn't have got someone else to do it.'

'Are you jealous?' Dan looked at her in surprise. 'There's nothing to be jealous about, Cordelia. Honestly. Ash and I are – well, I guess platonic is the word.'

'Platonic!' Cordelia laughed. 'There's no such thing.'

'There is,' Dan said. 'Honestly. I like her, but that's all.'

'I don't see why,' said Cordelia. 'She's such a milk and water kind of person I can't imagine why you even get on with her.'

'She's easy to get on with,' said Dan. 'And she's good at what she does.'

'Cook!' Cordelia's voice was scornful. 'It's not exactly a glittering career, is it?'

'Oh, I don't know,' said Dan mildly. 'What about Delia Smith and Darina Allen? They've done pretty well out of being cooks, haven't they?'

'Because they've expanded into other things,' said Cordelia. 'Let's face it, the Smith woman is never off the telly and Darina Allen is a one-woman industry what with her classes and ice creams and goodness knows what else. Is your precious Ash going down that road?'

'I don't think so,' said Dan.

'Limited vision,' said Cordelia. 'She might be a nice

person – I'm sure she is a nice person – but she'll never amount to anything, Dan.'

'I don't think she wants to.' He recalled her dismissal of the idea of running a restaurant or compiling a recipe book. 'But maybe the world doesn't need everyone running around trying to build successful empires.'

'Yes it does.' Cordelia lay down beside him again. 'But I'll concede your cook, Dan, once you promise me that you won't lay a finger on her.'

'Cordelia!' His voice was horrified. 'Of course I won't. I don't find her attractive in that sense at all.'

'Good,' said Cordelia as she rolled her body on top of his. 'Because I'd find it very, very disappointing if you did.'

Chapter 23

Mediterranean Cod
Cod fillets, butter, garlic, onion, oil, tomato and tomato
purée, courgettes, marjoram, salt and pepper
Cook garlic and onion in oil, add tomatoes and courgettes.
Place cubed cod fillets into casserole dish, cover with mix-
ture, cook in warm oven

Jodie hurried up the steps of the Chatham building past the knot of smokers who weren't allowed to indulge their habit inside. She was late and it was a bad start to the day to be late because Ash would get annoyed with her and she couldn't take Ash being annoyed with her today. She'd intended to be early, of course. She'd intended to be early enough to bring up the subject of Ash and Alistair and the whole break-up. But her carefully laid plans had come to nothing because of the body blow she'd been dealt last night. She sniffed as she pushed at the revolving glass door. She'd thought about ringing in sick but she hadn't been able to do that because she knew that she'd be letting Ash down. All the same, she really and truly did not feel like coming in to work today.

She took her security pass from the receptionist and pinned it to her jacket. Her fingers trembled and it took her a couple of attempts to do it properly. Bloody Chris, she thought, as she waited for the lift to arrive. Bloody, bloody, Chris. The bastard.

She swallowed. She'd been going out with Chris for almost a year and she'd thought things were going pretty well. This was the longest she'd ever gone out with anyone – as far as she was concerned they might as well have been an old married couple. She loved him. She thought he loved her. He made love to her often enough! But last night it had all gone horribly wrong. She'd decided to drop over to Alistair to see how he was getting on. She wasn't fooled by his light-hearted jokes about breaking up with Ash. She knew, too, that since he'd sold out Archangel to Transys and made so much money he didn't have as many friends as he used to. And that the ones he had now treated him differently. But she'd known him since they were kids and she'd never treated him differently. So she'd rung Chris, told him that she was going to see Alistair, and left the apartment.

Alistair hadn't really been in the mood to talk. He was working, as only he could, on some part of a project and he was deeply immersed in it. 'Losing myself in my work,' he'd grinned at her and Jodie had nodded and told him that she was glad he was OK. She'd thought about ringing Chris from Alistair's and trying to meet him in town for a drink, but she'd decided that maybe she'd just go home and wallow in a hot bath instead.

But when she arrived at the apartment Chris was already there. With Stefanie. Her physiotherapist flatmate. Who was doing things to him on the living-room rug that definitely weren't in the physiotherapist's handbook.

Jodie had stared at them, too shocked to believe what she was seeing. It happened in movies, she thought frantically. And in books too. But she never thought it actually happened in real life. She never thought that people could walk into their homes and find the person that they loved (that they thought loved them!) having it off with their best friend on the living-room floor.

She hadn't been able to say anything at first and then she'd gone berserk – throwing things at both of them, swearing at them, using language that she hadn't even realised she knew. She'd told them both to get the fuck out of the apartment and hadn't even allowed Chris the time to put on the leather jacket that he'd left in the kitchen. 'What about my stuff?' Stefanie had wailed and Jodie had snapped that she'd send her stuff to Chris's place.

She had no intention of sending Stefanie's stuff any-where. She might burn it – and anything she had that belonged to Chris. Why had he done it? Why had she trusted him and believed in him and cared about him when all the time he was lusting after the admittedly more voluptuous Stefanie? What was it about men, she muttered, as the lift stopped and the doors sighed open, that made them all such absolute shits?

Maybe Ash had the right idea after all, she thought wanly as she took a deep breath before going into the kitchen. Leave them before they leave you. Don't get involved. Don't get hurt. Jodie had forgotten what feeling hurt was like. She'd felt sorry for Alistair when he told her about Ash because she knew he'd liked her, but maybe it was Ash she should be feeling sorry for. After all, Ash wasn't used to being given the elbow, even if she deserved it. So maybe, awful and all as Jodie was feeling, Ash was feeling a hell of a lot worse. But – Jodie gulped – but Ash hadn't come home to find Alistair bonking someone else in her apartment. That definitely entitled her to feel the worst of all.

She pushed the door open. Ash was slicing a courgette, her movements quick and economical. Jodie was always amazed at the speed at which Ash cut, sliced and chopped food. It was as though she was a machine as she took a whole vegetable and turned it into even bite-size pieces before it had time to protest.

'Sorry I'm late,' she said as she hung her jacket on the back of the door. She felt her voice wobble.

'Better get the table set.' Ash didn't look up.

'Sure.'

'Only five today,' said Ash.

'Who's missing?' Jodie had her voice back under control.

'Dunno.' She turned to Jodie. 'You'd better get on with it, they'll be up soon.'

'Right.' Jodie opened the cutlery drawer. 'What's for starter?'

'Minestrone soup,' said Ash. 'I know it's a bit warm for soup but—'

'Doesn't bother me.' Jodie interrupted her. 'I'm not eating it.'

'You think it's a bit warm for soup too?' Ash looked at her anxiously.

'No,' said Jodie. She glanced at Ash. The girl looked exactly the same as always, she realised. Her skin was clear, her eyes weren't bloodshot, she didn't look as though her world had fallen apart. How the hell could that be? She really mustn't have cared a jot for Alistair. Otherwise she'd surely have the decency to look a little bit rattled.

Ash stared at Jodie. 'Are you all right?' she asked.

'I'm fine,' said Jodie. She wanted to tell Ash about Chris and she wanted to tell her that she knew about Alistair, but she was suddenly quite unable to talk about either of them.

'If you're sure.' Ash shrugged. 'It's cod for the main course,' she added as Jodie continued to rummage in the cutlery drawer, 'and lemon tart with banana pastry for dessert.'

'Fine,' said Jodie.

She went into the dining room to set the table, relieved that Ash hadn't nagged her for being late like she usually did. Maybe, thought Jodie, that was how Ash was suffering. Maybe she was really churned up inside. But she didn't look like someone who was churned up inside.

A tear trickled down her cheek and plopped onto the shiny polished surface of the table. She wiped at it with a linen napkin. If only, she thought, as she set the cutlery at each place, Chris hadn't betrayed her with that sycophantic bitch, Stefanie. Stefanie who'd moved into the apartment and told Jodie how great it was to live there. Who'd bought some new prints for the wall and potted plants for the sunny window ledge. Who'd always seemed so sweet and helpless and just plain nice! So nice that Jodie had believed them when Chris had told her that her physiotherapist flatmate was treating his sore shoulder! How naïve could she actually be? Jodie asked herself as she rearranged the water glasses. How naïve, how stupid, how incredibly dense was she not to have known that it wasn't his bloody shoulder that Stefanie was massaging! She wondered if there was a rule about physios getting involved with their patients. And if she could get Stefanie struck off for what she'd done with Chris. The thought cheered her and she managed a weak smile through her tears. And she remembered hurling the potted plants at both of them, which had given her a little bit of satisfaction.

Ash had moved on to slicing peppers when Jodie came back into the kitchen.

'All done?' she asked.

Jodie nodded. She looked at Ash and wondered whether or not she'd cried when Alistair told her it was over. Whether or not she'd even cared. Right now, with Chris's betrayal stabbing her in the heart with every beat, she could understand exactly why Ash treated men the way she did.

Ash frowned a little as she looked at Jodie but said nothing. Then both of them heard the ping of the lift as it arrived and the voices of the partners as they walked into the dining room. Ash took the bread rolls out of the oven and put them on a wire rack.

'Better get in and pour them a drink,' she said.

'I know what to do,' said Jodie sharply. 'This isn't the first time I've done this, you know.'

Ash looked at her retreating back in surprise then slid the cod into the warm oven. But she really didn't feel like talking to Jodie about her rudeness today. She didn't feel like doing anything today. She was exhausted. She hadn't had any sleep because she'd spent the entire night dozing and then snapping into wakefulness, which was more tiring, Ash thought, than if she'd stayed awake all night. She'd got up at four in the morning and looked at her pots of cold soup and wondered again what the hell she was going to do with all of them. She'd stood, barefoot, in the kitchen for a while and then she'd emptied all of her cupboards and cleaned them thoroughly before replacing all the tins and packets in graduated ranks on the shelves. They looked exactly the same as they'd done before. It was impossible to make her cupboards any tidier.

Jodie and Ash didn't have time to talk during lunch. Ash concentrated on the food while Jodie whizzed in and out of the kitchen, trying to keep her mind on what she was doing, when really she just wanted to be at home, the duvet pulled up under her chin while she overdosed on daytime TV and dreamed of ways of getting her revenge on Chris and Stefanie. She wondered if it would be possible to put wintergreen ointment into Stefanie's moisturiser jar before she slung it back at her with the rest of her stuff but, regretfully, decided that the smell of menthol and camphor would give it away.

But there must be something, she thought, something she could do to give the cheating, robbing, lying bitch what she deserved.

'Oh, shit, sorry!' She'd turned without looking and knocked the glass cafetière full of hot coffee out of Ash's hand. The cafetière hit the tiled floor with a crash, cracking on impact and sending a flood of hot coffee cascading across the floor. Jodie looked at Ash in horror, waiting for the tirade that she knew would happen, for the lecture on looking where she was going and standards of professionalism and then Ash's barbed comments about breakages coming out of salaries. She could see that Ash was winding up for something because her brown eyes were hard and her jaw was clenched and Jodie had a horrible feeling that whatever Ash said would make her cry. And she didn't want to cry in front of her. Ash just wasn't the sort of person who was sympathetic towards tears.

'Are you all right?' asked Ash.

'Yes, fine.'

'Put on another pot while I clean up,' said Ash.

Jodie stood still, blinking furiously. She was waiting for the onslaught which she knew would happen.

'Everything all right in here?' Ross Fearon poked his head round the door. 'There was the most awful crash. Anyone hurt?'

'No, Ross, everything's fine.' Ash smiled at him. 'Just a slight accident with the coffee. I'll brew some more.'

'Don't worry about it,' said Ross. 'It's probably good for us to stay off the coffee for a day.'

'But—'

'Really, Ash. It's busy downstairs anyway. Markets are having a rough ride today and we should be there, not here.'

'If you're sure.'

'I'm sure.'

'OK, then.' She nodded. 'You could ask Steve Proctor to send me an e-mail if he thinks I should sell some stock.'

Ross grinned at her. 'You know how it is,' he said. 'We always advise people that they should be holding for the long term and not to sell into some short-term weakness.'

Ash grimaced. 'That actually sounds like I should sell something before I lose my shirt.'

Ross shrugged. 'It's up to you.'

He closed the door and both Jodie and Ash heard the partners leave the dining room.

'I'm sorry,' said Jodie as she picked up a mop. 'It shouldn't have happened.'

'I know it shouldn't have happened,' said Ash. 'You know it shouldn't have happened. What's the point in telling you that again?'

Jodie stared at her. 'Oh, come on, Ash. Why don't you just shout at me and get it over and done with?'

'It wasn't your fault.' Ash bent down to pick up some of the bigger shards of glass. 'I wasn't looking either.'

'That normally doesn't make any difference,' muttered Jodie.

Ash stared at her. 'What do you mean?'

Jodie swallowed. She wished she hadn't said anything. Now she'd actually have to talk and she didn't think that she could talk without making a fool of herself.

'Nothing,' she said eventually. 'Just that you usually blame me if something goes wrong in the kitchen.'

'No I don't,' said Ash, horrified.

'Yes you do.' Jodie's voice was stronger. 'If anything goes wrong you blame me, not yourself.'

Ash pulled at her plait. 'Do you really think so?'

Jodie nodded.

'If that's the case, then I'm sorry,' said Ash.

'Oh, don't!' cried Jodie suddenly. 'Just don't!'

'Don't what?' Ash looked at her in amazement.

'Don't be nice to me today! I can't put up with someone being nice to me today. Be your usual cranky, perfectionist self and do me a great big favour!'

'Jodie!' Ash put her hands on Jodie's shoulders. 'What on earth's the matter with you?'

'That shit Chris is what's the matter.' Jodie couldn't keep back the tears any longer. 'He's having it off with my fucking flatmate. I saw them at it. I loved him, Ash, I really loved him. And he's gone and dumped me for someone with big tits and a small brain.'

'Oh, Jodie.'

'And don't tell me that there are other fish in the sea,' said Jodie fiercely. 'I know there are but I loved Chris. I really did.'

'I know.' Ash pulled Jodie towards her so that her head was resting on her shoulder. 'I understand, Jodie.'

'How can you?' Jodie's voice was muffled. 'When

you've split up with Alistair and you behave as though nothing had happened?'

How the hell did Jodie know about that already? wondered Ash. What was it about people that made them tell each other about break-ups and dates and boyfriends and – it must have been Alistair who told her, she realised. She shuddered at the thought of what else Alistair might have told Jodie.

'Were you talking to Alistair?' she asked.

'For a while,' said Jodie. 'I guess I kind of brought you two together. So it's not surprising I should be there when you split up.' She looked at Ash. 'Though it's a bit of a new departure for you, isn't it?'

'What is?'

'Having him break up with you instead of the other way round.'

Ash said nothing.

'How do you feel about it?' asked Jodie.

'What's there to feel? He thought the time had come to call it a day.'

'Oh, Ash, don't tell me you're not upset! Don't tell me you can just get on with your life as though it never happened.'

'Of course I'm a bit upset,' said Ash calmly. 'But what do you want me to do, Jodie?'

'Scream. Cry. Throw a tantrum. Say he's a bastard and a shit and you never liked him anyway.'

Ash smiled wanly. 'I can't say that,' she said. 'Of course I liked him.'

'Liked! What about love?' demanded Jodie.

'What about it?' asked Ash.

'He loved you, Ash,' she said. 'He really did.'

Ash shook her head. 'He wanted to love me. But he didn't really. He thought I was one sort of person, Jodie, but I wasn't. And not the right sort for him.'

'But was he the right sort of person for you?'

'I don't know,' said Ash.

Jodie said nothing but scrubbed at her eyes with a piece of kitchen towel.

'Would you like a drink?' said Ash. 'A glass of wine or something?'

'There's some white wine left over,' said Jodie doubtfully. 'But I thought you didn't approve of us drinking the leftovers.'

'This time I think it's OK.' Ash went into the dining room and retrieved the bottle of Sauvignon Blanc. She took two glasses from the cupboard and filled them.

'Thanks,' said Jodie as she accepted one of them. 'I'm sorry.'

'For what?' asked Ash.

'For making a fool of myself,' said Jodie.

'You didn't.' Ash shrugged and sipped the wine.

'Oh, come on!' Jodie's voice was stronger now. 'Crying in the kitchen! Sniffling onto your shoulder. And for what? Just because my bastard of a boyfriend has found someone else. But you – you haven't shed a tear. You never make a fool of yourself, Ash. Never.'

Ash said nothing.

'You simply get on with it and cook a cheese soufflé or something,' said Jodie.

Ash smiled slightly. 'Soup,' she said.

Jodie looked at her. 'Soup?'

'I made lots of it. That's why we had minestrone today.'

'Oh,' said Jodie. 'Well, it just proves my point. I have a weeping fit and tell myself that my life is over. I break three pots complete with potted plants, a couple of plates and a photo frame. You get dumped and you do something constructive like make soup. It's terrifying how composed you are about it.'

'Composed?' Ash made a face at her. 'I don't think so.'

'Of course you are,' said Jodie. 'You come in here exactly the same as any other day. No matter what happens you're always serenely in control of things – you're nothing like the rest of us.'

'The rest of you?'

'Girls like me. Confused, unsure, brimming with low self-esteem.' Jodie laughed shakily. 'The rest of us are the usual collection of neurotic twentysomethings who haven't yet managed to decide what we want out of life, whereas you are so completely cool you have us all totally intimidated.'

'You believe that?' Ash looked at her in surprise.

'It's true,' said Jodie.

Ash took a gulp of her wine. She couldn't believe that anyone would consider her capable or unflappable or in control of her life. She knew that she tried to be that way in the kitchen but how could anyone possibly look at her and not know that she wasn't anything like Jodie's description of her. After all, she was the girl who went home and stuck her head in a paper bag because she was gasping with panic. She was the girl who never allowed men into her apartment. She was the girl with four huge Le Creuset pots of soup still sitting on the hob. And she was the girl who had turned around and gone back home that morning because she was convinced that she'd left the immersion heater on! It was just as well that the so-called 'rest of them' weren't anything like her.

'Jodie, I'm not at all like you think,' she said. 'I'm really not. I—' She broke off, uncertain what she wanted to tell her.

'You're not the sort of person who'd throw potted plants across the room,' said Jodie. 'Especially all the really good ones. You wouldn't stay up all night crying. You wouldn't burn a photograph of your boyfriend and then change your mind and try and rescue it and singe your fingers.'

Ash sighed. 'I guess not.'

'You have it all, Ash. And, if you want him, you have Alistair too!'

'Oh, Jodie, I don't think—'

'I bet you anything he'd get back with you if you wanted.'

'In which case why did he break it off with me?' asked Ash.

'Because you were so distant with him,' Jodie told her. 'If you really do care about people, you can't treat them as though they don't matter, Ash.'

Ash shrugged.

'Perhaps, though, you really do have it all worked out. Keep them guessing, wanting more. Alistair was gutted that you never even let him into your apartment but he still went out with you. Whereas Chris practically took up residence with me and now he's thrown me over for the physio cow. Of course,' said Jodie ruefully, 'maybe that's why he spent so much time in my place. He wanted to be with her.' She buried her head in her hands. 'I want to kill him,' she mumbled. 'But I want to kill myself even more.'

'Jodie!' Ash was shocked and a little worried. 'You don't really mean that.'

Jodie looked up. 'I suppose not.' She sniffed. 'It's just – why do I always get it wrong, Ash? Even when I think I'm getting it right?'

'I don't think that it's just you.' Ash sighed deeply. 'I think everyone manages to get things wrong more than once in their lives.'

'But not you,' Jodie told her. 'Not you, Ash. Things always work out the way you want them to, don't they?'

'Not always,' said Ash as she drained her wine glass. 'Sometimes it feels like hardly ever.'

Chapter 24

Pizza Napoletana
Pizza dough, tomatoes, sugar, seasoning, mozzarella cheese,
anchovies, oregano
Simmer oil, tomatoes, sugar and seasoning in pot for
about 10 minutes. Roll out pizza dough. Spread tomato
mixture evenly over dough, arrange slices of mozzarella
and anchovies over tomato mixture. Sprinkle with oil,
oregano and seasoning. Bake in hot oven until topping is
melted and dough risen

The Alitalia flight left Dublin airport at just after
eleven o'clock. Ash sat back in her window seat
and sighed with relief that she was leaving the country,
even if it was only for a few days. She'd had second, third
and even fourth thoughts about this dinner for Dan's
family, but now it seemed like a godsend. Because she
was cracking up at home.

Alistair was always on her mind but she couldn't trust
her feelings about him any more. Sometimes she felt as
though there was a frozen ring round her heart which

stopped her from feeling anything at all. But she was afraid to dig too deeply into her emotions because she was terrified of what she might find. And then, in the newspaper gossip column, she'd seen the picture of Alistair and another girl at a summer barbecue which had taken place the week after they'd broken up. And she knew that she was hurt and that she was jealous, and she'd bundled up the newspaper and thrown it into the corner of the room.

Michelle had seen the photo too and she'd phoned Ash to ask who the girl was and what was going on.

'Isn't there anything else you could be worrying about?' snapped Ash.

'Don't tell me you've fucked it up again!' Michelle's voice was tense. 'Don't tell me you've gone and lost the best man in the whole world for you.'

'I won't tell you that,' said Ash.

'Oh, Ash, I'm sorry. It's just that in the picture she's all over him. It doesn't look good.'

'We're not going out any more,' said Ash. 'But he ended it, not me.'

There was a blank silence at the other end of the phone as Michelle digested the news. 'He ended it?' she repeated eventually.

'Yes,' said Ash.

'Why?'

'Because I'm a flake,' said Ash. 'That's why.'

'He didn't say that, did he?'

Ash laughed tersely. 'You've said it yourself often enough.'

'Do you want me to come over?' asked Michelle.

'Not right now,' said Ash. 'I'm packing to go to Sicily. I've got a job over there.'

'You're emigrating?' squeaked Michelle. 'Don't you think that's a bit drastic?'

'I'm not emigrating.' Ash almost laughed. 'I'm just doing one function, that's all.'

'In Sicily?'

'Yes.'

'For who?'

'One of my stockbroking clients.'

Michelle was silent again.

'It's for a few days,' Ash explained.

'I've got to hand it to you,' said Michelle. 'Most girls would be devastated. But you're going to cater for a function in Sicily.' She sighed. 'It's hardly surprising people think you're flaky.'

'Thanks,' said Ash.

'Call me when you get back,' said Michelle. 'I think you need to talk about it.'

Ash didn't want to talk to Michelle about it. She didn't want Michelle's sympathy, or to listen to her cousin bleating at her for having let the millionaire slip through her fingers. She didn't want to talk about how she felt – why, oh why, she wondered, did so many people want to talk all the time? Jodie still hadn't shut up about her break-up with Chris and she really and truly expected to get some feedback from Ash. But Ash didn't know what feedback to give her and she was tired of trying to dodge the questions all the time.

The plane burst through the thin film of cloud and mist that had shrouded the airport and popped into the blue sky above, and Ash felt herself relax physically and mentally as Dublin disappeared behind her.

Buon giorno, she murmured under her breath. She smiled to herself. She'd only been to Italy once before, on a school trip to Rome, but she'd been captivated by the city and the people, the warmth and the light. She was sure that Sicily would be very different to Rome – she visualised it as an arid lump of rock off the toe of Italy, but it was Italian nonetheless and she was looking forward to being there. She glanced around the cabin at her fellow passengers. The flight wasn't direct and she was getting a connecting flight from Milan so there were a number of Milanese businessmen on board, looking incredibly well-dressed in their designer business suits and oozing charm, style and a completely different way of life. Maybe I'll meet a Sicilian, she thought suddenly. And maybe he'll be the man I've been waiting for all my life. She smothered a snort of laughter at the thought. To meet and fall for a Sicilian would be mad and impulsive and probably impossible in three days. And not the sort of thing she'd do anyway. But it would be nice, the thought formed in her head, it would be nice to come home with someone else after being dumped by Alistair Brannigan.

Your pride is hurt, she told herself, as she flicked through the in-flight magazine. And it's the only bloody thing about you that is hurt! Despite what Michelle might think. Despite what you want to think yourself. She desperately wanted to believe that.

Michelle had called her again before she left. 'Let yourself go while you're away,' she said. 'Nobody at home will know if you do anything really stupid and it'd be good for you.'

'The only stupid thing I'm likely to do is overcook the pasta or something,' Ash told her spiritedly.

'I thought you might have improved a bit,' said Michelle dryly. 'But I'm not so sure any more.'

Ash opened her bag and took out *Ferrari Vendetta*, which was the first in the Vanna Savino series by Joss Morland. The detective story was set in Tuscany as well as Sicily and Ash wondered whether Joss had a villa there too, where he could drink in the atmosphere. The books were laced with atmosphere – Ash could almost see the vine-clad hills, the red-roofed houses and, less charmingly, the corpses that littered the pages. But it was fun to read and it passed the time nicely until she reached Milan. There she had to wait for a couple of hours before she boarded her connecting flight to Catania, so she bought a couple of recipe books to study on the plane.

She'd asked Dan whether or not they wanted something very Italian to eat. She enjoyed Italian cooking, she told him, but if he thought that Joss would be fed up with pasta and tomato sauce she'd happily do something else.

'I'll leave it up to you,' Dan had told her. 'Joss only eats fruit, breadsticks and prosciutto when he's working so he'll be ready for anything. Bronwyn prefers vegetables to meat. I'll eat whatever you cook.'

The flight from Milan to Catania left on time. Ash

leaned her head against the window and ran through menus in her head. By the time they arrived at Catania airport she'd narrowed down her choices. But it would depend, ultimately, on what was fresh and good in the shops.

Warm air, tinged with the smell of jet fuel, wrapped itself around her as she walked out of the airport. She took off her faded linen jacket and stuffed it into her travel bag. She hadn't expected it to be like this, like stepping into a warm bath.

She looked at the address Dan had given her. Villa Rosa was in Taormina, a smaller town to the north of Catania. Hopefully, by now, Dan had already arrived. She knew that lots of things didn't faze her (as Jodie might have put it) but the idea of arriving at his father's house without knowing anybody else there certainly did.

She hailed a cab and got inside, relieved that it had air-conditioning because, by now, her cotton top was sticking to her. And it's only May, she thought. Imagine what it'd be like in August!

It was a long time since Ash had been anywhere hot, either in May or in August. Somehow she never seemed to have the time, although she knew that telling herself that was probably a cop-out. But for as long as she could remember she hadn't taken two consecutive weeks' holiday and the time she took off she normally spent in Ireland. Part of the reason was that she hated leaving Bagel for too long, especially since he sulked like crazy anytime she left him on his own for more than a couple of days. The longest she'd been away was eight nights – she'd booked him into a cattery then and when she'd brought him home again he'd shown his displeasure at the entire event by shredding the side of the sofa with his claws.

Her neighbours had stepped into the breach again this time, demanding that she bring back some extra-extra-virgin olive oil as compensation for feeding him, as well as a lump of lava from Mount Etna. Ash was confident that she'd manage to obtain the olive oil; she was a little less certain about bringing home volcanic rock.

It had been a long day so far, she thought, as they drove along the motorway towards Taormina. But interesting. And it was nice to be away from everyone and everything at home. The taxi driver shifted into a lower gear as they began to climb higher. Ash hadn't even noticed them leaving the motorway but now the road narrowed and snaked its way upwards through the hills. She gasped as the lights of the coast were left far below them and she gripped the door handle as the hairpin bends of the road grew even more pronounced.

As they rounded the next bend she saw a tourist coach bearing down on them and she had to fight the impulse to yell at the taxi driver. She couldn't see how they'd manage to pass each other on the road but they did, the driver hugging one side so that they were almost embedded in this hillside. Ash gulped. She could see why Joss Morland spent his time here – nobody could get to him unless he really, really wanted them to!

Eventually the driver pulled up beside a black wrought-iron gate at the side of the road. Ash couldn't see any villa in the darkness. She couldn't see any other houses either – all she could see were the cypress and pine trees that hugged the hillside against the backdrop of the star-laden sky.

'Villa Rosa,' said the taxi driver.

'Are you sure?'

'Of course.' He looked again at the map she'd shown him, where Dan had marked the location of the villa, and nodded. 'Villa Rosa.'

She peered at the iron gate through the car window. Perhaps he was right, she thought. There was obviously something behind it. But she was worried that he was leaving her here in the dark and in the middle of nowhere, although it was probably a picturesque nowhere in daylight.

He got out of the cab and took her bag out of the boot. Clearly he reckoned his work was done and wasn't hanging about to see whether or not she was in the right place. Since it was a thirty- or forty-minute drive back to Catania, Ash supposed that he wanted to get home rather than wait around for a stupid tourist who didn't believe she was where she was supposed to be.

She peeled some lire notes from the wad in her purse and handed them to him. He nodded at her and got back into the taxi, gunning it up the road and leaving her standing on the pavement, her bag at her feet. Even here, near the coast though higher up, the air was humid. She wiped the beads of sweat from her upper lip, picked up her bag and went over to the wrought-iron gate.

It was locked. She rattled it a couple of times, then saw

an intercom set into the side of the yellow-brick wall. She pressed the buzzer.

'Hello?' The female voice at the other end spoke English and Ash sighed with relief. At least this meant that she might possibly be in the right place.

'Hello,' she said tentatively. 'My name is Ash O'Halloran. I'm here to cook dinner tomorrow night.'

'Oh, yes, we're expecting you. Come in.'

'The gate is locked,' said Ash.

'I'll buzz it open for you,' said the girl.

There was a hum and a click as the gate opened and Ash stepped inside. She could see now what she couldn't see earlier: the roof of the villa, which was set into the side of the hill. A gravel path led round it, and steep steps brought her down to the level of the house.

The front door opened as she came down the last of the steps.

'Hello.' The woman who'd spoken on the intercom stood at the threshold and Ash knew instantly that she was Dan's twin.

'Welcome to Villa Rosa,' said Bronwyn. 'I'm glad you found us.'

'To tell you the truth I wasn't too sure.' Ash smiled faintly. 'The cab driver deposited me on the side of the street and I couldn't see the house.'

Bronwyn laughed. 'Lots of houses around here are set into the hill like this,' she told Ash. 'And you can't see them from the road. Which is nice really.' She ushered Ash into the tiled hallway. 'Can I take your bag?'

'No thanks, it's not heavy.'

'Would you like to join us for a drink on the terrace or would you like to freshen up first?' asked Bronwyn.

'I think I'll just go to my room if that's OK,' said Ash.

'Fine.' Bronwyn nodded and led her down a narrow corridor. 'But join us afterwards.'

Ash said nothing. She had no intention of joining the Morlands for drinks. She was here to do a job, not sit around sipping Cinzano or Pedrotti or grappa with them.

Bronwyn pushed open the door of one of the rooms and gestured Ash to go inside. 'There's a bathroom en suite,' she told her. 'If there's anything you need, just let me know.'

'I will, thanks,' said Ash.

'We think it's a real blast, Dan hiring someone to come and do the cooking,' confided Bronwyn. 'It's not a bad idea, actually, because we're all hopeless at it – I've been known to spoil pasta which, let's face it, isn't exactly the hardest food in the world to cook. And this is such a nice house to entertain in – we've always wanted to do something special here.'

'I think he's crazy myself,' said Ash. 'You could've got someone local for a lot less money.'

'Dan likes to make big gestures from time to time,' Bronwyn told her. 'And part of it is to get at Dad.'

'Oh?'

'Let him know that Dan's done well for himself,' she explained. 'That it's no trouble to him to fly you from Dublin.'

'Really?'

Bronwyn nodded. 'Dan's always trying to prove to Dad that, despite his desertion of us for a fictional woman who earns him a fortune, we've done well with our lives.'

Ash wasn't sure she wanted to get into the nitty gritty of Joss Morland's desertion of his family. And according to Dan it was Joss's wife who'd walked out.

'Is Dan here?' asked Ash.

'He's gone up to the town,' said Bronwyn. 'He'll be back soon. I don't know how he's still awake, he's been travelling since yesterday. Apparently he was in London on business and then went to New York to see Cordelia. He's been there for the last two days.'

'Did she come back with him?' asked Ash.

Bronwyn shook her head. 'No, the führer remains in New York.'

'The führer?'

'You've met her, haven't you?' asked Bronwyn. 'The bossiest woman in the world.'

'I didn't think she was too bad,' Ash protested and Bronwyn snorted.

'She's ideal for Dan,' said his twin. 'He's the kind of guy who needs someone to organise him and she does that. But she drives me nuts with all this power talk of how great she is and how important her job is and what it's like being a woman in a man's world.'

'I suppose she works hard,' said Ash noncommittally.

'Don't we all.' Brownwyn stepped out of the room. 'But we don't go on about it for every minute of the day.

See you later, Ash.' She closed the door behind her and left Ash to look round the room.

It was small but with a high ceiling that made it feel much bigger. The door to the adjoining bathroom was ajar and Ash pushed it open and turned on the light. The bathroom was lovely – tiled almost completely in white and with a clear glass door on the shower so that, once again, a relatively small space seemed much bigger.

She went back into the bedroom and across to the window over which heavy red and green striped drapes had been pulled. She heaved them open and realised that the window was, in fact, a pair of French doors which opened inwards. There was a narrow balcony outside, barely wide enough to stand on. But she didn't need to stand on the balcony to be awestruck by the night view. The hill below the villa seemed to fall away to nothing so that Ash felt as though she was suspended in mid-air. She could see down to the coast and the narrow ribbon of yellow lights which traced their way round the bay. The night sky was studded with stars, the moon reflected onto the calm sea beneath and, in the distance, the faint lights of the Italian mainland glowed.

It was, thought Ash, the most beautiful place she'd ever been. And she was only seeing it by night! She could understand why Joss Morland came here to get the atmosphere – the warm night air was laden with it, from the faint hum of the traffic to the occasional chirrup of the cicadas and the sound of voices and laughter floating around the hillside.

I could live here, she thought. I could live here and

cook pizzas and pasta for the rest of my life and I'd feel happy.

Odd, she thought, that she didn't feel as uncomfortable about being here as she thought she would. Usually she didn't like being in strange places, away from the familiar things that she knew. But this was so lovely that it was impossible to feel uncomfortable. She couldn't wait to see it in daylight and she envied Joss for having it.

She turned back into the room and unpacked her things, hanging her clothes neatly in the wardrobe and arranging her toiletries on the glass shelf of the bathroom. She hummed as she unpacked, laughing at herself for the fact that her song was '*O Sole Mio*'.

Next thing you know I'll be handing out Cornettos, she thought, as she kicked off her trainers and lay down on the bed.

Chapter 25

Seafood Risotto
Olive oil, butter, onion, garlic, red and green pepper,
carnaroli rice, fish stock, dry white wine, bay leaf, salt and
pepper, cooked jumbo prawns, cooked mussels, Parmesan
cheese
Heat oil and butter and fry onion, garlic and peppers.
Add rice and stir until coated. Add some stock and wine,
bay leaf and seasoning. Simmer gently until all liquid is
absorbed by rice. Continue adding stock and simmering
until absorbed. Remove bay leaf, add prawns and mussels.
Turn into serving dish and serve with Parmesan cheese

T he long gauze curtain billowed in the soft morning
breeze and the slight movement woke Ash up. She
opened her eyes and lay in the bed for a moment then
sat up and looked around her. The air was still warm
and distant sounds of conversation amid the clattering
of crockery wafted to her. She pushed the sheet out of
the way and padded over to the open French doors.

The sky was deepest blue and the morning sun was

already glittering on the surface of the sea. Directly below her, the garden of the Villa Rosa was a frenzy of brightly coloured flowers and shrubs, through which steep stone steps led further down the hillside and stopped at swimming pool and terrace. She leaned over the balcony to see further. To her right and below her was another, wider terrace where a table, in the shade of a huge umbrella, was set with breakfast things. A man sat at the table, reading a newspaper. He had silver-grey hair, a tanned complexion and wore a shirt and shorts. Ash guessed he was Joss Morland.

She hadn't met any of the Morlands the previous night. Bronwyn had knocked on her door about half an hour after she'd unpacked and asked Ash if she'd like to join them downstairs. But Ash had been uncomfortable about it, still feeling that she was here to do a job and not become friends with everyone. Besides, she didn't want to meet Dan yet. He might ask her about Alistair and she didn't want to talk about Alistair in front of people she didn't even know. Anyway, she wouldn't be able to talk about him. She'd blocked him out of her mind as though he'd never existed. So she'd told Bronwyn that she was really tired and that she was just going to sit in her room, read a book and relax for a while. Bronwyn had shrugged, mentioned to Ash that she could wander down to the kitchen and get something to eat if she liked, and then disappeared again. Ash had been more tired than hungry. She drank the bottle of Pellegrino that was on her bedside locker and sat beside the open window, reading, until her eyes started to droop. Then she went to bed.

Now, however, she was starving. She watched as an elegant, fair-haired woman wearing a soft green dress walked to the table carrying a basket of croissants and a pot of coffee. She must be Joss's ex-wife, Ash decided. She could almost smell the aroma of the freshly brewed coffee and taste the buttery pastry of the croissants. Her stomach rumbled noisily. She hurried into the bathroom, had the quickest shower of her life, dressed in a plain white T-shirt and blue jeans and went in search of something to eat.

The kitchen was at the back of the house, facing into the hillside. It was a shaded room but brightly decorated with a white marble floor and white painted walls on which someone had stencilled images of vine leaves and grapes.

Dan stood in the middle of the kitchen beside the huge wooden table, a glass of orange juice in his hand.

'Ash!' He put down his glass and kissed her, continental style, on both cheeks. 'Great to see you.'

'Great to be here,' she said.

'Where were you last night?' asked Dan. 'I thought you'd join us for a drink – we were on the terrace for ages.'

'I was tired,' she said.

'Tired!' He snorted. 'Wait till you've spent a few days in London and a few days in New York and then you can talk about tiredness.'

'How was New York? And Cordelia?'

'Great,' said Dan. 'Poor girl is just snowed under with work and the trouble with her is that she keeps on accepting more. She wants so much to prove herself.'

'I'm sure she will.' Ash desperately wanted to cut a slice from the loaf of ciabatta bread but she didn't want to appear ravenous.

'I know she will,' Dan said. 'She's doing the training course and she's been given the opportunity to work for a time with one of the legal guys, Mike Fuller, who's a top exec in the bank. She thinks he fancies her a little so I told her to make sure he knew that she was already spoken for!'

'And has she?' Her stomach rumbled but not loud enough for Dan to hear.

'Absolutely. She said she flashes her engagement ring at him every time she meets him.'

Ash smiled. 'Probably scares the life out of him,' she said. 'It's not exactly the world's most discreet stone.'

'You telling me I've no taste?' asked Dan.

'God, no, not at all.' Ash flushed. 'I just meant—'

'I know what you meant.' He grinned at her. 'Stop taking things so personally.'

'I don't,' she said.

Dan smiled and cut himself a slice of bread. 'Aren't you having any? And are you going to join us for breakfast this morning or stay locked away in your room?'

'Dan, I'm not a friend of the family,' she said. 'I'm here to do a job. I'll have some breakfast but I don't want to be introduced to everyone as though I'm on holiday.'

'Whatever you like,' said Dan. 'But nobody will take

much notice of you anyway. That's not the way my family works.'

Ash thought about the Rourkes and how everyone wanted to know everything about everyone else and she wondered which was best.

'Here you are.' Dan handed her a plate with two slices of bread. 'There's fruit on the table outside so if you want anything else, including coffee, you'll have to come out.'

'Oh, OK,' she said warily and followed him to the terrace where she'd seen his parents earlier.

But there was nobody there now, although the coffee pot was still warm.

'Dad's probably gone to read through his manuscript again,' said Dan disparagingly. 'We almost have to prise it out of his hands eventually because he'd change it the day it went to print if he got half the chance.' He glanced at his watch. 'And Mum's gone out for the day, she couldn't possibly stay around Dad for the whole time. I think she muttered something about Syracuse.' He looked at Ash. 'If you'd allowed me to give you an extra day or two here you could have gone to Syracuse yourself. It's worth a visit if you're into history or architecture. The place was forever under attack or under siege or something. It's littered with archaeological remains, if that's your thing.'

'Another time, perhaps,' said Ash. 'Today I want to go into the town and check out the food shops.'

'Check out the clothes shops while you're at it,' said Dan.

Ash grinned. 'I'm not all that into clothes shops

myself,' she told him. 'Waste of time and money. And too crowded. I hate crowds.'

He made a face at her. 'I've never known a woman not to like clothes shops before,' he told her. 'The shops here are small and I don't think they're ever crowded. Bronwyn spends a fortune every time she visits.'

Ash looked at him doubtfully. 'It's only a small town, isn't it? It's not as though you could spend a fortune.'

'Expensive shops,' Dan said.

Ash shrugged. She doubted that there would be anything worth buying in Taormina unless, perhaps, there was a shoe shop. Ash liked Italian leather. But she didn't have time to look at clothes shops or shoe shops, she had lots of things to do today.

She shifted in the wood and canvas seat so that she could look at the sea again and wished she'd worn her shorts. The air was still humid and the heat clung to her.

'Beautiful, isn't it?' asked Dan.

'Gorgeous,' she said.

'When we were younger we used to come here a lot.' He picked up a banana from the bowl of fruit and began peeling it. 'And then we went through a phase where we didn't get on so well with Dad and we didn't come for ages. But now everything's fine.'

'Good,' said Ash. She swallowed her cup of coffee in one gulp. 'I'd better get going,' she said.

'Do you want me to drop you up to the town?' asked Dan. 'It's about a fifteen-minute walk from here. Uphill.'

Ash shook her head. 'I enjoy walking,' she told him. 'And I'm not in a hurry.'

'Could've fooled me,' he murmured as she left the table and walked quickly back into the house again.

In the daylight, Ash realised that what Bronwyn had told her the previous night was perfectly true. Many of the villas were built at varying heights along the hillside so that roofs were at street level or below. All of them faced towards the sea and most of them were, like Villa Rosa, painted in pastel shades. The Villa Rosa was palest pink, with bright green shutters. It was oblong, like a tall coloured box jutting up from the greenery below. It was the prettiest house that Ash had ever seen.

She walked along the winding road, hugging the side so as to keep well clear of the endless number of Vespas that raced up and down it at breakneck speed. Ash was sure she'd seen a girl on her scooter talking into her mobile phone at the same time as she whizzed by, which, she reckoned, had to be illegal. Or maybe not, she told herself wryly; this was part of Italy after all.

A little later she arrived at the old gateway to the town. Three-storey buildings with long windows and wrought-iron balconies packed with urns of brightly coloured flowers lined the main street. Despite the bustling nature of the town, Ash felt as though she had stepped back in time.

More immediately, though, an ice-cream parlour attracted her attention. She was still hungry, not having felt comfortable sitting around the Villa Rosa for breakfast, so she bought herself a cone filled with creamy vanilla and sprinkled with chocolate. She licked the ice cream as she strolled along the street, past the ivy-clad shop whose antique silverware was laid out in front of it and past the souvenir shop where she realised she could buy some particularly tacky pieces of lava rock for her neighbours.

As she progressed along the Corso Umberto she stopped in surprise. She suddenly understood what Dan had meant when he said that the shops in Taormina were expensive. They were all designer boutiques. The one in front of her was Prada and the shop next door proclaimed that it sold Gucci and Armani. So much for a small town on a small island, she thought, as she looked at the extremely sophisticated window displays and remembered that her Italian teacher in school had once said that Italians didn't take out mortgages on their houses; they thought it more important to take out loans for their clothes instead.

I'm not here to gaze at Prada bags, she told herself as she swallowed the last of her ice cream and licked her fingers appreciatively. I'm here to buy olives and rice, meat and vegetables and whatever else I need for tonight. She didn't have to think about wine because Joss Morland had a well-stocked wine cellar which she'd discovered when she returned to the house after breakfast. After inspecting the racks of wine she'd spent some time checking out the kitchen, making sure that she had everything she needed. Joss might eat nothing but prosciutto, if Dan was right, but his kitchen was more than adequate for her needs.

She'd also spent time looking at the dining room which opened onto the terrace where she'd had breakfast. She wasn't sure whether or not the Morlands would prefer to eat indoors or *al fresco* but, either way, there was enough room to accommodate them. It would be a perfect setting for a perfect meal. A triumph, she told herself, of her cooking skills.

She walked on, mulling over the alternative menu choices. There were so many possibilities that each one she chose seemed more perfect than the last. She stopped in front of the next shop despite herself, even though it sold clothes not food, because the single dress in the window was so lovely that she found it impossible to walk by. It was ink-blue gossamer-fine net over silk, with a round neckline at the front and cut low at the back. Tiny silver beads had been sewn onto the net in an abstract design.

It was the kind of dress that she should have had when she'd gone to the K Club with Dan as his old friend. It was the kind of dress that she might have needed if she'd been sensible enough not to have scared Alistair Brannigan away. It was the kind of dress that would make anyone feel confident on any occasion. It was the first time Ash had ever looked at an item of clothing that couldn't be worn every day if necessary and wanted it anyway.

But, she thought, it was bound to be ridiculously expensive. Clearly everything on this street was designer wear and nothing would come with a Dunnes Stores or Marks and Spencer price tag. But it was so lovely, she sighed, as she gazed at it. So very elegant. And she really, really wanted it.

She shook her head and walked past the shop. Then

she turned round. They probably won't have it in my size, she decided and pushed open the door of the shop. And chances are it's one of those dresses that looks great in the window, tucked tightly round the display model, but looks terrible on a live person with curves ruining the line!

'*Belissima!*' cried the saleswoman as Ash stepped out of the changing room and stood in front of the mirror. '*Belissima!*'

Ash gazed at her reflection. The silk of the dress clung to her body and the silver beads sparkled under the spotlights of the shop. She was a different person in this dress, she thought, as she slowly turned round. She was a sophisticated Ash, the kind of Ash who wouldn't feel out of place anywhere. Well, she told herself, reality taking hold, she'd look completely out of place in the kitchen!

'How much?' she asked the saleswoman.

'In euros,' she replied, 'five hundred and fifty.'

It was a ridiculous price to pay for a dress, thought Ash. Even a dress that was as beautiful as this one. What's more, she thought, I couldn't wear it more than a couple of times. Buying it would be crazy.

'It's beautiful.' She turned in front of the mirror again.

The saleswoman said nothing but smiled at her encouragingly. I've never spent this much on one item of clothing before, thought Ash. Never. It's not the way I do things. I'll go away and think about it.

She went back into the changing room, slid out of the dress and back into her T-shirt and jeans. She pulled her hair into a pony tail and wondered how she could look so great a moment earlier and so ordinary now.

'I'll take it.' The words were out of her mouth before she even realised she was speaking. The saleswoman told her that it was a wonderful choice and very reasonable. Ash signed her credit card slip and wondered what on earth was happening to her. She'd never before gone out to buy olives and peppers and aubergines and had, instead, bought a dress for nearly four hundred pounds! She took the plain white carrier bag stamped with the shop's gold and black logo and stepped outside into the street. She felt as though her whole life had somersaulted in the last few days.

Not long ago I was going out with Alistair Brannigan, she mused, I could end it whenever I liked, my most important event was a dinner for six in Monkstown and the most expensive dress I owned cost seventy-five pounds and was nearly four years old. And now I'm on my own again, he was the one who ended it, I'm cooking in Sicily and I've made the first impulse purchase of my life. And it is a complete waste of money because, let's face it, without Alistair will I ever get the chance to wear it?

She'd heard about impulse shopping, she'd read about it, but she'd never done it before and never realised how wonderful the feeling could be. She'd always thought that it was done by stupid women with more money than sense. Or silly girls with no money at all who racked up scary credit card bills. She didn't even buy food on impulse, always as part of a plan. And yet she'd done it herself today and she'd liked it. She could almost understand what Michelle meant when she said how good it was when you were down. And, if she wasn't down, she certainly wasn't up. According to Michelle, most women bought clothes when they were upset. It helped, apparently. Now, for once in her life, she was behaving like most women and it certainly had helped!

She clutched the carrier bag tightly between her fingers as she continued her stroll through the narrow streets of the town. She stopped at a pasta shop to look at some of the fantastically shaped pieces and checked out the small fruit and vegetable shop nearby. It made her feel marginally more normal again to have noticed that the pasta was cheaper at this end of the street than the other.

The air was growing more humid and Ash's T-shirt was damp. She found a shaded stone seat almost opposite the old church, sat down and closed her eyes. Sounds of children's laughter as they ran round the square carried on the air, along with music from one of the open-air cafés. It was relaxing, soothing and would have lulled her to sleep if the seat hadn't been so hard.

She smiled to herself as she thought of what Michelle would say when she told her about the dress. Michelle thought she was an utterly hopeless shopper. The first time they'd gone into Drogheda together Ash had trailed behind Michelle, showing no interest whatsoever in the clothes even though she'd saved more pocket money and could have afforded almost anything in Penney's. She'd looked listlessly at the displays and had told Michelle that it was all rubbish. Michelle hadn't asked Ash to come shopping with her again. She'd told Ash that she wasn't normal, everyone loved shopping.

But she'd think I was normal now, thought Ash. She'd think that I was like everyone else in the world. In fact she'd probably think I was mad spending so much on one dress.

She opened her eyes and looked at her watch. Better get on with it, she thought. She'd identified the shops where she was going to buy her ingredients and she didn't want to hang around until lunchtime when many of them might shut. She bought garlic and rosemary, peppercorns, olives and capers to go with the chicken dish she'd finally decided on. She also bought tomatoes, green peppers and aubergines and a variety of salads. She'd decided against pasta but was going to serve a seafood risotto to start and she supposed that she should make her own version of tiramisu for dessert. It always went down well with her clients. She also bought some fresh fruit from a vendor on the side of the road, whose battered blue van was crammed with bananas, apricots, apples, oranges, peaches and, to Ash's surprise, coconuts. When she'd made her selection of fruit he threw in a coconut as a gift.

The bags were heavy. She trudged down the hill towards the villa, wondering if the weather would break. By now the air was so warm and humid that she felt as though she was drinking it rather than breathing it.

'My God, you've been busy.' Bronwyn came into the kitchen as Ash was unloading her bags. 'And how many of us are you expecting to feed?'

'Five,' said Ash. 'That's what Dan said. You, your boyfriend, your mother, Joss and Dan.'

'That's right,' said Bronwyn. 'It just looks like an awful lot of food.'

'It always does until people start to eat.' Ash filled the sink with water and threw the vegetables into it.

'What time are you going to serve dinner?' asked Bronwyn.

'Eight thirty?' suggested Ash.

'Sounds good to me.' Bronwyn nodded. 'You've got time to sit by the pool for a while.'

Ash shook her head. 'I've lots to do. I want to look at the dining room again and the terrace and check out a few more things in the kitchen. No time for lounging, I'm afraid.'

'You keep talking as though you're just the hired help,' complained Bronwyn. 'I thought you were Dan's friend. Though I'm not sure how Cordelia feels about Dan having women friends under the age of forty-five.'

'I'm more of an acquaintance,' said Ash. 'And Cordelia knows exactly how unimportant I am.' Just the cook, that was what Cordelia had said about her.

'Come and join us anyway,' said Bronwyn. 'You haven't even met Mum or Dad yet.'

'I've lots to do,' repeated Ash. 'Honestly.'

Bronwyn sighed. 'Don't say I didn't ask you,' she told Ash.

'I won't.' Ash smiled at her and returned to washing the vegetables.

Chapter 26

Sicilian Vegetables
Broad beans, artichokes, peas, extra-virgin olive oil, new
onions finely sliced, white wine vinegar, fresh parsley
coarsely chopped, salt and pepper
Gently fry onion and artichoke in oil until soft. Add
the rest of the ingredients. Cook slowly until vinegar has
evaporated

Ash thought that she was going to faint with the
heat. The villa wasn't air-conditioned and, despite
the extractor fan in the kitchen, the room was like a
furnace. She checked the risotto one more time and then
went outside to tell the Morlands that dinner was ready.

Dan's mother, Freda, stood at the opposite end of the
terrace to Joss. She was smoking a cigarette and the thin
blue-grey smoke spiralled into the air. Joss was leaning
against the rail, staring out over the sea.

Bronwyn and her boyfriend, Tony – a dark-haired man
with the build of a rugby-player – stood near the steps that
led down to the pool and closer to where Ash had set the

table. By common consent they were eating outdoors, which was hardly surprising given how warm it was. As a break from the heat, Ash had ventured down to the pool later in the afternoon when she could see that there was no one there. She'd had to push her way through the fronds and flowers of the overgrown garden and past the gargoyle that protruded from the side wall to get there. The gargoyle – a half-human, half-leonine face with a wide-open mouth – was, in fact, part of the gutter. Ash had pictured it as it would look when it rained, with water gushing out of its mouth, and wished she could see it like that.

The pool was small, but well positioned to catch the sunlight. Ash had trailed her toes lazily through the water and thought how nice it would be to have a swim. Perhaps tomorrow, she thought wistfully. Then she'd gone back to the villa to work.

She looked along the terrace for Dan but she couldn't see him. Bronwyn caught her eye and waved at her.

'Dinner's ready,' said Ash. 'Where's Dan?'

'In the living room,' Bronwyn said. 'He's on the phone to Cordelia.'

'Will he be ages?' asked Ash.

Bronwyn shrugged. 'Probably. He's besotted with that woman.'

'Why do you dislike her so much?' asked Tony.

'I don't dislike her but she's irritating,' said Bronwyn. 'Too pushy.'

'I like her,' Tony said. 'I like a woman who knows what she wants.'

'Maybe.' Bronwyn didn't sound convinced. 'It's just that she's so – so overpowering.'

Ash cleared her throat. 'Maybe you could get Dan to give me a shout as soon as he's finished,' she said. 'Then I'll serve dinner.'

What the hell could they be talking about? Ash wondered crossly as she lowered the heat still further under the copper pot. Wedding plans? Work troubles? Or maybe it was just a very intimate telephone conversation. She replaced the lid on the pot. Here she was again cooking for Dan Morland and, once again, he was making her wait. And the last time it had been because he was making love in the living room while she was working in the kitchen. It had been perfectly obvious that he'd been at it with Cordelia before dinner, she'd had that smug, self-satisfied look in her eyes all during the meal. Until he'd asked her to marry him.

Preliminary engagement discussions! It might have sounded sensible to her but, in reality, who on earth actually held preliminary engagement discussions? Except perhaps someone like Ivana Trump who probably had her lawyers hold the preliminary engagement discussions. Ash mused that she'd probably never get as far as preliminary engagement discussions herself. She'd run away from the poor bloke before he even had a chance to clear his throat.

'Oh, hi.' She looked up as Dan came into the kitchen. 'Are you ready to eat now?'

'Certainly.' He looked at her curiously. 'Is there a problem?'

'No,' she said. 'I thought you said half eight was OK.'

'It is,' said Dan.

'It's a quarter to nine now,' said Ash.

His mouth twitched. 'Fifteen minutes isn't a crime, is it?'

'No.'

'It is, isn't it?' He'd heard the badly disguised censure in her voice.

'Don't be silly.'

'You're mad at me because I've delayed you by fifteen minutes.' His voice shook with laughter. 'Oh, Ash, I'm sorry. I didn't realise it mattered.'

'It doesn't matter,' she said stiffly. 'I'm – it's just that I time things.'

'Surely you're meant to be flexible,' said Dan. 'It doesn't spoil because of fifteen minutes, does it?'

She shook her head. 'It's not the food, just me. Don't worry about it.'

'I was talking to Cordelia,' said Dan. 'I'm sorry.' He looked at her speculatively. 'That night you did dinner for us – our engagement dinner – we were very late, weren't we?'

'Yes,' said Ash.

'Were you annoyed then?'

'Oh, Dan, it's irrelevant.'

He laughed again. 'I didn't realise,' he repeated. 'It's the rebellion thing of course, isn't it? It's made you become one of those punctuality, just-so freaky kind of women.'

Freaky. Why the hell did they all call her freaky? Or flaky. Why did she let them? She wasn't really either of those things. She was – was – different.

'Go and sit down,' she told him, 'and let me dazzle you with my cooking.'

'To Dad.' Dan popped the cork out of a bottle of Dom Perignon and filled their glasses with champagne. 'And to Vanna Savino.'

They clinked glasses and sat down.

'It's my best yet,' said Joss. 'It combines passion, fiery tempers and murderous intent.'

'Your books always do that,' said Bronwyn. 'That's why I never know which one is which.'

'Monster child!' Joss looked at her indulgently.

'It's true,' she told him. 'I prefer romance to murder.'

'Don't worry, Joss,' said Freda. 'From the day I no longer had to live with Vanna I liked her.'

'Thanks.' He drained his glass of champagne.

'I like her too,' said Dan. 'And Cordelia loves her. She's read them all.'

'Pity she couldn't be bothered to come here and say so,' said Bronwyn.

'Will you give it a rest?' demanded Dan. 'I know you don't like her but you don't have to snipe at me all the time. You know she would've been here if it was at all possible.'

'Sorry,' said Bronwyn unrepentantly.

'How's she getting on?' Freda turned to Dan.

'Great,' he told her. 'Working hard. Doing her course. Getting lots of experience before she comes home.'

'Experience for what?' asked Bronwyn. 'Ireland will seem as dull as ditchwater to her after Wall Street. Her experience will be more useful there.'

'Experience is experience,' said Dan. 'It doesn't matter where you get it or where you use it.'

'But what'll she do when she gets back?'

'Work for Harrison's. They have an office in Dublin. No reason why she won't.'

'Will it be that easy?' Joss asked.

'Of course,' said Dan. 'There are plenty of jobs in Dublin.'

Ash walked out onto the terrace and set the plates in front of them.

'I think she's a very nice girl,' said Freda as Ash spooned some of the steaming risotto onto her plate. 'And you could do a lot worse than a wife with some passion for life.'

'I know,' said Dan.

'Cordelia is strong and ambitious and knows what she wants. I'd hate to think of you with a mousy girl who doesn't know her own mind.' Freda picked up the bottle and poured the last of the champagne into her glass.

'Mum, you know and I know that Cordelia knows her own mind.'

'I spent a long time not knowing mine.' Freda glanced at Joss. 'And I spent a lot of time festering away, knowing that I was capable of better things.'

'Oh, change the record, Freda,' moaned Joss. 'Every time!'

'I just want them to know how important it is to be true to yourself,' said Freda. 'Even Bronnie and Tony, wonderful match though they are.'

'Mum, please!' Bronwyn flushed.

Ash glanced at Bronwyn as she walked round the table to serve Joss.

'Make sure you keep your job,' said Freda. 'Don't be dependent. They can leave you, you know. Or even worse, they can replace you!' Her eyes narrowed as she looked at Joss.

'She'll have to keep her job,' said Tony. 'I'm not in Joss's league when it comes to money.'

'Joss wasn't in Joss's league when I lived with him,' said Freda spiritedly. 'He didn't have the decency to earn anything until I left!'

'I didn't have the peace to write anything until you left!'

Ash scurried back to the kitchen, wondering whether or not Joss and Freda were going to have a row. Please don't, she begged as she mixed lemon, tomato purée and wine together to pour over the chicken pieces. Please don't ruin my dinner by having a fight.

It's their dinner, she reminded herself as she added tomatoes to the chicken dish. If they want to fling the food at each other it's entirely their prerogative. But hopefully not. I've worked so hard at it and I want everyone to have a good time.

It would take another twenty minutes or so for the main

course to be ready. She opened the side door and sat on the tiled step. Snatches of conversation wafted up to her but not distinctly enough for her to be able to understand any of it.

Maybe if I'd stayed with Alistair we would have ended up like Freda and Joss. We were too different, really, for all that I tried to be right for him. Or for all that he tried to be right for me. She chewed at her lip. Maybe I should change. People do. People go off and climb the Himalayas or sail single-handed round the world, they do all sorts of things that nobody would expect. Maybe it's really in my blood to be a wandering sort of person and not a settled sort of person. Maybe I've tried too hard to be a settled sort of person.

She frowned. She couldn't quite imagine herself climbing the Himalayas or sailing single-handedly round the world. But she could imagine Julia doing it. Her mother would have looked at it as a challenge, thought Ash. And she probably would have enjoyed it.

She realised, suddenly, that she didn't feel the spurt of anger that she normally did when she thought of Julia. In fact thinking of Julia climbing Mount Everest had made her smile.

'Fuck you!'

The words were as clear and distinct as if Freda Morland had uttered them beside her. Ash jumped up and went back into the kitchen. But she leaned out of the window so that she could hear better.

'Fuck you and your women and your books!'

Ash stood, immobile, by the window. It was Freda's

voice but the words seemed totally inappropriate to the elegant lady she'd met.

'You do this on purpose, don't you, you fucking bastard!' And this time Ash heard the sound of glass breaking and she could picture, as clearly as if she was there, one of the beautiful crystal goblets flying through the air and landing on the terrace.

'Don't be so stupid.' Joss Morland's voice was deep and authoritative.

'Don't call me stupid you – you – you baby-snatcher!'

Ash didn't know what to do. This clearly was the kind of row where no holds were barred. She knew that kind of row, she'd lived it with Julia whenever her mother had argued with one of her boyfriends. Things had sailed through the air fairly often in their lives together, from cups and saucers to wooden ornaments and real pearl necklaces. Ash listened for the sound of more breaking glass and was rewarded by another thud and a crack although this time it sounded as if a plate had ended up on the ground.

She chewed at her thumbnail. It was now over twenty minutes since she'd served the risotto, the main course was ready, so was her wonderful vegetable accompaniment, and she should really go and clear away the starters. But not if they were having a row – she didn't want to intrude on a row.

She gave it another five minutes then tentatively made her way to the terrace. She hadn't heard anything at all in that time and when she reached them the Morlands were sitting in stony silence. Ash experienced a sense of déjà vu yet again. If the delayed start had been like her dinner with Dan and Cordelia, she now felt as she had when she'd walked in after he'd proposed and Cordelia told him she was going to the States. The atmosphere, despite the humid air, was frigid.

Freda's plate and glass were both missing. Ash glanced around and saw the shattered glass at the other end of the terrace. It had clearly been flung at Joss and had missed. The broken plate was on the ground beside Freda. Ash couldn't help feeling pleased that at least Freda had eaten all of her risotto.

She went round the table and cleared away the empty plates.

'Would you like the main course now?' she asked.

'I don't want anything,' said Freda. 'I'm not hungry any more.'

'For goodness' sake, Mum!' Dan sounded angry. 'Have something to eat.'

'Don't speak to me like that,' she snapped. 'And I don't want anything to eat.'

'That's fine, Mrs Morland.' Ash's voice faltered as she realised what she'd said.

'Not Mrs Morland,' hissed Freda. 'Ms Forrest. Dan did tell you, I presume, that Joss and I are divorced. Although that took a long bloody time.'

'Of course,' said Ash.

'So I don't go round using his name any more. At least that way people don't ask me if I know him!'

'Of course,' said Ash again, furious at herself. She went indoors and brought out the dinner plates.

'I suppose you think this was an appropriate occasion, do you?' Freda asked Joss who was sitting at the opposite end of the table. 'A dinner that's supposed to be a celebration between us? And you think it's OK to inform me, your first and only wife, and our children that you're screwing an eighteen-year-old?'

'That's not what I said.'

'You can hardly say that you're not screwing her!' Freda spat the words at him.

Ash moved away from the table and into the dining room where she could still hear every word.

'If you're involved with her you're screwing her, aren't you?' demanded Freda. 'You say you come here to work but all you do is look around for nubile young things so that you can check out the accuracy of your sex scenes!'

'Mum!' Dan's voice was urgent. 'It doesn't matter to you any more. You know it doesn't.'

'Well, why does he have to boast about it?' demanded Freda. 'Arrogant fucker.'

'Because he's a man,' said Bronwyn.

'Now hold on a minute, Bronnie,' Tony protested.

'He's a man and he doesn't really give a shit,' continued Bronwyn. 'And he was a useless father to me.'

'But you never sent back any of the money I gave you,' said Joss.

'I deserved it,' snapped Bronwyn. 'For having had to put up with you.'

'Bullshit!' Joss snapped back at her. 'At least Dan had the decency to go out and earn his own living.'

'I earn my own living!' cried Bronwyn. 'I hold down a damn good job.'

'So you could've given me back the money any time. But you didn't.'

'I told you, I deserved it,' she said.

'Did you know,' asked Freda loudly, 'that he was having an affair before I left him? Of course you did, for all that I tried to keep it from you. But it was impossible.'

'Mum, please!' Dan sounded agonised.

'I said that I left him because of the books and of course it *was* because of the books in a way but it was really because of the slut he was seeing at the time.'

'Freda.' Joss's voice was firm. 'That's enough.'

'But you were,' said Freda. 'You modelled that Savino bitch on her, didn't you? Olive skin, dark eyes, dark hair – generously rounded breasts! Hah! As if you didn't know all there was to know about her generously bloody rounded breasts after you'd had your hands on them!'

There was a sudden silence round the table. Ash was almost afraid to breathe.

'Mum, you're tired,' said Dan.

'No I'm not,' said Freda. 'He tries to change history, you know. He says things like we split up because of the pressure of his work. He knows that's complete rubbish. It was because he was seeing the tart – not that she lasted long because none of them ever do and this one won't either, will she? Not past her nineteenth birthday anyway!' She glared at Joss, breathless and defiant.

'I gave you a good life,' said Joss.

'Oh, please!' Freda raised her eyes to heaven. 'You gave me a crap life. I'll admit you paid for it afterwards but it was a rotten life and you made me miserable and for all of those years afterwards when we couldn't get a divorce you made it hell.'

'Mum, that's not true,' said Dan. 'Dad looked after us, you know he did.'

'I didn't want that sort of looking after.' Suddenly Freda's face crumpled. 'I wanted him to love me.' She leaned forward, put her head on the table and burst into a paroxysm of sobbing.

Oh my God, thought Ash. What the hell am I supposed to do now?

There was a scuffling noise on the terrace and she ducked out of sight behind one of the drapes. She saw Dan lead Freda through the dining room and she stood, hesitantly, beside the open doors to the terrace.

'Great work, Dad.' Bronwyn's voice was full of controlled fury. 'What in God's name possessed you to tell her about your latest child lover tonight of all nights?'

'She needed to know,' said Joss.

'No she didn't.'

Ash heard Bronwyn's chair scrape along the terrace and she ducked out of sight again. The girl stalked through the dining room, followed a couple of seconds later by Tony.

That only left Joss, thought Ash. She waited for him to leave the terrace too but he didn't. Then the smell of sweet pipe smoke wafted in towards her. It didn't look as if anyone was going to eat her Italian chicken with Sicilian vegetables. Or her creative tiramisu.

She picked up the serving dish and carried it back to the kitchen.

It was half an hour later when Dan pushed open the kitchen door. Ash was eating the leftover seafood risotto starter. She swallowed quickly and it went down the wrong way, making her cough and her eyes water.

'Here.' Dan filled a glass from the jug on the table.

'Thanks,' said Ash when her coughing had subsided.

'I have to apologise to you again,' he said.

'No.'

'Yes,' said Dan. 'That wasn't supposed to happen. Dad is such an asshole sometimes.'

'Was she drunk?' asked Ash.

'No,' said Dan. 'Just furious that he chose tonight to tell us that he has a new girlfriend.'

'You told me that your mother has a boyfriend,' Ash pointed out.

'Joss's girlfriend is eighteen,' Dan said.

'So I heard,' admitted Ash.

'She flipped.' Dan sighed. 'Although everyone thinks that Joss is the volatile one, it's actually Mum. That's why she couldn't live with him. She'd want to argue, he'd clam up. He'd ignore her and retire to his study and tell her he was writing. Half the time it was just an excuse to get out of the way.'

'Why does it still matter to her?' asked Ash.

'I don't know.' Dan leaned against the wall. 'I don't know how much you heard, Ash, but when she left him it was because of a girl, not really because of the books. We all pretended it was the books because she wanted us to and in some ways the two were interlinked anyway. Even when she left, she didn't stop loving Dad. Maybe you never really stop loving someone. She knew she had to get out of the relationship and she did, but Joss is still the man she married.' He rubbed his forehead. 'Perhaps you try to replace the same person over and over again even though you know they're wrong for you. She's never got over the fact that he replaced her with a younger woman, though, even though it didn't last. And doing it again – he's such an idiot!'

'Dan, I don't need to know this,' said Ash. 'I'm really sorry things haven't worked out.'

'Oh, it happens.' He grinned suddenly. 'We had a blow-up at the end-of-book dinner three years ago too and I can't even remember what that was about. She threw a knife at him then – fortunately her aim is awful and it was a butter knife anyway. We'll get over it. She'll get over it. Dad gets over everything, he has his head in the clouds most of the time. He'll get over this poor unfortunate eighteen-year-old too. Hopefully, she'll also get over him.'

'Hopefully,' said Ash.

'You went to so much trouble,' said Dan, 'and we didn't even get to the main course!'

'It'll keep,' Ash told him. 'You can heat it up tomorrow.'

'It's not quite the same, is it?'

'Sometimes the flavour improves with waiting,' said Ash.

Chapter 27

Italian Chicken
Chicken, tomatoes, tomato purée, garlic, basil, oregano, dry
white wine, lemon, olives, salt and pepper, olive oil
Make marinade with garlic, basil, oregano, lemon juice,
salt, pepper and oil. Cut chicken into pieces, rub with
marinade and chill. Brown chicken. Mix juice of lemon
with tomato purée and wine, pour over chicken, stir in
tomatoes. Add herbs and simmer. A few minutes before
serving add halved olives and simmer again

S he was in her bedroom, sitting in the gentle breeze of
the open windows, when Dan knocked at the door a
couple of hours later.

'Hi,' she said as she opened it.

'Can I come in?' he asked.

She opened the door wider and he walked by her.
He sat down on one of the armchairs beside the open
window.

'Mum has moved to the hotel down the road – Dad's
paying for it. Dad has gone up to town, presumably to

see his latest lover. Bronwyn and Tony have gone out. And I came to say that I ate some of the chicken dish and it was really gorgeous.' He grinned at her. 'And as for the vegetables – out of this world!'

She smiled. 'I'm glad you liked it.'

'I wish we'd managed to stay civilised enough for everyone to eat it.'

'It doesn't matter,' said Ash.

'I wanted everything to be so good.' Dan sighed. 'I thought that it would be perfect.' He made a face at her. 'My track record in dinner organisation isn't great, is it?'

'Not really,' she told him. 'Maybe some day I'll cook a meal for you and you'll actually manage to get as far as dessert.'

'I bet there's some deep psychological thing about me,' said Dan gloomily. 'I'm sure that I keep organising dinners out of some sense of family which is totally misplaced and all to do with the fact that mine broke up.'

'Probably,' said Ash. 'My shrink was always going on about my fragmented childhood. Or rather, she was always trying to make me go on about my fragmented childhood. You know – "Why do *you* think you're a complete loony, Aisling?"'

'We'll be on TV yet,' Dan told her. 'Children of neurotic parents.'

'I'm glad you didn't say neurotic children of neurotic parents,' said Ash. 'After the way I lectured you about timekeeping.'

He laughed. 'There's probably something very deep about that too.'

'I'm sure.' Ash sighed.

'I wish you could've enjoyed your time here.'

'Oh, but I did!' Ash looked at him in surprise. 'I had a great day today, even if nobody ate anything! I walked around the town and the shops – I even bought a dress and I *never* buy dresses. I had a good time.'

'You've hardly had time to enjoy anything,' Dan objected.

'I enjoy cooking.' She grinned at him. 'I know it must seem mad to you, but I love to cook. And cooking Italian food in Sicily – well, it's been great.'

'It's still your job,' he told her. 'And obviously you have to be paid.' He took a chequebook out of his pocket.

'Don't be stupid,' she said. 'You brought me here, that's enough.'

'That's ridiculous,' said Dan. 'I'd expect to be paid for my stockbroking advice whether or not my client made any money. You should be paid for cooking whether or not we actually ate anything. Your time is money after all.'

'Dan, if you write a cheque I'll rip it up.'

'Better give you cash.' He smiled at her.

'I'd rip that up too. Besides, I still owe you money anyway. From the night at the K Club. When you bought me my raffle ticket.'

'For heaven's sake, Ash.'

'I mean it.' She grinned. 'Even though I didn't win.'

'I'd try and persuade you to stay an extra few days here instead but I guess you wouldn't want to do that either.'

'I took Monday off,' she told him. 'But I have a function on Tuesday. I have all day tomorrow here, though to tell you the truth I was wondering if I couldn't change my flight to the one tomorrow evening. I don't think—'

'Please don't try to change it,' said Dan. 'Stay until Monday.'

'I'll be in the way,' said Ash.

'No you won't,' Dan told her.

'Look, Dan, your family is going through a bit of a trauma. You don't want other people here.'

'You're not other people,' he said. 'Anyway, with Mum in the hotel, the catalyst for our arguments has gone. And don't look so shocked,' he added. 'We'll see her every day.'

'She doesn't look like the sort of woman to throw such a complete wobbler,' said Ash.

'I know,' said Dan. 'But she's never really forgiven Dad for being successful after she left him. And she's right about Vanna Savino – he was having an affair with an Italian student when he wrote the first book. He wasn't exactly the world's most faithful husband.'

Ash looked at Dan sympathetically.

'However,' said Dan briskly, 'he's Joss and I'm me. I can see what happens when it all goes wrong.'

'Me too,' said Ash wryly. 'Even if Julia didn't quite get as far as the husband.'

Dan laughed. 'You will stay tomorrow, won't you?'

She nodded. 'I'd love to. I really want to swim in your pool.'

*   *   *

The house was still quiet when she woke up the following morning. She got washed and dressed as quickly as she could, grabbed a couple of croissants from the kitchen and slipped out of the house before she met anyone.

Ash supposed that she should be used to family drama but it was completely different when it was somebody else's family. From what Dan had previously told her, she'd pictured Freda as the placid mother struggling to do her best for the children, yet Freda was very different to the docile woman of her imagination. She was very different to the woman she looked, too – Ash still couldn't get over how the elegant woman had turned into someone shouting and screaming and throwing plates around the terrace.

Eighteen years old, though. She grinned as she walked up the steep road to the town. Joss was in his sixties. He was an attractive man, she conceded, but what on earth made an eighteen-year-old girl decide to have an affair with a bloke in his sixties? Money? A lot of it came down to money, Ash decided, as she jumped out of the way of a blue Vespa being ridden at speed by a girl wearing cutaway jeans and a bikini top. Every day the papers were full of stories of ancient men and their trophy wives or girlfriends. She wondered if Alistair had thought of her as a trophy girlfriend. Probably not, she decided. She was too old to be a trophy! She'd bet anything that his next girlfriend would be younger than she was. The girl in the newspaper picture had looked younger.

She pulled a damp strand of hair away from her fore-head. It was more humid than ever today and her body glistened with perspiration. She bought an ice cream (it was true they were nicer here than anywhere else in the world) then followed the street up towards the ancient Greek theatre and paid at the desk to wander around the ruins.

The view was spectacular. She stood on the highest tier of the theatre and looked through the gaps in the broken walls over the town below. Pink and white villas and houses clustered around the bottom of the mountains while the sea shimmered silver-blue in the heat haze.

She walked around the theatre and realised that from the side overlooking the sea she could make out the ochre-tiled roof of the Villa Rosa where it nestled between the trees. It looked peaceful and serene, hardly a venue for heart-stopping drama.

Eventually she left the theatre and walked down the narrow street, stopping at some of the souvenir shops to buy a couple of ceramic plates inscribed with images of Medina, the island's symbol, as well as the lava rock and olive oil for her neighbours. She also bought a ceramic tile which said *Attenti al Gatto*, meaning Beware of the Cat. She wasn't sure where the brightly coloured tile would look best in her pale yellow and white apartment, but she bought it anyway because Bagel would be furious with her when she got home so she'd have a bit of bewaring to do!

She was hungry. The streets were now full of families taking a morning stroll although heavy grey clouds had begun to roll in from the mountains. But it was still incredibly warm. She found a seat at a pavement café and ordered cappuccino and waffles. She was surprised at herself for ordering food – the croissants earlier had been delicious, she'd just eaten an ice cream and she couldn't understand why she was hungry again. But she was.

The cappuccino was hot and aromatic. She tore the top from a sachet of sugar, poured it over the white froth and stirred it slowly as she inhaled the fragrance of the coffee.

'Ash!'

She hadn't spotted Dan who'd entered the square from another side. He was wearing a black T-shirt, blue jeans and, with his dark hair combed back from his face, he looked like a Sicilian himself.

'Hi, Dan.' She waved at him lazily.

'How are you?' He pulled out a wicker chair and sat beside her. '*Bierra, per favore*,' he said to the waiter who'd immediately rushed out to serve him.

'Thirsty?' asked Ash.

'I need a beer,' said Dan. He stretched his legs out in front of him. 'I've spent the last two hours mediating between Mum and Dad. What is it about parents? You'd imagine that either or both of them would've got a bit of sense by now but when I listen to them it's like listening to them as they were twenty years ago.'

'Why does your mum still see your dad if she knows about the women and it upsets her so much?' asked Ash.

Dan shrugged as he accepted his glass of beer from the

456

waiter and took a deep drink. 'A self-destructive thing?' he wondered. 'I can't help thinking that, no matter what she says, she likes the whiff of unpredictability that Dad brings to everything. And she likes the fact that she's the only one he married.'

Ash laughed. 'I prefer predictability myself. But I can understand your dad's attraction. He's in pretty good shape for his age.'

'I know,' said Dan ruefully. 'If I'm half as good . . .'

'No reason why not,' said Ash. 'You look more like him than your mum.'

'Thanks, I think,' said Dan.

They sat in silence together, watching the crowd in the square ebb and flow.

'I came looking for you to see if you'd like to do some sightseeing today,' said Dan after a while. 'And to ask you if you'd like to come to dinner with me tonight – you don't have to cook it, I promise. I just wanted to say thanks. Since you're going to rip up my cheque.'

Ash shook her head slowly. 'That's nice of you, but I'll probably just get a pizza or something later. And there's no need to take me sightseeing, Dan.'

'But it's a lovely island,' he protested, 'and you should see more of it.'

'Really, there's no need to bother.'

'It's not a bother,' he told her. 'I'd like it.'

'I – well, OK, then,' she said before she could change her mind because it seemed a shame to pass up the opportunity. 'Why not?'

Dan beckoned the waiter, paid for the beer and Ash's

coffee and waffles, and led her out of the town to a parked Fiat.

'It's Dad's car,' he told her as he opened the door. 'He never drives.'

'Where to?' she asked.

'Let me surprise you,' said Dan.

Ash didn't tell him that she didn't like surprises. She sat back and allowed Dan to drive where he pleased, which was higher and higher through the hills and towards Mount Etna. The road narrowed into a series of hairpin bends as they passed through a small village which was, Ash realised, covered in soot.

'It hasn't erupted violently recently,' Dan told her. 'But it spews cinders and soot all the time.'

'It's spectacular,' said Ash, just as the car bumped and slewed across the road. She grabbed Dan's arm and shrieked as he fought with the steering to bring the car to a stop.

'What was that?' she asked, her heart beating rapidly.

'Tyre,' he said. 'I don't believe it.' He got out of the car and inspected the front wheel. 'I don't know how that happened,' he called to her. 'But it's ruined.'

'Have you a spare?' she asked.

'Of course I have a spare.'

She got out of the car while he jacked it up. It was cooler this high up but the air tasted of cinders and burning. What on earth possessed people to live up here, she wondered, when it was so lovely near the coast?

'It'll take a while.' Dan was wrestling with the nuts on the tyre.

'Aren't you supposed to loosen them while the car is on the ground?' asked Ash.

'I did,' said Dan through gritted teeth. 'But not enough, obviously.'

She sat on a rock while he changed the tyre, and closed her ears to his muttered curses. When, eventually, he was finished, she suggested that they abandon the rest of the ascent to Etna and return to the villa for him to clean up.

'You know, I really *would* like to go somewhere with you that didn't end in some kind of disaster,' said Dan as he turned the car round.

'I do seem to be a bit of a jinx,' she admitted. 'I'm sorry.'

'Never mind,' said Dan. 'You can come to dinner with me tonight and lay that particular jinx to rest for good.'

She'd objected to the dinner plans because she felt she should, rather than because she didn't want to go. When Dan told her that he'd reserved tables at the neighbourhood's poshest restaurant she thought he was joking. But he wasn't. She was secretly delighted to have the opportunity to wear her new dress although, she thought regretfully, she hadn't got a really decent pair of shoes to go with it. She'd brought a pair of light mules with her but they were well worn and not really what her beautiful new dress deserved. They'd have to do, though, because her only other footwear was her trainers and, much as some people could make a statement by wearing an evening dress and a pair of trainers, Ash knew she wasn't one of them.

She wore her silver earrings but nothing round her neck. The dress was high enough not to need anything and the only chain she had was the gold necklace that Alistair had bought the night of the movie premiere, which didn't go with it.

Suddenly her heart constricted and hot tears flooded her eyes and spilled down her cheeks. He won't be there when I go home, she realised. He won't have left a message on my answering machine or an e-mail on my computer and he won't ring me to find out what I'm doing. And she knew that she'd miss the fact that he wouldn't be there. And she realised that she'd miss knowing that there was someone in her life. She felt a surge of loneliness and misery that she hadn't even known she could feel. This was why she'd been right never to get involved before. When you got involved and when you split up, the hurt was real and she could feel it gripping her inside and surging through her.

She lay down on the bed and buried her face in the pillow. I was a bloody fool, she told herself. I didn't even try to make him love me. So how can I blame him for leaving me? What if I never meet anyone again? The thought came to her and she sat up, pulling the plain white bedspread round her shoulders. What if no one ever wants me? The possibility was chilling. She'd always supposed that some day there'd be someone, somewhere, who'd meet her exacting requirements but now she realised that it was highly unlikely. If she hadn't been able to get it together with Alistair Brannigan then who in the whole world was left? If she hadn't been such an idiot. If she hadn't been (to use everyone's words) such a flake. If she hadn't been thinking of goddamed Julia at a time when she should have been thinking of her boyfriend. Honestly, she thought, as the tears trickled down her cheeks and plopped onto the sheet, how many sane, ordinary women think about their mother when they're lying in their boyfriend's bed?

But every time she went out with someone new she thought of Julia. And every time it got serious she thought of Julia. And every time she kissed them and told them goodbye she thought of Julia too. And she thought of Julia's boyfriends and wondered which of them, herself or Julia, had got it right.

Neither of them had, she realised with a pang. Julia had been hopeless with men and she was just as hopeless. And maybe every time she'd broken it off with someone to protect herself, she truly had hurt them. She'd never considered that they might be hurt. She'd imagined it was something they'd get over quickly. But why, she asked herself, would I think that? Why should they be any different to me?

All her efforts to protect herself from feeling unhappy had probably only made other people unhappy. And, in the end, she hadn't protected herself at all. She remembered the night of the dinner at the K Club with Dan when he'd told her that getting hurt was part of the territory. She hadn't wanted it to be part of the territory but of course it was! How could she ever have thought any differently?

She lay back on the bed with her eyes closed. I'm such

a moron, she told herself. No wonder people don't like me very much.

She hadn't realised she'd fallen asleep but a sudden sound startled her into wakefulness. She glanced at the bedside clock and saw to her horror that she was supposed to be meeting Dan in fifteen minutes to go to a posh restaurant for dinner. She'd never felt less like going out to dinner in her life before.

Perhaps, she thought, I could just tell him that I don't feel very well. She got up from the bed and looked at herself in the mirror. Her eyes were red and puffy and her cheeks were streaked and blotchy. She didn't look like the kind of person anyone would want to take to dinner. And Dan probably didn't really want to take her to dinner anyway. But he'd offered. And he'd reserved a table. And it would be a selfish rather than a selfless act to tell him now, with a quarter of an hour to go, that she didn't feel like it.

I'll go to dinner with him, she said. I promised. I'll even try to be nice. I'll stop thinking about how I feel and think about how someone else feels instead.

She splashed cold water onto her face and put some Optrex drops into her eyes. They were still red, but didn't look quite as much like a pair of stoplights as they had before. She rummaged in her bag for some foundation – she hardly ever bothered with foundation but she needed to do a repair job on her face – and she smoothed it on with the tips of her fingers. By the time she'd put on some mascara and lipstick, she looked almost OK.

She slid into the blue dress and put on her mules.

Now I *do* look OK, she said to herself as she looked at her reflection in the full-length mirror. I've been such a clothes slob in the past. I've missed out so much on all the shopping stuff because I thought of it as a chore instead of something that can be fun. Maybe, if I can be a different sort of person in the future, I'll actually get to enjoy shopping. After all, I enjoyed buying this!

She picked up her bag and walked along the short corridor to the living room. Bronwyn was sitting there, reading a copy of *Hello!*.

'My goodness,' she said as she looked up and saw Ash. 'You look – different.'

'Thanks,' said Ash dryly as she thought of how puffy her face still was.

'Lovely different,' said Bronwyn. 'That dress is gorgeous. Where on earth did you buy it?'

'Here,' said Ash. 'Yesterday.'

'It's fantastic on you.' Bronwyn looked at her critically. 'You look great but – are you feeling all right?'

'Why?' asked Ash anxiously.

'No reason.' Bronwyn wondered why Ash's eyes were red-rimmed. 'Don't mind me. What size are you?'

'Twelve,' said Ash. She paused for a moment and then carried on. 'But I've got kind of wide hips which I hate. I struggle with narrow cuts.'

'You don't look as though you have wide hips,' said Bronwyn.

'Oh, I have,' said Ash forcefully. 'And I have stubby nails.' This is OK, she thought. I can talk to someone about dresses and nails and not make an idiot out of myself. 'I try not to bite them and mostly I don't but I can't grow them. I'd love to have long, elegant nails.'

'Fake it,' suggested Bronwyn.

'It's too much trouble,' Ash told her. 'What with the cooking and everything, I really need to keep them pretty short. I'd just like to have long ones, that's all.'

'The risotto last night was wonderful,' said Bronwyn. 'And so was the chicken – we lashed into it today. As for the dessert! Fabulous.' She grinned. 'Did we scare you with the row?'

Ash shook her head.

'Poor Mum,' said Bronwyn. 'She's great most of the time but occasionally she just loses it. Dad has the absolute worst effect in the world on her. When he's not around she's perfectly rational.'

'Why do you bother with this book thing at all?' asked Ash. 'If it means your Mum gets so upset.'

'She doesn't always,' said Bronwyn, 'and she likes to keep in touch with the old bugger because she wants to be left something in his will.'

'Oh, Bronwyn, it's not that mercenary surely.'

Bronwyn shrugged. 'Maybe. Maybe not.'

'Hi, girls. Are you ready, Ash – oh, wow!' Dan strode into the room and stopped. He looked at Ash in surprise. 'You look wonderful,' he said.

'So I was telling her,' said Bronwyn. 'But she says she has wide hips.'

'Not from where I'm standing,' said Dan.

'I have,' said Ash.

'Women!' Dan looked at them in disgust. 'There's always something. With Cordelia it's her nose.'

'Not surprisingly,' said Bronwyn and Dan shot a daggered look at her.

'Will we go?' said Dan.

Ash nodded and said goodbye to Bronwyn.

'It's only a five-minute walk,' said Dan. 'So I thought you'd prefer that rather than taking the car.'

'That's fine,' said Ash as they stepped outside into the soup-warm air. They didn't talk as they walked to the restaurant but Ash half wished she'd suggested taking the car anyway because her mules weren't made for anything other than just being on her feet. Walking obviously hadn't been part of the designer's brief. But Dan was right and it took only five minutes to reach the restaurant which was, like everywhere else, set down from the road.

'You'll like it,' said Dan, 'truly you will. Anyone who is anyone in Taormina comes here.'

'Does your dad?' she asked.

'Oh, Dad!' he said in disgust. 'Dad sits at home with his books and his prosciutto and he doesn't bother with anything else.'

'Except eighteen-year-olds,' said Ash as she walked through the gates with him.

Chapter 28

Tomato and Mozzarella Steaks with Basil
Fillet steak, salt and pepper, garlic, beef tomatoes, mozza-
rella cheese, fresh basil
Crush garlic and fry. Add steaks and cook to taste. Place slice
of tomato on each steak and season. Place basil leaves on top
of tomato and a slice of mozzarella on top of the basil. Cook
under hot grill until tomato is warm and cheese is melted

It was a beautiful restaurant. Like the Villa Rosa, it had a long terrace which ran the length of the building although this one opened into a circular area which, Dan told her, was sometimes used for dancing.

'It's like being on the set of *La Dolce Vita* or something.' Ash looked around her with interest. 'Everyone looks so fabulous.'

'So do you,' said Dan.

'Thanks.' She grinned at him as a waiter led them to a table for two on the softly lit terrace. 'Oh, Dan, this is really lovely. I would've been quite happy with pizza but this is wonderful.'

'I knew you'd like it,' he told her. 'The food is utterly fantastic.'

She looked at him expectantly.

'What?' he asked.

'I'm waiting for you to tell me that it'll give me loads of ideas,' she told him.

'Why?'

'Because everyone always does.' She laughed. 'I get really pissed off with them when they do.'

'I'm glad I bucked the trend,' said Dan.

'So am I.'

The waiter handed them some menus and Dan ordered a bottle of champagne. Ash looked at him in surprise. 'What's that for?'

He shrugged. 'I like it. I always have. I thought it'd be fun.'

'Champagne gets me drunk,' she told him. 'I try not to get drunk because I'm quite silly when I'm drunk.'

'Are you?' He looked at her over the top of his menu. 'I think I'd like to see you being silly.'

'No you wouldn't.'

'I would.' He smiled. 'You always look too sensible by half to me.'

'No, I'm not! I'm a complete fool about a lot of things.' Her face clouded for a moment then she grinned. 'What about all the times you've invaded my kitchen and seen me mopping up spilled oil or slicing my finger with a knife. Not the actions of a sensible woman.'

'True,' he said thoughtfully, 'but you still seem to be cool when you're having a crisis.'

'You've never really seen me in a crisis.' Ash pictured herself with her head stuck in a brown paper bag or, as she'd been just a short time earlier, sobbing her heart out in the bedroom.

The menu was superb. There were at least four different mushroom dishes, half a dozen delicious-sounding pastas, chicken, beef and fish courses, all of which were done in different local styles. Ash could feel her mouth begin to water. It seemed ages since her waffles earlier in the day and she hadn't bothered with anything since. She wondered if having a broken heart made you hungry. According to everyone she'd ever met, being rejected usually meant that you weren't able to eat at all. But, she mused, since she'd been so bloody different about her whole attitude to men up until now, maybe her reaction to heartache would be to eat instead of starve.

'I'm going to have the mushrooms,' she said. 'Followed by seafood pasta.'

'And I'm going to have the ravioli,' Dan told her. 'And the beef. What wine would you like? Red or white?'

'I don't mind,' she told him.

'A nice rich Barolo,' he said. 'It'll be good after the champagne.'

'I'll be too hungover to go home tomorrow,' she said.

'I never get hungover here,' Dan told her. 'It's something to do with the air. Although,' he added, 'maybe not at the moment. I think it's more humid now than it was earlier.'

Ash nodded in agreement as the waiter arrived with the Dom Perignon. He popped the cork expertly so that it came out of the bottle with a discreet sigh then filled their glasses.

'Thanks for everything,' said Dan as he tilted his glass to Ash.

'For nothing,' she said ruefully. 'And it was going to be such a good dinner!'

'Oh, you've done other things,' he said. 'The engagement night, coming to the ball with me, organising the caterers for the wedding. It seems strange to me that we'd hardly exchanged more than a few words a year ago and now you've become my emergency friend.'

'At least we've proved it can be done.'

'What?' he asked.

'Men and women. It is, after all, possible to be friends.'

'To friendship,' he said as he tilted his glass towards her.

The champagne was deliciously cool and bubbly, she thought as she sipped it. Perfect for drinking on the terrace. And perfect for making you feel as though things weren't so bad after all. She sat back in the comfortable chair and looked over the balcony towards the sea.

'It's lovely, isn't it?' said Dan.

'Beautiful.'

'I can see why Dad stays here.'

Ash nodded. 'Me too.'

'Maybe I'll retire here,' said Dan. 'When I get burned out by the markets.'

'Will you get burned out?' asked Ash.

He shrugged. 'Maybe.'

'But Cordelia will step into your shoes.' Ash looked at him from beneath her dark eyelashes.

'I guess so,' said Dan. 'It's strange that she's such a determined person whereas I—' he smiled at her, 'this is for your ears only, Ash, not for the partners in Chatham's – I'm not that bothered any more.'

'I thought everyone who worked in Chatham's bothered,' said Ash. 'I thought it was all you cared about.'

'Oh, I care,' said Dan. 'But it's not the only thing I care about. It used to be, of course, but somehow I can't help feeling that there are more important things in life than work.'

'Like what?'

'I'll sound too wimpy if I say things like being happy,' said Dan. 'But in the last year or so I can't help thinking that you've got to get the most out of life that you can. And killing yourself to do it isn't always the best way.'

'So you're thinking of retiring to a remote mountain top?' asked Ash.

'With Cordelia in tow?' Dan laughed. 'I don't think so! However, I'm quite happy to let her be the ambitious one for a while.'

'What would you do if you didn't work for Chatham's any more?' Ash really couldn't imagine Dan loafing around doing nothing. No matter what he said.

'There's the problem,' said Dan. 'I'm not qualified to do anything else. I wish I had a talent like you.'

'Anyone can cook,' said Ash dismissively.

470

'You know that's bullshit,' Dan told her. 'The only reason I've survived till now has been the business lunches! Otherwise my diet would be mainly takeaways.'

Ash laughed.

'It's true,' said Dan. 'And Cordelia was saying the exact same thing to me. She's fretting because she's put on a few pounds and now she's spending her free time in the gym losing them again. Actually, I think she's lost weight since she went over there.'

'She doesn't need to lose weight,' said Ash.

'I know,' said Dan. 'I keep telling her that she's perfect the way she is but she insists that she needs to use the gym every day. Actually, I think it's partly because everyone else does.'

'That must be awful,' said Ash. 'I'd hate to work in a place where body pump classes are mandatory.'

Dan laughed. 'I'd be afraid to body pump.'

'So would I,' admitted Ash. 'I've no sense of rhythm and at the best of times any aerobic class I ever went to was a nightmare. Every time the class clapped to the right, I'd be stumbling around to my left. So I'd be lethal doing it with weights.'

'I'm not great with any of those classes,' said Dan. 'And I hate the way the instructors whoop and shout all the time. It's so nerve-wracking.'

'We sound like a couple of pensioners.' Ash giggled as the waiter put their starters in front of them.

'We'll both have to do a couple of classes after this.' Dan smacked his lips appreciatively. 'Looks fantastic.'

Ash nodded as she ate her mushrooms. They were

absolutely delicious, she thought, cooked to perfection. She liked wild mushrooms, ones which simply burst with flavour, so different to the insipid plastic mushrooms that supermarkets sold.

'Of course, Cordelia complains that it's so easy to put on weight in the States,' Dan said. 'She says it's impossible to get small portions of anything.'

'Small and the States don't exactly go together,' said Ash. 'Especially in the food department.'

'Do you remember that?' asked Dan.

She shook her head. 'Not really. But I do remember that, in one of the places we lived, there was a diner that allowed you to eat whatever you could from their buffet for a fixed price. I can't remember what it was, but every so often Julia would take me there and we'd eat like pigs.'

'Did you actually go hungry when you were small?' asked Dan.

'No,' replied Ash. 'At least, I didn't. But maybe Julia did.' She ran her finger round the rim of her champagne glass. 'I've never thought about it before.' But she thought about it now and remembered how Julia would sometimes say that she didn't feel like anything to eat herself but would make Ash eat. And she wondered whether or not her mother had lied to her.

'Are you OK?' asked Dan.

'Of course.' She smiled faintly at him. 'Just remembering.'

The waiter arrived with their main courses and filled their wine glasses, even though they hadn't yet finished the champagne. I'm sorry, Julia, thought Ash. I'm sorry for being such a selfish, horrible, insensitive daughter. You did your best and it was never good enough for me. I did nothing but criticise you and I was so very, very wrong.

Dan watched her as she pushed her pasta round her plate. He'd never seen her look so serious before.

'Sure you're OK?' he asked again. 'Only Vittorio won't be very happy if you send back the food.'

'I'm fine,' she said. 'Really.'

'How's Alistair?' Dan reckoned that he should shift the subject away from Ash's past life but the expression on her face made him realise that he'd just made a terrible blunder.

She put down her knife and fork. 'I'm not sure.'

'Not sure?'

'Alistair and I – well, we've sort of broken up.'

'Ash! You're joking. You should have said something before now.'

She shrugged. 'No reason to.'

'I thought you two were so right for each other.'

'I'm not actually right for anyone,' she said ruefully. 'And I've only just realised that.'

'But why?'

'Look, Dan, I really don't want to talk about it.'

He regarded her thoughtfully. 'Did you end it or did he?'

'Does it make a difference?'

He shook his head. 'I guess not.'

The waiter cleared their plates and looked in disappointment at the amount that Ash had left. She was

473

surprised at having left it herself and thought that maybe the not being able to eat after your boyfriend dumped you scenario was true after all.

'You must be feeling a bit cut up about it all the same,' said Dan.

'I'll get over it,' she said shortly. 'So will he.'

'I'm sorry,' said Dan.

'Don't be.' Ash swallowed the lump in her throat. 'How about finishing off that champagne?'

The waiter filled their glasses before Dan had a chance to and they sat in silence, gazing out at the faint ribbon of lights that was the Italian coast.

'I had another invitation from Honor Carmody,' said Dan eventually.

'Oh really?' Ash looked at him with bright eyes. 'To what?'

'Garden party,' said Dan. 'In the grounds of her house. She has a wonderful place in Enniskerry.'

'Will Cordelia be home in time for it?' asked Ash.

'I'm not sure,' Dan said. 'But if she's not, you don't have to worry, Ash. I didn't accept the invitation this time so you won't be press-ganged into it at the last minute.'

'I didn't mind,' said Ash. 'It was fun, really.'

'I'm glad you thought so.'

'It was interesting meeting all those women who knew you.' She smiled at him.

Dan made a face at her.

'Just how many girlfriends have you had?'

Dan sat back in his chair and considered. 'Ten, twenty – I don't know. Do you count one-night stands?'

'I didn't mean how many you'd slept with!' cried Ash. 'I meant – you know, how many girls have you gone out with?'

'Ten, twenty – I don't know,' repeated Dan.

'OK. How many have you slept with?' she asked.

'I thought you didn't want to know!'

She smiled. 'I just wondered.'

'Not that many,' he admitted.

'Less than twenty?'

'Good God, yes.'

'Less than ten?'

'Is it demeaning to admit to less than ten?' he asked.

'Possibly.'

'In or around ten,' said Dan. 'What about you?'

'I've gone out with loads of blokes,' she told him. 'But I don't – well, I haven't slept with too many of them.'

'That's good, isn't it?' asked Dan.

'God knows,' she sighed.

'At least you cared about the guys you slept with.'

She said nothing.

'You didn't care?' he asked.

'Does it matter?'

'No,' he said. 'And I'm sorry, it's none of my business.'

'Forget it,' she told him.

'OK,' he said. 'You can tell me to sod off if you like, and I know you don't want to talk about it, but why aren't you and Alistair right for each other?'

'Because I'm an idiot.'

Dan laughed.

'I am!' Ash smiled a little herself. 'Let's face it, Dan, he was the most eligible bloke I've ever met and what did I do – well, you don't want to know, but the bottom line is that I'm back on the shelf and he's holding off the hordes.'

'You're not on the shelf,' said Dan. 'I bet hundreds of blokes are falling over themselves to ask you out.'

She laughed out loud. 'I doubt it, but thanks.'

'You'll find someone else,' Dan told her.

'It's not a question of finding someone else,' said Ash. 'It's a question of . . . oh, Dan, I was horrible to him.'

'I've been horrible to women in the past,' said Dan. 'We don't always behave the way we should.'

'How have you been horrible?' asked Ash.

He shrugged. 'I once went out with a girl for a bet. She was a really nice girl but I treated her terribly – wouldn't return her phone calls or anything. I've gone out with loads of women just once and not bothered to call them afterwards. I pretend it's because I'm not very good with them but actually I just haven't cared enough about them.'

Ash blinked. 'You sound like me.'

'I'm not like you at all,' said Dan. 'I've been dumped loads of times! I was crazy about a girl called Veronica. Went out with her for months. Bought her flowers, chocs, jewellery – did all of the things that are supposed to melt them at the knees. And she left me for someone with a bigger bank account.'

Ash smiled at him.

'*She* sounds a bit like you, doesn't she?' asked Dan.

'A bit,' admitted Ash. 'That's why Michelle, my cousin, thought Alistair such a good match.' She ran her finger up and down the stem of her wine glass. 'She used to tease me when we were at school because I opened a Post Office savings account with my pocket money.'

'Nothing wrong with that,' said Dan robustly.

'I saved more than I spent,' said Ash. 'I was such a bore.'

'And now?'

She took a large gulp of wine. 'Now, I'm not much better.'

'Oh, come on!'

'No really. I'm not a fun kind of person, Dan. I was thinking about it earlier. I'm not the kind of girl that gets drunk every night and who doesn't know where she's left things and who's only got tights with ladders and who's pining for a bloke all the time.'

'I know that,' said Dan. 'You told me. You're neat and tidy.'

'Which is all very well,' said Ash, 'but who really wants to date neat and tidy?'

'Plenty of people,' said Dan.

'Not really,' said Ash. 'They want to go out with you for a while but they're probably secretly relieved when it's over. Men don't want neat and tidy, they want fun and loving.'

'You can be both,' said Dan.

Ash shook her head. 'Not me.'

The waiter returned with dessert menus but Ash said that, even in the interests of research, she couldn't eat anything else. They ordered filtered coffee and sat back in their chairs again.

'Perhaps I should have talked to Cordelia about getting married here.' Dan decided to change the subject for a while. 'It'd be lovely, wouldn't it?'

Ash nodded.

'Romantic.'

'You're into romance, aren't you?' she teased. 'Remember your engagement night, you wanted romance then too.'

'Is there anything wrong with that?' asked Dan.

She shook her head. 'Nope.'

'Well then.' He looked at her defiantly and refilled her glass.

'I'm getting drunk,' she told him.

'Good,' he said. 'So am I.'

It was nice to be drunk, thought Ash, as she squinted at Dan. It was nice to be miles away from everyone and everything and not to have to think about things. She wondered, briefly, whether or not she'd remembered to unplug the TV before she'd left.

There was a sudden eddy of activity at the entrance to the terrace as a waiter led a couple to a table at the opposite end. The man was around the same age as Joss Morland, Ash estimated, while the girl was in her early twenties. Daughter or lover? she wondered as she drank more Barolo. Then the girl giggled and leaned across the table towards the older man and kissed him provocatively on the cheek, which answered the question for her.

'Don't they realise how stupid they look?' asked Dan, who'd watched the couple arrive too.

'If they care about each other, what does it matter?'

'Oh, come on, Ash.' Dan looked at her impatiently. 'That old geezer, that young girl – Dad and his latest flame – what is it about men?'

'I don't know.' She grinned at him. 'You tell me. You're the one who'll be out looking for teenagers when you're sixty-five.'

'I won't,' said Dan. 'I'll be happily married.' He got up abruptly. 'I'm going to the men's room. Back in a minute.'

Ash sat back and waited for him. He was really upset about this thing with his dad, she realised. She wasn't sure why it bothered him so much. The girl at the other table was popping green olives into the older man's mouth. She couldn't be more than twenty, Ash decided, as she studied her more closely. Her skin was smooth and clear although her eyes were hidden behind a pair of Armani sunglasses. Maybe she's famous or something, thought Ash, since she feels the need to wear sunglasses at night. Maybe Dan and I have got it wrong and she's the dominant person in the relationship. But she knew that they hadn't got it wrong.

'You look very thoughtful.' Dan sat down at the table again.

'I've been trying to work out the intricacies of the couple over there,' she told him. 'I was secretly hoping that maybe she was the rich bitch and he was the arm candy but somehow I don't think so.'

'If you were going for arm candy, would you go for a bloke in his sixties?' asked Dan.

'The way I'm going I'll be in my sixties myself before I manage to hold on to a man,' she told him wryly.

'I doubt that,' said Dan.

'You wanted to know why I split up with Alistair?' She drained her glass of wine. 'It's the same reason as why I split up with everyone. I'm afraid, Dan. Afraid of letting them in and doing anything I haven't already worked out in considerable detail beforehand. I'm afraid of doing anything spontaneous and loving and fun.'

'Why?' he asked.

'Because –' she reached for the wine bottle and refilled her glass. 'Because Julia did all of those things and Julia got killed.'

'Ash!' He looked at her, horrified. 'That's crazy.'

'I know.' She smiled tentatively at him. 'I know I'm crazy. I know I'm fucked up. I know I should just go with the flow – but I can't.' She took another gulp of wine. 'You know Jodie? The waitress I work with?'

Dan nodded.

'Jodie broke up with her boyfriend and she threw potted plants at him. And she told me all about it. And apparently she's spent every night since talking to her friends about it and sitting in with them watching videos of Julia Roberts and Meg Ryan and Sandra Bullock all being strong women. And she went into town and spent a fortune on clothes and got her hair done. When they got tired of that they went out and got pissed together. And what did I do when Alistair and I split up? I made fucking soup, that's what I did. I was really sensible and made four pots of soup.'

Dan looked at her and said nothing.

'I know I need to cut loose. Everyone tells me that,' she told him. 'It's not that I don't see it. It's just that I can't do it.'

'Because Julia got killed?'

'Partly. Maybe. I don't know,' she said.

'You're not Julia,' said Dan.

'I know.' She bit her lip. 'I've spent my whole life not being Julia. And now I wonder if she wasn't right about things after all.'

'Do you love Alistair?' asked Dan.

Ash rubbed the back of her neck. 'I don't know that either,' she said. 'So I suppose I mustn't because if I did I'd be able to tell you.' She sighed. 'He tried to make love to me one morning and I just shoved him away and he got mad at me and I don't blame him. That's the actual reason why it's over, Dan.'

'I'm sorry,' said Dan.

She sighed. 'So am I.'

'What you need,' he told her as he topped up her glass again, 'is to get blitzed tonight and do something really silly and impulsive and very, very girlie and you'll realise that the world won't stop turning if you do and you can go home and make it up with Alistair.'

'He wouldn't make it up with me,' she said. 'He was furious with me.'

'You should do something silly and impulsive anyway,' said Dan.

'Like what?'

'Go for a midnight swim,' he suggested.

Ash laughed. 'It's not impulsive if I plan it.'

'I guess not.' Dan was pleased to hear her laugh.

'Maybe you're right,' she said. 'It's just hard to change.'

'I know,' said Dan.

She sat back in the seat and closed her eyes. She'd already done something silly by drinking so much, she thought. Her head was light and she knew that when she got up to walk she was going to be unsteady on her feet.

'Would you like me to get the bill?' asked Dan.

'Yes please,' she said.

She closed her eyes again. She heard him ask for the bill and she sensed the waiter coming to the table with it. But she felt as if she was floating on her chair.

'Come on, Ash.' Dan was beside her, his hand under her arm. 'Best get back, I think.'

He was nice, she thought. Really nice. Cordelia didn't know how lucky she was. Imagine going off to the States and leaving such a nice, nice man behind. A man that anyone would be happy to have.

'Careful,' said Dan as she stood up and wobbled. 'I think maybe some of that wine has gone to your head.'

'You told me to get blitzed,' she said.

'I didn't realise it was happening to you already.'

'Let's look at the sea,' she said. 'I want to look at the sea.'

They stood beside the stone balustrade and she gazed across the inky blackness of the water. Julia had loved to swim in the sea. Julia had been like a fish, cleaving her way confidently through the water. Ash loved the sea too. Swimming was the one thing she had shared with Julia.

She leaned forward and Dan held her arm more tightly. Then she stumbled and her mule slid off her foot and through the gap in the balustrade.

'Oh shit,' she gasped in dismay. 'My shoe.' And then she started to giggle helplessly.

Dan peered over the stone. 'I can't see it,' he said. 'But it's probably just below us.'

'It doesn't matter.' Ash couldn't stop laughing. 'They were a cheap pair of shoes anyway. Not suitable for my very expensive dress. Which, actually, was a kind of impulsive purchase. So maybe I'm changing after all.' She hiccoughed and looked at him in surprise. 'Oops. Excuse me!'

He couldn't help laughing at her himself. 'Come on,' he said. 'I'd better get you back before you lose the other one.'

'One isn't much good to me,' she said. She leaned down and took it off her foot. 'Maybe the best thing is to get rid of it too.'

'Ash, don't!' He caught her hand.

'Why not?' She grinned at him. 'It's only an ordinary old size five from Marks and Sparks. It deserves to end up in the sea!' And she threw it in a wide arc out towards the dark water.

She noticed that the hum of conversation in the restaurant had suddenly stopped. And she realised that everyone was looking at her.

'I know I said silly and impulsive,' said Dan. 'I didn't quite realise how literally you were going to take me.'

I'm so drunk, she thought as she allowed him to lead her out of the restaurant and past the curious glances of the other diners. I'm drunker than I've ever been before. And I don't care. Because I know that I can be a different person. A silly person. If I want to be.

The road back to the Villa Rosa was covered in gravel and old pine needles. She picked her way gingerly over them while Dan supported her. She swore softly as she stepped on a bigger stone and Dan offered to carry her.

'No,' she told him. 'I'm a big girl. I can do it all on my own.'

'Ash, at the rate we're going it'll take us an hour to get back to the villa. If I carry you it'll take ten minutes.'

'Don't be utterly, utterly silly.' She was finding it quite difficult to string the words together. 'I'm perfectly capable – oh!' She stumbled again and he was convulsed with laughter.

'Don't laugh!' She squinted at him. 'Don't you dare laugh at me.'

'I'm not,' he lied. 'Really.'

'You can give me a piggyback,' she said.

'OK.'

She fastened her arms round his neck and clambered onto his back. Here I am, she thought, doing something mad in Sicily and nobody but me knows. Michelle was right after all. When you go away you can be a completely different person. If Jodie could see me now she wouldn't be able to believe her eyes.

The Villa Rosa was in darkness. Ash slid from Dan's back while he opened the door and let them inside.

'I had a really good time tonight,' she told him as she stood barefoot in the hallway.

'So did I,' said Dan.

'And I was kind of impulsive, wasn't I?'

'Very,' said Dan. 'You've become a spontaneous, impulsive, lunatic Sicilian!'

She smiled at him and then she kissed him. She hadn't intended to kiss him. She'd intended to hug him. But when she leaned towards him with her face raised, her mouth was suddenly on his and she felt the softness of his lips and the unexpected strength of his hand on her bare back. She held him more tightly and he held her and she didn't know what made her break away from him.

'Oh God,' she said shakily. 'That was – I'm sorry. I didn't mean to do it.' And she gathered her dress in her hands and stumbled up the stairs away from him.

She fled to her room and almost slammed the door closed behind her. Her heart was still racing but not in the frightening way it did when she was panicking about something and needed a brown paper bag, but in a different, more exciting kind of way.

It was only a kiss, she told herself. An unexpected kiss. One that had happened without her realising it. But, God, she thought, she'd never kissed anyone and felt her lips on fire before. She'd never kissed anyone and felt as though she wanted to keep on kissing them for ever. She'd never felt as though the kiss itself was the most wonderful thing that could happen to her.

You've never been blind drunk when you kissed anyone before, she told herself as she slumped onto her bed. It's something you should consider for the future.

Dan was standing by the window in his room when the phone rang.

'Hi, Dan!' It was Cordelia, her voice as clear as though she was standing right beside him.

'Hi.'

'Guess what?'

'What?'

'I've got a salary increase.'

'Why?'

'Why d'you think?' Cordelia was offended. 'Because I'm good at my job and they've recognised that.'

'You're coming home to get married in a couple of months,' said Dan. 'Have they recognised that too?'

'Don't be silly,' she said.

'Or have *you* forgotten about it?'

'You're not being very nice tonight, Dan, did you know that?'

'I'm sorry,' he said. 'I'm tired. Yesterday was traumatic and today—'

'How are your folks?' Cordelia thought that the row between Freda and Joss was hilarious.

'Much better,' said Dan.

'So, all's well and that sort of thing?'

'More or less.'

'No need for you to feel tired then.'

'I suppose not.'

'How's the chef?'

'Pardon?' Dan held his left hand out in front of him and realised that it was shaking. He couldn't believe that Cordelia didn't know, didn't sense that he'd just kissed Ash O'Halloran and it hadn't been the sort of friendly peck on the cheek he'd given her before.

'Has she recovered from the fact that you flew her out for a meal that people actually chucked all around the place?'

'Nobody threw the food anywhere,' said Dan.

'Nobody ate it either,' retorted Cordelia.

'Ash is OK,' said Dan.

'I'm glad she's not doing the wedding all the same,' said Cordelia. 'Have you talked to Gillian lately?'

'Gillian?'

'The girl who *is* doing the catering? The company that the chef put you in touch with?'

'Oh, no. Not lately.'

'I'd like to see her menu ideas.'

'I'll phone her when I get home,' said Dan. He wondered was Ash OK. He knew she hadn't meant to kiss him. She was drunk. He was drunk. God, he thought, what is it with me when I get drunk? When Cordelia went to the States the first thing I did was get drunk and go to a bloody nightclub and meet pneumatic Barbie. And now I get drunk again and allow Ash O'Halloran to kiss me. He could still taste her on his lips.

'Sorry?' He hadn't heard Cordelia's last sentence, he'd been too busy trying to blot Ash out of his mind.

'I said I was going to Chicago on Thursday,' said

Cordelia irritably. 'Really good stuff, this, Dan, because Chicago is terribly important.'

'Is there anything about Harrison's that isn't?' he asked wryly.

'Don't be like that,' she said. Her voice suddenly softened. 'Do you miss me?'

'Of course I do,' he replied.

'Well, think of me,' she said softly.

Oh Christ, he thought. Not tonight. She loved this, he knew she did and so did he, but not tonight.

'Think of me as I take off my blouse, Dan. I'm taking it off now.'

He was silent.

'It's sliding down my arms. Down my back.'

He said nothing.

'Are you still there?' she asked.

'Yes,' he croaked. 'I'm still here.'

'It's on the floor, Dan. I'm wearing a white bra today.'

'Are you?'

'Sure am. With little lacy flowers on it. And I'm taking it off now.'

Oh, don't, Cordelia, he thought. Please don't. I just can't cope with this right now.

'And it's on the floor too. Beside my blouse. Are you still there, Dan?'

'Of course,' he said.

'And I'm wearing a long skirt. It's linen. Crisp white linen. But I'm taking that off too. Can you hear it sliding down to the floor?'

'I – yes.'

'So the only thing I'm wearing now is my thong.'

He closed his eyes and tried to picture her.

'It's a white thong. I'm very virginal tonight, Dan. For you.'

'Oh, Cordelia—'

'I want you to imagine me like it was the first time.' Her voice was throaty.

'I am,' he said.

'Because I'm thinking of you.' She sighed softly. 'I'm thinking of you and I'm thinking there's no one in the world like you.'

That's true, he thought wildly. There's no one like me. I'm talking to my fiancée and I'm thinking of another woman. Not because I love her or anything but because she kissed me. And it was exciting.

'And I'm thinking of you with me, Dan. Where you should be.'

He desperately tried to get into the spirit of it. But he couldn't.

'And I'm thinking how much I want you.'

He was silent. She groaned softly and he wanted to groan too. But it was because the only image he could see in his mind was of Ash O'Halloran, standing barefoot in the hall, hair falling from the pretty blue clips that had held it in place, her full, pink lips turned up to him and the only thing he could think was how soft they'd been beneath his own.

Ash couldn't sleep. She couldn't understand why she hadn't passed out with the effects of the champagne and the wine. Usually wine sent her to sleep. But not tonight. She tossed and turned in the bed until the sheets were drenched with perspiration. Finally, at almost half past two, she got up and pulled on a T-shirt. She poked her head out of the window and felt the air more turgid than ever. I need to swim, she thought. I need to cool down and stay cooled down. And I need to do something active, something to work off the energy that's fizzing around inside me. She put on her trainers and picked up a towel. Then she opened the door of the bedroom and walked quietly out of the house.

The steps down to the pool were in darkness. Suddenly she was nervous about being here alone in the dark. She gritted her teeth and pushed her way through the greenery, past the gargoyle, and made her way towards the dim light of the pool.

At last she was beside it and out of the gloom of the steps and she wasn't scared any more even though she could now see that the sky had clouded over which was why, for the first time since she'd arrived, there was no light from the moon. She undid the laces of her trainers and peeled off her T-shirt.

Then she almost cried out loud because there was someone in the pool and she hadn't noticed before because they'd been swimming underwater. Her hands flew across her breasts and the top of her legs.

'Christ, Ash, you gave me a fright.' Dan held on to the edge of the pool.

'Sorry,' she said.

'Were you going to swim?'

She nodded.

'Come on, then.'

She hesitated for a moment then dived neatly and cleanly into the pool. It was deliciously cold. She stayed underwater for a full length before breaking to the surface and shaking the water from her face. She looked round for Dan. He was at the deep end, treading water and watching her.

She swam towards him slowly, wondering if he'd move. But he stayed where he was. He's horrified at me, she thought. He's horrified that I kissed him. It's like breaking a trust or something. She slid underwater and surfaced again in the same place. He hadn't moved either.

'I'm sorry,' she said.

'Sorry?'

'About earlier.'

'It's nothing,' said Dan. 'You'd had too much to drink. So had I. Don't worry about it.'

'I think I kind of got carried away with the spontaneous impulsive stuff.'

He smiled. 'No problem.'

She drifted towards him. 'It didn't mean anything, of course.'

'Of course,' he said.

'The water's lovely,' she said.

'Yes.'

She didn't know how or when she wrapped her legs round his body or how or when they suddenly started to kiss again. And then she wasn't able to think at all because she was completely caught up in the exquisite pleasure of the moment, of feeling as though she was part of him and he was part of her and it was all right to be like this.

Finally he let her go.

Her heart was thumping so quickly and so loudly in her chest that she was afraid it would explode.

'Unfinished business,' he said.

'Yes.'

'It seemed the right thing to do.'

'Spontaneous and impulsive,' she told him.

He nodded.

'And wrong. Really wrong. A big mistake. Huge. Massive.'

'I know.'

She hauled herself out of the water and wrapped the plain white towel around her.

'This was a one-night thing,' she said.

'Sure.'

'I shouldn't have done it.'

He could hardly see her in the shadow of the bougain- villaea that grew near the pool.

'Ash—'

'I've got to get back,' she told him. 'I have an early flight tomorrow. I need to get some sleep.'

She picked up her trainers and T-shirt and disappeared up the pathway before he managed to get out of the pool himself.

Chapter 29

Sicilian Sauce
Onion, peppers, garlic, tomatoes, aubergine, olives, capers,
chilli, basil
Finely chop the onion, peppers and garlic and simmer
over low heat. Chop tomatoes and aubergine, add to pan,
simmer. Finally add capers, basil, olives and chilli and
simmer again

T he low rumble of thunder woke her from a fitful and
disturbed sleep. It was almost half past six. She got
out of bed and looked out of the window. The clouds
were low in the sky, the air was warmer than ever and
the thunder was still in the distance.

Ash went into the bathroom and looked at herself in the
mirror. Her hair was in disarray. Her waterproof mascara
had smudged under her eyes so that she looked like a
panda and her face was pale and tired. She stepped under
the shower and tipped half a bottle of Clairol Herbal
Essences onto her head.

She'd been hoping that it was a dream, that the entire

evening before had been a dream brought on by rich food and wine and champagne. But it hadn't been a dream. Her damp T-shirt still lay on the floor where she'd flung it when she came back from the pool and there was a small bruise on her arm from where he had held her tightly.

She closed her eyes and thought about it again and she was horrified to feel the same stirring of passion within her. How could it have happened? she asked herself. She liked him. You didn't suddenly get the hots for someone you liked. You usually got the hots for someone you hardly knew and by the time you learned about them, your interest had waned. Which was why you didn't bloody well jump on them straightaway. Which was why you planned things. I'm not a spontaneous, impulsive person, she told herself as the water cascaded over her face. And now I know why. But, she thought bitterly, there is something seriously wrong with me as a person if I think it's OK to have sex with a man who's engaged to somebody else. Somebody I've met. Somebody I – well, I don't exactly like Cordelia but I don't dislike her either.

She turned off the shower and stood dripping in the stall. I don't think it's OK to have sex with a man who's engaged to somebody else, she told herself. It's absolutely, definitely, not OK in fact. It's completely wrong. I shouldn't have done it.

But what about him? Did he think it was OK? Did he think it was fun? Was that why he'd been urging her to loosen up? Did he think that plying her with drink and then letting her kiss him and then making love to her was a reasonable thing to do? Had he felt anything at all for her other than amusement? But why should he, she asked herself as she rubbed herself briskly with one of the bathroom towels, when I don't feel anything for him. What *I* was feeling was revenge. Getting back at Alistair even though Alistair didn't know anything about it. I did it because it made me feel good. Christ, she thought, I'm a complete bitch.

She didn't bother to dry her hair but simply combed it through and tied it back in a thick plait. She dressed in her black jeans and a black cotton top before packing her bag for the return journey home.

Her flight was at eleven. She would walk up to Taormina now and get a taxi to take her to the airport where she could have a coffee and a pastry for her breakfast although, at this moment, the thought of coffee and pastry made her stomach heave. She suddenly realised that she had a blinding headache. But she should leave now, before anyone else was awake so that she didn't have to see them. Things would be different back in Dublin. She could forget it even happened back in Dublin; she could forget all about this impulsive sex and shopping nonsense. She'd think before she acted, as she'd always done before.

The rain came just as she stepped out of the villa. The drops were huge and heavy, warm pellets of water falling from the glowering sky. She swore softly under her breath. She tried to walk under the shelter of the trees that overhung the road but she was getting drenched all the same. Raindrops slid from the leaves of the trees and down the back of her neck, making her feel even more uncomfortable. A car pulled to a halt a couple of feet ahead of her and the driver rolled down the window.

'Get in, Ash,' said Dan.

She shook her head. 'It's OK.'

'You're getting soaked,' he told her. 'Get in.'

'No,' she said.

'For Christ's sake, Ash, don't be so fucking stupid and get in the fucking car!'

She looked at him for a moment then walked round to the passenger seat and got in, throwing her bag into the rear.

'I'll drive you to the airport,' he said as he executed a U-turn.

'Drive me to the taxi rank,' she said.

'I'll drive you to the airport.'

'Dan, I really don't feel like talking,' she told him. 'Drive me to a taxi rank.'

'I never said anything about talking.' Dan overtook a spluttering truck. 'We can drive to the airport in silence if that's what you want but that's where I'm bringing you.'

'Fine,' said Ash tiredly. She shivered. Her top was wet now and so were her jeans and trainers.

Dan drove quickly down the hill, negotiating the bends with practised ease. Normally Ash would have worried about the speed and the twists and turns of the road but her head hurt and she was beyond caring.

'I guess you want to take the "last night never happened" approach,' said Dan as he was finally forced to stop to allow a tour bus to pick up some passengers.

'Yes, absolutely,' said Ash quickly.

'You don't think there was a reason—'

'The reason was that I was drunk and so were you,' said Ash. 'And I was stupidly trying to act like all the girls in the world that do stupid things.'

'You're certain?'

She glanced at him. 'Dan, you're engaged to Cordelia. You love Cordelia – you've told me so a thousand times. And I was trying to get back at Alistair.'

'What?'

'I've tried my whole life not to get hurt and I tried to tell myself that I didn't care enough about Alistair to be hurt but I was and kissing you and – and – everything – well, it was getting back at him.'

'Thanks,' said Dan.

'I'm sorry,' said Ash. 'I really am. This is why I don't do impulsive, Dan. Because my impulses are pretty damn silly.'

'There's no way Cordelia will get to hear about it?' He looked at her.

'Not unless you tell her,' said Ash wryly. 'Which I guess wouldn't be a great move.'

'Not great,' agreed Dan.

They were silent again as the rain came down even harder and made driving almost impossible. Ash suddenly remembered the gargoyle at the Villa Rosa and wondered whether the rainwater was gushing out of its mouth now.

'I have to stop for a minute,' said Dan. 'Let this ease off.' He pulled the car into the side of the road, overlooking the sea which was a fury of white-topped waves. 'I've never done anything like that before,' he said after a few minutes. 'I know I said that I've treated women badly sometimes but—'

'You didn't treat me badly,' said Ash. 'If anyone should feel bad about it, it's Cordelia.'

'But Cordelia won't know,' said Dan.

'Like I said,' Ash told him, 'not unless you tell her.'

'Thank you,' said Dan.

'No problem.' Ash kept her voice as light as she could.

'I truly am sorry.'

'Look, Dan, please don't spend time telling me how sorry you are. We said we'd pretend it never happened, didn't we? I got into the car because you said that we'd drive to the airport in silence. I don't want to spend the next half hour analysing why I was so bloody stupid and so thoughtless and so – so –'

'Abandoned,' said Dan. 'I never imagined you could be abandoned. You were quite something, really.'

'Oh, God, Dan – don't say things like that! I was quite something stupid!'

'I shouldn't have let you,' he said.

'It wasn't your fault,' she told him. 'Stop talking as though you were the lord of the manor and you tumbled with the servants. You couldn't have stopped me.'

He laughed. 'You sound like someone who was suddenly unleashed.'

'It's not funny,' she said.

'I know. But I thought I should lighten the atmosphere a little.'

'Do me a favour,' said Ash. 'Don't.'

'OK. But maybe we really should talk about it.'

'No,' she said vehemently. 'What good would talking do? Lead us into thinking there was anything more for us? Which there isn't. Because I don't love you, Dan. And you don't love me either. And, even if you broke it off with Cordelia and started to go out with me on the basis of one insane moment of lust, I'd still end up dumping you. That's what I do.'

'Not with Alistair,' he reminded her. 'He was the one that left you.'

'So I react by jumping on the first bloke I see,' said Ash. 'Even if that bloke is you.' She shivered suddenly.

'You should change out of those wet things,' said Dan.

'I will,' she told him. 'When I get to the airport.'

The rain eased a little and Dan started the car again. They drove in silence. When they pulled up outside the airport, Ash leaned into the back to grab her bag. She got out of the car and slammed the door shut.

'Ash!' Dan rolled down the window.

She turned back towards him and looked at him. Then she turned away and walked into the terminal building.

The rain and the storms had delayed all of the flights out of Catania. Ash changed out of her wet things, repacked her bag, and sat down in the terminal to wait until her flight was called. She bought some paracetamol and a newspaper but the words were a jumble of letters in front of her eyes and she couldn't concentrate on them. Occasionally, she drifted into sleep, only to wake up with a jump a few seconds later. By the time she eventually boarded the plane, three hours later than scheduled, she was exhausted. As the plane climbed into the sky, Ash could see fingers of lightning in the distance, illuminating the clouds in a spectacular display.

She'd missed her connection from Milan and had to wait for another, still later, flight. By the time she reached Dublin she felt as though she'd been travelling all her life.

Everyone else on the flight seemed to have someone to meet them. Ash felt very alone as she pulled her bag through the arrivals hall and out of the airport. The temperature in Dublin was distinctly cold in comparison with Sicily and she pulled her jacket round her as she queued for a taxi.

Her one bit of luck today, she thought as she huddled in the back seat of the cab, was that she had a non-talkative driver. She leaned her head against the window and wondered whether or not she'd ever manage to take control of her life again. It had all been so simple before. And it would be simple again. All she had to do was remember what mattered to her. Her job, her apartment and her cat. There was a reason, she realised, that those madcap thirtysomethings were always drunk and in a flap over things; it was because they couldn't get to grips with what life was all about. But she'd already done that. And, even though it had got away from her a little in the last few weeks, even if it had somersaulted last night, she could get it back again. She wasn't the sort of person who went into a decline and hit the bottle. She knew she wasn't. She wasn't the sort of person who got depressed and slept with the first unsuitable man she met. Not really. Just because she'd made one mistake didn't mean that her life would now be a collision of other mistakes. She wasn't, after all, Julia. Dan had said so.

She paid the taxi driver and tipped him extravagantly because of his silence. He smiled at her and thanked her and offered to bring her case into the apartment for her.

'No, thanks,' she told him. 'I can manage.'

I've always managed, she muttered to herself as she waited for the lift. I've always managed because I've always had to manage and that's the sort of person I am.

She unlocked the apartment door and went inside. Everything was as she'd left it, neat and tidy, and she was comforted by it and by the fact that the TV was unplugged as it should be. She unpacked her bag and threw her wet clothes into the laundry basket. Already Sicily was taking on a dream-like quality in her mind; it was hard to believe that the T-shirt had been soaked in another country.

She went across the hallway to exchange the bottle of olive oil and lump of volcanic rock for Bagel. Her neighbours wanted to hear about her trip and despite the fact that she didn't want to talk about it at all she obliged them with edited versions of the dinner party for the Morlands (she left out the bit about Freda throwing plates around the place), her trip up Etna (she didn't mention the puncture) and her meal with Dan (she just said that the food had been great).

'Sounds fantastic,' sighed Rhoda. 'I wish I'd had a break like that.'

'It was great,' lied Ash. 'It's terrible to be home.' Bagel squirmed in her arms and she told them that she'd better get back to the apartment. 'But you must come over for dinner sometime,' she said, surprising herself because she'd never invited them over before.

'Great.' Rhoda smiled widely at her. 'We'd love to.'

What on earth am I doing? Ash asked herself. I'm still acting without thinking. I need to get a grip on things.

Bagel expressed his displeasure at her desertion of him by sharpening his claws on the sofa. She didn't bother trying to stop him. Then he stalked into the kitchen, sat down by his bowl and mewed loudly.

She filled it with Whiskas and watched him as he wolfed down the food. Comfort-eating, she thought. I'd comfort-eat myself only I don't feel in the slightest bit hungry.

She went back into the living room and turned on her computer. The only e-mails in her mailbox were newsletters from some of the services she subscribed to. There was nothing from Alistair. She hadn't expected a message from him, of course, but she couldn't help feeling that her life must be a complete bore if all she ever got were messages from book clubs telling her that there was another Delia Smith for her to buy. There must be something more to it all than being able to boil an egg perfectly.

There were no messages on her answering machine either. She went downstairs to check her postbox. At least there were a few envelopes there but, she realised, they were all brown envelopes which meant that they were all bills.

Is this it? she asked herself. Is this all I am? Four utility bills, a letter from the bank telling me I can borrow up to ten thousand pounds and a circular from my local politician telling me that he's working hard on my behalf.

She brought the bills upstairs and placed them in the in-tray on her desk. Then she sat back and looked round the apartment. The cornflake-yellow walls seemed to close in on her.

It's time I redecorated again, she decided. Bagel jumped up on her lap and began to knead her stomach.

Chapter 30

Sourdough Bread
Sourdough starter, lukewarm water, sugar, salt, melted
margarine, flour
Mix sourdough, water, sugar, salt and margarine. Add
half the flour and beat until smooth. Allow to stand for 15
minutes. Add flour to make soft dough. Knead and con-
tinue adding flour until dough is no longer sticky. Place in
large bowl, cover and allow to rise until volume doubles

C ordelia had ordered ham and mustard on sourdough bread for her lunch. She ate it at her desk as she read through a report on a toy company the bank was working for. But she couldn't concentrate on the report and, after three pages, she put it to one side and picked up the wedding dress brochure again. The one on page four was absolutely gorgeous but so ridiculously expensive that Cordelia wondered if she should be locked up for simply thinking about it. It was only one day, after all. It was insane to spend a few thousand dollars on a dress you'd only wear for a day.

Her phone buzzed and she reached out for the receiver.

'Cordelia Carroll,' she said, unable to keep the slight American twang out of her voice these days.

'Hi, Cordelia. I was wondering if you could drop up to my office for a moment.'

She opened her eyes a little wider. 'Mike? Now?'

'Yes, now, if you're not busy. You know where it is?'

'Of course.' Cordelia could feel her heartbeat quicken. She wiped sourdough crumbs from her lips, threw the remainder of her roll into the trash and walked over to the elevators. She was nervous but curious. Mike was one of the executives who could hold her future in the palm of his hand. She'd cultivated a very casual friendship with Mike because he was in the gym every morning and she always smiled at him and said hello as he pounded the treadmill. Occasionally he'd ask her how one or other of the projects was coming along and he always seemed interested in her replies. Mike Fuller, thought Cordelia, was a useful person to be friendly with.

She was surprised to see Melissa Kravich in his office too. As always, Melissa was perfectly groomed and manicured and looked as though she'd stepped out of an advertisement for Power Women.

'Sit down, Cordelia.' Mike's hazel eyes were warm and friendly and she could feel her nervousness, if not her anticipation, disappear.

'Melissa and I have been talking about further developments in mergers and acquisitions,' said Mike. 'And your name was mentioned.'

'Oh.' Cordelia glanced from Mike to Melissa, suddenly nervous again. This wasn't some sort of set-up, was it? she wondered. They couldn't fire her for something, could they? They'd only just given her a raise. But you never knew on Wall Street. Anything could happen.

'Melissa thinks you're an extremely able kind of person. And so do I.'

They weren't going to fire her! She breathed a sigh of relief.

'A position has become available. I've spoken to Melissa and she agrees with me that you would be perfect for the job.'

'Really?' Cordelia tried to keep her voice unemotional.

'It's in our Chicago office,' said Mike. 'Which, as you know, is the biggest outside this one. They were very impressed with you in Chicago the other day. You'd be working as assistant vice president with responsibility for special projects, with a guaranteed promotion to vice president after six months.'

Vice president! Cordelia felt her head swim. Vice president! OK, so it was true that everyone was a vice president but you still had to reach that position. And she was being offered it – ahead of DeVere Bassett and anyone else in her department. There was the slight disadvantage of moving to Chicago but she could get over that. And Mike was right, it was a big office; there'd be plenty of opportunities for her and it was everything she'd ever wanted.

'We'd expect for you to start in August,' said Mike.

August. That word brought her back to earth with a bump. She was getting married in August. She couldn't start a job in Chicago when she was getting married the same month. Cordelia struggled with her mixed emotions. She wanted this job so badly it almost hurt. She glanced at Melissa again. The older woman was watching her.

'Is there a problem?' asked Melissa.

She knows I'm due to get married in August, thought Cordelia. I've spoken to her about it. She frowned slightly. Was this some kind of test? she wondered. To prove her loyalty to Harrison's? Was she supposed to say that she didn't care about getting married to Dan, that her career was more important to her than anything? That was the way Melissa would be about it, she knew. A woman who could drink cocktails and chat with board members when her son had been carted off to hospital wouldn't let something like a wedding disrupt her career plans. Melissa would see Cordelia's wish to get married as a weakness which would work against her in her future career.

Cordelia wanted to be successful. She craved success. But did she crave it at all costs? If she took this job would she, one day, become the sort of woman who'd drink cocktails at a corporate function while her nanny stayed with her son in hospital? Or was she getting everything out of proportion?

'It's a fantastic opportunity,' she said carefully, looking at Mike. 'I'm utterly delighted that you've considered me. There is one slight drawback, though.'

'And that is?' Mike regarded her thoughtfully.

'I'm getting married in August. I was supposed to take up a new position in Dublin in September.'

'I know about the Dublin position,' said Mike. 'But you're hardly comparing like with like, Cordelia. Dublin is a small operation beside Chicago.'

'I know,' she said.

'Do you want to go home and get married and spend the rest of your life in the Dublin office?' asked Melissa.

Cordelia shot her a glance. She wants me to say yes, Cordelia realised. She wants me to say that I'm the kind of woman who'll give up everything to get married. She wants me to fail. Suddenly Cordelia realised that Melissa was one of those women in power who resented other women. Who wanted to be the only one doing well. Who enjoyed being the only woman in a room full of men.

'Perhaps,' said Cordelia carefully, looking directly at Mike Fuller, 'we can work something out.'

'Like what?' asked Mike.

'I can't change the date of my wedding,' said Cordelia. 'And, let's face it, Mike, you'd think I was a pretty sad individual if I tried.'

He grinned at her.

'But I'm sure you can be flexible about my starting date in Chicago. After all, a week here or there won't mean much in the entire scheme of things.'

'The project we have in mind is particularly urgent,' said Melissa.

'But you don't need me in Chicago until August so it can't be that urgent,' said Cordelia reasonably. 'So there's already an element of flexibility.'

'You have a point,' said Mike.

He wants me to get this job, she realised. He likes

me. He knows I can do it and he knows that Melissa is deliberately trying to be obstructive.

'How about I sit down with you and work out exactly when I can come back from Ireland?' she suggested. 'I'm sure we can agree something that'll keep everyone happy.'

'Sounds reasonable,' said Mike.

'If you think so,' said Melissa.

'I'm so glad you've given me this opportunity.' Cordelia beamed at them both and thought about her strategy for getting Dan to agree to a change of plans.

Ash cleared away the dishes and stacked them in the dishwasher. Today's lunch had been for four and so she didn't need a waitress and she did everything herself. Normally she didn't mind but today she wished that Jodie had been around because she'd woken up with another massive headache but this time accompanied by a sore throat. In the last few minutes she'd started to sneeze and she knew that she was coming down with a cold. Ash didn't believe that you could get colds simply from sitting around in wet clothes but she couldn't think of any other way she'd managed to pick it up. There was a very small part of her that believed she was being punished for her night of passion with Dan which, she told herself, was extremely silly. But she couldn't help feeling like that. She rubbed the back of her neck and wished she was at home, curled up on the sofa with Bagel at her feet. Not that Bagel was much comfort at the moment – he was still ignoring her, letting her know that she couldn't just leave him whenever she liked.

I wish everything was the way it was before, she thought. She switched on the dishwasher. I wish I'd never gone to Sicily. I wish I'd never met Dan Morland. Or Alistair Brannigan. I wish I hadn't got involved.

Things had been much simpler when she hadn't got involved. She'd always known that.

Dan and Bronwyn were sitting on the terrace at the Villa Rosa. Dan's legs were propped up on the wrought-iron table, catching the early evening sun. Bronwyn was painting her nails a bright orange.

'It's so much easier to sit out now that the air has cleared,' said Bronwyn. 'I bet you're glad you were able to stay for an extra week.'

'Mm.'

'I'm not surprised that Mum flipped at the dinner. It was so hot that even I felt out of sorts and you know that I'm normally the most even-tempered of people.'

Dan snorted at his sister.

'I am!' Bronwyn held her hand out in front of her and nodded approvingly. 'What d'you think?'

'Don't ask me,' Dan told her. 'I'm hopeless at what's *de rigueur* in women's fashion.'

Bronwyn giggled. 'You sound like a middle-aged man.'

'I feel it sometimes,' said Dan. 'Putting up with Mum and Dad. Trying to keep everyone happy.'

'You don't have to do that,' said Bronwyn. 'Besides, everyone *is* happy. The fact that they fight all the time is irrelevant.'

'I used to think so.' Dan sighed. 'Now I'm not sure.'

'Poor Dan.' She leaned over and hugged him. 'You want so much for people to do what you want them to do.'

'Is it wrong?' asked Dan. 'To want a normal kind of family life?'

'What's normal?' Bronwyn took off her sunglasses and looked at him. 'Nothing's normal. Every family has a wardrobe full of abnormal skeletons.'

'We don't have skeletons,' said Dan. 'It's just – I'd love to have had parents who got married and stayed together. Maybe a father who had been a bit more nine to five than Dad.'

'You want a lot.' Bronwyn smiled at him. 'Life's not like that, Dan. It probably never was.'

'I know,' he said. 'I'm a fool, really.'

'No, you're not,' she told him. 'You're a great brother. You just feel too responsible, that's all. Remember when Mum left? And you spent the whole time doing housework?'

He nodded.

'You looked so daft,' she said. 'Pulling that huge vacuum cleaner around the house. Walking around with bottles of Jif.'

'Mum wouldn't do it,' he said defensively.

'It didn't mean you had to.' Bronwyn uncapped the bottle of nail varnish again and began to coat the fingers of her other hand. 'And you don't have to try and make the end-of-book dinner into some spectacular family event either.'

'I wanted to.'

'I know. And I know that we say we'll have a big do every year. But it's better that we don't.'

'If you think I'll ever try anything like this again, you've another think coming!'

'It was a nice idea. But mad.'

'She's a great cook though,' said Dan.

'Absolutely.' Bronwyn nodded. 'And you fancy her, don't you?'

'Good God, no!'

'Come on, Dan. It's me, your twin. You can't keep secrets from your twin.'

'I'm not keeping secrets.'

'Dan, she's a really nice, really attractive girl who cooks. She fulfils all of those little domesticated fantasies that you have of a wife in the kitchen and two kids in the garden!'

Dan's mouth twitched. 'You think so?'

'Of course. I'd have been shocked if you didn't fancy her.'

'So, that doesn't mean I should break it off with Cordelia?'

Bronwyn sat bolt upright in the chair and nearly sent the bottle of nail varnish flying off the table. 'You're thinking of breaking it off with Cordelia?'

'Of course not,' said Dan vehemently. 'I just meant that – well, if I fancied Ash a bit it wouldn't mean that I didn't love Cordelia.'

'You're sure you do love Cordelia? Even though you fancy Ash?'

'Yes,' said Dan firmly. 'And the Ash thing – it's nothing really.'

'You know Cordelia's not exactly my cup of tea. But, to tell you the truth, I suppose she's better for you than your fantasy woman, Dan. At least she won't disappoint you because she knows what she wants out of life.'

'Ash isn't my fantasy woman,' said Dan. 'And why would she disappoint me if she was?'

'Because no woman these days is content to cook and look after a man. And that's what you really want, Dan. Someone to look after you.'

'If that's what I really want, then why did I get engaged to Cordelia?' he asked.

'Because you've always been a sucker for long legs.' Bronwyn laughed.

'Another fantasy?' asked Dan.

'Possibly,' said Bronwyn.

Dan was silent.

'She's a nice girl,' said Bronwyn.

'That's the first positive thing you've ever said about Cordelia,' said Dan.

'I didn't mean Cordelia.'

Dan made a face at her. 'I admit that Ash is a nice girl,' he said. 'But not for me.'

'Why?' asked Bronwyn.

'She's got problems,' said Dan shortly.

'Haven't we all.' Bronwyn looked at her nails again. 'D'you think I should've done them in purple instead?'

Ash had more vegetables than she knew what to do with piled on her worktop. Tomatoes, red cabbage, carrots, peas, onions, leeks, peppers and corns were spread out on every available surface. Bagel had seen the bags and had disappeared out of the open kitchen window. Ash took her biggest, heaviest pots out of their cupboards and put them on her hob.

She hadn't decided yet what she was going to cook. Not soup because she still had a freezer full of soup. But anything that involved chopping and peeling and slicing was therapeutic and she wanted to chop and peel and slice. She needed comfort right now. Her head was pounding, her throat hurt and another sneeze wasn't far away.

And although she didn't feel as though she was going to have a panic attack, she left a brown paper bag on the counter, just in case.

Chapter 31

Lamb Cutlets
Lamb cutlets, garlic, salt and pepper, rosemary, thyme
Crush garlic, salt and pepper, mix with herbs and spread
over cutlets. Cook under warm grill to taste

Dan was finding it hard to concentrate, even though markets were having a terrible day and he was constantly on the phone executing orders for his clients. Most of them were yelling at him that they wanted to sell stocks but all of them wanted to sell at prices that simply weren't available any more. Some people just didn't believe him when he quoted levels for shares which were twenty or thirty per cent lower than they'd been the previous night and he knew that many of them believed that they were being ripped off. But they weren't – it was the kind of day where the state of the world markets would be headline news at six o'clock and on the evening bulletins too.

He looked at the flashing lights on his telephone board and sighed as he picked up the phone and listened to yet another client complain that he hadn't sold shares fast enough. Dan made all the right noises even though he knew that it wasn't much good to the client, but he sympathised at the right time and pointed out that, when markets were as volatile as they were today, it was impossible to get anything done. And he agreed when the client fumed that someone, somewhere was making a lot of money. Actually, on a day like today, nobody was making much money. He glanced at his screen and saw that both Archangel and Transys were being marked down again. The way things were going, Alistair Brannigan was going to be a very ordinary millionaire before too long. Maybe he'd done Ash a favour by dumping her after all. He shook his head to dislodge Ash from his mind. He hadn't thought of her at all since he'd come back to Dublin; there had been other things to think about. Like Cordelia's wonderful new job in Chicago.

'I have to take it, Dan. I really do.' Her voice had pleaded with him across the Atlantic.

'And what about me?' he asked.

'Dan, you'll get a job here. You know you will.'

'It's not that easy,' he said.

'You can get something with Harrison's. They'll sort it out. I told Mike about you. That you were in financial services in Dublin. He's sure they'll have something to suit you.'

How could he say no? And maybe he'd be better off in the States, where he'd have to be ambitious and aggressive all over again, instead of settling for just being OK in Dublin.

She'd arranged a meeting for him with Mike Fuller. He was going to New York the following weekend. He'd better get the job, he thought. Ross was already annoyed at him for taking another couple of days off just when he'd come back from Sicily.

He finished with the client and leaned back in his seat. Steve and Jim were still on the phone but there was a sudden lull in activity and Dan was relieved not to have to talk to somebody else straightaway. It won't be like this in Harrison's, he told himself. There, any second not on the phone would be a wasted second. He looked at his watch. Nearly twelve thirty. Nearly time for the partners' lunch. It would be quick today because people wanted to be at their desks as much as they could, but they'd spend a bit of time talking about their strategy for the week ahead and trying to decide whether today was an aberration or whether markets were going to collapse. Dan hoped not, it would be terrible for business, but he couldn't help feeling relieved that he'd followed his instincts and sold a lot of his shares before now. To renovate the bathroom, he remembered. But there was no point in renovating it if he was going to spend the next couple of years in the States.

He rubbed the back of his neck. He'd rent out the house, of course, because he still intended to come home some day. There was no point in selling it when it was located in such a great part of town and he could get a good rental income from it. Then, when Cordelia was ready to settle down, they'd come back. He hadn't talked to Ross Fearon about his move yet. He wanted to wait until he had something definite from the Yanks. You could never be certain until the contract was there in black and white. And they might hate him. In which case he didn't know exactly what he and Cordelia would do.

Ross came out of his office and signalled Dan that they were ready to go to lunch. Dan nodded at the managing director and got up from the desk. Today would be the first time he'd seen Ash since Sicily and he wasn't looking forward to it. Having managed to put her out of his mind so successfully, he now dreaded the idea of seeing her again. And, even worse, remembering how much he'd actually enjoyed being with her.

You are a complete shit, he told himself as he walked towards the lift. He knew that if he ever told his mates about his night with Ash it would be in a triumphant, boasting kind of way, so that they'd be envious of him and admire his good fortune in securing such an attractive bit on the side while the gorgeous Cordelia waited for him in New York. But he didn't feel fortunate or triumphant or like boasting today. He felt guilty.

Bronwyn had tackled him on the subject of Ash again before he'd left Sicily and had asked him, outright, if he'd ever been to bed with her. Not for the first time, Dan wished she wasn't his twin. She knew things about him that he didn't even know himself. He'd always found it difficult to keep a secret from her. He'd been able to deny it by telling himself that making love to Ash in the swimming pool wasn't the same thing as actually going to bed with her but he knew that Bronwyn didn't really believe him. Yet he couldn't tell her the truth. He'd never lied to her before but he couldn't talk to her now.

The partners of Chatham's sat round the dining-room table and Jodie set plates of smoked salmon in front of them. Dan squeezed some lemon over his salmon and realised that he wasn't hungry.

'We need to get a research note out,' said Ross Fearon. 'I've spoken to James O'Driscoll about it and he's working on something that we can e-mail to clients this evening. What we have to decide is whether or not to advise them to sell or to sit tight.'

The partners offered their opinions – as divided as any group of non-experts would be. Dan said nothing but pushed his salmon around on his plate.

'Dan, you were very bearish about things earlier in the year,' said Ross. 'What d'you think now?'

'I think they're going down more.' Dan could hardly keep a coherent thought in his head. This had never happened to him before. Until now he'd always been able to separate his personal and his professional life, and his personal life had never plagued him during working hours even though his professional life had sometimes caused him heartburn at home.

'So you'll be recommending selling?' Ross hated to hear his dealers recommending that people sell.

'Some of the stocks,' said Dan. 'I reckon they should buy the big names that have taken big hits.'

'Sounds good.' Ross preferred that tack. 'Switch out of

the poor performers into ones that have just got bashed on indiscriminate selling.'

'Something like that.' Dan put his knife and fork on his plate. He hadn't managed to eat any of the salmon.

Jodie came in and cleared away the plates while the partners continued to discuss the type of stocks they would recommend that their clients buy.

Dan was thinking of Ash. Knowing that she was so close to him made it impossible not to think of her. And it was hard to believe that she was next door cutting and chopping and slicing and doing whatever it was she did in the kitchen and the food was appearing in the dining room and nobody knew that he, Dan Morland, had made love to her in a swimming pool in Sicily. The thought was so unbelievable that he could hardly accept it himself. And that night was a memory blurred by the fact that he, as well as Ash, had drunk too much. Why, he asked himself furiously, do I always do such stupid things when I drink too much? But she'd been great. Whatever he felt about anything else, she'd been great!

He sat up straight in his chair. There is something seriously wrong with me, he thought, that I'm thinking about sex on a day when the company has seen the worst fall in equity markets since the Asian crisis of 1997. I can't believe I'm thinking about it when there are other, serious issues for me to be thinking about instead. And, worst of all, I'm thinking about sex with somebody other than Cordelia.

He thought of Cordelia in her white linen suit wearing

nothing but her white thong underneath. It helped. But not as much as he'd have liked.

Jodie came back into the dining room, carrying plates of lamb cutlets. Dan made a face as she put them in front of him. Lamb wasn't his favourite dish and rare lamb was something he liked even less. Ash hardly ever served lamb. He wondered if she was deliberately punishing him. And then he realised that she didn't know that he didn't like lamb.

He ate some of the side portion of vegetables but very little else. He listened to the other partners as they talked and tried to keep his mind on what they were talking about. And all the time he thought that, after lunch, he should go into the kitchen, say hello to Ash and make some harmless comment so that she'd see that he'd completely forgotten about what had happened between them.

But maybe I should do nothing. He ground his teeth. I don't usually agonise like this. I didn't when I slept with Roisin McGrath and then told her that it was over afterwards. I felt bad about it but it didn't gnaw at my insides like this is doing. I didn't feel like such a total shit even though I was and even though I know Roisin was hurt. It was the only time he'd ever done that.

'Not hungry?' murmured Jodie as she cleared away the plates.

'Not very.' Dan looked up at her. 'Tell Ash it was nothing to do with her cooking.'

'Ash isn't in today,' said Jodie. 'It was Lauren.' She moved on round the table leaving Dan feeling as though

521

she'd hit him. Where was Ash? She wasn't due to be off, was she? Was she sick? Was she afraid of seeing him? Oh God, he thought, was she pregnant?

He hadn't even considered the idea before but now it took over his entire mind. She couldn't be, he thought. She wouldn't even know if she was and she certainly wouldn't be out sick yet. But the thought terrified him all the same. What if she was pregnant? What then? What the hell would Cordelia say? How could he keep that from her?

What in God's name was I thinking of, he asked himself for the hundredth time, when I gave in to her impulse too?

Ash sat at her computer and looked at the news headlines about carnage in the stock market. It didn't bother her as much as it would have done a few months ago. She'd sold most of her shares the last time there'd been a wobble – Steve Proctor had tried to talk her out of it but she'd been adamant – and now she only had a few hundred pounds invested and the rest of her money had been safely put in a deposit account. But she wanted to redecorate again and so she'd have to take the money out of her account and sell the rest of the shares so that she could turn the cornflake-yellow walls into something else. Blue perhaps. She liked blue. She looked at Archangel's share price and bit her lip. Poor Alistair would be having a fit. The value of his company had almost halved in the last month and she knew that he would be gutted by it because he really cared about the company. She knew that his personal wealth was relatively OK because he'd got the cash payment as well as the share options. But the share options wouldn't be worth much right now.

She sneezed abruptly and rummaged in her bag for another tissue. Her cold was almost better and she probably could have done the lunch today but she hadn't been able to make herself go in. She didn't know whether it was because she was unwell or whether it was because she wasn't able to face Dan Morland. If, indeed, she'd come face to face with him at all, which wasn't really likely. In the end she'd decided that it was because of her cold – after all, it wouldn't exactly be hygienic to sniffle around the kitchen. So she'd rung Lauren and asked her if she could stand in for her again and Lauren had agreed.

Except she now wished she'd gone in. There was no real reason for him to know that she hadn't turned up, the partners very rarely came into the kitchen anyway. But, in case he had, she should've been there. Because not being there might make him think that she cared. That she'd been upset by the incident in Sicily. She was calling it the incident now and it made her feel better to think of it like that. She wanted him to be sure that she wasn't thinking about him or worried about him or – well, she wanted him to know that she'd recovered from her mad, impulsive moment. To know that she was the same Ash as she'd always been. To know that everything was in its rightful place once more.

Chapter 32

Cookies
Self-raising flour, sugar, margarine, egg yolk, cinnamon,
lemon juice, water
Cream margarine and sugar. Add egg and beat. Fold
in flour, cinnamon, lemon juice and water to make soft
dough. Roll out and cut into circles. Bake on greased tray
in moderate oven

The next morning (another day with no bookings – she felt as though she should panic but she didn't have the energy to) she got up late and had a leisurely breakfast. At least, she had a leisurely cup of coffee because she still had no appetite. After Bagel had munched his way through his own breakfast she opened the kitchen window and he disappeared onto the roof.

She decided to go for a walk to clear her head. It was a mild day, not exactly warm but not cold enough to need anything other than a light jacket. Her lightest jacket was about five years old, she realised, as she took it out of the wardrobe. It was utterly out of date and she hadn't even particularly liked it when she'd bought it. She should buy a new one. She sighed. She didn't want to go shopping in Dublin. It had been different in Taormina.

She walked along the Liffey past Temple Bar and Wood Quay where she crossed the river. Normally she only came this way in the mornings when she was going to the fruit market but today she walked the route because she liked it.

She caught sight of her reflection in one of the glass doors as she walked into the recently renovated Smithfield Village, a place that always made her feel like a tourist in her own city. Medium height, blonde hair pulled back, wearing a pair of newly washed and somewhat stiff Levi's and her unfashionable pink jacket. Did she look like any of the thousands of twentysomething girls walking around the city? she wondered. Or could people tell by looking at her that she was someone who was so confused about her life that she'd had to check three times this morning to see if she'd turned off the taps in the bathroom?

Why did you have sex with Dan? The question popped into her head as it had popped into her head at all sorts of unexpected moments since she'd come home. And she was never able to answer it, she just pushed it into the recesses of her mind and hoped that, one day, she'd be able to forget about it. She didn't want to think about sex with Dan. She didn't want to think about sex with anyone.

Michelle had phoned her since she came back and Ash had pleaded her rotten cold as a reason for not being able to talk. Michelle asked if she'd had a good time and Ash said of course she had but she felt really terrible at the moment and could she call Michelle back when she felt better. Only she hadn't called her back yet and she knew that her cousin would soon get annoyed at her silence. Funnily enough, she thought, I understand why she'd get annoyed. I'd want to know about someone's working holiday in Sicily too.

She walked out of the shopping area and stood at the lift to the top of the Jameson chimney. It had been built in 1895 and when the area had been regenerated a glass observation platform had been added to the top of the 175ft stack so that people could look over the city. She'd gone up in the lift when it had first opened to the public but she hadn't been here since.

There were half a dozen people already on the platform. Ash stood at the window and looked along the Liffey, towards Howth and Dublin Bay. She knew where her own apartment building was from where she stood, although it was just a jumble among the other buildings along the quayside, so many of them built in the last ten years. Very new, she thought, in the lifetime of an old city.

She felt different. She couldn't explain why she felt different but she did. It seemed to her that the other Ash, the confident but panic-stricken Ash, had been replaced by someone who looked like her and spoke like her but who didn't think like her any more. She still hadn't figured out exactly how she was thinking but she knew that she was thinking differently. She wasn't sure, though, that it was a good thing.

She stared at the second chimney in the complex and

at the date 1819 which was etched into the bricks. She wondered whether anyone who lived over a hundred and eighty years ago had spent time worrying about being the right sort of person and living the right sort of life and being concerned that they'd had sex with someone else's fiancé. She wondered if they worried about having problems with commitment. Not likely, she told herself, they just worried about earning a living. Nobody in 1819 went to see shrinks because they had issues in their lives. Or because they had problems with commitment. Or because they'd done something incredibly stupid in a swimming pool. They just got on with it. So why couldn't she just get on with it? Why did she spend so much time thinking about things instead of getting on with doing things?

And then she realised, wryly, that she had just done something without thinking about it, and it had been something incredibly stupid.

But, she insisted to herself as she pressed her head against the glass, nobody had to know about it and nobody had to get hurt. It would be something that, sooner or later, she'd forget about. Like she forgot about all of those guys she'd gone out with – and all of those guys she'd made love to just once. It didn't mean anything.

She moved along the platform and stared out over the church spires towards the Dublin mountains. What would Julia do now? she wondered. If she was alive, what would she have said?

Nothing, obviously. Julia would have shrugged and

told her to forget it. Julia had never really given Ash advice when she was smaller. She'd held monologues with her from time to time, had talked about the importance of being true to yourself and not letting yourself be caught up in the trivia of day-to-day living.

I know what she meant, thought Ash. I know what she was trying to capture. That feeling of complete abandon. The feeling of living for just one moment. The feeling that everything was absolutely perfect. Poor Julia, thought Ash. She never could find absolutely perfect.

She waited for the wave of helplessness and panic that always caught her when she thought of Julia but it didn't come. She could see Julia more clearly in her mind now than she ever had before – a pretty, ditzy woman with masses of curls, wide eyes and a huge, beaming smile, looking for perfection. Julia would hate to think that I lived the sort of life I do, thought Ash. She'd want me to have fun, to be with people, to sit around with my girlfriends and sleep around with my boyfriends. And not feel guilty about it.

I can't not feel guilty about Dan, she thought. But I can sure as hell stop feeling sorry for myself.

The lift arrived to take people back to ground level.

'Are you coming?' asked the lift operator.

Ash shook her head. 'I'll stay up here a little longer,' she said.

'It's a wonderful view,' said the operator.

'Yes, it is,' said Ash.

It was another hectic day at Chatham's. Dan sat back in his seat and watched as the US market went lower again. Some people were being badly burned, he thought. People who had loans backed by the value of their shares were hurting too. The banks were getting worried that the share holdings weren't covering the loans and were starting to call some of them in. Which meant that they were having to sell shares which was driving the price down even more. Two of his best clients had liquidated large parts of their portfolios that afternoon at horribly low prices.

He'd sold shares for his father too. They'd talked about it while he was in Sicily and Joss had asked Dan whether or not he thought that the falls that had already happened might continue. When Dan said that it was possible, Joss had asked him to sell everything. 'And talk to Freda, too,' Joss had added. 'I know she holds chunks of stock and she hasn't the faintest idea what they are or how much they're worth. You'd better do something before they're suddenly worthless and she starts tapping me for cash!'

Dan leaned forward and punched his father's phone number again.

'Yes?'

He wished Joss was less abrupt on the phone.

'It's me,' he said. 'I sold everything. I talked to Mum and I sold everything she owned too. I'll be sending you a cheque in a few days' time.'

'Lodge it to my account,' said Joss. 'I'll be home soon anyway.'

'How soon?' asked Dan.

'Two weeks,' said Joss. 'I want to stay with you for a couple of days, then I'll go to Cork.'

'Fine,' said Dan. 'Will you be on your own?'

Joss laughed. 'Yes. Carlotta isn't coming with me.'

'Are you still seeing her?'

'Oh, Dan, you sound like my own father! It's a bit of fun, Carlotta and me. I don't know whether I'll see her again or not.'

'Then why the hell did you have to tell Mum about her?' asked Dan.

'I can't help it.' Joss sighed. 'That woman just makes me do stupid things. She always did.'

'You ruined the dinner.' Dan couldn't keep the annoyance out of his voice.

'Oh, come on, it was fun!' protested Joss. 'It would have been very boring otherwise.'

'The poor cook—'

'Now don't go on about the poor cook,' warned Joss. 'You flew her over and took her to dinner and spent a very enjoyable fifteen minutes with her in the pool. She do—'

'What do you mean?' interrupted Dan.

'You think I'm blind?' asked Joss. 'Hell, Dan, I might be sixty-five years old but I can see when my son has the hots for someone. All that crap about her being such a wonderful cook – Carlotta is just as good!'

'She's a fantastic cook,' said Dan.

'And was she good in the pool too?' asked Joss.

'How do you know about the pool?' demanded Dan.

'I woke up,' said Joss. 'Maybe it was all the people prowling round the house that woke me. I remembered I'd left my pipe on the terrace and I went out to get it. I heard splashing. I saw you.'

'Bloody hell.'

'So don't preach at your old man,' said Joss.

'You're unbelievable.'

'So are you,' said Joss. 'What about your fiancée?'

Dan sighed. 'What about her?'

'How d'you think she'll react when she finds out about the cook?'

'She won't find out,' said Dan. 'Because nobody's going to tell her.'

'Which means that the cook was just your hors d'oeuvre?' asked Joss.

'I'll lodge the money to your account,' said Dan. 'Let me know when you're coming over.'

It was a long walk from Smithfield to Connolly Station. Ash didn't come back along the quays but walked instead through Mary's Lane to Mary Street and along Henry Street where the crowds were milling around the shops. She stood in front of Arnott's window and coveted the lemon-yellow snakeskin jacket which was almost seven hundred pounds. I might be a newly converted impulse shopper, she thought, but I don't have seven hundred to blow on a jacket. She frowned. The shares that she'd sold a few months ago had been worth about eight hundred pounds. She'd put the money in a savings account to wait for a time when prices fell and it would be worth getting back into the market again. And she'd earmarked some of it for her redecoration of the apartment. But, she thought, maybe a yellow snakeskin jacket would be much better for her than boring bank shares and different coloured walls. The shares and the walls would always be around but someone else might buy the yellow snakeskin jacket. She took a deep breath and pushed open the doors to the store.

It looked great on her. Despite the fact that her eyes were red-rimmed from lack of sleep and her nose was still red from her cold, and despite the fact that she'd walked out of the apartment without a shred of make-up on her, the jacket looked fantastic. She turned in front of the mirror a few times and looked at herself from every angle. It suited her. It really did. She nodded her approval to the salesgirl who folded it up and put it into a bag for her.

Then, on her way out of the shop, she stopped and bought a bottle of Eau d'Issey for herself, and Shalimar, which she knew Michelle liked, for her cousin.

She sat on the DART to Killester and wondered what Michelle would say when she arrived, unannounced, on her doorstep.

Michelle looked at her in astonishment.

'What are you doing here?' she asked.

'That's all I get?' Ash raised an eyebrow. 'A "what are you doing here?" No "it's nice to see you"?'

'Ash, in your entire life you've never called on me without ringing first,' said Michelle. 'Are you surprised that I'm in shock?'

'Not really,' said Ash. 'But can I come in?'

'Of course.' Michelle was flustered. 'The house is in a state.'

'That's OK.' Ash picked her way through Brian's Lego, Lucy's selection of Barbie dolls, a plastic bicycle, a set of junior golf clubs and a pile of laundry.

'Ash! Ash!' Lucy ran towards her and hugged her. 'We're having a tea party. Do you want to come?'

Ash was dragged into the back garden where she spent twenty minutes eating and drinking imaginary tea and eating imaginary cakes with Lucy and Brian before she managed to return to Michelle in the kitchen.

'She's going to be like you,' said Michelle. 'She loves pretending to cook.'

'I'm glad that gene came out somewhere else,' said Ash. 'I was beginning to think I was the only one.'

'So what's the matter?' asked Michelle as she closed the door on the dishwasher. 'What's dragged you out here?'

'I wanted your advice,' said Ash.

Michelle stared at her. 'My advice!' Her voice was incredulous. 'You're asking me my advice on something?'

'Yes,' said Ash.

'Are you feeling OK?' asked Michelle. 'You haven't banged your head or anything, have you?'

'No,' said Ash. 'I've been shopping, actually.'

'Shopping!' This time Michelle's voice was a squeak. 'You don't shop, Ash.'

'I did today. Nothing much,' she told Michelle hastily. 'In terms of volume anyway. But I saw it and I liked it so I bought it.' She took the snakeskin jacket out of the bag and showed it to her cousin.

'Good God!' Michelle stared at the jacket and stroked

the skin. 'This isn't the kind of thing you usually wear, is it? But it's gorgeous. And it looks like it cost a fortune.'

'I know.' Ash put it on. 'I feel good in it. I bought you something too.' She reached into the bag and gave Michelle the bottle of Shalimar.

'OK, now I know that there's something seriously wrong,' said Michelle. 'You don't go round buying people presents. It's not you, Ash. It really isn't.' Suddenly her mouth dropped open and she stared at Ash again. 'It's the multimillionaire, isn't it! You're back with the multimillionaire! That's what this is all about.'

'In a way.' Ash slipped the jacket from her shoulders and hung it carelessly over the kitchen chair. 'I haven't got back together with him, Michelle. I haven't spoken to him since we split up.'

'So what's with the shopping?'

'I – I'm trying to be different.'

'Different?' Michelle looked at her in puzzlement. 'How different?'

'You know, more – less – nicer.'

'Nicer?'

'Stop repeating everything I say,' said Ash. 'I'm trying to be more relaxed and less boring.'

'And this is because of the multimillionaire?'

'He said some things about me that were true,' said Ash. 'I didn't want them to be true but they were.'

'So you're going to be – different.' Michelle scratched her head. 'I guess shopping is a good start, Ash. But, you know, I'm not sure you should try and change that much. You can't be the sort of person you're not.'

'You're always on at me to change!' cried Ash. 'You're the one that tells me I'm flaky and neurotic and don't do the things that ordinary people do.'

'True,' admitted Michelle. 'But, let's face it, Ash, you are who you are. You can't turn into a shopaholic in a day.'

'I rather think I have.' Ash grinned. 'I bought a dress in Sicily and it seems to have sent me along a slippery slope.'

'Oh yes, Sicily!' Michelle beamed at Ash as she picked up the kettle and began to fill it. 'Tell me all about Sicily.'

Ash pulled at her plait. Should she tell Michelle all about Sicily? She'd come to her cousin's house to talk but she still hadn't decided exactly how much talking she was going to do. She realised that she'd never talked very much with Michelle before – they'd usually simply argued. Or else apologised for arguing.

'It was hot,' said Ash. 'And really humid. The air seemed to wrap itself round you.'

'Ash, I don't want a meteorological report.' Michelle put the biscuit barrel on the table. 'What was it like? Where did you stay? Was the dinner successful?'

'I stayed with the people I was cooking for,' said Ash. 'You'll never guess who they were, Michelle.'

'Who?'

'Joss Morland.'

Michelle frowned. 'The name's familiar.'

'The Vanna Savino series on TV? The books?'

'Oh yes!' Michelle's eyes lit up. 'He's your stockbroker client?'

'Dan Morland hired me. He's the client. He's Joss's son.' She knew that her heart was beating faster. She'd have to tell Michelle. She was bursting to tell someone.

'And what were they like, the Morlands?' asked Michelle. 'Isn't he divorced?'

Ash nodded. 'But they get together for the dinner. It's traditional.'

'How civilised,' said Michelle dryly.

'Actually not,' Ash told her and proceeded to relate the events of the night.

'Wow!' Michelle's eyes were wide. 'I bet you could sell that story to a gossip columnist.'

'I couldn't!' Ash looked shocked. 'It would be a – a violation of trust.'

'I suppose so,' sighed Michelle. 'But it's a great story.' She got up and made the tea while Ash broke a cinnamon cookie in half.

'I slept with the son.'

Michelle was so astonished at Ash's sudden announcement that she poured tea all over the table and the two of them had to mop it up with paper towels.

'You what?' asked Michelle when the table was dry again and their cups were full. 'I did hear that properly, didn't I?'

Ash nodded.

'You slept with him? Do you fancy him? Are you going

out with him?' Michelle heaved a sigh. 'You are a real pain, aren't you? Just as you break up with the multimillionaire you fall into bed with the son of a megastar writer.'

'I didn't quite fall into bed with him,' said Ash. 'We had sex in their swimming pool.'

'Ash!'

'And he's engaged to somebody else.'

'Ash!' But this time Michelle's voice was more serious.

'I know I shouldn't have done it,' said Ash. 'I know it was a terrible mistake. I know that I'm a bitch and a cow and God knows what else. But I couldn't help myself.'

'Does this have something to do with the being different thing?' asked Michelle.

'Sort of.' Ash held her face in her hands. 'Oh, Michelle, I just don't know about anything any more.'

Michelle looked at her cousin, got out of her chair and put her arms round her. 'You are an awful eejit, aren't you?' she told Ash.

'Probably,' muttered Ash.

'Tell me about it.'

So she told Michelle about Dan and Cordelia and the preliminary engagement discussion dinner and Cordelia's job in the States. And she told Michelle about buying the dress in Sicily and getting drunk and kissing Dan. And finally about diving into the swimming pool beside him.

'You really know how to live,' said Michelle. 'All the time I get at you for your lack of commitment and all sorts of things but I'm probably really just jealous.'

'No you're not.'

'Well, maybe not. But you've got to admit, Ash, your life is not exactly boring, is it?'

'It's supposed to be,' said Ash bitterly.

'What's the story with this bloke now?' asked Michelle. 'Do you love him or was it mindless drunk sex? Does he love you? What about the fiancée?'

'We both agreed it was a terrible mistake.' Ash sniffed and then took a sip of tea. 'And it was, Michelle, I know it was. But all of a sudden I thought that I could live with him. I could be happy with him.' She rubbed her nose. 'Probably I couldn't really but it was the first time I ever thought like that. And it scared me.'

'So what do you want to do now?' asked Michelle. 'See him again?'

'What should I do?' asked Ash. 'This is what people do, isn't it? They ask for advice. I'm asking you for advice.'

'People ask for advice but actually they only want to hear what they want to hear,' said Michelle. 'And I can't advise you, Ash, when you tell me you don't know what you want. Is this Dan bloke likely to break it off with his fiancée?'

Ash shook her head. 'He loves her.'

'Funny way of showing it then,' sniffed Michelle.

'He was drunk too,' said Ash.

'No excuse.'

'Maybe not.' Ash broke another cookie in half. 'I'm wondering if maybe I should try and get back with Alistair.'

Michelle looked at her. 'You want to get back with the

multimillionaire who dumped you? As a result of sleeping with someone else?'

'Alistair was right for me,' said Ash. 'I pushed him away when I shouldn't have. That's why we split up. But I think I could work it out with him.'

'And is that what you want?' asked Michelle.

'I think it is,' said Ash slowly.

'Do you love him?' asked Michelle.

'He's the best person in the world for me.' Ash was more forceful now. 'I was a fool not to realise it before. Of course I love him.'

'Well, if you want to try and get him back then that's what you should do.'

Ash smiled at Michelle. 'I knew you'd be able to tell me what to do,' she said. 'You were always good at telling me what to do.'

She stayed in Michelle's all day. She helped to get the children ready for bed and then she sat in the living room with Michelle and Emmet watching TV. Emmet offered to drive her to the train station but she shook her head and told him that she wanted to walk. She hugged Michelle at the doorway and Michelle told her to take care and let her know how things turned out. And she thanked Ash for the bottle of Shalimar and told her that the lemon-yellow snakeskin jacket was lovely on her. And that she should go shopping more often.

Bagel was sitting on the windowsill, staring placidly out over the courtyard behind the apartments. He got up and stretched when he saw her, and turned in that heartstopping way he did, so that he could get in through the window which she'd opened. He head-butted her a few times before sitting in front of his empty food bowl and looking at her expectantly. She opened a sachet of Whiskas and squeezed it into the dish.

She walked into the living room and looked at her computer in surprise. The fruit screensaver she used was on the monitor. She'd obviously gone out without switching it off.

But nothing really awful had happened. In fact, she'd enjoyed the day.

Chapter 33

Gooseberry Fool
Prepared gooseberries, sugar, double cream
Purée gooseberries, add sugar to taste and chill. Whip the
cream then fold into chilled fruit purée

S he took the curried parsnip and apple soup out of the freezer for Monday's lunch at Chatham's. Strangely, she felt all right about Chatham's this week. She wasn't worried about seeing Dan Morland, she wasn't afraid of panicking and she wasn't even concerned about the thought of him coming into the kitchen to say – well, what on earth could he say to her? They'd apologised enough to each other already and they couldn't keep on saying they were sorry. Besides, seeing him so much over the last few months had been unusual. Normally she'd see the partners a couple of times a year. Chances were he wouldn't bother coming into the kitchen at all. But if he did she knew she could cope with it. Her conversation with Michelle had helped her get things into perspective and she'd spent the weekend thinking about Alistair and wondering if she couldn't get back together with him again. After all, she'd changed. And she'd changed into the sort of woman that, just maybe, Alistair would like better than the sort of woman she'd been before. It would be the first time she ever attempted to get back with someone. But her life suddenly seemed to be filled with first times.

Jodie walked into the kitchen as Ash was pouring herself a glass of water.

'Hi,' she said. 'How are you feeling?'

'Fine,' said Ash. 'My cold is better and – well, I feel fine.'

Jodie looked at her curiously. 'You look different,' she said.

'How?'

'I don't know,' said Jodie. 'Just different.' She grinned. 'Maybe it was the result of a few days lying out in the sun.'

'I wish,' said Ash. 'It was warm but cloudy a lot of the time. And there was a storm.'

'So tell me all about it,' demanded Jodie. 'What was the Morlands' place like? Did Dan's fiancée turn up?'

Ash gave Jodie a very watered-down version of events. She had no intention of telling her about the fracas at dinner. And, of course, she had absolutely no intention whatsoever of telling her about anything else.

'I'm not sure I could go to dinner with my divorced husband,' said Jodie when Ash commented that the atmosphere hadn't exactly been cordial. 'I mean, it's over, isn't it? Once it's over, what's the point in trying to stay friendly?'

'Speaking of friendly, how are you and Chris?'

'Not friendly,' said Jodie. 'Although I thought the better of burning everything belonging to him and just packed it all into a refuse sack instead. I left it outside the apartment door, rang him and told him where it was. I said that if he didn't come round and pick it up pretty quickly, it would disappear. The refuse sack was gone the next time I looked so I suppose he got everything.'

'What about Stefanie?' asked Ash.

Jodie shrugged. 'I did the same with her things. The cheating bitch.'

'Maybe they'd only slept together once,' said Ash. 'Maybe it wasn't the big thing you thought.'

'It was,' said Jodie gloomily. 'There was no way I walked in on a first time between that pair. And even if they had only done it once, it's the principle of it, isn't it? He was my boyfriend. He shouldn't have slept with her at all.'

Ash knew she shouldn't pursue the conversation but she couldn't help herself. 'But what if it was an – an aberration?' she asked. 'What if Chris *had* only slept with her once? Would you forgive him? Or her?'

Jodie stared at her. She never had this sort of discussion with Ash. Maybe being dumped by Alistair had wrought changes in her that nobody could have imagined.

'Cheating is cheating,' she told Ash firmly.

'What if you didn't know about it?' asked Ash. 'What

if he'd slept with her, just once, and you never found out?'

'Not much I could do about it,' said Jodie. 'But I'm sure I would find out in the end. Women do.' She looked at Ash curiously. 'Why?'

Ash shrugged. 'I just wondered how you'd feel.'

'Did Alistair cheat on you with someone?' asked Jodie. 'Is that really why you split up with him?'

'Surely he told you why we split up.' Ash opened the oven door to check on the duck. 'I behaved stupidly and I blew it, Jodie.'

'I can't see it,' Jodie told her. 'You behaving stupidly doesn't fit into my picture of you.'

'You've no idea how stupidly I can behave.' Ash closed the oven door again.

'I think I heard the lift,' said Jodie. 'I suppose I'd better get in there and start doling out the mineral water.'

The lunch went off without a hitch. All of the partners were there, Jodie told Ash, and they were still debating the pounding that the markets had taken over the last month or so.

'What did you do with your shares?' asked Jodie when she returned from handing out the gooseberry fool. 'Did you sneak out of the markets and are you getting ready to sneak back in again?'

'I sold them all a while ago,' Ash told her. 'Well, I've got a few left but I'm selling them too because I bought some new clothes and I need the money.'

Jodie looked at her in surprise. 'I thought the shares were your pension. I didn't think you'd exchange them for clothes!'

'I'm going to put a bit more into my regular personal pension,' said Ash. 'I might buy and sell shares again sometime but for the rest of this year I'm going to spend the money I made from them instead.'

'On what?' asked Jodie.

Ash shrugged. 'I don't know yet. Holidays. Jackets. Dresses.'

'Are you sure you're feeling OK?' asked Jodie. 'That doesn't sound very like you, Ash.'

Ash switched on the coffee filter. 'Have you talked to Alistair about me?' she asked.

'Not much,' said Jodie cautiously. 'He told me that he'd cared about you a lot. But that he was turning his attention to cheap and cheerful now.'

'Cheap and cheerful!' Ash laughed shortly. 'I suppose I can understand that. I wasn't the most cheerful person to go out with. Not cheap either, I guess,' she added as she thought about the gold necklace.

'Alistair is a decent bloke,' said Jodie.

'I know.' Ash leaned against the worktop. 'I'd like to get back with him, Jodie.'

'Really?' Jodie looked at her in astonishment.

'I made a mistake about him,' said Ash. 'And, before you get the wrong idea, I don't want to get back with him just so's I can dump him later! We suited each other. I liked him. He was fun to be with and we enjoyed the same things.'

'He told me that you were difficult,' said Jodie reluctantly. 'That you wanted too much.'

'Do you think he'd see me again?' asked Ash. 'If I rang him up, would he meet me?'

'I don't know,' said Jodie. 'But I'll put in a good word for you if you like.'

'Thanks,' said Ash as she put the leftover gooseberry fool in the fridge.

She half expected Dan to come into the kitchen but he didn't and she was relieved about it. If he'd come in she was ready to say that she'd already forgotten about Sicily and that she was fine about it and she was sorry that it had happened but they could both now just get on with their lives. But she hadn't needed to use her carefully rehearsed speech and, as she packed up to go home, she was glad. There was a part of her that would've liked the opportunity to talk to him again. For closure purposes. Her shrink had been big into closure and now Ash knew why. There was a time when you had to put things behind you and move forward and she'd reached that time now. She was comfortable about being Ash O'Halloran, aged twenty-nine and eleven months, single woman with cat. She was comfortable about the fact that one day she might not be single any more. But kind of glad that the day wasn't exactly imminent.

'Ash!' Pauline, the receptionist, called to her as she was walking across the glossy marble tiled floor. She turned back.

'I was asked to give you this,' said Pauline and handed Ash a paper carrier bag taped closed at the top.

'What is it?' asked Ash.

'I don't know,' said Pauline. 'Daniel Morland, from the third floor, asked me to give it to you.'

The new, carefree Ash felt her mouth go dry. But she wasn't going to panic, she knew she wasn't.

She took the bag from the receptionist and walked out of the building. Copies of Joss's books? she wondered. She strode rapidly across the bridge towards her apartment. A payment in kind for her work?

She didn't open the bag straightaway. First, she fed Bagel who'd scented the liver she'd bought him and practically threw himself at her in joy at the thought of it. Then she made herself a strawberry milkshake and crumbled chocolate flakes over the top. She stood at the window and drank it while she watched the toll bridge slowly rise so that a ship could come further up the river.

Eventually she opened the carrier bag.

The box inside, which she'd thought might have held Joss's books, actually contained a pair of shoes. Delicate wisps that were hardly shoes at all, in shades of blue. Perfect for her ink-blue dress.

The card with them was brief.

'Sorry about everything,' wrote Dan. 'You said that you took size fives. I hope these fit and replace the ones you lost. It was a great spontaneous moment. Be happy.' He'd scrawled his initials at the end.

She couldn't accept them, she knew she couldn't. But she tried them on anyway. They fitted perfectly.

Chapter 34

Apple Pie
Shortcrust pastry, cooking apples, sugar, cinnamon, cloves
Peel, core and chop apples. Roll out half of the pastry and
place on ovenproof plate. Place apples on pastry, sprinkle
with sugar and cinnamon, add some cloves. Brush edges
of pastry with water. Roll out remaining pastry and cover
apples, press edges firmly together to seal, trim excess pastry.
Glaze top of pie, make small hole in centre and cook in
moderate oven until brown

Dan had hired a company to clean his house from top to bottom so that it would look good for the guy from a letting agency, who was calling around to look over it in an hour's time. As well, of course, as looking good for the wedding in August. Dan found it hard to believe that a few weeks from now he would be married to Cordelia and living in Chicago. There were worse things, he told himself, than living in Chicago, particularly when he'd been offered such a good job with one of Harrison's subsidiary companies. And Cordelia was ecstatic about her promotion which had acted like an aphrodisiac on her on his long weekend in New York. 'It's a power thing,' she told him when she woke him up at six in the morning by sliding her body along his and caressing his lips with the tip of her nipple. 'I know I have it. I know you have it. We're going to be such a great couple and it really, really turns me on.'

It really, really turned Dan on too. But afterwards he felt terrible. He wanted to tell Cordelia about his night with Ash and tell her that it had meant nothing to him. But he knew that telling her would be a big mistake. He remembered reading articles in Bronwyn's magazines when they were younger and they all warned about the dangers of confessing to something just to assuage your own feelings of guilt. It had happened. It was meaningless. There was no point in jeopardising the rest of their lives together because of one night of insanity on a heat-soaked lump of rock in the middle of the Mediterranean. Besides, he thought, Cordelia would kill him if she knew.

So he hadn't told her and he knew that he'd made the right decision and he was glad that Ash O'Halloran had obviously made the right decision too because she hadn't said anything to him about the shoes that he'd very stupidly bought for her. He'd walked into Taormina the day before he came home and he'd seen them in the window of one of the many shoe shops and he'd thought of how well they'd look with her lovely ink-blue dress. And he'd bought them on the spur of the moment, remembering her size and thinking that giving her the shoes would, in some way, make up for everything.

After he'd done it he'd thought that maybe it hadn't been such a good idea after all. So he hadn't brought them in for that first lunch afterwards, the one that she hadn't actually cooked for anyway. But then he'd changed his mind. He thought it would be a nice gesture and would draw a line under what had happened. And clearly it had. Ash might have been foolish and impulsive when she was away, thought Dan, but thank God she'd regained her senses when she got home again.

Ash was on the sofa, her knees pulled up under her chin, a pile of menu sheets scattered around her. Bagel was sitting on the one for baked trout as he licked his paw and rubbed it over his face. She chewed on her pencil as she thought about the eighteenth birthday party she'd been asked to cater for. Maeve Heaney had called her and said that it was for a friend of a friend who'd been let down by the people she'd booked and she knew that it was extremely short notice but would Ash by any chance be available? The party was scheduled for the day that Dan and Cordelia were getting married. It was just as well, thought Ash, as she flicked through some of the sheets, that she wasn't involved with Dan's wedding any more. And she was glad that she'd have something to do on the day of his marriage so that she wouldn't think about him and Cordelia and feel bad about everything all over again.

She hadn't heard anything more from him after Pauline had given her the bag containing the shoes. They were still in the bag in the back of her wardrobe. Giving them back would have meant contacting him and she didn't want that. The mature approach, she decided, was to do nothing. And the mature approach had been the right one because he hadn't come into the kitchen and she hadn't been out in the dining room and they hadn't bumped into each other anywhere in the Chatham office building.

She missed that. She hadn't realised how often she'd seen him and spoken to him and how much she'd enjoyed being friends with him. And she couldn't help wondering whether, even then, she'd wanted to make love to him. She didn't think so, but she was perfectly prepared to accept that her unconscious mind (not to mention her unconscious body) might have wanted to hop into bed with him long ago even though she hadn't realised it at the time.

Cordelia leaned back in her chair. I'll have a leather chair in Chicago, she thought gleefully. Vice presidents had leather chairs. And I'll have an office of my own, even if it does have fibreglass partitions and not much space. But I'll be in charge of things. I'll be the one making decisions. I'll be the one people are scared of. She didn't mind the idea of people being afraid of her. She knew that most women who struggled in business had trouble because they wanted to be liked. Because they hated appearing rough and tough and hated making other people feel uncomfortable. But Cordelia knew that she could cope with that. You didn't have to be liked. She'd found that out from Melissa. You only had to be respected. Cordelia knew that she didn't like Melissa very much. And she knew that she still felt uncomfortable about the way Melissa had reacted to her son's accident the night of the cocktails on the thirty-third floor. But not liking Melissa was irrelevant in the whole scheme of things.

DeVere Bassett walked up to her desk. 'Gloating?' he asked.

She grinned at him. 'Nope. Just happy with life.'

'You worked hard,' said DeVere. 'You deserve it.'

'I know.' She sat up straight.

'How does your fiancé feel about working in the States?' asked DeVere. 'I hear that Mike Fuller had to pull some strings to get him a job.'

Cordelia shrugged. 'Dan's extremely good at what he does. It was just getting him legal in the States that they had to work at.'

'Will you earn more than him?' asked DeVere.

'I hope so.'

'Will he cope with that OK?'

'Would you?'

DeVere exhaled slowly. 'Actually, I'm not sure. I know I should but I'm not sure I would.'

'Dan is the perfect man,' said Cordelia. 'He does what I tell him and he feels good about it.'

'Poor bloke!'

'I'm lucky to have found him,' said Cordelia. 'I know lots of guys wouldn't have been as understanding as Dan but he's a real gem.'

'I wish I could get the time to come to your wedding,' said DeVere. 'I wanted to meet this paragon of manhood.

The one that makes me feel that I'm totally insensitive for telling my girlfriend that we weren't going to see no damn chick flick last night but we were going to see a good action movie instead.'

Cordelia laughed. 'Dan won't go to chick flicks either. He hates romantic comedies or anything with stars who have been on American sitcoms.'

'He's right,' said DeVere robustly.

'I'm not sure,' Cordelia said. 'There are only so many times you can watch someone in a green vest save the world and not feel cynical about it.'

DeVere laughed. 'I would've pegged you as the sort of woman who'd like action movies,' he told her. 'You're an action kind of girl, aren't you?'

'I have a soft side,' she said.

'I never realised! But, a word of advice, Cordelia, don't show your soft side in Chicago.'

She looked at him from beneath her black lashes. 'I haven't shown it here. Why should I show it any-where else?'

Chapter 35

Cocktail Sausages
Place on oven tray and cook in hot oven until brown. Serve
with or without spicy dips

Since she'd talked things over with Michelle, Ash had made up her mind to call Alistair but she didn't have the nerve. She kept picking up the phone, listening to the hum on the line and then putting it down again without dialling his number. Sometimes she thought it would be easier to contact him by e-mail so she sat in front of her computer and composed long messages to him which she never sent. Expecting rejection was hard, she thought as she deleted the fourth e-mail she'd written. Even though you steeled yourself for it, even though you told yourself that it wouldn't be the worst thing in the world, it was still difficult to put yourself through it.

Yet maybe he wouldn't reject her again. She bit her lip as she thought about it. They'd parted bitterly but she knew that Alistair wasn't a bitter person. He was, despite his status as a go-getting businessman, a caring sort of person. The sort of person she should never have pushed away from her. The sort of person who wouldn't dream of having sex with a person if he was engaged to someone else. God, she thought as she rubbed her temples with the tips of her fingers, will I ever be able to put that out of my mind? But it was hard to forget the pleasure she and Dan had given each other. Part of her didn't want to forget it.

The worst thing that can happen is that Alistair will tell me to sod off, she told herself as she picked up the phone again. And I can live with that. People live with no all the time.

'Mr Brannigan's office.' Natascha's voice was clear and confident.

Ash tried to speak but couldn't. She wished she'd phoned Alistair at home. But she'd always called him at the office before.

'Mr Brannigan's office,' repeated Natascha.

'Hi, Natascha.' The words seemed to be coming from someone else. 'Is Alistair there?'

'Ash?' queried Natascha. 'How are you? No, Alistair's not here right now.'

'Could you ask him to call me when he gets back?' asked Ash.

'I'll pass on the message that you called,' said Natascha. 'But he's away at the moment. He's on vacation for a week, then he's meeting some people in the States, after which he's going to Germany. He may be back for a day or two in between but I'm not certain yet.'

This is horrible, thought Ash. She gripped the receiver

more tightly. I definitely should've phoned him at home. Natascha must know I've split up with Alistair and now she thinks I'm some sad reject trying to get him back. She hated the idea that Alistair's secretary might feel sorry for her because she'd been dumped by her boss.

'You can always e-mail him,' added Natascha helpfully. 'He picks up his messages every day.'

'Sure, Natascha, thanks.' Ash hung up and stood by the telephone. Her hands were shaking.

The idea of a party to celebrate her thirtieth birthday came to her in the middle of the night. She'd never had a birthday party before because catering for other people's put her off the idea of doing anything for herself. Besides which, she knew she wasn't a party person. But organising it gave her another focus and she was happy about that although suddenly quite nervous because the whole thing was new to her.

'It won't be a terribly raucous party, I'm afraid,' she told Jodie as she handed her an invite. 'Not the sort of thing you're probably used to . . . but I'd really like it if you could come.'

'Of course I'll come!' Jodie was utterly astonished at the invitation. 'I'd love to come, Ash, I really would.'

'It's not that there'll be loads of singing and people going mental with drink,' Ash said. 'I've invited all of the Rourkes of course, so that drags up the average age. And I've invited Seamus and Margaret and my neighbours across the hall. As well as some of the clients that I do a lot of work for. But it's not – well, it's not a *young* party.'

Jodie grinned. 'You're thirty, Ash, not a hundred and thirty. And what, exactly, do you think goes on at *young* parties?'

'Drugs, I suppose,' said Ash. 'And people getting utterly pissed and passing out in the bedroom where they're having it off with someone totally unsuitable.'

'I haven't been at a decent drugs party in years,' said Jodie, 'but maybe I go to the wrong sort of parties! Ash, it'll be great fun.'

'I hope so.' Having issued the invitations while she was still enthusiastic about the idea, Ash was now terrified that it'd be the biggest flop that anyone had ever gone to. She kept wondering what she should do to make things fun for people.

'It's going to be great,' Michelle told her when she rang her cousin in a panic to ask her if there was something she'd forgotten. 'Honest to God, Ash, you're paranoid.'

'I know,' said Ash ruefully.

'You can't plan every little detail,' Michelle said. 'You can't order people to enjoy themselves. But you can have a good atmosphere so that they will.'

'I'm good at intimate atmospheres,' Ash said. 'I'm good at sophisticated atmospheres. I'm just not sure about party atmospheres.'

'You've done twenty-firsts, haven't you?' demanded Michelle.

'Yes, but this is different. It's nine years older, for starters,' objected Ash.

'Once you don't have the place intimidatingly tidy you'll be fine,' said Michelle. 'And me and Emmet are really looking forward to it. So's Mum; she was on the phone to me earlier and we were chatting about what to wear.'

'What to wear!' Ash was horrified. 'What d'you mean, what to wear? It's a party, Michelle. It's informal.'

'I know.' Michelle laughed. 'But I'm still going to buy something new. It's a great excuse.'

'Oh.'

'You'd better have something new too,' said Michelle. 'Something slinky and gorgeous.'

'But—'

'Oh, I know you're saying informal,' said Michelle. 'But I want to dress up a bit. Why not?'

'How dressed up are you going to be?' demanded Ash who was now in a terror about her own wardrobe.

'I saw a fabulous top in Debenham's,' Michelle said. 'Black, almost see-through – which means you can get a good look at my baby-enhanced boobs as supported by my Wonderbra. And there was a lovely skirt to go with it.'

'I was going to wear my jeans,' Ash faltered.

'Come on, cousin!' Michelle snorted. 'Party time. Party clothes.'

'Bloody hell,' muttered Ash. 'What have I let myself in for?'

'Ash, you're young, free and, at the moment, single. You've got to get into the spirit of it.' Michelle's voice softened suddenly. 'How are you feeling? Have you done anything about Alistair yet?'

'He's away at the moment,' said Ash. 'He went on

holiday and then he went to the States. I think he's in Germany now.'

'Have you been talking to him?'

'I spoke to his secretary,' said Ash.

'But not to him?'

'She said she'd pass on a message that I called,' said Ash. 'But he hasn't got back to me.'

'If he's away he mightn't have had the time. Why don't you ask him to the party?'

'I don't think so.'

'But it'd be a good idea, Ash. If he accepts then you'll know he's still interested. If he doesn't – well, at least you'll have a gang of friends round you!'

'Maybe you're right.' Ash was uncertain.

'I'm always right,' said Michelle. 'You'll be fine, Ash. Honestly you will.'

'I know I will,' said Ash. 'It just seems to take a long time to get to the fine stage.'

'Has the writer's son been in touch?' Michelle asked casually.

'Of course he hasn't been in touch!' cried Ash. 'I told you, it was – well, I suppose it was just casual sex.'

'He's a right bastard,' said Michelle. 'He should have at least called you.'

'Absolutely not.' Ash decided against mentioning the shoes he'd left for her. 'It was one of those monumental mistakes, Michelle. I don't want to ever hear from him again.'

'All the same . . .' Michelle's voice was supportive.

'All the same nothing,' said Ash. 'I don't even want to think about him.'

'Then ask Alistair to your party,' Michelle said firmly. 'If he turns you down you can forget him and start all over again.'

'I know.' Ash sounded unconvinced.

'You have to move on,' said Michelle. 'One way or another.'

On the Wednesday before her birthday Ash catered for lunch at Banco Brava and then went shopping. She hit Grafton Street and wandered round the shops for ages before buying a blue wraparound skirt, a pale pink top embroidered with purple and blue flowers and a pair of soft pink shoes. She also tried on a very flattering pair of rather expensive acid-green trousers and a bright yellow shirt. She was tempted to buy the trousers and the shirt too but common sense reasserted itself. What with the party and all the other things she'd spent money on lately her finances were running low. And she wasn't quite prepared to start living her life on an overdraft. But, she told herself, when she had a few quid again she'd think about acid-green trousers.

She hadn't intended to go to the hairdresser's but her attention was caught by one of the styles displayed in the window. She looked at the photograph of the model for almost five minutes before she pushed open the door and told the stylist that she'd like something like that too.

I look kind of kooky, she thought as she gazed at her reflection in the mirror when she got back to the apartment. Not half as sensible as I normally do. She added some extra pink lipstick and blew kisses at herself. Then she shook her head and decided that she'd lost her marbles completely.

On the Saturday of the party she got up early and cooked. Jodie had told her that she was out of her mind to cook things herself, that she should just walk into Tesco or Marks and Spencer and buy trays of party food but Ash couldn't bring herself to do that. So, as she did for any other party she catered for, she made her entire range of finger foods and nibbles. After all, she murmured to herself, this is my job, I'm supposed to be good at it.

And it looked great. By eight o'clock when she was sitting in the living room and drinking a large glass of Pinot Grigio, the food was arranged in appetising piles on the table, there were bowls of savouries and nuts scattered strategically round the apartment and it looked very, very partyish.

But Alistair hadn't been in touch. She sighed deeply and wondered if she'd finally become the sort of person she'd never expected to be, waiting hopelessly for a phone call from someone who didn't care any more. She got up and switched on her computer. There was always the chance that he'd e-mailed her back. Or, she thought, as she waited for Outlook Express to start up, maybe he'll turn up unexpectedly. That'd be a romantic sort of thing to happen . . .

Her eyes widened as she looked at the screen. There was one new message and it was from Alistair!

'Hi, Ash,' he wrote. 'Sorry I haven't replied to you

before now but I've been really busy. As you probably know the markets have turned against my kind of business lately and it's been difficult to organise the sort of financing we need, particularly because Transys have been under the cosh themselves. But I've been in the States for the last few weeks and it looks like I've managed to put something good together. I nearly fainted when I got your party invite. You – party – your apartment??? What's happened to Little Miss Ice Cool? I was so intrigued I nearly hopped on a plane straightaway! Too busy at the moment though. All the same, perhaps we might get together for a drink when I get back? It won't be for another few weeks as I've still lots to do here and in Germany. I don't know if we can get it back together, Ash, but it might be worth a try. I do like you a hell of a lot, you're the sort of girl who gets under a man's skin. Unfortunately! Talk soon. Alistair.'

Her heart was still thumping with a mixture of emotions when the doorbell rang. She switched off the computer, then checked her appearance nervously in the mirror before buzzing the intercom to let Molly and Shay inside.

'You never cease to surprise.' Molly kissed her on the cheek then stared at her. 'I was all geared up for white walls and black carpet, or mango walls and yellow floorboards or pink walls and—'

'I get the drift,' Ash interrupted her. 'Mango walls and yellow floorboards! You make me sound like an episode of *Changing Rooms*.'

'But not this time,' said Molly. 'This time it's just – changing you!'

'Normally when you come to visit I've had the apartment done and you've had your hair done.' Ash grinned at her and ran her fingers through her newly shortened locks. 'I decided not to bother with the apartment this time and do me instead. D'you like it?'

'Yes, yes, I do,' said Molly slowly. 'It's very different, Ash. You look like someone else altogether.'

'I know.' Ash smiled. 'But it's been a warm summer and I thought – well, you know, a change would be good and so I went in and got it cut.'

'You look more like Julia now,' Molly told her. 'I don't know whether that's the right thing to say.'

'Julia's hair was much longer,' said Ash.

'I know. But – well, you do look more like her.'

'You look great, Ash.' Shay hugged her. 'And so does the apartment.'

'Thanks,' said Ash. 'Where are the boys?'

'Coming in a convoy,' Shay told her. 'They should be here any minute.'

But it was Michelle and Emmet who arrived next. Michelle, too, couldn't take her eyes off Ash's hair. 'Plus, you've completely thrown me by that outfit,' her cousin said. 'You look about twenty, not thirty.'

'Really?' Ash beamed at her.

'That doesn't have to be a compliment!' But Michelle laughed. 'And I love the pearls. They're so prim and the rest of you isn't.'

Ash's hands flew to her neck and touched them. 'They

were Julia's,' she told Michelle. 'I don't think Julia was ever prim.'

'Not from what I've heard,' said Michelle.

'I love what you're wearing too,' Ash said. 'And I see what you mean about the boobs. They look great.'

'I'm trying to drive Emmet into a frenzy of lust and desire,' said Michelle. 'Since the birth of Shay junior I've been too knackered to consider lust and desire with any degree of enthusiasm. But I've suddenly rediscovered the urge and I want to make it all worthwhile. Oh, and by the way, happy birthday.' She handed Ash a parcel which, when opened, revealed a pale purple Edina Ronay cardigan.

'It's lovely,' said Ash.

'It fits in with your new look,' Michelle said. 'Though that wasn't deliberate. I just thought it would suit you.'

'Thanks.' Ash held it up against her chest. 'Thanks, Michelle.' She hugged her cousin.

Molly and Shay had bought her old-fashioned weighing scales which, she remembered, she'd once mentioned to Molly that she liked very much. Then her male cousins arrived, along with Irina and Nancy, and she was suddenly doling out glasses of wine and beer while more and more people seemed to be filling her apartment.

It had never buzzed with so much life and noise before. Bagel took one look at the increasing crowd and disappeared out of the open kitchen window. Jodie arrived with a tall, blonde and extremely handsome man in tow.

'This is Harry,' she told Ash. 'I met him last week. I hope you don't mind me dragging him along.'

'The more the merrier,' said Ash as she handed him a beer.

Rhoda and Jim from across the hall arrived, so did Conal and Petra from next door. And Ash noticed that people were wandering around her apartment, putting glasses down on her highly polished surfaces, spilling crumbs on her beech floorboards and generally being totally unaware that they were in the home of a well-known neatness freak.

And she didn't mind. Well, almost. She had to clamp down on a feeling of panic when Rob Rourke knocked over a bottle of Budweiser and the golden liquid spread across the floor. But Mo Harper, one of her regular clients, grabbed some kitchen roll and mopped it up before Ash had time to say anything.

'I love your place.' Margaret, Ash's alternative waitress, stood beside her with a glass of wine in one hand and a cocktail sausage in the other. 'It's so bright and cheerful.'

'Thanks,' said Ash.

'Is it true that you don't allow men into it?'

'No,' said Ash. 'It's only a vicious rumour though it does have some foundation in fact.'

'It's a brilliant idea,' said Margaret. 'They mess up the place something shocking. My brother is living with me at the moment and you should see the bathroom! A complete nightmare. He shaves and – oh, well, you don't want to know, Ash.'

'Possibly not,' agreed Ash. 'Thanks, Charlie.' Her eldest cousin was doing the rounds of the room, topping up wine glasses.

'Yo, Ash!' Jodie was on vodka and bitter lemon and had knocked back a number in quick succession. 'Mind if I put on one of my heavy metal CDs?'

Ash had been playing Dire Straits at a volume something below what the group themselves would consider average.

'Sure,' she said lightly.

'God, you must be on happy pills or something.' Jodie laughed. 'That was a joke!'

'Oh,' said Ash. 'Sorry.'

'We'll give it a bit of Cher, though.' Jodie sifted through Ash's CD collection. She slid a CD into the deck and accompanied Cher in asking whether or not Ash believed in life after love.

I suppose I do, thought Ash. Alistair's e-mail was still in her mind as she smiled at Jodie. It's a bit of a roller-coaster, she thought, this relationship thing – but maybe it's better not to always know how things are going to turn out. She walked over to the window and stared out over the river.

'You OK?' Michelle joined her.

'Yes,' said Ash. 'I am.'

'Enjoying yourself?'

Ash looked around. The room was full of people, laughing, talking and, in Jodie and Rhoda's case, singing. Rhoda had a pretty good voice too, Ash realised. She hadn't known that her neighbour could sing.

'Yes,' she answered Michelle's question.

'You don't sound completely convinced,' said Michelle.

Ash grinned at her. 'Would it be really awful and boring

and terrible of me to say that, much as I'm enjoying it, I'd probably prefer a dinner party?'

'Yes!' cried Michelle. Then her voice softened. 'But I suppose Rome wasn't built in a day. And the fact that you've allowed all of these strangers to mess up your personal space is something.'

'I'm not that bad,' said Ash defensively.

'You – oh, well, maybe not,' said Michelle. 'But I bet you go round with your Mr Sheen tomorrow giving every single surface the once over until it gleams.'

'Sod off.' Ash's voice was amiable.

'I'm right, though.'

Ash hesitated and Michelle roared with laughter.

'Oh, Ash, come on and join us.' Jodie had a group of girls singing together. 'We can form a group. The Party Animals.'

'I don't think so,' said Ash.

'Come on,' persuaded Jodie. 'You can be our lead vocalist.'

'Jodie, I'd empty the place. I can't sing.'

'Even for me?' said Jodie. 'Even to keep me happy?'

'There are some things that even I won't do,' Ash told her. 'I'm not going to make a complete fool of myself, thanks very much.'

'Ash, you can make a fool of yourself at a party,' said Jodie. 'It's practically obligatory.'

'I – oh, all right.'

'Way to go!' cried Jodie and promptly launched into a version of Wannabe which had everyone in the room whooping in enthusiasm. While Ash, uncoordinated as ever as far as the dance steps were concerned, tried to copy her friend, failed miserably and finally sat down on the floor engulfed by hysterical laughter.

She had a raging thirst. She got out of bed at five in the morning when the early sun was already turning the sky flaming orange outside her window. She padded down the stairs and opened the fridge door. Her only remaining soft drink was a carton of cranberry juice and she poured some of it into a long glass which, for some reason she couldn't fathom, was also in the fridge.

Bagel was on the windowsill outside. Ash let him in and the cat leaped into the kitchen to survey the damage to his territory. He picked his way through the debris of empty cans and discarded paper napkins and sat in front of his bowl. Ash opened a fresh tin of cat food and tried not to breathe as she spooned some into it.

'I could throw up,' she muttered to the cat. 'It's times like this, Bagel, that I wish they didn't add the smell to cat food.'

Bagel ignored her and began to eat savagely. He'd missed supper last night because of the party and he wanted Ash to know that he was hungry.

'I was going to tidy up before I came to bed,' she told him. 'Which was only an hour and a half ago anyway.'

Bagel glanced at her and resumed eating.

'But I didn't have the energy.' She looked round the kitchen. 'It's not that bad, I suppose. And now I know that I've changed beyond all recognition,' she murmured, 'because the kitchen is a disaster area and the living room isn't much better.'

She walked into the living room, sipping her cranberry juice. The CD player was still switched on, she noticed. She went over to it and hit the off button. Then she looked around. It was a complete mess, she thought, but nothing she couldn't handle. And she remembered Michelle's comments about the Mr Sheen and regretted that her cousin was probably right about that. But not straightaway. She needed to rehydrate before she could even contemplate tidying up. The answer machine was blinking at her. She squeezed her eyes together and looked at it again because she certainly didn't remember the phone ringing. Although if it had rung during the party (especially when they were doing their Spice Girls impressions) she wouldn't have heard it anyway. But she hadn't noticed that it was flashing when she went to bed. Shit, she thought, maybe Alistair had phoned to say hello!

She rubbed her eyes as she walked over to it and pressed the play button.

'Hi, Ash, it's me, Gillian. I meant to call you last week but I got really tied up with a few bits and pieces so this was the first chance I got. Sorry I've missed you and this is probably old news to you now anyway, but just in case you haven't been talking to him I thought I should tell you that the wedding reception you left me in charge of – Mr Morland – has been called off! I had to come to a settlement with him over fees and everything but he was more than amicable. He's actually rather cute, don't you think, but clearly a man with commitment problems! Let me know the next time you have something big on and I'd love to help. Talk to you soon. 'Bye.'

Chapter 36

Ratatouille
Potatoes, onions, courgettes, peppers, garlic, tomatoes, olive
oil, salt and pepper
Slice potatoes, onions, courgettes and peppers. Add to heated
olive oil in pan. Chop garlic and tomatoes and add to pan.
Season. Cover and simmer for around 40 minutes. Uncover
and simmer again until most of the liquid has evaporated

O n the day she was supposed to have married Dan Morland, Cordelia sat in her leather chair on the fifteenth floor of Harrison's Chicago office and stared at her computer screen. Her mother had phoned that morning and asked her if she was all right. Linda had told Cordelia that she was thinking of her and hoping that she'd make a real success of her career. Cordelia had heard the unspoken message that her mother thought that she'd have to make a real success of her career since she'd so clearly blown her chance at a highly suitable marriage.

She watched the screensaver on her computer generate a random whirl of colour. She felt as though she was a whirl herself today, for the first time in a long time uncertain about what she was doing.

When Dan had arrived at her apartment in New York a few weeks ago, she hadn't even sensed that anything was wrong. She'd prattled on about Chicago and the opportunities for both of them as she offered him juice or a smoothie or (horror of horrors these days) rich, strong, non-decaffeinated coffee. But then she realised that he wasn't even listening to her, that whatever was going on in his head was miles away from Harrison's and his new career.

'What's the matter?' she asked irritably after he'd looked at her blankly when she asked whether or not he wanted Java or Colombian coffee.

'Nothing,' he said.

It was the way he spoke the word that made her realise that there was something.

She turned round and looked at him. 'Dan?'

'I don't think it's going to work, do you?' He blurted it out and stopped, horrified at himself.

'What?'

'There's something – I—'

'What the fuck is the matter with you?' she asked dangerously. 'What exactly isn't going to work?'

'Me, here in the States. I don't want to be here, Cordelia. I never did. I don't want to work for Harrison's and I don't want to live in Chicago.'

'Great,' she said. 'Wonderful. I bust a gut to get a fantastic job for you and now you're telling me it's not going to work? Are you out of your mind?'

'No,' he said. He rubbed his hands over his face. 'I'm sorry, Cordelia. But I never wanted you to bust a gut to get me a job. I never wanted to work here. I wanted you to come home.'

'Well, sure,' she said. 'But that was before the opportunity came up. You couldn't expect me to turn down the opportunity, could you?'

'You said you would, you know.'

'Pardon?'

'Last time you were in Dublin. You said you didn't get off on mergers and acquisitions like you did with me. And that you'd be able to leave it all behind.' He sighed. 'Everyone told me that you'd hate coming home but I told them they were wrong.'

'I would've come home if I hadn't been offered this job,' said Cordelia. 'Of course I would. But this changes everything. It's important, Dan. Really important.'

'More important than us?'

'What the hell's the matter with you?' she demanded. 'It's arranged, Dan. It's sorted. You agreed. We're living here.'

He shook his head. 'I don't want to live here, Cordelia. I never did. But I thought—' He broke off. 'I was wrong.'

'And me?' she asked. 'Were you wrong about me too?'

'What do you think?'

She stared at him. 'I think you're trying to break up with me,' she said.

'I—'

573

'Christ.' She stood still. 'You *are* trying to break up with me.'

'Cordelia, I always thought you were the one. You know I did. I never felt for anyone like I felt for you.'

'Don't give me that shit!' Her voice was angry. 'What the hell do you think you're doing, Dan?'

'I didn't come here to break up with you,' he said. 'I came here to change things.'

'Because you don't like how they are?'

'Because they're not what I expected.'

'There's someone else, isn't there?' The realisation hit her like a physical blow. 'You've found someone else.'

'Not the way you think,' he said.

'Oh, come on!' She looked at him, her eyes flashing anger. 'We wouldn't be having this conversation if it was just about you living here, would we? If you loved me it wouldn't matter where we were.'

'If you loved me you'd come back to Dublin,' said Dan.

'Don't try to make it my fault,' she snapped. 'I'm not the one who—' She broke off and he could see the sudden fury in her eyes. 'It's the fucking cook, isn't it?' she demanded. 'You've fallen for the fucking cook.'

'Cordelia, it's not like that.'

'You bastard! All the times you said you liked her or felt sorry for her or that it was just a platonic thing! You swore you'd never touch her! And now you've fucking screwed her and you prefer her to me!'

'No,' said Dan.

'Don't even bother lying to me about it,' she said furiously. 'Don't.'

He stood silently in front of her. She had a right to be angry, a right to lash out at him and a right to feel hurt. And he felt terrible. But he wondered if she'd be as angry if she knew that Ash O'Halloran had made it clear that she never wanted to see him again. God, he thought, I'm useless with women. Truly useless.

'Why did you say you'd marry me?' he asked suddenly. 'That night. You were going to the States anyway and you didn't need the complication of being engaged. So why did you say yes?'

'I wanted to be part of a couple,' she said simply, the anger suddenly gone from her voice. 'When you asked me to marry you I was surprised. And at first I was going to say no. Then I thought of how good we were together. Because we *are* good together, Dan. We suit. We understand each other's work. We're great in bed together. And I liked the idea of going to the States already committed so that nobody could come on to me too much. That's why I said yes.'

'Very businesslike,' he said dryly.

'And I thought I loved you,' she said. 'I thought you loved me too.'

'So did I,' said Dan. 'But I realised that I couldn't love you as much as I thought if—'

'If you could hop into bed with the cook at the first available opportunity,' she finished tartly.

'It wasn't like that,' said Dan. 'It was a one-off.'

'And what about her boyfriend?' asked Cordelia.

'They split up.'

'Is that what people around you do?'

'Cordelia, I didn't mean to – it just happened.'

'Spare me,' she said. 'That's male bullshit.'

'I know.'

'We'd have been a *great* couple here,' she told him. 'Successful. With a great apartment in a great neighbourhood. Going to really nice places and meeting really nice people. We'd have had all the things we wanted, Dan. All the things you used to work for. I thought you wanted the same as me.'

'It's not enough for me any more,' said Dan. 'Once it would have been, Cordelia, it's not that I have no ambition. God knows, I trampled on enough toes in Chatham's in my time. But now – now I don't think so.'

'And you think you'll find what you really want with the cook?'

'No,' he said. 'I don't think I have any chance with her. But in the end it wasn't about me and her, Cordelia. It was about me and you.'

They looked at each other in silence for a full minute. Then she took the enormous sapphire and diamond ring off her finger and handed it back to him. He told her to keep it but she shook her head. And she did nothing to stop him when he picked up his case and walked out of the apartment.

The computer screen went blank and the screensaver began to generate a new pattern of colours. Cordelia rubbed her eyes. I'm twenty-four years old, she told herself. I've got years and years to find the right person. The man who'll share my enthusiasm for getting ahead. The man who'll crave success as much as I do. But right now I've got something else. Something more important than any man. I've got my office and my leather chair and my business cards with 'Vice President' embossed on them and nobody's going to take that away from me.

She hit a key on her keyboard and the screen cleared to show her organiser. She clicked on Mike Fuller's number. She wanted to set up a meeting with him to talk about the Chicago project. She had a lot of really good ideas about the Chicago project. And, if she was right, maybe by next year those business cards would say President. And she'd have a bigger office and a better chair. And that was what mattered most to her now after all.

Michelle helped Ash to carry the huge pots of chicken curry into the van that Ash had hired for the day.

'Why don't you buy your own?' she asked as Ash closed the doors.

'Not worth it,' said Ash. 'Most of the time I'm cooking in someone else's kitchen so I only need to bring pots and things. And I'm usually working in the city centre so it's easy for me to walk and I'd never get parking. This damn party was different. I can heat the food up again there but I couldn't have cooked everything. It was simpler like this.'

The cousins got into the van and Ash slid the key into

the ignition. She glanced at Michelle who was tightening her seat belt.

'I don't drive very often but I'm OK at it,' she told her. 'I promise not to turn the van over.'

Michelle giggled. 'I didn't mean it to look so obvious,' she said. 'Come on, Ash, let's go.'

The party, the one that Maeve Heaney had asked her to do for the friend of a friend, was being held in a community hall, which surprised Ash because she assumed it was going to be a more upmarket affair. But when she'd been put in touch with Ian Madden, the young man had told her that he wanted to have it in a place where it didn't matter if they got raucous and loud and, possibly, even sick. 'You're sure you actually want food?' asked Ash in amusement and Ian had laughed and said yes but they only wanted curry. So Ash had gone along to inspect the community hall. She'd looked in despair at the feeble gas ring and had decided that she'd do all the cooking at home and heat it up when she got to the hall. She planned to get there early enough to ensure that the food was piping hot so that the entire guest list wouldn't come down with food poisoning.

She'd had a nasty shock when she'd phoned Jodie in advance and asked if she was available that Friday. Jodie told her she was going away with some girlfriends that weekend. And neither Seamus nor Margaret were available either, which threw Ash into a mild panic. She'd sat in the apartment and wondered why it was that everyone seemed to have things to do while she was the one who'd been able to agree to cater for this party without even having to think about it. Eventually she'd asked Michelle, feeling sure that her cousin would say no. But Michelle had said that she'd love to help out and Ash knew that she meant it.

She drove carefully through the city and out towards Lucan while Michelle chatted happily about the fact that Lucy had sprung up another couple of inches almost overnight and Brian was incredibly well co-ordinated – Emmet, she told Ash, thought that Brian had a good chance of being a professional footballer when he was older.

'So tell me,' said Michelle after a while. 'What's the story with Alistair?' Ash had already told Michelle about his e-mail on the day of the party.

'He sent another e-mail from the States,' she said. 'We're getting together when he arrives home.' She glanced at Michelle. 'He's finishing some business first. The bank that the writer's son's ex-fiancée works for is involved in it.'

It took a moment for Michelle to work out what Ash had said. 'Ex-fiancée?' she squeaked. 'Ash, what the hell happened?'

'I don't know,' said Ash. 'I got a phone call from Gillian who was doing the catering and she told me it was off.'

'But why?' demanded Michelle. 'Because of you?'

'I don't know why,' said Ash irritably. 'I haven't been talking to him. I won't be talking to him.'

'But—'

'But nothing,' said Ash firmly as she overtook the car

in front. The pots in the back of the van rattled and she slowed down again.

'And is the ex-fiancée working with Alistair?'

'I don't know,' replied Ash.

'What if she tells him?'

'It's up to her. If she meets him. If she has anything to do with it.' Ash kept her voice even.

'Ash, are you sure you're OK about this?' Michelle looked at her cousin but Ash's eyes were fixed on the road ahead. 'You're so calm but I know if it was me . . .'

'Michelle, I'm fine. Haven't you ever had a one-night stand before?'

'To tell you the truth, no.'

'Well, I have,' said Ash. 'And what I had with Dan Morland was a one-night stand.' She turned the van into the tarmacadamed area in front of the community hall. 'Now come on, Mrs Somers, earn your keep and start unloading.'

'Whatever you say.' Michelle looked at Ash but her cousin was busy with the keys to the van and Michelle couldn't read the expression on her face.

Sicily in August was an inferno. Even at midnight the heat was still in the air. But it wasn't as humid as it had been a couple of months ago. Now the days burned with a dry heat while the nights were so warm that it was impossible to sleep with anything more than a sheet covering your body. And even that was too much, thought Dan, as he pushed his body from the bed and got up.

He'd gone to bed early, tired from a day spent out

on the boats with one of Joss's friends. But he'd tossed and turned and found himself quite unable to sleep even though he'd been sure that, this time, he'd go out like a light.

It seemed like for ever since he'd last had a decent night's sleep. He couldn't even remember a time when he'd got into bed and just slept although he knew that those times had existed. But nowadays sleep eluded him at every turn. Now, when he got into bed, all he could think about was Cordelia and Ash and how he'd done the right things but for the wrong reasons. Or maybe how he'd done the wrong things for the right reasons. He simply wasn't sure any more.

When he'd come back from the States he'd thought about calling Ash. But he hadn't been able to do it. He'd waited for her to ring him, hoping that when she heard the news about the break-up of his relationship with Cordelia she'd call. But she didn't. And, that being the case, he wasn't going to call her because she'd made it perfectly clear to him that she wasn't inter-ested in seeing him or talking to him and that their night together had been a huge mistake. Even then he'd picked up the phone a few times and begun to dial her number but he'd replaced it again because what was the point? He could almost hear her tell him that she didn't want to be Cordelia's cast-off, thanks very much. And maybe he was flattering himself to think that she'd even care.

He slid on a T-shirt and trainers and opened his bedroom door. The house was silent. He walked along the narrow corridor, down the marble stairs and out onto the terrace. Then he went through the stepped garden and down to the pool.

The water was lukewarm. He swam up and down it, his arms pumping and his legs thrashing until his heart felt as though it would explode with the effort. When he stopped he hauled himself out of the water and stood by the railing overlooking the sea. He grinned to himself as he remembered Ash throwing her shoe over the balustrade at the restaurant. Trying to be mad and impulsive. He'd liked her mad and impulsive. But he liked her the other way too. Prickly and freaky.

'Can't sleep either?' asked Joss.

Dan whirled round. 'Don't sneak up on me like that,' he snapped. 'You scared me half to death.'

'I didn't sneak,' protested Joss. 'You just didn't hear me.'

'You still gave me a fright.' Dan knew that his voice sounded boyish as he spoke. He suddenly felt as though he was a child again and that Joss was about to berate him for sitting in his study or messing with his papers.

'You're jumpy these days,' said Joss. 'Though I suppose any man who's chucked in his job and chucked in his fiancée has a right to be jumpy.'

Dan looked at his father wryly. 'Thanks.'

'What are your plans?' asked Joss.

'I don't know,' said Dan.

'You going to rejoin your old firm?'

'Maybe.' Dan leaned against the railing. 'Ross told me that I was welcome to come back. And I'd only be a talking point for a day or two. But I haven't made up my mind yet.'

'You could work for me,' said Joss. 'Look after my investments. The business side of my life.'

'You have an agent,' Dan pointed out.

Joss chuckled. 'His job is just to get me as much money as is humanly possible for everything I write. How I spend that money is entirely up to me.'

Dan smiled. 'Thanks for the offer, Dad. But I'm not sure I'm cut out for it.'

'What are you cut out for?' asked Joss.

'God knows,' said Dan.

'Have you seen the cook since?' Joss looked at him inquiringly and Dan exhaled slowly before shaking his head.

'Dan, did you love her?'

'I don't think so,' he said.

'Pretty emphatic,' said Joss dryly.

'I thought I loved Cordelia,' said Dan. 'And then I realised that I did, but not enough. It was a frightening thought.'

'Maybe you did,' said Joss, 'Or maybe you're like me – always looking for something better. In which case, don't ever get married.'

Dan looked at his father. 'That's your word of wisdom to me?'

Joss laughed. 'I was a rotten husband,' he said. 'But I'm a great lover. I don't regret the rotten husband bit and I enjoy being a great lover. But I wish I'd been a better father.'

Dan said nothing.

'And please don't break in with "you were a great father",' said Joss wryly.

'You weren't,' said Dan. 'But you've been pretty good since. And I'm grateful for you letting me stay here.'

'You don't have to be,' said Joss. 'But – and this is my word of wisdom to you, Dan, take it or leave it – you're not really like me at all. There's room in the world for only one Joss Morland.'

This time Dan laughed. 'Arrogant sod.'

'That's me,' said Joss.

'Thanks,' said Dan.

'You're welcome,' said Joss and walked back to the villa.

Chapter 37

Just Desserts
Cream cheese, 4 eggs (separated), lightly whipped cream,
vanilla essence, caster sugar, selection of fresh berries
Lightly whip cream. Beat whites of eggs. Beat cream cheese
until smooth and whisk in cream and egg yolks. Fold in
caster sugar, vanilla essence and egg whites. Pour into lined
deep cake tin and freeze until firm. Turn out before serving
and decorate with berries

O n the last Saturday in September, Ash woke up
with a hangover. Not a serious head-pounding,
stomach-churning, stale-mouth kind of hangover, just
a general sense that she'd had too much to drink the
night before and that she could really, really murder a
long, cold glass of water.

She got up and went into the kitchen. The sun was
streaming through the window and Bagel was stretched
on the narrow window ledge basking in it. Ash poured
some water from the fridge into a tumbler and drank it
gratefully before letting the cat in and shaking some dried
cat food into his dish.

Bagel mewed at her and practically fell into the dish. He hadn't been in the apartment since the previous afternoon because he never stayed around when she had visitors, and last night she'd fulfilled her promise to her neighbours Rhoda and Jim by inviting them over for dinner. She'd asked her other neighbours Conal and Petra too and they'd spent a very enjoyable evening chatting and drinking and generally getting to know each other better. It was a sad reflection on her, thought Ash, that she'd been living in the same building as these people for years – and that she'd even asked Rhoda and Jim to keep an eye on Bagel from time to time – but she knew nothing about them as people. And she knew nothing about Conal and Petra either. She'd said so late at night when they'd demolished a few bottles of wine but Conal had laughed at her and said it wasn't her at all, it was modern living and it was a shame that people didn't know their neighbours any more but that not everyone would be lucky enough to have someone who cooked like Ash anyway.

It had been fun, thought Ash, as she poured herself another glass of water. Not something she'd want to do every weekend, but fun to do once in a while. And it was interesting to actually get to know the people who shared her building.

She put the empty glass into the dishwasher and walked into the living room. She'd tidied up when her neighbours had gone home, unable to face the thought of leaving the apartment in a mess overnight. The only time she'd managed that had been the night of her thirtieth birthday party. And Michelle had been right about her behaviour the following day – she'd spent hours with her duster and polish, getting the place clean again. And she'd done it all in a daze because she'd been reeling from the shock of the fact that Dan Morland and Cordelia Carroll weren't getting married after all. And she'd been reeling from the awful, awful feeling of guilt that it was because of her that it had happened. She just couldn't seem to get Dan and Cordelia out of her head.

It wasn't my fault, she told herself again as she left Bagel to his breakfast and went upstairs to her bedroom. Cordelia didn't have to know about it and if he told her and she freaked out – she sighed. She wished she knew what had happened but maybe it was as well that she didn't.

She wondered what Dan was doing now because she knew he hadn't been back to Chatham's. She'd rung one day and spoken to Steve Proctor and asked him some inane question about share prices which he answered, like all stockbrokers, as seriously as though it had been an intelligent question. She'd wanted to ask him about Dan but she'd lost her nerve.

'It doesn't matter any more,' she muttered, as she showered and then dressed. 'I have Alistair in my life now anyway.'

He'd phoned her when he came back from the States, delighted that the deal with Rodotronics had gone through. He sang the praises of Cordelia Carroll too and Ash had agreed with him that she was clearly extremely talented. 'Which is why, no doubt, she gave Dan Morland the boot,' Alistair told her. 'He thoroughly deserved it by all accounts.'

'Why?' Ash froze at the mention of Dan's name. What had Cordelia told Alistair?

'I'm not certain,' said Alistair. 'Obviously it wasn't something we talked about very much but it seems that she got him a job at Harrison's and then he turned it down or something. She was furious with him.' He laughed. 'I always knew that he couldn't really cut it.' At which point he changed the subject and Ash had mentally counted up to fifty to get her breathing under control again. She'd been convinced that Cordelia and Dan had split up because of her and yet Cordelia clearly hadn't said anything to Alistair about it. So perhaps she didn't know about her after all. Or if she did, Ash thought nervously, maybe it was something that Cordelia was keeping in reserve so that one day she could destroy her relationship with Alistair just as she had destroyed Cordelia's with Dan. Or maybe it had nothing to do with her after all. Then she'd told herself that she was getting obsessed and tried to push all thoughts of Dan Morland to the back of her mind. When she went out with Alistair she tried to be happy and light-hearted and fun to be with and she didn't allow herself to worry about the future.

Being with him now was different to before, although she wasn't exactly sure how. He seemed happy to be back with her again and, the second time they went out, she brought him back to her place where he grinned at her and expressed disappointment that it was, after all, just an ordinary apartment. Then he'd made love to her on her futon and it didn't even occur to her that this was the first time she'd slept with a man in her apartment.

I think I'm getting it together, she thought, as she put on a light pink cotton dress and flicked a brush through her hair. I think I have it all under control again.

She had nothing to do today. But, because it was warm and sunny and because she thought that being outdoors would be good for her, she decided to catch the DART out to Howth and walk along the pier. She liked sitting on the end of the pier at Howth, watching the sailing boats bobbing across the bay and listening to the clanging of the masts of the boats already in the harbour. Sitting out there would help, too, with her project of putting together a book containing some of her favourite recipes which she thought she might be able to sell to some of her clients. She'd thought of it the evening she'd talked to Dan about his wedding reception and dismissed the idea as unworkable because she'd have to be precise about the recipes. But, in the last couple of weeks, she'd changed her mind and was beginning to enjoy working on it. She was thinking about the fish section at the moment and she hoped that the tang of the sea air would inspire her. It would be kill or cure, she decided. If it didn't inspire her it would just make her feel even worse.

Howth was full of people with the same idea. At least, the same idea of walking along the pier. It was crammed with couples and families all wanting to catch the end of summer. It wouldn't be long before walking along the pier became an exercise in hardiness as they battled with the icy winds that blew in off the bay. But, right now, it was blissful.

Ash stayed in Howth for the entire day, going for a walk up the hill in the afternoon and sitting at the summit overlooking the sea before finally catching a bus back to the city centre. Her legs were sore from climbing the hill and she knew that she was a little sunburned too. The tip of her nose was red and her cheeks glowed.

She pushed open the glass doors to the apartment building and got into the lift. She was far too tired to climb the stairs.

The doors opened and she stepped into the hallway. Then she gasped in surprise and almost dropped her carrier bag. Dan Morland was sitting on the landing outside her apartment, his back against the long window, his legs stretched out in front of him.

'Hi, Ash,' he said.

'What the hell are you doing here?' It came out more abruptly than she'd intended.

He got up. 'I'm not sure,' he said. 'I wanted to see you and – well, I guess you've heard by now?'

She wanted to say no and ask him what on earth he was talking about but she couldn't.

'Yes,' she said. 'Gillian left me a message a while ago.'

'Nice girl, Gillian,' said Dan.

'What happened?' asked Ash.

'We decided that we wanted different things from life,' said Dan.

'Why?'

'And in the end she wanted more from me than I realised I could give her.'

'Oh, for heaven's sake,' said Ash. 'That's nonsense.'

'Ash, I gave up my job for her. And my house for her. I was moving to the States to be with her because she landed a really important position in the Chicago branch of Harrison's.'

'And then you changed your mind.'

'She thinks I lack ambition,' said Dan.

'That's the only reason?'

'Pretty much.'

'Nothing to do with – with what happened. You know. You and me?'

'Is there a you and me?' asked Dan.

'Don't be stupid.' Her eyes glittered. 'Did you tell her? Did you – confess?'

'I didn't need to,' said Dan. 'She guessed. Women usually do.'

Ash swallowed. 'I'm sorry.'

'It was a catalyst,' said Dan. 'If it hadn't been you and me it would've been something else.'

'Would it?' Ash looked up at him. 'Really?'

'Oh yes,' said Dan. 'Because, in the end, I didn't love her enough. I thought I did. I loved her dynamism and her go-getting nature and the fact that she didn't take no for an answer. Which was fine until I realised that her whole life was like that. And I didn't want to be married to her and living in the States and living the lifestyle she wanted.'

'Why?' asked Ash. 'Most people would love to spend

a few years in the States. I bet you'd have come back eventually.'

'Maybe,' admitted Dan. 'But I just didn't want to go. So she was right about me. I do lack ambition.'

'What'll you do now?' she asked. 'You've resigned from Chatham's, you've broken it off with your fiancée . . .'

Dan smiled wryly. 'And I've no ambition. I sound like some New Age hippie.'

'Julia would be proud of you,' said Ash.

'Would she?'

'Probably.' Ash shrugged. 'She was the kind of person who'd do something stupid like chucking in her job before she knew what else she was going to do.'

'I didn't chuck it in before I knew what else I was going to do,' said Dan. 'As far as I was concerned, I was going to go to the States and be the person that Cordelia wanted me to be. But the night before I went, I realised that was impossible. Nobody can be the sort of person that somebody else wants them to be. No matter how much they might think they can. We don't change.'

'Oh, I don't know,' said Ash lightly. 'I've become a slightly different person over the last couple of months. You know, less freaky.'

Dan chuckled. 'I like you freaky.'

'No you don't,' said Ash.

'Of course I do,' said Dan. 'And I liked you mad and impulsive too.'

Ash said nothing.

'Ash—'

'I'm seeing Alistair again,' she said quickly. 'We got back together.'

'Oh.'

'He's right for me,' she told him. 'He's a good, decent, caring person.'

'Of course he is,' said Dan. 'And he's done great things with the company, I believe.'

'Absolutely,' said Ash.

'Was looking at losing all his money a few months ago and now might even double it because of Rodotronics.'

'I don't care about his money,' said Ash. 'It was never that important.'

'I know,' said Dan. 'I'm sorry.'

She pulled at the ends of her hair.

'So it's serious between you and the Technology King?'

'Perhaps.'

'You're not going to dump him like all the others?'

'Don't patronise me,' she snapped.

'I'm sorry,' said Dan again. 'I guess I wondered if—'

'And don't wonder,' she interrupted him. 'There's nothing to wonder about. I'm sorry about you and Cordelia, I really am, but that doesn't mean you can just turn up on my doorstep and expect—' She broke off and rubbed the back of her neck. 'It was great, that night. It really was. But it was just one night. And I'm not going to hurt Alistair for just one night.'

'Of course not,' Dan said. 'I know I was stupid to come here, Ash. But I haven't been able to get you out of my mind and I thought – oh, it doesn't matter, I suppose.'

'You broke up with Cordelia and that was your decision,'

said Ash. 'It wasn't my fault, Dan. I didn't ask you to. And I don't want you running to me to justify why you did it.'

'I'm not trying to justify anything,' said Dan. 'I didn't contact you before now because I wanted to get things straight in my head. I'm not a total bastard. Not really. I didn't want to break up with one girl and then rush off with another. Besides, I didn't want you to think – I'm not like my father, you know.'

'Of course not,' said Ash. She opened her bag and took out the keys to her apartment. 'Look, I'm sorry, but I had a late night last night and I'm really tired and I've just got to sit down for a while,' she told him. 'It was nice of you to come and see me and everything but I don't think there's anything else to say.'

'You sure about that?'

'Absolutely,' said Ash.

'So I've wasted my time coming here.'

'You should have phoned me first,' said Ash. 'I'd have told you about Alistair. Then you wouldn't have wasted your time.'

'I didn't think,' Dan told her.

'Impulsive,' said Ash.

'Just thoughtless.'

Ash opened the apartment door. 'I've got to go,' she said. 'I'm sorry.'

'OK,' said Dan slowly. 'I'm sorry too, Ash. I'm sorry that I messed with your life. And I'm sorry that things weren't different. But I'm glad that I realised that I was making a mistake with Cordelia even if you got caught in the middle. And I'm glad you've worked things out for yourself too.'

'You'll find someone else,' said Ash. 'That's the way things happen.'

'Sure.' Dan smiled. 'What with my boyish good looks and fatal charm . . .'

She smiled back at him. 'Yes.'

'I'd better go,' said Dan. 'But can I tell you before I do that I like your hair like that? It suits you. Makes you look less icy. More cuddly. And I rather like your sunburned nose too.'

'Stop it, Dan,' said Ash. She suddenly realised that they were having this conversation on the landing of the apartment block and God only knew how many of her neighbours were listening to it. Having them over to dinner was one thing but having them listen to her private life was something entirely different.

'I'll go now,' said Dan. He looked at her. 'I guess sometimes you hope that things will work out the way you imagine but they never do, do they?'

'Maybe it's better that way,' said Ash.

'Maybe.' He smiled at her. 'Goodbye, Ash.'

'Goodbye, Dan.'

Ash watched him walk down the stairs of the apartment block. She stood outside her apartment door and realised that her body was trembling. And that her breath was coming in short gasps. If I'm not careful, she told herself, I'll need a brown paper bag. And I've thrown out all of my brown paper bags. She wrapped her arms round her body and leaned against her wall.

She tried not to think of what it must have been like between him and Cordelia in the States. She wondered if there had been the faintest chance that they could have worked things out. She couldn't help feeling that they should have worked things out. After all, they'd come through the preliminary engagement discussions, hadn't they? Perhaps Dan was right after all, though, and the go-getting brunette just wasn't what he needed. Maybe he meant it when he said that he wasn't ambitious enough for her or for the States or for the life she wanted to live. Maybe they were both lucky that they hadn't made an awful mistake. If a night with her had been enough to make him realise that he was making a mistake, it was worth it.

Ash closed her eyes again and recalled that night. She could see him sitting opposite her at the restaurant, laughing with her. Standing beside her as they looked over the balustrade at the dark blue of the sea. Looking at her in shock when she'd thrown her shoe into the water. Giving her a piggyback over the pine needles because she could hardly walk. She could remember those moments much more clearly than afterwards, in the pool. That had been pleasure but the other – the other had been sharing. He'd been good to share things with.

But she had Alistair now. She could share things with him instead. She'd worked hard to get it together with Alistair again. She'd turned into the sort of person he wanted to be with. And everyone said that they were great for each other. Everyone. He'd hate her for ever if she dumped him now. She didn't want him to hate her and she didn't want to dump him. She wanted to love him. So, she told herself, she wouldn't do anything now that she'd regret in the future. She knew better than that. She'd always known better than that.

She walked slowly into her apartment and closed the door behind her. She leaned against the wall and closed her eyes while Bagel twined his body round her legs and mewed loudly. She opened her eyes again and followed him into the kitchen where he stood beside his empty bowl. She spooned some Whiskas into it, put it in front of him and stood watching him.

Alistair didn't like cats. But he put up with Bagel because of her. That showed how much he cared.

She took a deep breath and strode quickly through the living room, leaving Bagel to gobble his food alone. She opened the apartment door and stood, indecisively, on the landing. Then she ran down the stairs, two at a time, until she clattered to the ground floor and almost catapulted into the empty lobby of the building. Don't do anything stupid, she told herself. Nothing you'll regret. Be sensible. You're good at being sensible.

She pressed the buzzer, released the glass door and stepped outside. The sun reflected off the opaque water of the Liffey, almost blinding her.

He was further along the quays, walking towards the mouth of the river, his hands thrust deep into the pockets of his jeans. She stood on the pavement for a moment looking after him. Don't do something stupid, she repeated to herself. Don't.

'Dan!'

He stopped and turned round.

She walked towards him. He waited for her. She felt as if she was outside herself, watching herself walk to him in slow motion, as though she'd walk towards him for ever. But finally she was beside him. He looked at her uncertainly, then put his arms round her and kissed her. She'd never been kissed in the street before. At least, never in broad daylight. Where anyone could see her. By someone who didn't seem to care that they were making a show of themselves!

Finally he took his lips from hers but continued to hold her in the circle of his arms. Her heart was pounding but her breath was almost even. His eyes crinkled at the corners and he smiled at her.

'Ash?'

'Yes?' She was surprised that she could speak.

He touched her lips with the tip of his forefinger. 'Ash, if that's how you give the brush-off to someone, I have to tell you that it's a damn sight better than anyone else's way of doing it. And it'll go down as my all-time favourite goodbye. It's no wonder you do it so often when it's so bloody good.'

'Does it have to mean goodbye?' Ash bit her bottom lip then smiled at him, a smile that spread across her face and lit up her eyes. 'I'm rather hoping that it might actually mean hello.'

Anyone But Him

Sheila O'Flanagan

Andie Corcoran and her sister Jin have never seen eye to eye. Andie doesn't envy Jin her wealthy husband and luxury lifestyle, while Jin can't believe Andie's happy with her quiet and man-free existence (if only she knew!).

But when their widowed mother Cora comes back from a Caribbean cruise with more than just a suntan, Andie and Jin are united in horror. Who is this gorgeous young man who's swept their mother off her feet? And what exactly does he want? On top of this, both sisters are about to face crises of their own.

What they really need is a friend to set the world to rights with – but can they ever be friends with each other?

Praise for Sheila O'Flanagan's bestsellers:

'Highly readable' *Daily Express*

'The Sheila O'Flanagan guarantee is a pretty powerful one' *Irish Independent*

'Another fantastic book' *Irish News*

'Witty and touching' *Family Circle*

0 7553 0758 5

headline

SHEILA O'FLANAGAN

Too Good to be True

Can love at first sight last a lifetime?

Air-traffic controller Carey Browne is used to handling unpredictable situations. So when Ben Russell, a man she's known all of five minutes, proposes, she calmly deals with the matter – and accepts, much to the horror of her family and friends.

Has the woman gone completely mad?

Despite their disapproval, and the icy reception from Ben's sister, Freya, Carey is determined to make the marriage work. She knows she's found her soulmate. If only everyone would leave them alone.

But it seems that Ben hasn't been entirely honest about his past, and Carey soon starts to wonder whether she's made a dreadful mistake. After all, something so perfect must be too good to be true . . . mustn't it?

Praise for Sheila O'Flanagan's bestsellers

'The Sheila O'Flanagan guarantee is a pretty powerful one' *Irish Independent*

'Hugely enjoyable' *Best*

'A must-read' *Woman's Own*

'Another fantastic book' *Irish News*

0 7553 2380 7 (A format)
0 7553 2994 5 (B format)

headline
review